DESDEMONA

To Roz —
Thank you for your
support.

1

DESDEMONA

By Darryl Alexander Hines

The Media Group, Publisher

Atlanta, Georgia

Acknowledgments

Too many to mention but you know who you are.

Desdemona second printing 2012

Other books by the author

*Sketches (to be released Summer, 2012)
Tales From A Twisted Brotha (Winter, 2012)*

Contact the author: darrylahines@gmail.com

Or visit the website: www.darrylahines.com

Chapter One

"One roundtrip ticket to New York," she said.

"Penn Station? Amtrak stops all over New York." The ticket agent kept his head down, as his eyes seemed to reach over his bifocals. He studied her face, waited for his answer.

His nearsighted stare made her shrink away and she turned to give him more of a profile than a post office style headshot, straight away. She kept her left eye, the one with the angry bruise, away from the man's view.

"I'm going to the city. Penn Station?" She posed her answer as a question because she wasn't sure which stop was closest to Times Square.

"That'll be a hundred and fifty-six dollars."

She nodded then dug deep inside her purse. Rummaged through her personal items: hairbrush, makeup kit, cellphone, iPod, condoms and gun. She glanced up momentarily checking to see if the man at the ticket counter had seen the weapon. She breathed easy as he seemed to have not noticed the small caliber pistol secreted away inside her handbag.

He kept his head down, rubber stamp in one hand, pencil in the other. Heavy thump from one hand with the words: Originating city, Washington, DC – Destination New York, NY making an impression in ink on her ticket. He made a repetitive tapping on the counter with his pencil occasionally looking up to see if she was finally ready to pay.

She grabbed at a wad of bills, smiled uneasily and began unfolding the crumbled up currency. She seemed apologetic as she handed him a hundred dollar bill. "Hundred dollar bills are all I have."

"I've got change. That's one ticket. Return when?"

"Tomorrow."

"Name?"

"Huh?"

He exhaled hard. "Your name, Miss."

"Oh, Charity Trudeau."

She watched as he typed her name into the computer. She had second thoughts about using her real name. Derek told her that catching the train wouldn't involve the scrutiny passengers undergo when they fly the friendly skies. No metal detectors, no driver's license or picture I.D. required. But she shrugged off the thought that anyone could trace her movements no matter how she traveled.

The agent slid Charity's ticket and change across the counter in one motion. She swept everything into one hand careful not to open her purse again for the world to see her secrets.

He said, "Train's leaving at Gate 7. Better hurry or you'll miss it."

She followed the signs to Gate 7, listened to the hiss of the train's hydraulics that sounded like a snake then surveyed the platform for faces. Charity found an open seat in a car that wasn't half full and settled in for the trip to New York City.

Minutes into the ride the porter strolled through the car asking for tickets. She was a middle aged black woman with a small frame and stoic expression. She stopped at every occupied seat asking for the rider's ticket. The porter examined with her eyes and punched a hole in the ticket before sliding it into a slot on the back of the rider's seat.

When she got to Charity she stood there looking at the young woman who was half asleep. The porter cleared her throat, which got the girl's attention.

"Ticket please."

Charity pulled her ticket out of the pouch attached to the seat in front of hers. She had realized that opening her purse was a risky venture so she took no chances. She handed her ticket to the porter without looking directly at the woman. She remembered Derek's words: "Don't make eye contact with anyone, but don't look away either. You don't want people to identify you if something goes wrong."

The porter went about her task punching Charity's ticket as she had with the other passengers then started to meander down the aisle. Charity breathed a little easier thinking that she had safely passed the second test until the porter stopped in her tracks and started walking back. She stood by Charity and stared at her purse.

"Is that a knock off?" she asked Charity.

The young woman felt a lump grow in her throat then swallowed it away. "Ah, no. It's real."

The porter shook her head unable to contain her own amazement. "What does a purse like that cost? About nine thousand dollars?"

Charity stared at the back of the seat in front of hers and not at the porter. "Yes, I think."

"Girl, if I sold everything in my apartment, furniture, refrigerator, T.V. and all my clothes I couldn't buy that purse." The porter twisted her mouth, looked Charity up and down. "Scores?"

"Huh?" Charity looked up at the porter, but still avoided the other woman's eyes.

"You dance at Scores? Lots of pretty girls do. Nothin' to be ashamed of. I hear girls there make two-three hundred thousand a year just shakin' their asses."

"No ma'am. I'm an actress."

The porter slowly moved away and continued down the aisle. She huffed and walked away mumbling. "I ain't never seen her on television or in the movies. Actress my ass."

Charity smiled at the thought that she actually had two purses like the one she carried. The other was folded and tucked neatly inside the purse the porter had admired. Derek told her it was large enough to carry the two hundred and fifty thousand in cash she was to bring back for him.

She reached inside her purse for her compact. Looking in the small mirror she could see the dark ring around her eye thinly disguised with beige colored makeup over her beige colored skin. She cursed Derek every time she thought about what he did to her eye and although she was making this run for him her thoughts spoke of revenge.

All of the apologies in the world couldn't undo what he did to her. A backhand to her face unexpected, but not a shock to her. She told Derek she didn't want to make this run for him. It didn't feel right. But her protests were met with his forceful persuasion.

She thought: *He'll pay for this. I swear.*

She lamented the fact that she wasn't in control of the situation---not over Derek, not over her own life. His dominance over her was obvious. What better evidence could there have been to prove it. She was making the run, black eye, bad feelings and all.

When Charity arrived at Penn Central she wasted no time getting off the train. She made her way out of the station and on to West 34th Street. She could see Madison Square Garden in the background. She stopped and took in the scenery for the moment then raised her hand to attract the attention of one of the many taxicabs parked near the station.

She told the driver, "The Four Seasons Hotel."

Easy directions, easy to remember.

Charity opened her purse as she kept a careful eye on the cab driver. She took out the brown envelope and peeled away the flap for the first time because her curiosity was getting the best of her. She wondered what was inside that envelope that was worth a quarter of a million dollars.

She looked at the envelope's contents and felt a sudden rush of anger as she read. She whispered, "Son of a bitch!" then put the items back inside the envelope.

A few minutes later Charity was standing in the lobby of the Four Seasons Hotel waiting for the man that Derek told her to give the envelope to, the man who would give her the money. He said nothing when he found her sitting in the hotel lobby other than hello.

His unsmiling face, bald head set on top of a wide muscular frame was intimidating enough to make her want to run away. She thought: *Screw this. Screw Derek.* But it was too late. She followed the man without a will of her own as they headed to the elevator and to his room on the fifth floor.

Her fear mounted as she walked. She wondered why Derek sent her on this particular run. It was different, not like the others. Of course, he told her that she was the only person he could trust. Besides, he gave her the gun just in case. He told her there was nothing to worry about.

The man, of Asian background, remained straight-faced until they walked into his room. "You black girl, no?"

Charity didn't answer. She thought her racial background was obvious.

The man speaking in halting English leered at her for a moment. "Ever been to Thailand?"

She shook her head.

"Not many black girls there. You do well dancing in go-go there. Blond girls and black girls make lot of money there." His smile turned lascivious. "Girl like you do well. Men give you jewelry. Give you gold. Give you diamonds. They pay lot of *baht.*"

She felt her impatience start to rise. She wanted to get the hell out of that room. Get away from the man who stood there leering at her, leering at her the way men did at the club. But they paid for their visual intercourse and fantasy rides. This man was taking her in like he'd put her on a plate and sop her up like a biscuit. And the money he'd pay was Derek's money---all Derek's.

She thought about the envelope over his idle chatter. The anger returned. She gritted her teeth. She had reached a crossroad in her life. It was unplanned, unrehearsed.

"You got the money?" she said.

The man nodded.

"Derek said you need to show it to me before I give you the envelope."

He smiled. "Derek. He not a trusting man. You just little girl. I could simply take it and keep the money." He moved closer to her. "I could take you, as well."

He was adding insult to injury. You don't disrespect anyone with the power of life and death---even if she is a scared young girl. It was the final straw. She reached inside her purse, pulled out the chrome plated .380 and pointed it at the man's head.

"Why don't you just give me the money and shut the fuck up!"

Her voice was high-pitched and loud. She felt the adrenalin course its way through her veins as her chest heaved. Her expression was deadly. He realized right then that she would pull the trigger and ignite the firestorm that would end his life.

He did as he was ordered handing her the bag. "The envelope please," he said.

Charity gave him an angry scowl in return to his demand. She took the bag with the money and stuffed it inside her purse to the point where it bulged at its designer seams.

"What about my envelope?" The man's face was wrought with confusion. He was almost begging.

Charity twisted her mouth, made her pretty face look angry and menacing even if she couldn't scare a three year old with that expression.

"I should blow your ass away just because of what's in that envelope. Trust me, you'll never get it."

The man's face hardened. He spoke through clinched teeth. "You give me envelope and I forget this little incident. Maybe, I spare your life. Maybe, I won't have Derek's ears put in jar. Maybe, my associates won't pay a visit to your mother and father."

He smiled menacingly and waited with his hand outstretched.

Charity shook her head. Her gun was power, transforming her from an eighteen year-old exotic dancer from a small town in Georgia to an angel of death. The weapon emboldened her and made her convincingly real like the times when she starred in her high school plays.

The cold press of the weapon's grip, its weight made her want to squeeze the trigger, hear its angry report, watch this man's blood run.

"Take off your clothes! All of them!"

"You make big mistake little girl. Derek tell you who I am? Who I work for?"

"No. And I don't care." She leveled the gun at his head. "Do it!"

He unbuttoned his shirt and reluctantly pulled it off. Then came his pants. He twisted his face in confusion. "Underwear?"

"Them too," Charity said.

He did as he was told.

She looked at him, smiled inside. "You must've just taken a cold shower. O.K. Pick up your clothes."

She surveyed the suite still trying to decide the best way to stop him from following her. She thought about locking him inside the bathroom, but like most rooms the door only locked from the inside. She thought: *The balcony.*

She used her gun to point to the balcony. "All right, I think you need some fresh air."

"You cannot do this. People will see me out there."

"It's up to you. You wanna be a little embarrassed or a lot dead."

He mumbled something as he waddled ahead of Charity to the balcony some five stories in the air. When he stepped outside he quickly covered his most private parts and turned to face Charity. "I will see you again and when I do it will be a most unpleasant encounter for you. Where I come from death is a sport and killing someone, especially a young, pretty girl is to be savored and enjoyed like sushi. I will taste you one day soon, Tell Derek he will be *kon dta-gla.*"

"Yeah? Well back at cha----whatever you said."

Charity locked the patio door and slowly backed out of the room. She took the stairs down to the lobby, just in case and jumped into a cab waiting in front of the hotel. "Greyhound Bus Terminal!" She barked at the driver.

Charity rode to the terminal thinking about her next move. She had changed Derek's plan abruptly. She was operating on the fly, creating as she goes. Derek would be waiting for her call. The plan was that he would meet her the next day at Union Station in D.C. He had allowed her a day to do some shopping at the stores along Fashion Avenue. He would be at the station at the appointed time waiting for the money, but what was done was already done.

Charity had made an irrevocable move and it was too late to change it. She'd slip into D.C. by bus not the train as planned, catch a cab to some nondescript motel outside the city and decide what she should do from there.

Charity sat at the rear of the bus where no one could see her. She opened the sack she had taken from the man, kept a wary eye trained towards the front of the bus in case someone might venture to the back where she sat. There were stacks of bills inside with money wrappers designating a thousand dollars per stack. She counted two hundred and fifty stacks of bills or two hundred and fifty thousand dollars.

It was still more money than she'd ever have all her own. Charity clutched the bag and wrapped both arms around it. Derek would never see the money or Charity again if she had her way. She just had to figure out how to elude him.

Chapter Two

One day earlier

I thought it was to be an innocent meeting, but it turned out to be fateful. It was also the first time I met *him*.

Charity called me earlier. She wanted to meet me for lunch at J. Paul's, an upscale restaurant down in the Georgetown section of Washington. Nothing unusual for sisters. Actually, we're half-sisters, but the label was merely semantics. Her father, my mother made us sisters. But Charity is a Trudeau and I'm a Reynolds.

We hadn't talked in a couple of weeks, but it was a typical *Charity* kind of call, tense and needy. She had that sound of trouble in her tone that I could feel, my ears acted like some kind of sensor. Charity's problems, which were many, always seemed to supersede mine and made them almost non-existent like I was a pimple on an elephant's ass. But that was the way it was when we were growing up so I didn't expect things to change.

"Dahlia I really need to talk to you real bad." Charity said those words through the telephone without saying hello. A distress signal from my past that occasionally surfaced into my present then dissipated leaving me wary of the future.

I had reluctantly agreed to meet her. I invited my friend El to join us, hoping she'd keep Charity at bay. El had just returned home from vacationing in Africa, a rare break for a hardworking government attorney. El would be the buffer I needed to put some distance between me and the whirlwind Charity called her life.

I was the first to arrive at the restaurant that day. Upscale restaurants, boutiques and townhouses were its legacy, but Georgetown was more than Rodeo Drive on the Potomac. Its brick and cobblestone streets spoke of a history that preceded Coach, Prada and Givenchy. But I wasn't exactly dressed for the occasion. I remember walking into J. Paul's with my image cast back at me in the full-length mirrors that surrounded its entrance.

I tried to shrink my five foot, nine inch image, hunching my shoulders with my arms folded across my chest and afraid to look directly at any of the well-heeled and better dressed patrons in the restaurant. I thought: *what am I doing here?* I was wearing a plaid dress looking like a refugee from the Holy Mother of the Sacred Cross School for Girls.

I sat down and reached into my purse, found my compact and opened it so I could look at the mirror. I regarded the face that was looking back at me and concluded that it only looked well.

Charity would be running late and El, later. I wasn't surprised because that was Charity's way and El had already told me that she was swamped with work at the office, but she'd break away to see me.

I looked around the restaurant hoping that I'd see my friend hanging around the door or chatting with some gorgeous guy that she always seemed to find. I was feeling a little insecure sitting all alone in a large booth.

Everyone else at J. Paul's was suitably teamed up with lunch dates, business partners and of course, lobbyists and politicians. This is D.C.

A strange mix of people was in the restaurant that day, so I people watched while I waited. A long-legged blond was playing footsie with her date, a man who was probably married judging by the way he nervously glanced over his shoulder whenever she displayed any affection towards him. There was a table full of Middle Eastern-looking gentlemen whose animated conversations blended perfectly with the clatter of silverware and china. And there was a couple of young black men dressed in their urban gear that I considered as the signature of my twenty-something generation.

I couldn't help but size them up. *Hilfiger and Sean John,* a mixture of the latest oxymoronic urban chic that seemed to define a generation, looking more like disparate uniforms than a fashion statement.

I quickly shifted my eyes and my thoughts away from the two men and continued to pan across the restaurant. My eyes settled on a man sitting at a table a few feet away. Seeing him gave me a jolt. I shook my head slightly as though he was some kind of an apparition. "Can't be him," I mumbled.

I stole a quick glance then pretended to read my menu, but my eyes inexplicably returned for more. It was probably the way he was dressed in an impeccably sharp gray suit, ultra-white Egyptian cotton shirt with gold cufflinks barely peeking from underneath his jacket sleeves and polished Italian loafers.

Beautifully colored skin, neat salt and pepper hair, white hair around his ears that swept down from his temples. Sported a thick evenly trimmed mustache that framed his lips and made them look like a DaVinci work of art. He looked better in person than he did on the big screen.

He had company. An exotic-looking Asian woman, older than me and stunning, sat across the table from him. She had her hair in one long braid that wrapped around the side of her neck and draped over her shoulder past her right breast like a snake. Silk dress, stiletto heels---tight dress, high heels accented her well formed bare skin legs. She sat with her legs crossed under the table. Intense stares across the table at him. His every word met with a head nod like she was being scolded.

She leaned forward, said something that caused him to shake his head. Fell back against her chair. Head down, eyes followed. Violet, catlike eyes with perfect brows surveyed the room. Caught me looking. I jerked my own eyes away and found my menu. The waiter was my savior.

"Madam, are you ready to order?"

"Not quite yet, thank you. I'm waiting for my friends," I answered.

"How about something to drink? We have a special on the house, Chardonnay."

"Can I ask you something?" I motioned for the waiter to come closer. I used my eyes to direct him to the couple across the room. "Isn't that…?"

The waiter smiled. "He gets that all the time. Everyone thinks so. People stop him in here asking for autographs all the time."

"Oh."

I glanced over at the couple. She was playing with her food. Full lips in a pout. He ignored her, sipped from his glass of wine. I could see frustration turning to anger. She dropped her fork into her plate. Stood up. Angry words I couldn't quite hear preceded her napkin being tossed on the table then her departure.

She cat walked past my table, gave me an angry stare. Angry violet colored, almond shaped eyes---she could've been the dragon lady herself---made me want to be invisible. I looked over at him. He gave me a half-hearted shoulder shrug then smiled. I looked away.

"The house wine is fine," I told the waiter.

13

Chapter Three

I hadn't noticed someone approaching. It was Charity.

"Sorry, I'm late. I know you were about to leave, right?" she said.

She gave me one of those hugs, the kind that spoke of obligation without real warmth. We were going through the motions the way kin do when there's no real kinship.

I forced a smile. "Yeah, I was ready to leave. I only got an hour for lunch." I paused. "El's going to meet us here, too," I said.

Charity gave me a hard sigh then blew out her exasperation at hearing my announcement. She slumped hard into the seat across the table from me. "Damn, Dahlia! I told you I needed to talk to you---in private! Besides, she always gives me that lawyer's look, like she's trying to cross-examine my thoughts. Hate that bitch!"

She sat there with her bottom lip poked out, pupils cut away from me and her arms folded. Looked like a little kid, a spoiled rotten little kid. Looked like the teenager that she was, looked like someone who was moments away from being sent to timeout with her forehead pressed up against the wall.

"You didn't say it was something private, Charity." I looked around making her aware of our surroundings, a busy restaurant packed full of people talking and eating was hardly the place for discreet conversation. "Besides, El called me first," I told her thinking that a lie would get me off the spot.

"It ain't that heavy. I can make it quick, but if I dummy up when she gets here just remember that you invited her not me. I don't like her ass," she said.

Charity dummied up on me even before El arrived. Blackberry in one hand, iPod in the other and a cell phone on each hip she rivaled any wartime command center. Anxious fingers had her text messaging until she noticed that the waiter was bringing my glass of wine. She reached for it and took a sip without asking. "I need this," she told me.

"Oh, it's like that, huh?" I asked.

I watched her as her eyes shifted nervously from side to side without focusing on anything or anyone in particular then I noticed the dark, angry halo around her left eye, made it look like a firecracker had exploded on her face. Charity's prophylactic attempt to disguise her badge of dishonor was some honey-colored foundation that brought more attention to her face than detracted away from it.

"What the hell happened?" I asked, but I already knew the answer to my question. "That son of a bitch! Son of a bitch! You reported this, didn't you?"

Charity shook her head, let her shoulders drop in resignation. "I'm scared, Dahlia. What if they lock him up? I wouldn't be safe even if they sent him out to Lorton and put him under the jail."

"Then you need to leave. Pack your stuff and move out," I told her.

"Where am I going to go? To your place?' she said. "He knows about you. So do his people."

That fact had already flashed through my thoughts, didn't bring me any comfort in knowing that I could be collateral damage like a victim of a misguided missile screaming through a neighborhood in Baghdad or the West Bank. I knew that the best thing for me was to lay low, not bring the warfront to my own door.

"What about moving back home?" I asked.

Another heavy sigh. Charity propped up her face with her hand and elbow to stop it from sinking from the weight of heavy thoughts. Going home was a form of suicide. We both knew that. She eased her hand from her chin to her hair, twisted her fingers around a lock of straight hair she'd bought from some unknown third world donor and integrated with her own. It looked natural with her light skin.

The twisting was something she'd do when she was a little girl. Charity would twist and twist until her own head was ravaged, made barren in spots, a poster girl for relief aid for Darfur.

"Actually, that's the reason I called you. It's about the folks. Have you talked to mom, lately?"

"No," I answered.

"Somebody broke into their house."

My heart felt like it was on pause. "She's all right, isn't she?"

"Their *both* fine," Charity said. Nonchalance resonated in her tone.

"I don't get it," I said. "There's nothing to steal, except your father's flat screen T.V. He loves that thing more than mom."

'Your words Dahlia. Anyway, they didn't take anything from the house, just tore it up. Mom said it was like they were looking for something. Mostly, they ransacked Grandma's old room."

That was like a spear being run through my heart. My grandmother had passed away almost a year ago and my mother kept her old room like it was some kind of shrine. The fact that someone would tear up her room must have devastated mom.

I thought about the only thing that kept me connected to my late grandmother, other than fond memories----the old quilt that now hung on my living room wall. Nana had inherited it from her mother. It had been in the Reynolds family for years. No one knew who made it or why, but Nana always said it told a story, probably about my family's story.

Charity twisted her hair and her mouth with her lips drawn tight. She said, "Look, I'm worried about them."

"Your paranoia must be hereditary, Charity."

"You can ignore me if you want to, but I'm telling you that we all need to be careful."

Charity started rummaging through the large purse she had unceremoniously thrown on the table right in front of me. She had her head down, focused and determined to find whatever prize she'd hidden in her large Gucci bag that doubled as a suitcase.

"I need a cigarette," she said.

"You know you can't smoke in here," I told her.

I looked down, saw something strange through its unzipped opening. I could see steel, shiny and deadly with a mother of pearl handle, pretty yet capable of so much destruction.

"What are you doing with that?" I asked her nearly whispering.

"It's just for protection."

"Well, you should've *protected* yourself against Derek when he was smacking you around. You got a license to carry that thing?"

"Of course not, Dahlia. But neither does half the people walking around this whole damn country. Everyone's strapped like they gonna take a trip to Iraq."

I was a little freaked out, not at the gun I'd grown up in the country, but the person carrying it made me uneasy. People like Charity were the very reason for gun control.

I was shaking my head, something wasn't adding up.
"There's something you're not telling me, Charity. I'm not stupid.

16

The gun, the way you seem all freaked out. You're into something deeper than what you're saying."

She frowned. "Like I said, it ain't that serious. The piece is for my protection. It's dangerous out here. Some maniac at the club thinks because I dance for him that we got some kind of thing going, a connection, a fantasy relationship. It happens all the time. The gun's in case they want to go there and I ain't trying to follow."

I couldn't help but feel skeptical, but it wasn't my problem. Sounded cold, but I'd warned her about coming to DC instead of going to college. And working as a stripper was her idea. Of course, she told me that she was dancing to save up for college.

Some hip-hop artist named, Buck Wild coming from the command center on Charity's right hip, rapping about "A Pimp's Life". Charity's cellular spoke the lyrics, "I' ma pimp, I' ma pimp. Ya'll know what I am."

It was Derek.

His special ringtone. I'd heard that song before. Always embarrassed by its sound. That it was wrapped around a classic Motown beat was sacrilegious.

Rhianna playing on Charity's left hip, the command center was going off like Shock and Awe II was raining down on us.

I tried to give her the most disapproving look I could find. "Derek?" I said.

Charity shrugged. "Yeah, the first one. Second was my agent." She huffed. "Look I really need to talk to you about...."

Our conversation was short-circuited when we heard El laughing. She was talking to the two young men I had noticed earlier. She did that classic move as she reached into her Coach handbag and pulled out a silver cardholder. With a smile and a wink of her eye, El handed each man one of her business cards and started walking in our direction. She raised her eyebrows and added a little extra hip action to her walk; cheeks bouncing like an Iverson crossover dribble and giving the two men a full view of her more than ample junk-in-the-trunk.

Charity frowned. Whispered her disapproval, "She's such a hoe,"

This was typical El, coming through like a brown tornado and gathering up everything that got in her way. She was a woman that couldn't be missed in a club or crowded room.

"That was Jamil Forrest, running back and MVP of the league last year. He got a big, fat contract extension this year worth about ninety million. Gorgeous brother, I figured he might need a good lawyer some day. Don't want him to go the way of Mike Vick," El said.

She and Charity exchanged disapproving looks, but my sister quickly redirected her gaze, didn't want to invite an inquisition. She stared out the window instead, pretended the sights on the outside were much more interesting than El's arrival. I noticed that Charity was careful not to display her bruised eye so that my friend could see it.

I stood up and greeted El with a real hug. It had been nearly a month since we'd seen each other and I could tell that her vacation had done her some good. Clear eyed and smiling wide, El grabbed a seat beside me in the booth right across from Charity. I squirmed when my sister moved over directly in front of me like staring at El would give her some kind of disease.

El gave her a cool, "hello". She quickly picked up a menu, scanned the list of entrees and seemed to settle on something. "Still dancing, Charity?"

"It pays the bills. Still sending brothers up the river, El?"

"Those who go send themselves. Kind of like pole dancing. We all make our own choices."

I cleared my throat, looked over at Charity and gave her a timeout nod. "You ladies ready to order?"

"I ain't hungry. Where's that waiter?" Charity asked.

I could sense her impatience, watched my sister carefully as she tapped the table with her fingernails. Looking around and tapping, steadily. Twisting her hair once again then tapping. She had much too much energy for one person. Charity's energy without direction was spreading and making me uneasy.

I'ma pimp, I'ma pimp.

Charity said, "Damn!" She just stared at her phone.

When the waiter came she quickly snapped her order. "Vodka martini. Grey Goose."

El said something about drinking in the middle of the day instead of eating a good meal, which sent Charity back to a tit for tat exchange with my friend.

I played with my water, stirring my slice of lemon 'round and round with my spoon. My eyes drifted away from our table to the

18

man I'd noticed earlier. He was still sitting there, eyes trained on the newspaper and occasionally taking a sip from his glass. He seemed unfazed by the confrontation with the dragon lady. I watched as he looked up to speak to the waiter and flashed a hundred watt smile. Charity and El's conversation became background noise to my pre-occupation with him.

I started wondering who he was. His nonchalant reaction to the Asian woman's departure heightened my curiosity. *Heartbreaker,* I thought.

My thoughts were more intoxicating than the wine I was drinking. Stolen glances, intermittent thoughts of a handsome stranger sobered by Charity and El's bickering.

The waiter bringing our food and Charity's drink signaled the combatants to go to a neutral corner.

Charity tapped her fingernails, twisted her hair while El and I caught up on each other's current events. She reached for her cell phone again and started sending text messages, taking herself out of our conversation and into her own wireless world.

El mentioned Walter, her boyfriend.

"Yeah, Walter the strong silent type," Charity said. "I don't think I've heard the brother put two sentences together."

"Yeah, kinda like the men you talk to: 'How much for a lap dance, baby?'"

That was the last straw for Charity. She downed her martini, chewed the olive and spit out the seed into her glass. It rattled against the sides of the glass, ringing like the bell for Round Ten had ended the fight and everyone was waiting for the judges to add up the scorecards. Mine told me that El was the winner and still champion.

"I gotta go, Dahlia," she said. "I'm catching Amtrak so I have to get over to Union Station. I've got an audition in New York."

"Video vixen?" El said. It wasn't really a question.

Another tight-lipped narrowed eyed look from Charity directed at her antagonist. She turned to face me. "We need to talk real soon when we have some privacy, Dahlia. You need to call the folks, find out if everything's alright."

Charity gave El a parting frown then disappeared into the crowd and out the door. We could see her on the street in front of the restaurant with her arm extended, flagging a taxicab.

"She's got some issues," El said.

"Always had," I replied. "She's always thought that our mother favored me over her. I guess because I never knew my father and hers was there."

"She's had eighteen years to deal with it, but I guess that's not much time. She's still so young. Hope she'll learn to deal with it."

"You shouldn't ride her so much, El. She's family," I said.

"So am I, sort of, but you're right. I guess I've seen too many young women like that be left to their own devices when nobody cares enough to say a word to them."

"It's how you say it, El. You know that better than I do. Besides, don't judge her. I mean, I'm not a fan, but she's doing what she does so that eventually she can go to Julliard."

"I guess that includes living with a drug dealer," El said.

"What can I say? Charity thinks she's in love just because."

Suitably chastised, El stabbed her salmon with her fork, continued, "Don't want to be nosy, but what's the problem with your family?"

"Somebody broke into the folks' house down in Georgia. Charity said they didn't take anything. I think it was probably some of those rug rats she used to hang out with before she moved up here."

"She's been known not to have the best judgment when it comes to picking her friends," El said. "I mean, look at the company she keeps. I think Derek and his crew are on DEA's radar screen."

"You know something I don't, El?"

"Nah, just speculating. No insider information. Drug enforcement isn't my department."

"Charity's carrying heat," I told El.

"Uhmmm, that's a little extreme even for her. I'll check around see if any of my friends at the Justice Department have any unclassified info about Charity's friend and his associates."

"How's your salmon?" I asked. I figured we'd spent more time on Charity and her issues than she deserved, but I couldn't get her swollen eye and the gun she was carrying out of my mind. It was time to change the subject, to talk about something lighter. "How's your love life?" It was more of a statement than a question, something we always did to jumpstart a conversation.

"Good and bad," El answered.

My thoughts flashed back to the man eating alone, the one I'd been studying. "What do you think of that man over there?" I asked motioning in his direction.

"He looks like that actor. You know, what's his name? Is that him?"

"No. I already asked the waiter." I felt a little embarrassed by my confession. "You ever thought what it would be like to date someone much older?" I asked El.

She smiled. "I saw you checking him out. Don't know, to tell the truth. I'd keep an open mind. I'm a confident woman, but I have to be on the same level as the man I'm involved with. I'm twenty-six just like you. I'm hip-hop, Generation Next. I guess I'd wonder if I could keep a man who's refined and cultured interested in me. Then, there's the sex part. I haven't even reached my peak yet. How would a man who's past his keep up with me?"

I took another sip of wine, cut the man a side glance. "I guess it depends on the man."

He caught me looking again. Nodded, smiled gently. I shifted uneasily in my chair. A lump gathered in my throat, I swallowed hard hoping to regain my composure. My chest heaved. I guess I should've worn a bra.

I was breathing hard, almost hyperventilating the way I'd do to the point of nearly passing out whenever I was in an uncomfortable social situation. I nervously pretended to focus on the last few morsels of food on my plate.

I saw him rise up from his chair. He was taller than he looked sitting, about six-two or six-three. Shoulders widened a little by the padding in the shoulders of his suit. The suit fit him perfectly, made him look like a cutout doll for some high fashion magazine or a woman's fantasy.

He was walking in the direction of our table. I thought for a moment, *Oh, my God, he's coming over here. .* He gave us a slight nod, acknowledging our attention like a man accustomed to being admired by women, but we played coy and didn't speak acting as though we hadn't noticed him at all.

I turned around to get another look at him only to lock eyes with his. He had stopped in his tracks, turned and was heading straight to us. I gave El a nervous look that she, in turn, shrugged off. She smiled, fluffed her hair and waited.

He greeted us with a smile. When he spoke his voice resonated with a rich baritone vibrato that made my juices start to flow. I squirmed slightly in my seat when he said, "Hello, ladies. Don't want to intrude, but I noticed you sitting here. Thought I'd introduce myself and give you my card."

El spoke up. "Well, hello. I'm El Porter. This my friend Dahlia Reynolds."

I nodded.

He said, "Pleased to meet you both." And extended his hand. "Mackenzie Powell. Everyone calls me, Mac."

El seized it, held it with the tips of her fingers like she was staking a claim on it. He quickly released her grip and reached for my hand, held it like a flower. I could feel his energy through soft hands that hadn't known manual labor. He smiled down at me, let his eyes hold mine like he wasn't going to let go. His eyes, green and gray at the same time in stark contrast to his tan skin had a catlike intensity, left me mesmerized.

I said, "Pleased to meet you."

"Look, I have an art gallery and antique shop not too far from here off Wisconsin Avenue and R Street. My address is on the card. We're having an exhibition next week. Like for you both to come. I think I have something that would interest you."

He looked only at me.

El and I nodded like we were responding to a command. I took his card without reading it and put it in my purse.

"It was a pleasure meeting you," he told us, but he was still looking directly at me. Another dimpled smile and he retreated towards the exit.

My thoughts turned sexual, my fantasies took flight for a split second.

"He's real cute," El said.

"What?" My trance had been broken.

Our eyes followed him as he left the restaurant. He walked up to the group of young men who valet parked cars. El made an unintelligible sound. I looked up in time to see him slide into a sparkling, shiny black Bentley with white leather interior.

El said, "Uhmm, Bentley Continental GT. Seen it in The Dupont Registry. Two hundred grand for a car," she paused. "You know fifty or even, sixty ain't that old." She had this goofy look on her face as she ogled the man and his car.

I considered telling El about the "Mac's" tense encounter with his drop dead gorgeous Asian friend, associate, lover? Take your pick. But I thought better. I had no idea what had happened or why she stormed out of the restaurant or why she gave me such a hard look and I thought I'd probably never know.

Chapter Four

I thought of Charity taking the train to New York, riding with her hopes and dreams wrapped around her heart. Singing and acting, her passion.

Charity chasing her singing/acting career like Don Quixote chasing dragons. Strippers don't usually become stars. But she was young. I'm cynical.

But Charity carrying a gun wasn't art or passion. Even I knew that people pack a weapon for a reason. Most because they're either carrying a lot of loot or they're planning to steal some. Others become gunslingers because they're scared.

Charity had no real money to speak of, living off tips by crotch riding the doughboys or the occasional middle-aged man who by drunken circumstance allowed his foolhardy libido to override his common sense. Ignoring the dangers he ventures into some seedy strip club on Capital Ave. The club where Charity danced was no Scores, the New York strip club where girls made well into the six figures. Lap dances fifty dollars a pop.

I figured that my sister had no good reason for toting a fire breathing death instrument unless she was scared. Maybe, it really was Derek. Maybe, there was more to her black eye than what she'd told me.

I thought about her words, telling me to call the folks and check on them, which was the first thing I did once I got home from work that day.

"It's Dahlia, mama."

Hi baby.

"Just checking on you." I made some small talk knowing that things don't change much in Waycross then I said. "Charity told me you all had a break-in."

Yes, strange thing. They didn't take nothing. So I calls the police and two men in suits come by. They ask a couple of questions about what was missing. I says, nothing. Then they started asking me questions about your father. I didn't know what that was all about. I think they were foreigners.

"You mean Rufus?"

No. Your father. Your real father.

It was strange for anyone to ask about my father, the man who seemed to have vaporized from the Georgia clay and planted his seed. Later, when I was about eleven, my mother told me he was dead, killed in a car accident the day I was born. I thought, what's foreign anymore. This country is so diverse, but that's my mother--- old school.

I hung up not feeling any better than I did when I first called, but not any worse, either. My mother wasn't too concerned about the break-in or the men asking questions about my real father, but her reaction was strange itself. I wanted to ask her about the questions

I decided to file my concerns away not knowing that these things would someday come back and bite me, except it was more like a beast trying to devour my body whole.

Chapter Five

A voice from the squawk box followed by the irritating sound made by my building's front door buzzer. Persistent buzzing at my door, like a magazine salesman trying to make quota. I'd been sitting on my sofa marinating in my mother's words for too long, wondering if I should've told her about the blue-black gift from Derek that Charity was wearing around her eye, wondering what Rufus would do if he knew. The buzzer broke my trance.

I flipped on the television, turned it to Channel Three, studied the image of a young man looking straight up into the lobby camera.

"Antoine," I said under my breath.

I hadn't seen or talked to him for several weeks and when those lapses in time occurred I would wonder whether he was in jail or shacked up with some chick. Antoine was young and women said he was *pretty* and it wasn't beyond the realm of possibility that some older woman was taking care of him. So when I saw him that day outside my building looking like a puppy dog in the security monitor I was surprised.

I wasn't ready to have company and it was a Wednesday night. Unlike Antoine, I had to get up early for work the following day. My hair, still in a bun with a scarf wrapped around my head, didn't make me look very sexy. Most of all, I wasn't physically or mentally ready for an all-night sex-fest with a man who always acted like the Energizer Bunny on steroids.

For a moment I stood there looking at his image on the screen without speaking, trying to make up my mind whether I should let him in or not. I eased out a heavy sigh from deep within full of resignation. *Even unfulfilling sex is better than none at all.* Reluctantly, I pressed the buzzer and when he spoke I said, "C'mon up," sounding as matter-of-fact as I could.

Antoine was a stud and I knew that was unlikely to change for many years, but I was no longer enamored with his good looks and ripped body. He had long been nothing more than a blow up doll, the male version, and he might as well have had the vacant eyes and expressionless face of a manufactured man with a big ego and a penis that inflated and deflated on command. I knew what to expect

26

when I opened the door---the smile, framed by dimples and heightened by his green-brown eyes that always seemed to draw me in and The Look that broadcast to me and probably the entire world---*You know you want me, real bad.*

"Hey, stranger," I greeted him as he walked past me and straight to my sofa.

He smiled and planted his six-foot, two-inch frame in a sprawling position that covered more than half of its seating area. As usual he was empty handed. No flowers, no candy, nothing but himself and that "drill" he carried between his legs. For some women that was enough and for the moment, as it had been with virtually every moment I was with Antoine, I was one of those women.

He quickly removed his sweatshirt and made himself comfortable. It was clear that he was planning to stay for a while. He sat there in his sleeveless tee shirt, the kind some people call "wife-beaters" which was loosely covered up by a Wizards basketball jersey. I couldn't help but notice how cut-up his arms, shoulders and pecs were.

"Looks like you've been spending a lot of time in the gym, lately," I said.

"Yeah, trying to get ripped."

"Must be nice to have that kind of time on your hands to spend hours in the gym everyday," I said.

I was trying not to sound too sarcastic, but I was feeling a little envious because I had to work everyday yet I could barely afford to buy a workout tape and I didn't have the luxury of spending hours in an egotistical, voyeur's pit called a "fitness center."

Displaying his body had always been Antoine's version of seduction and I had to admit that seeing him like that was turning me on. For us, carnality was strictly physical without pretending that there was some kind of spiritual or emotional bond. It was sex for the sake of sex.

Antoine was sagging like many twenty-something black males who wore their pants low and their underwear pulled up high, prison code for saying, "I'm available." He looked like one of hip-hop's soldiers wearing his parade dress of baggy pants, basketball jersey with someone else's name on it as unpaid advertisers for the

No Boys Allowed league and topped off with a baseball style cap. His cornrow braids were squeezing his brain.

"Hey, baby," rolled from his lips like slow thunder. His voice was deep and raspy. Antoine attributed that quality to all of the weed he smoked growing up and his continuing mission to get high on a daily basis. "I was in the neighborhood. I thought I'd give you a holler."

"Yeah, I bet," I replied unable to disguise my skepticism.

"No, seriously, I been in the studio a lot lately. Working on something that's hot, real hot! Told my dude that I needed some R & R and I needed to chill. So I was rolling out this way to score some trees and I thought I'd just swing by old girl's place and see what's up."

I twisted my lips, gave him that look like I knew it was all bullshit. But it really didn't matter because my emotional investment in Antoine had been spent months ago.

"You got a car?" I asked.

"Yeah, I got wheels. Brand new Escalade with some spinning twenty-fours. Dat shit is hot!"

"Uhmm, maybe, you can finally take me out on a date," I said, again my comment was reeking with skepticism.

He'd never taken me anywhere during the entire year I'd known him. I remembered how we met that time when El dragged me out to *Dream*, a D.C. nightclub. Even I could tell that Antoine and I seemed a most unlikely pair, but I thought that there was definitely a connection between us then. In fact, although a lot of beautiful women were throwing themselves at him that night Antoine ignored them all. He took me home and I, uncharacteristically, had sex with him. That one night defined the parameters of our relationship and it hadn't changed.

I sat down beside him realizing that we'd have one of those awkward moments when nothing was said by two people who had little in common. Antoine asked the usual questions like how were things at my job and about my friends, but nothing deep or probing about me in particular. It quickly became obvious that our effort at small talk was futile and only a waste of precious time better utilized for sleeping after sex.

"I'm going to bed," I told him. "You can follow me or you can chill right here. It's up to you. Don't be offended but I have to get up early and go to work."

I guess my words were music to Antoine's ears. "I'm right behind you," he said.

I took off my robe revealing my nude body underneath. This was nothing special that I did for him. I always slept without any clothes on anyway and he no doubt, enjoyed the visual. I had a king-size bed that was perfect for two people who'd seek refuge in one of its expansive corners once they had finished coupling. I busily pulled back the comforter and fluffed the pillows that matched it as though I was oblivious to Antoine's presence there.

"Damn, girl! You got a beautiful body. I don't know why you always hide what you got. Shit, I peeped you the first time we met, all conservative and shit, but I saw right through that. I guess that's what attracted me, you know, the low-keyed, subtle thing about you."

His words rang empty against my sleepy consciousness. I was already in bed, lying on my side with my back to him. His words now totally garbled by the sleep that was trying to overtake my body and mind seemed to melt together. Still, I could feel the weight of his body as he climbed in bed and immediately pressed himself against me. He removed the scarf and loosened my hair. The few kisses he would deposit on the back of my neck would be the sum total of his efforts at foreplay.

"Are you wearing some protection?" I asked.

"Of course. I never go raw, even if it's with your fine ass," he said.

Already erect, Antoine slid between my legs and buried himself into me. He seemed to fill me up, as he started slow and steady then quickly followed with his rapid fire thrusting.

The redundancy of his lovemaking brought no surprises. It was always the same. He would lift me up so my ass would be the mountain he'd try to conquer. Position me on my knees while he "hit it from the back", doggy-style. From this angle it was never slow and gentle, but always pounding like a jackhammer's staccato-like destruction of everything it touched, like the pounding of a man determined to get his first.

I could hear his groans and the slapping of his pelvis against my buttocks and feel the pounding inside. There was no pain and little pleasure, at least not the kind of pleasure that would send me into an orgasmic frenzy, but he did feel good.

Strange as it seems I had never had an orgasm, not from someone else's doing. Charity said she had them all the time with Derek. El said depending on the man she'd have one. But I wondered what it would be like to explode, to have my mind lobotomized by pleasure, leaving me stupid and drained. With Antoine I'd come to the brink and then it would fade away, obscured by his "me first" attitude towards lovemaking. Frustration would take the place of orgasm.

I was trying to force one that night as he banged away at me. Gradually, I could feel the intensity of something building inside my body. *Maybe just maybe, this would be the time.*

We were both breathing hard and as Antoine increased his thrusting I pushed back in rhythm.

I thought, *Just a little more, I'm almost there.*

But when he screamed out in that primal cry of a man who had reached his climax of pleasure I knew that I would go unfulfilled. He quickly pulled out and rolled over on to his back as I fell onto my stomach, exasperated. Seconds later we both lay there asleep without touching, oblivious to each other's presence.

Chapter Six

Six a.m. I was already up, getting dressed for work. I'd washed off Antoine's scent in the shower and along with it the memory of our being together. I guess it's kind of a sad thing when you have sex with one man and wake up thinking about another, but I was thinking about Mac as I showered. I guess it was his eyes and the self-assured manner he had when he approached El and I. Whatever the reason, I couldn't get him out of my head, which is probably the reason I didn't notice that Antoine was already up sitting at my computer.

I guess I must've surprised him when I walked into the living room. He looked nervous, quickly made the screen fade to black, didn't run the protocol to turn off Windows, made me suspicious.

"What are you doing?" I asked. I tried to sound matter-of-fact.

"Nothing, nothing."

"Probably looking at some porn," I said. Judging from the guilty look that was etched on his face I thought I was probably right.

Antoine laughed. "Nah, not like that. That's for dudes who can't get none." He hastily got up, headed down the hall toward the bathroom.

I was sitting at the kitchen table when he sauntered in and sat down.

"Can a brother get a cup of coffee?" he asked.

"How you like yours?"

"Black."

I could feel his eyes watching me as I stood and walked to the stove to pour him a cup. I figured he was having one of those morning-after moments, the way he always did after we had sex. But there was something different about him this time. His eyes weren't filled with lust or that look of longing for more. I could tell that there were heavy thoughts behind those green eyes.

"What's bothering *you*?" I asked him. I fought my own skepticism, but it obviously came through in my tone.

"Why does something have to be bothering me?" he asked.

"It was my question for you to answer. Not the other way around," I said. "Kinda defensive, aren't you?"

"Nah, I'm all right. Just got a lot on my mind, that's all."

He said that then retreated back inside his thoughts and interacted only with his cup and the coffee in it. I backed off of my question.

"What's up with Charity?" he asked.

I could tell there'd been a shift from whatever weighty thoughts he'd had before when he asked about my sister, but the question caught me off guard. They'd only met once and their interaction was limited to an introduction and casual conversation so I thought it was strange for him to ask about her. I decided it was simply out of courtesy.

"She still dances over at Club 55."

Antoine twisted his face like he'd just bit into a lemon. "Rough place, kind of. Dollar lap dances don't bring out the real big spenders or the classy old guys willing to drop a few hundred just to hang out with something young and fresh."

"You know Derek Horne?" he asked. "Runs with a crew of thugs off Rhode Island Ave."

"Yeah, calls himself Derek D." I laughed a little behind Derek's lack of imagination.

Antoine gave me a knowing nod. "That's what I wanted to talk to you about."

I was confused. "You want to talk to me about Derek?"

"And your sister. I really didn't want to get into it. I guess that's why I said nothing about it last night," Antoine said. He paused.

"You've gone this far, Antoine might as well finish."

"Your girl's in trouble big time."

I shook my head. "That asshole Derek's the one in trouble. If you'd seen what he did to her. She's walking around with a black eye and trying to audition for plays in New York."

Antoine gave me a slight laugh. "Yeah, right. Auditions." He took a deep breath and exhaled slowly like he was preparing himself for a speech. "She went to New York earlier today to deliver something and hasn't come back. Derek's pissed. I mean, really pissed. Says Charity ripped him off for some cash. Took a quarter of a million from him. He's telling everyone she's dead sister walking."

It was my turn to take a deep breath and release my disappointment with a sigh. My mind went into hyper-drive. I hadn't heard from her not since we met at the restaurant. I could feel my stomach churn. But I figured she was safe, otherwise it wouldn't be Antoine talking about my sister----it would be the coroner.

"Yeah, Derek needs to take a powder and I don't mean that stuff he sells. She's probably up in the Big Apple shopping," I said.

"I don't know nothing. I'm just letting you know what's happening."

I thought about how Derek kept calling Charity while we were sitting in J. Paul's. The urgency was compelling. I guess a quarter of a million does that to people. "I'm sure she'll give him his money."

"It's not just the money," Antoine said. "Charity didn't make the delivery."

I could feel my blood boil. "He's got her delivering drugs?"

"Don't know about that. Might be dope. Could be a lot of things. Derek's doin' shit all over the place. Point is she didn't make the drop and she's got the goods. People in New York want what their money paid for."

"So what should she do?" I asked.

Antoine shook his head. "She's got three strikes against her. Took Derek's money. Kept the goods and stuck a gun in the face of a real dangerous Asian mob guy. Nothing, but keep hiding, keep running, if that's what she's doin' cause no apology and no amount of money's gonna save her now. Guess you haven't heard from her."

I shook my head. No sense being subjected to questions I couldn't answer. Of course I thought about the gun but I couldn't imagine Charity using one to rob a man. Guilt washed over me. *Maybe if I'd been a better big sister,* I thought.

"Look, maybe I can help her. If she kept the package, tell her to call me. I know Derek well enough. He might let her slide on the money end, but he doesn't want it to look like he got punked. It's bad for his street cred. But he can maintain it if she returns the goods and suffers whatever consequences he has in mind. I don't mean like he'd kill her, but there would be consequences."

I said, "That's two out of three."

"If the Asian dude gets his package, he'll probably forget about some little chick threatening to blow his ass away. From what I hear it was kind of funny. He laughed about it."

To me it wasn't funny.

"If you still need that ride I'm ready to roll."

I needed to think. I knew Charity would call me eventually and I had no idea what I'd say to her. Most of all I didn't know how to save her.

Chapter Seven

The Metro train was crowded like every day with what seemed like all of humanity pressed shoulder to shoulder and riding in a sardine can at seventy miles an hour. I was fortunate that the place where I got on was at the start of the line and the car was relatively empty. The closer to downtown, the more crowded the train became; a seat was cherished like having the exact change for a token.

For a moment I thought I saw a black Bentley like the one Mackenzie was driving. It was cruising beside the train on Georgia Avenue before the Metro became subterranean. I looked hard to see the driver, but I couldn't distinguish a face through its tinted windows. I thought that it might be him, after all, how many black Bentley's are there even in Washington, DC. But as I looked closer I noticed that the car wasn't a Bentley at all, just a Chrysler 300M look-a-like.

I thought about the card he had given me the day before and rummaged through my purse to find it. *Mackenzie Powell, Antiquities Dealer,* was written in gold embossed letters with a fancy cursive font. I rubbed his name with my fingers, brought back the image of his face and I daydreamed.

Seconds later the train was underground and hidden from the streets, a sardine can moving at eighty miles an hour. I usually felt a little claustrophobic in the tunnel so I'd study people as a diversion.

Most of the people on the train had their heads buried in a newspaper or a book. Others hammered away at their laptop computers, their PDA's or Blackberry's. As for my part, I just watched them impassively until I felt that someone was watching me.

At first, I dismissed the idea that the man in the gray suit was being overly attentive and reacting to my every move because when I looked at him he'd look away. He didn't smile or nod, didn't acknowledge me in any way. I could see the remnants of a face, brown and angular, that chilled my spirit and sent shivers through my body. *Just ignore him,* I thought, but that was hard to do.

He was wearing a hat, detective-style with the brim pulled down low and wearing sunglasses that left only his nose, mouth and chin exposed. My imagination went into overdrive, sending my thoughts to spiral into some 1940's type spy movie with this guy right out of central casting.

The announcement over the train's intercom that the Pentagon was the next stop shook me from fantasy and slammed me back to reality. In a few minutes I'd be sitting at my desk, eyes trained on a computer screen and realizing that my life was as flat as the images it projected.

By 7:30 a.m. I was following the herd of people getting off at the Pentagon station as they all stutter stepped to keep from walking on top of each other. I was aware that the man I saw on the train was behind me. I quickened my pace trying to put some distance between us.

I thought I was being paranoid-it was early in the morning and he probably worked at the Pentagon like thousands of others.

Once on the safe side of the security checkpoint I turned to look back into the crowd, hoping he had re-appeared and I could get a good look at the man so that I could file his image in my memory, but he was gone.

Chapter Eight

My desk was no different than it was any other day: Laptop computer with a screen saver spiraling traces of a wand waved by an invisible fairy, notepad as blank as my enthusiasm and a picture of my mother with my stepfather's hand around her shoulder and his face torn out.

I clicked on my laptop and typed my password, downloaded an Excel document that had been sent by my supervisor and daydreamed over the numbers. I thought briefly of Antoine and then drifted to the beautiful older man I'd seen at J. Paul's the day before. Wondered what it would be like to be with him.

I thought about the feel of Mackenzie Powell's hand as he held mine. But mostly, I envisioned his eyes. Eyes like jade with hints of gray set in sepia-colored skin held some kind of mystery or something more like a secret. I thought about Antoine and his green eyes, probably the same color as Mac's but green not jade in my mind's eye.

There were physical similarities between the two men. Same height, eye color, but a chasm of about thirty years between them and probably light years in everything else. It wasn't just Mac's Bentley versus Antoine's Escalade it was different styles, generations---old school versus new school. But it was my fantasy that ruled me. I didn't know Mac at all.

I limped through the rest of the day thinking about Charity, Mackenzie and Antoine. It was the thing that Antoine told me, Charity taking a gun and robbing a man, a very dangerous man and I thought about the trouble she was in. I needed to talk to her, but I wasn't sure what I was going to say. I'd play big sis the way I always had. Yell at her, scream and cry. In the end I'd make everything better for her.

I was back on the Metro on my way home. I settled back into my seat, thoughts taking me out the window as the world flashed by and the tin can with wheels was hurling me up north to my place in Silver Spring. My cell phone rang, rather it sang. I'd downloaded Eryka Badu's "Otherside of the Game", was using it for my ring tone. It fit my mood at the time.

I looked at the telephone number, recognized it as Charity's. I took a deep breath and pushed "talk".

"Dahlia, it's Charity. Just wanta let you know I'm at your place so you don't freak when you come in."

"No problem" I hung up the phone. My sister's telephone call had taken the air out of my balloon. It wasn't good news, her telling me that she was at my place and there was an alarm in her tone. I could tell that she was scared and for good reason.

I just wondered if she'd tell me what she did on her own or whether I'd have to pry it out of her.

I mumbled, "I gotta get my extra key back from her."

*   *   *

Charity sat on the floor in my living room, legs crossed lotus-style, rocking with the rhythm beaming from the private world of iPod. This was her way of telling me that something was bothering her, her not talking in huge gaps of time. Eventually she'd open up with one of those, "what would you do if you were me type questions."

I looked up from my book, *The Complete Taoist Teachings of Mantak Chia,* looked at the young woman sitting on the floor with earphones glued to her head, her inner ears being blown out by the existentialistic styling of some rapper whose view of the world is limited to its bitches and hoes. I shook my head, but I guess I'd been where Charity was eight years ago.

"Charity!"

I was standing over her, looking down on top of her head and extended hair. She sensed my presence, felt my heat.

"What?" she screamed.

She took off her earphones.

I said, "I thought you stopped by to see me."

She nodded. "I did. I was just relaxing before I tell you the good news."

"How was New York?" I interrupted. "Did you get that audition? Don't tell me---you got the part!"

She laughed.

"Thought I had a chance as a stand-in for a part in an off Broadway play about the life of Hannibal," she told me.

"You mean the guy who ate people? Wore that scary mask in the movies?"

She smiled at me like I was the naïve eighteen year old. "No, silly. Hannibal, the dude from Carthage kicking the Romans' asses. That Hannibal," she said. "Sang better than the other girls who auditioned. They said I was too light-skinned. And I was like, what the hell? Hannibal and his people were all different colors."

"Didn't they know that before they called you?" I asked.

"Well, they saw my picture, but you know, I had the photographer make me look darker."

I was skeptical, still thinking about the bruise around her eye, thought about the gun she had, doubted if she even had an audition at all. Thought about what Antoine had said about her and hoping it wasn't true. I remembered Charity as the little girl who'd twisted her hair like she wanted to be ugly.

I looked at her real hard. Charity was shorter than I, about five foot, five inches tall and with a body most women would die for. Her round face made her look even younger than her eighteen years, but her womanly curves betrayed her youth.

I sat down on the floor across from her. "So what's bothering you?"

"Why you say that?" Charity answered.

"I know you, Charity," I said trying to sound like the big sister I was. I was hoping she'd come right out and tell me.

She gave me a wide smile that lit up her eyes along with it. I watched her reach into her purse and fumbled around the large bag. A fleeting thought: *I hope she doesn't accidentally grab the trigger on that gun.* Finally, Charity pulled out a wad of stacked fifty- dollar bills with the bank's wrapping band still around it.

"Remember how I stayed with you here for like six months without paying any rent?"

I couldn't forget that. Blamed my mother everyday Charity was there because she begged me to let her come up to DC. I gave Charity a quieted, "Yes."

She started bouncing on her haunches with her legs tucked underneath, twisting her head from side to side. "Here," she said, holding the stack out towards me. "It's five thousand dollars---for you."

"What? Look, Charity you staying here was not a problem. I mean, it was just a little inconvenience. Didn't really cost me much to have you here at that time."

I shook my head. "Where'd you get this money Charity?"   I already knew the answer. My worst fears were confirmed.

She stood up and walked over to the quilt hanging on my wall. Touched it lightly with her fingers, seemed to admire its detail. It was obvious that she wasn't going to share any of her problems with me.

"I remember looking at this when I was a little girl. I always thought it was so pretty," she said. "I always wondered why Nana gave it to you before she died."

"What? You think you should've gotten it? You don't even have your own place."

Charity seemed to recoil from my comment. She took a step back, looked longingly at the quilt and then gave me some sad eyes. "Makes you feel like you belong to something, doesn't it?"

I didn't know how to answer her question, just joined her in admiring the quilt.

"Do you know what the symbols mean? I always wanted to know what these symbols meant." Charity was pointing to a section of the quilt made of calico and patchwork and symbols that I understood to be our family tree.

"Didn't Nana ever tell you?' I asked.

"She told me certain things. She'd smile and say other things were secret, like there was some big mystery."

I smiled. "Don't know what the big mystery is. It's just family history, that's all."

"Yeah, I noticed the stick figures, used to ask Grandma who was who. She said the one with the halo was you. I'd always ask her why you were the only one with a halo and she'd smile and say you were her angel."

I'ma pimp, I'ma pimp. Buck Wild virtually unintelligible. It was my sister's ringtone embarrassingly alerting her that someone was calling.

Charity let her cell phone speak the rapper's lyrics, allowed it to fall on deaf ears.

I waited for her to answer Derek's call, but she didn't. She allowed her voicemail to quiet Buck Wild and answered my unspoken question wondering whether she was going to answer her phone.

Our talking about the quilt was a temporary diversion and we both knew it. I had backed off asking Charity about what happened in New York, but the telephone call that I knew had to be Derek put me back on track.

"So what's up with you and Derek?' I asked.

Silence.

I'ma pimp, I'ma pimp. Charity's ringtone returned with an incessant persistence that made my stomach churn.

She stared at her phone with angry eyes. "Shit! Shit! Shit!" She hit the mute button on her cellular.

I locked my eyes on her, refused to let her wiggle free from my stare. I waited for the answer that I knew would come. Charity rarely dropped by to see me for just a social call. Her visit that day signaled that she needed to talk to me about something serious although she was trying her best to avoid the inevitable conversation.

"You're in trouble, aren't you?" I asked. I didn't want to tell her that I knew everything.

She nodded, bit down on her bottom lip and resumed her seat on the floor like it would be easier to talk sitting down. Her body language displayed fear, submission.

"I didn't go to New York for an audition," she said.

I laughed slightly, in part because I knew she hadn't; not with a bruise around her eye that broadcast a beat down.

"There'll be other auditions," I told her trying to stay on a positive note.

"You don't get it, Dahlia. I went to New York, but I lied about having an audition. I went there to deliver something for Derek."

That really was trouble.

"I had to deliver something for Derek to this guy and he was to give me some money for it," Charity told me.

"Drugs?"

She poked out her lip like a misbehaving four year old. Shook her head. "No, it wasn't about no drugs. It was a package and I didn't deliver it. I took the money instead," she said.

"What do you mean you took the money?"

Charity opened her purse, let me see the gun. "I *took* it."

"And what was in the package Charity?" I had to ask her again.

"Can't tell you. Trust me it's better this way. Besides I'm rich, Dahlia."

"And what does Derek think about your new found wealth?" I asked her

"Haven't seen or talked to Derek."

Bigger trouble.

I felt a lump gathering in my throat. I thought about what Antoine had told me about Derek. No self-respecting thug would accept being ripped off even if it was by his girlfriend---*especially* if it was his girlfriend.

"You gotta call him Charity. You gotta give him his money."

"No and no! I've already turned that corner. Besides, you see what he did to my face. He owes me, damn it. The little punk-ass nigga owes me."

I closed my eyes, imagined the unthinkable. Charity lying in a ditch with her head blown off, thrown there the way someone would discard a bag of old clothes. Body parts strewn all over the highway like socks, shoes and soiled underwear.

"Charity, you gotta give it back! Find some way to give it back!"

I stood up and paced around my living room. Started pulling at my own hair as though I could release a solution to her dilemma from my brain.

"Maybe, maybe we can talk to El. She's got all kinds of contacts with the local and federal authorities. Maybe, she can mediate some kind of exchange. Like Derek will get his money and he won't get arrested for whatever he's doing!"

It was a proposal from the panicked. I knew that no one who could do anything would buy into it. Charity just shook her head. She had made up her mind to keep the money and hide out from Derek.

"Dahlia, I got a quarter of a million cash. I can do anything with that money. I can go anywhere."

"Like where, Charity?"

"Shoot, who knows? Hollywood? Change my name, you know. You know a lot of people got their careers started overseas. Maybe, I'll go over to France or someplace, become a big star like Josephine Baker." She smiled, feigned a sophisticated pose with her head cocked to the side and pouted lips.

I shook my head. "Dumb move, Charity. Real dumb move. Antoine says Derek and his people are doing business all over the country. They probably have contacts everywhere. Anywhere you go they'll find you and kill you."

It was obvious that Charity's plan wasn't a well thought out one. Taking the money was the easy part, not getting found was hard.

"Whatever you're going to do you need to get right on it. The longer you're around the more likely he'll catch up with you," I told her.

She was still holding back, not telling me everything. She hadn't told me that the guy she robbed was some big time gangster. I decided that it was time to get it all out on the table.

"Look, sis. I didn't want to say anything because I wanted you to tell me yourself, but Antoine was over here the other night. He told me everything. He talked to Derek and of course, he's pissed off, but maybe you can work it out with him."

"Work it out! Dahlia, you can see his version of working things out! Look at my eye! Fuck him!"

"Honey, you need to do something because according to Antoine that's the least of your problems. That guy you robbed was some big underworld gangster. Derek might be forgiving but this guy won't be," I paused. "Maybe, if you give him whatever it was you were supposed to deliver to him."

Charity's face became reflective. "I'd rather die first," she replied in a soft and sullen tone as though she was taking some kind of secret blood oath.

Charity stood up, paced the floor back and forth. She started talking like I wasn't there. "I can't leave the country, not yet. I don't even have a passport. I gotta go someplace where they can't find me. I gotta disappear like I never even existed."

It was a hopeless situation, we both knew it. Hopeless and irrevocable. Charity had painted herself into a corner and she had me tiptoeing along with her.

"I need time to think," I said. "Where have you been staying the last couple of days?"

"Hiding out in a motel out in Gaithersburg."

"Well, you need to go back out there and lay low until we think of something. Damn Charity, damn!"

Frustration ruled me. I had been living a safe life, no drama and no real excitement, just work and now I was scared for both of us.

"I'll call you a cab. You go straight to the motel and don't do anything to bring attention to your self. Don't go anywhere, don't do nothing. If you need to get out of there you can come here, but make sure no one's following you, O.K.?"

Charity nodded. "All right, but I don't need a cab. I drove over here."

"You did what? You drove? But, you don't, you don't"

She was now beaming, smiling even wider than she did before. "I bought a car. Come see."

She pulled me over to my front window that looked out over onto Connecticut Avenue three flights down. She was smiling hard, was even giddy like a child with a new toy. She pointed to the black Chrysler 300M with a rear spoiler, ground effects and a hood that looked like something ready to funnel air into a supersonic jet. Wide oversized tires and chrome wheels made the car as subtle as Snoop Dogg's minister-bishop pimp.

I looked at her, couldn't believe my eyes. "Are you crazy?" I asked her. "You might as well put a bull's eye on the side of the car and your name on the back."

"No one knows it's mine. I just bought it yesterday."

"And you paid cash, right?"

She nodded. "Fifty grand. It's a custom job."

"You should've added some neon lights to your *custom job*. Did you put the car in your name?" I asked.

Charity laughed. "I might be dumb, but I ain't stupid. I made up a name. They don't ask for any I.D. when you pay cash."

"Well, what name did you use, Einstein?"

"Desdemona. Desdemona Smith. It's a name I got from grandma---the Desdemona part. Smith was my idea. Nana always said Desdemona was a pretty name. Shakespeare used it in Othello. Figured I'm going to be a great actress someday so it fit."

I'd run out of words. I just reminded her to stay out of sight and try to be low-key until she figured out her next move. I told her to call me everyday, once in the morning and again before midnight. "Make it a habit," I said.

I sat on the floor long after Charity had left my place, still looking at the quilt. My grandmother had always told me that the symbols on it meant something. To my ancestors it was a map that led some of them to freedom on the inspirational train they rode on the Underground Railroad. She told me that it would offer me a different kind of freedom and would answer many of the questions I had growing up---I just had to figure it out.

But there were no answers for Charity woven in fabric, no pathway to her own liberation, just my own feeling that she was doomed by events brought on by a provocation all her own and we were joined at the hip in our fate.

Chapter Nine

I studied his business card hard and long, repeated his name like a short poem. "Mackenzie Powell."

He quickly became the itch I couldn't scratch. I thought about the way he just approached and introduced himself to El and I, but somehow I felt it was me he wanted to meet, to know.

I needed to clear my head because Charity was foremost in my thoughts. I ventured over to Old Town in Alexandria, Virginia, a stone's throw away from the Pentagon. I could lose myself in this neighborhood full of brownstone houses and small stores that sold antique furniture and pricey clothes. Lose the thoughts of my sister and slip into my own little fantasy world with no problems and no drama.

I browsed window after window and occasionally entered one of the boutiques lined up on King Street. It didn't take long before I grew tired of looking at things I couldn't buy so I found a jazz club nearby in the heart of Old Town. I wasn't really into jazz but I liked the atmosphere of the converted four-story brownstone that served as a place for people to congregate and enjoy music that wasn't frenetic and mind numbing.

I stood in front of the Café Alexandria for a moment contemplating whether I should go inside or take a ride on the Metro back home. I could hear the sound of a live band oozing outside through the front door whenever someone more determined than I scurried past and stepped inside. I took a deep breath and walked in. I made a beeline right into the ladies room, gave myself a once over in the mirror.

Mine was the look of a working girl and not the kind that sold themselves on the corners along K Street just a stone's throw away from the Whitehouse. Instead, I was in a dressed down plaid suit with the skirt hanging just below my knees, a white blouse that screamed for a fashion intervention and flat shoes from the Wal-Mart couture collection. Good judgment would have told me to leave the club immediately but I decided to stay.

This was the kind of club I could see my friend El frequenting someday after she turns thirty-five and her prey had advanced from young pro-athletes to some middle-aged and married, rich cat who craved to have a beautiful woman playing arm candy to the bittersweet memories of what he once had been.

I walked out of the bathroom with my head held high, made my way to the bar. I didn't realize how crowded the place was when I first walked in the door, but getting to the bar was like weaving my way through the mass of humanity on the morning train.

There were men lined up along the bar watching every woman who walked by like they were judges in the Miss America contest. I imagined them holding signs rating each woman and I shuddered to think how they would rate me especially considering my outfit but still I pressed on.

I found an open seat at the bar, flanked on one side by two thirty-something divas with short skirts and long legs, holding court to a pack of men playing the usual ritualistic mating game of who could be the most charming. I made a quick study of the two women.

Their laughing became intense. Thought they might be laughing at me, but I knew they weren't. I was virtually invisible.

I compared the fun that they were having to my anxiety filled mood, wondered why I was in a nightclub in the first place when my world was slowly colliding with everybody else's.

I looked over at the man sitting to my left. I could see the profile of his face with a sharp nose, gray stubble sticking out like barbed wire and probably just as sharp to the touch. He looked like he was at least eighty-years-old and was drinking alone, oblivious to the crowd of people jockeying to order drinks at the bar. And there I was in the middle of it all, lucky to find a place to sit.

"I'd like a glass of Shiraz," I told the bartender.

I took a sip and looked over at the old man sitting beside me with his drink as his company. He held his glass up as though he was toasting my arrival and took a sip. I smiled.

"Pretty girls should never drink alone," he said.

At first I thought it was a line, an attempt on his part to come on to me, but he quickly turned and looked straight ahead at the mirror behind the bar. I joined him in that furtive stare, beheld my own image reflected in the mirror that didn't lie. "What makes you think that I'm not meeting someone?" I asked him.

He didn't turn to face me, allowed his eyes to embrace both of our images in the mirror. He took a hard sip of something strong that must've burned his throat as it filtered its way down into his stomach. I could see him grimace from the effects of the alcohol like it had lit a fire inside his belly. He coughed once, nodded at my image.

"You're here to think. I see it in your eyes. You're carrying something with you," he said. "Let go of it."

I turned away and spun my bar stool around to face the jazz combo pushing music to the crowd. Most of the men in the club were wearing suits like they'd gone to the Café Alexandria right after leaving their offices, calling their wives to tell them they were working late. I thought about the sign in the club's entrance that read: No jeans, No tennis shoes, No baseball caps. That meant no 23-year-old brothers standing around with straws stuck in bottles of Moet.

My eyes drifted around until I settled on a table across the room and a couple engrossed in conversation. It was Mackenzie Powell this time with a beautiful mocha-colored woman, her hair jazzy and short the way Halle Berry once wore hers and with a prominent streak of silver peeking through her flaxen waves.

Seeing him so unexpectedly made my heart race. I inhaled deep, closed my eyes for a second and exhaled all the feelings that made me want to run out of the place. I looked nervously toward the old man sitting beside me to see if he had noticed my reaction, but he was still absorbed in the parameters he'd established for interacting and I wasn't in it.

I glanced over at the group of two women and four men huddled near me on the other side, but the women were too self-absorbed to notice my urchin-like presence and the men were equally caught up in them except one, that is. A big man with a shaved head was looking right at me with his eyes narrowed displaying a look of feigned concern for me.

"You all right?" he asked.

"I'm fine," I answered, unable to steady the slight tremor in my voice.

I watched him as he moved away from the group and closer to me. I braced myself for the inevitable and often clumsy introduction between strangers.

"Hi. My name is Joe," he said.

The hot air from his breath told me that he'd been drinking for a while, must've gotten off work early and came here for the happy hour discounted drinks and buffet. He extended the hand that wasn't holding a glass and waited for mine to connect.

"Dahlia," I replied.

He stared into my eyes and held my hand for too long, gave me the feeling that he wasn't going to let go. His quirky smile and clammy hand made me feel uncomfortable. I felt like he was trying to suck out a part of my soul through my appendages.

"You work at the Pentagon," he told me.

My mind reeled. I thought about the man on the train who kept staring at me the other day and followed me all the way to the security gate. I thought: *They're following me.*

"How do you know where I work?" I asked.

I eased my hand from his grip, wanted to run unable to disguise my panicked tone.

He smiled, easily. "Relax, just a guess. Most people who come here work in Pentagon City. Judging by the way you're dressed I'd say you came here from work."

"I guess that makes you a real detective," I said. I was trying my best to hide my sarcasm but it was clear and he apparently didn't care.

"Do my best. I can size up a woman from jump. Know everything about her after giving her a once over."

He leered at me like I was a t-bone steak. I was waiting for him to drool all over his cotton blend and polyester suit.

"Have we met somewhere before?" I asked.

"Hey, that's my line."

"No, seriously. You look familiar."

"I guess I got one of those faces. You know, hard to forget."

I looked away from Joe and his "unforgettable face" over at Mackenzie Powell and the woman who was entertaining him. I thought back to a couple of days earlier when I met him in the restaurant. He was with "the dragon lady", that Asian beauty who'd left J. Paul's in a huff. Now he was with another woman, just as beautiful and she was laughing and gazing at his green eyes like he was the only man alive. I imagined my own light hazel colored eyes turning green as I watched them.

Joe leaned close to whisper in my ear. The smell of martinis, beer and incongruent alcoholic beverages all mixed together nearly overwhelmed me.

"Does she know?" he asked.

I pulled back and looked at him, a puzzled expression rooted all over my face.

"Does who know what?" I asked.

"Your boyfriend over there. Does his wife know about you and him?"

He was looking directly at Mackenzie Powell.

"I don't know what you're talking about. That's not my boyfriend," I said. I turned away to face the bar and my image again in the mirror while Joe stared out into the club.

He leaned against the bar, made an indignant huffing sound, as he seemed to size up Mackenzie then turned in my direction. I tried to ignore him by staring in the mirror, but he moved close and wrapped his arm around the back of my chair. I tried to twist my seat away from his grip.

His beer-laden breath whispered the words in my ear, "What's the problem, baby? You ain't got a man and here I am, six-foot, five and two hunnert and fitty pounds of prime beef."

His lips were nearly touching my ear. I leaned back, but he only pulled me closer. Pushed his gut up against my hip, answered the unasked question---boxers not briefs. I felt slightly ill and mostly helpless.

I looked over at the old man sitting on the other side making love to his drink, still oblivious to my dilemma. The bartender was feverishly serving a thirsty crowd and the club had no security guards or bouncers---this was a jazz set.

I pulled my face as far back as I could without falling into the old man. Told Joe; "I have to go to the ladies' room." I stood up, but he was blocking my path.

He sneered. Grabbed my arm and held it real tight. "I know what you're about. You think you'll just play me off, head to the bathroom and keep on stepping out the door."

I pulled away from him, but my arm was in his vice grip. I spoke through locked teeth. "What's your problem, asshole? Let go of my arm!"

I didn't see him approach us, but I heard his voice deep and purposeful. "The lady's with me." He stepped between Joe and I, left hand on Joe's arm, sparkle from his Rolex catching our attention like a beacon from a lighthouse. He pulled the other man's hand away and stood between us. It was Mac.

"Who the fuck are you?" Joe asked. "A few minutes ago you were playing real cozy with that fine ass chocolate sister and now you're all up in my face trying to block my action. Can't you see she's with me?"

Mac turned to face me. I shook my head. "I guess that answers the question. Do your self a favor and step away," he told Joe.

"And if I don't?" Joe belly upped to Mac.

Mac smiled. It wasn't a nervous smile, but a self-assured one. Joe's size and bravado didn't intimidate him. "Old friend of mine used to say, you got two choices. You can choose the road less traveled and take your drunk ass out of here, or...."

Joe looked around. Snarled. "Don't see your friend around here to help you." Tightened his jaws. "I'll take my chances on the 'or what'," he said.

"You don't want to know the alternative," Mac said.

Joe looked around at the small crowd. We all were holding our collective breaths, waiting and watching to see what would happen next.

It was obvious Joe's ego was on the line. "Like I said, I'll take the 'or what'." He puffed his chest out. Took one large hand and wiped his mouth with it. "We can go outside old man, settle things there."

"Suit yourself," Mac said. He started heading for the door with Joe right behind. Mac turned around and opened up his jacket and casually put his hand in his pocket. He whispered something to Joe but I couldn't quite hear. I thought I saw a flash of steel tucked down inside his belt. Joe froze. He looked at the people at the bar, gave us all a weak smile.

Mac stood there stern-faced. Waited.

Joe blew out a heavy sigh. His shoulders slumped downward. "Man, I ain't gone fight you. I'd probably go to jail for manslaughter or some shit."

Mac smiled, flashed his bright white teeth, reminded me of a shark's deadly grin. "You probably would," he said. He stuck out his hand towards Joe who grabbed it with his own. They shook hands, exchanged tense smiles and I watched as Joe left the club. I finally exhaled.

Mac coolly walked towards me, let a dimple cut into his left cheek, a smile emanating from his eyes. "Are you O.K.?"

I nodded.

He said, "Look, I'm getting out of here. Can I drop you off someplace?"

I hesitated. "What about your friend? The lady I saw you with at your table."

He shrugged. "What about her? She's gone."

He extended his hand towards me, dimples cut deep into his face, eyes warm and soft. I reached out and touched his hand, drifted to him like a character in a Spike Lee film. My legs had no conscience or fear. He could take me anywhere.

Chapter Ten

I followed Mackenzie Powell to his car parked on the street a few doors down from Club Alexandria's. I hadn't noticed it when I first walked into the club. I might've kept walking if I had, too much of a coincidence, I thought.

He opened the door on the passenger side, allowed me to slide inside his car. White leather seats caressed me, made me feel safe. I thought about Antoine for a moment, then my mother's words. "You can tell a lot about a man by the way he acts not by what he tells you," she'd say. Opening a car door, a small gesture, spoke volumes about a man. Antoine never did that for me.

Mac climbed inside. Took the steering wheel like a jet pilot. I watched without saying a word as he started the Bentley's engine. Digitized lights in fluorescent orange made the interior of the car look like the inside of a spaceship. He said, "CD player on." I reacted with a slight jerk of my head. He smiled. "Is there anything you want to hear?"

I shook my head. "Whatever you like," I said.

"Miles Davis," he commanded. "Birth of the Cool."

The CD player responded with an audible beep as it searched for his selection. Seconds later the sounds of a soulful trumpet infiltrated the cabin, pushed out by twelve speakers. I felt like I was at a concert in the Kennedy Center.

"Where do you live?" he said.

"Silver Spring on Aspen Hill Road, but you don't have to take me all the way out there," I said. "If you just drop me off at the closest Metro station I can take the train home."

"It's not a problem. Besides, it's late. Train stations aren't the safest places for a woman alone at night."

He was right. I settled into the ride not knowing what else to say.

I exhaled slowly, letting all of the air seep out of my lungs and then purposely slowed my breathing. The car was filled with a kind of tension, not the uncomfortable kind but the sexual tension that permeates the space two people occupy when they're thrown together for the first time.

I said without looking at him, "Thanks for getting that guy to leave me alone. What did you say to him? I mean he looked like he'd seen a ghost," I said.

"I introduced him to my associate, Mr. Friendly."

"Mr. Friendly?" I asked.

Mackenzie opened his jacket with one hand. I caught another glimpse of the chrome-plated pistol tucked inside a holster. My eyes widened. Seeing it gave me a rush of adrenalin and instantly filled me with a sense of intrigue or danger.

"You a cop?"

He shook his head. "It's a deterrent. I carry it for protection."

His greenish eyes softened as the thought of Joe and their confrontation passed by like it had never happened. "I was surprised to see you out in the club tonight," he said.

"I was surprised to see you there, too." I hesitated. "Was that your wife you were with?"

"No, Felicia's a friend. We met for a drink."

"You must have lots of women friends," said.

"Why do you say that?"

"That day I met you at the restaurant. You were with another lady. Real pretty, Asian. Is *she* your wife?"

He responded with a broad smile. "You're getting kind of personal, aren't you?"

"I'm sorry. It's just I couldn't help but notice you. I mean, notice her. She seemed angry when she left J' Paul's. She gave me this mean look when she walked by my table"

He nodded, but kept his eyes on the road. "You're very observant, young lady. What do you do for living? FBI? CIA?"

I sunk low into my seat. "No, nothing so exotic. I work at the Pentagon crunching numbers."

He eased out a sigh. "I guess that makes you a very analytical person."

I replied, "Probably."

I thought about his comment and took it as an offhand insult. Analytical didn't mean "sexy" in my book. *Anal*, the root of the word, said I was uptight.

He guided his car through downtown Washington, onto Constitution Avenue caught the Baltimore-Washington Parkway heading towards the Beltway. Miles' music relaxed me. I listened for a moment without saying a word and Mackenzie drove, his thoughts were somewhere outside of the car. I looked at his profile---rugged, handsome, noble.

"You don't look like an antiques dealer, Mr. Powell."

"Call me Mac," he said. "Well, you don't look like some analyst working for the military-industrial complex."

"Excuse me?"

He laughed. "Loaded response. I'm a child of the Sixties. You know, Woodstock, Chicago Democratic Convention, Huey Newton, Eldridge Cleaver's anti-establishment mantra. I was in it. I was there. Loved Hendrix---still do."

"I read about that time period," I said.

"Seems like ancient history to you, I bet. I lived it. Woodstock was surreal."

I laughed. "I can see you now with your long hair and bell bottoms. So you were at Woodstock?"

"Well, sort of. I was in a band that played there. Kind of a warm up act."

"My father was a musician back in the day," I said.

"Does he still play?"

I let out a small sigh. "No, he's dead. He died years ago, right before I was born. I never knew him."

"I'm sorry. I'm sure he would've been proud of the young woman you've become."

I said. "How do you know?"

"Know what?"

"Know what kind of woman I am."

He turned his eyes away from the road ahead, looked right into mine. "I can read people. I see something in your eyes. There's character there and beauty that comes from within."

"That's just another way of saying I'm ugly."

Mac shook his head. "Have you really looked at yourself? You're a very beautiful young woman, Dahlia Reynolds. Take off your glasses."

I did.

"Look at me," he said.

I squinted, saw a blurred image of a man with a mustache and salt and pepper colored hair. "You're blurry."

"Have I changed?" Mac said. "No. I'm the same person no matter how the world views me."

I knew I had a confused expression all over my face.

55

"The point is---you are who you are, regardless of how I view you and how the world perceives you. My perception of you is that you're very beautiful and to me that's more important than how you might perceive yourself."

I put my glasses back on, let my thoughts play with his words. I gave him a timid smile not knowing what to say.

Mac said, "You *are* very beautiful."

For some reason I knew that he wasn't just feeding me something I wanted to hear. There was sincerity in his tone that made me believe him.

"Why me?" I asked him.

Mac said, "What do you mean?"

"I mean everything. The way you introduced yourself at the restaurant. The way you stood up for me back there. Of all the pretty women in your world, why me?"

He took a deep breath and exhaled slowly like he was searching for the perfect answer. "You remind me of someone I used to know."

He turned silent after that as though that was explanation enough, but the question lingered in my thoughts. *Why me?*

He touched my hand that was on the armrest between us. I recoiled from his touch, pulled my hand away and rested it in my lap.

"I'm sorry," he said. "Don't get me wrong. I'm not trying to come on to you. It's just that so much can be said about a woman by touching her hands."

"Sounds like a come on." I smiled. "You're real smooth."

He laughed. "No, just being real."

"Trust issues, I guess." I gently placed my hand back on the armrest. "You want to read my palm?"

"Well, I'm driving and this car doesn't have autopilot." He touched my open hand, rubbed his fingers along mine from base to tips. "Do you play?"

"What?"

"You know, music. Do you play?"

"Not really. I wanted to play the piano growing up but my family couldn't afford lessons or a piano."

"Too bad. Dainty fingers, nimble hands capable enough to manipulate the keys."

I gave him a wary look. "Are you talking about music or something else?"

He smiled. Miles played on.

"Connecticut Avenue's my exit," I told him. "Over to Aspen Hill Road. That's where I live."

Mac listened as I directed and we talked like we'd known each other for years. I grew bolder with every mile we'd driven. "You have any children?"

"A son. He graduated from Yale last year. I'm hoping he'll go on to law school," Mac said.

"Are you close?"

"No, not really. Trust issues. He thinks I abandoned him and his mother when he was a little boy."

"Did you?" I said.

Mac's smile evaporated. "There were circumstances that were beyond my control. Kept me away."

"Divorce?" I said.

"That was part of it."

"We were pretty young when we got married. A couple of kids living in the country near Lafayette, Louisiana," Mac said.

"You're kidding!" I said. "My father was from Lafayette. Did you know him? Richard Reynolds? You had to have known him. He was in a band. Don't remember the name of the group."

"Serendipity, I guess."

I said, "What do you mean?"

He rubbed his chin. "Your father coming from my hometown. He's probably my age, or would've been my age. Us meeting in J' Pauls'. You being at the club tonight, destiny, fate---I guess we were meant to meet," Mac said.

We glided on Connecticut Avenue. I was looking out the window as the terrain changed from the urban landscape with its concrete façade to Washington's suburbia of neatly trimmed lawns and Sixties-type definition of the American dream.

"Do you have any family here in Washington?" he said.

"Sort of." The question slammed Charity back into my thoughts. "I have a younger sister living in the area."

"Does she work for the government, too?"

"No, she's an entertainer," I said.

I was relieved to see my building, knowing that I wouldn't have to tell Mac anything else about my sister. "That's my building just ahead."

Mac slowed to a stop and parked behind a dark car with tinted windows. He turned to face me. "Look you were almost right about something you said. There was a reason for us meeting. That day in J' Paul's I noticed you. Saw a certain sadness in your eyes. A distress call there. It drew me to you."

I folded my arms across my chest. Pouted a little. "You feel sorry for me?"

"Not hardly. I see myself in your eyes when I was your age. The world was getting the best of me," he said then paused. "There were circumstances that I couldn't control that were pressing me."

His words made me think about my sister. She was my circumstance. I felt like telling him right then hoping that he could relieve my fears and anxiety about her plight.

Mac got out of the car and walked over to my side. He opened the door and extended his hand towards me. "I'll walk you to your door," he said. "Are you coming to my party?"

I frowned. "I'm not sure. I looked at your card. It sounds like it's going to be a real dressy affair."

"You'd be stunning no matter what you wear," he said.

I smiled slightly and unlocked the front door to my building. "I'll see. Maybe my friend El will come along."

He looked real soulful, eyes like lipid pools of sensuality. He said, "I'd love to see you again." Mac turned and started walking back to his car. He flashed his perfect white teeth. "Remember what I said, it's all about your perception of yourself. That's all that matters."

Chapter Eleven

I called Charity from my office the day after I ran into Mac at Club Alexandria's, but she didn't answer her phone. I called her on her other cell phone, the left one, and she still didn't pick up. I didn't panic, but I needed a moment to collect myself. I thought: *She doesn't know my office number.* I pulled out my own cell phone and called.

"What up?" Charity's usual greeting. Slurred words told me that my call had awaken her and I could almost see her lying on a motel bed that she'd made queen size by pushing the two small ones together.

"Dahlia?"

"Yeah. You all right?"

"Yeah, I'm cool. Just bored as hell out here."

"Bored is better than dead."

Charity blew into her phone. "Not so sure."

"Look, I'm trying to figure out an angle for you. Don't you know anyone you can go and stay with? Somebody on your father's side? Somebody they can't trace you to?"

"Dahlia, you know as well as I do that my father doesn't keep in touch with anyone in his family."

Charity's exasperation was obvious. I thought for a moment that a smart girl would've thought all this out before she made her move, but she was more intelligent than smart and everyone knows there's a difference.

"Don't worry about it Dahlia. I'll fix this thing. Don't worry."

I didn't say anything for a moment and neither did Charity. We were both holding onto to our thoughts.

Finally. "Charity. And the package? If that's what they want just give it to them."

"I can't give it to them."

"Why not Charity."

"You don't need to know nothing else, trust me."

She was starting to annoy me with all the intrigue and secrets. "It's your life. Just do me a favor," I told her. "Call me once a day like I asked, let me know everything's fine. Would you?"

"Yeah, I'll do that. Morning or at night?"

"At night. Always call me at night Charity."

I spent the day at work trying to figure out an angle, a way to extricate my sister from the trouble she'd gotten into. Her father couldn't help and God knows I didn't want any fallout from her misdeeds to touch our mother. I knew my mother and she had enough to worry about, starting with the man without a face who'd dropped by asking questions about me and the father I never knew.

I guess my mind was full, so full that I hardly noticed the black Mercedes parked in front of my apartment building that day when I was coming home from work. Aspen Hill Road is always busy during the afternoon rush hour. Cars and people line the street, taxis dropping off residents in the row of apartment buildings and condos that dot the street make any parked car an ordinary part of the urban landscape. I didn't see the two men inside the car until I heard one of them call out my name.

I stopped and turned around. I looked. It was Derek sitting on the passenger side of the car with the window rolled down. He was slumped way down into the car seat so that the only part of his body showing was a baldhead that looked like a brown skull with a thin layer of flesh stretched over it. High cheekbones and deep set eyes contributed to that skull and crossbones look that made him all the more sinister. It made me wonder what Charity ever saw in him.

His being there in front of my building and calling out my name gave me a jolt. I wanted to run inside and lock the door behind me, but I didn't. I stopped in my tracks, but didn't come close to Derek and the car, kept my distance. I gave him a: *what do you want look?* It was difficult to hide my feelings. Something bordering on hate always hit me whenever I saw Derek or heard Charity speak his name. I often thought if I could kick his ass I would---gladly.

"Seen Charity?" he asked almost shouting through the opened car window.

I shouted back. "No, haven't seen her! Why?"

Derek cocked his head, shrugged his shoulders until they rose to the same level as his head. He leaned over and stuck his bean-shaped head through the window, outside the car like he wanted me to take in his face and its sinister glory. He had real thin lips, which looked unnatural for a black man, so when he spoke they curled with each word.

He cupped his chin with his thumb and forefinger, rubbed it. "She went out of town to New York. Haven't seen her. Was hoping you had."

"Well, I haven't," I said.

"What?"

I repeated, "I haven't seen her!"

"What?" he said. "I can't hear you." He motioned for me to come over to the car.

That he couldn't hear me was a lie. I looked at the front door to my building. I could see the young security guard through the glass. I was sure Derek saw him, too. I fumbled nervously for my keys. I said, "Look, I haven't seen her for a few weeks."

He shouted back, "Oh yeah, that's interesting. Charity said she was having lunch with you the other day in Georgetown. It was the same day she went to New York."

I'd been busted. I grabbed my keys, but dropped them on the sidewalk leading to my buildings entrance. I reached over to pick them up as everything came spilling out of my purse. "Shit!" I mumbled. I stooped over and began picking up my things. "Be cool," I whispered. "Just be fucking cool."

But it was too late to be cool. Derek was already out of the car, hurrying to help. He bent down on one knee, started reaching for items like mascara, lipstick, business cards, pens and pencils.

"That's O.K. I got it," I said. I was scooping up my belongings right into my open purse---along with a little dirt and errant blades of grass left on the walk.

Derek stood up, smiled. Wicked. "Looking good big Sis." Then his jaw stiffened. There was no smile on his face, not even a forced one. "You tell Charity I need to get with her, you hear me? Tell her I said, she needs to come back home. That thing she did. She knows what I'm talkin' about was just a little misunderstanding. It's forgotten, she's forgiven."

I nodded. I slowed down, purposely took my time and pretended I was putting the contents I'd shuffled back into my bag in order. I didn't want to face him or look directly into his eyes.

I saw his shoes carry him back to the car. He climbed inside and shut the door. His partner, the driver, started the engine.

I looked up. Derek was looking at me hard. He twisted his lips, mouthed the words, "See you later" and pointed his index finger at me. He had his thumb held straight up then brought it down slowly against the top of his pointed finger. Did a recoil motion with his hand and blew at the tip of his finger.

It was a chilly reminder that I couldn't trust anything he said. He was going to kill Charity whenever he found her. Derek had caught me in a lie when I told him I hadn't seen her in weeks. He knew it would only be a matter of time until she'd show up again at my place or that I'd lead him right to her. And if all else failed he'd try to force me to tell him where she was hiding.

I figured Derek would wait before taking drastic measures. He'd rely on patience and take advantage of my fear. That's the way it worked: predator waiting patiently for the prey to make a stupid mistake, out of fear. It isn't the predator that causes the prey's undoing---it's the fear.

Chapter Twelve

It all started with Antoine's visit and the things he said. They say, don't kill the messenger and you probably shouldn't, but sometimes you have to keep a close eye on anyone who bears bad news.

I was sitting at my desk when I was summoned to the personnel office. A pretty young blonde-haired girl was sitting at the receptionist's desk with a stack of papers in front of her and a wad of chewing gum jammed into her mouth. Occasionally she would bite down on a bubble of air trapped inside the gum and it would pop with that aggravating sound that drives teachers to distraction and makes you want to slap the gum chewer in the mouth.

She told me to fill out some paperwork and that the agency had to re-certify all of its employees who had their files corrupted and information deleted.

"What do you mean, re-certify?" I asked her.

"Your security clearance. You have to be re-certified for your clearance status."

I let her comment roll around in my head. Then thought about some of the things El had told me about the government's scrutiny over every little piss-assed blemish on its employees' records. I thought about my student loans, federal-insured, that had gone delinquent and on the verge of going into default.

I thought about how I could not only lose my clearance, but my job along with it. They'd think that someone who owes almost a hundred grand in student loans could compromise government secrets for money.

"You'll have to fill out these papers."

The young woman had a bureaucratic sense of nonchalance, detached with that "I'm just doing my job" attitude.

I finished filling out forms like the ones I'd filled out when they first hired me. I had to give them every little detail about my life. Answered questions about my mother, stepfather and my deceased biological seed planter, finished and handed them to the gatekeeper.

"They're running your info through the computers today. You should have something back before the day is over," she said without looking at me.

The walk and elevator ride back to my office was a long one with thoughts of my career's demise dominating my journey, but as bad as it was it was better than to think about Charity. I thought about the different scenarios and how they'd play out.

I remembered once when a girl was fired and how they had security with guns wearing Gestapo type, drag clothing, escort her out of the building. She'd committed no crime but that's how they did things, fearful that some hundred and twenty-five pound, five foot-six female might go postal and annihilate us all.

The rest of the day was wasted by worry and I sat at my desk waiting for that fateful email or the Gestapo goose-stepping their way to my cubicle. Later, I got the email from Mr. Rhinehart. It read: *Dahlia Reynolds, I need to see you right away.*

The walk down that long, narrow hall to Mr. Rhinehart's office was something like rolling in a Spike Lee movie. My feet had no feeling, never seemed to touch the cold marble floors. Familiar droplets of perspiration gathered right around the bridge of my nose like dew. I used my open hands to fan my face as I walked, happy that there was no one else in the hall to see me flapping my wings as though I'd take flight. I hesitated when I reached his door, but then I took a deep breath and knocked.

"It's open!" He said.

I turned the doorknob slowly and walked in. He wasn't alone. There were two other men there with Rhinehart as he sat at his desk with this stoic expression on his face. The other two men were in chairs with their backs to me. Rhinehart forced a weak smile and motioned for me to take a seat beside his desk. It looked like a scene from Gitmo before they break out the board and start dousing me with water.

"This is Agent Robinson and that's Agent Liles," Rhinehart said.

I nodded politely and they both responded with grimfaced salutations. "Hello, pleased to meet you." They spoke in one voice like it was part of their routine honed to perfection from countless encounters with people as a duo.

"They're with the FBI," Rhinehart added.

Those words hit me hard, reverberated through my body and settled somewhere between my stomach and my heart. Both organs reacted. My stomach churned and felt queasy. My heart raced with intermittent palpitations inserted to slow its pace. In my mind I put together, FBI and Charity. *But what do I have to do with all this?*

I was tempted to start talking before they even asked a question. Tell them I know nothing, tell them that I'm not involved, tell them that Charity and I are only half-sisters.

Robinson, no first name, was the first to speak after our introductions. He sensed my anxiety. "There's nothing to be concerned about, Ms. Reynolds. We just want to ask you a few questions."

I had learned a long time ago that whenever someone started a conversation with those fated words "nothing to worry about" it meant that trouble was on its way. I didn't respond, just waited for the questions.

He had a manila folder balanced on his lap that was in stark contrast to his large dark brown hands. I squirmed uncomfortably as he deftly opened the folder and read something to himself before he began to speak.

"It's about the background investigation the agency conducted," he told me.

I relaxed for a moment realizing I had nothing to hide. My student loan was public record and I thought that if the FBI was getting into the collection business for every delinquent student loan then the country was really in trouble. I just thought, *please don't ask me about Charity.*

"Do you know a Mr. Antoine Blackwell?"

I nodded. He smirked.

"You need to watch the kind of company you keep," he said.

"I'm not sure what you're talking about, Sir," I replied.

I squirmed again in my chair like my thong panties were riding up on me. My body language was going to send me to the electric chair for a crime I didn't know I had committed. I cleared my throat.

"I mean, I know he smokes a little weed now and then but…"

"Don't try and be coy with us," said the second man. Agent Liles broke through. Robinson gave him a stern look, smiled slightly and with a gesture of his hand held Liles at bay.

"I apologize, Ms. Reynolds for my associate's remark. Like I said, we just want to ask you a few questions," Robinson said.

I picked up on their act right away---good cop, bad cop---a time worn cliché, but still no less intimidating. This was the salt and pepper version. I figured that it was Robinson's role as my African-American brother to make me feel at ease while Liles would be "the man", my oppressor ready to shackle me and take me away. "I'm sorry, I guess I don't know why you're asking me about Antoine," I said.

"How well do you know him?" Robinson asked me.

"Not that well. I mean, we're friends, sort of but…"

It was Liles' turn again. "You don't know him that well and you're sort of friends but", he paused and glanced at Robinson's open folder. "He's spent the night at your place twice during the last couple of months and he was there just a couple of days ago."

My mouth dropped open. I looked at Mr. Rhinehart for help, but he simply shrugged his shoulders.

"I didn't know that's a crime," I said. I fought against the desire to go off on him. They were spying on me. "Do I need to call my lawyer?"

Robinson leaned close, flashed his big brown eyes, curled his lips and displayed some of the whitest teeth I'd ever seen. He spoke in an almost whispered, "You won't need a lawyer. Like I said, we just want to ask you some questions. Do you know what Mr. Blackwell does for a living?"

"Music producer." I decided right then to keep my answers short.

He smiled even wider. "He ever talk about any of his associates in *the music business?*"

I detected the *music business* sarcasm. "No."

"Well, if he does anything in the music business it's on the side," Robinson said.

"So, what are you telling me? Is he involved in a gang? Drugs?" I asked.

Liles was chomping at the bit, waiting for his chance to jump into the interrogation.

"Yeah, Antoine's in a gang, alright," he said.

Robinson gave his partner another look as if to say, you'll get your turn, just wait.

"I guess you could call it gang activity but at a different level," he told me. "They're a lot more sophisticated than your typical red shirt-blue shirt guys. I guess you'd call them smugglers or maybe import-export entrepreneurs."

"I don't understand what any of this has to do with me," I replied.

Robinson gave Liles the nod. It was tag team time and like a television wrestler he was already climbing over the ropes to deliver his own kind of smack down.

"It's got plenty to do with you, Ms. Reynolds. Wire transfers of large sums of money from your home computer to foreign banks puts you right smack dab in the middle of all this," Liles said.

My mouth dropped open. "Are you saying that you monitored my home computer? Isn't that illegal or something?"

Liles smirked. "We got all the law we need on our side. It's called The Patriot Act. So why don't we just stop playing games, Ms. Reynolds."

"I don't know what you're talking about. I mean, Antoine's been over to my place lately and he's used my computer to surf the net or play video games, but that's all." I could feel my emotions gaining a stranglehold around my brain, but I fought back the tears that were beginning to well up in my eyes. I needed to think clearly. I shook my head. "I haven't done anything wrong," I added.

I watched as Liles reached for the folder and pulled out a sheet of paper. He unceremoniously placed it on my lap. It was a bank statement from a bank in Antigua with my name at the top. My eyes skimmed over the statement and rested at the bottom where it read: *Account Balance: $250,000.00.* For a moment I froze unable to even blink my eyelids.

"That's a lot of money for a twenty something, forty thousand dollar a year government employee. Isn't it?" he said.

I could feel six eyes all trained on me, waiting for my response. "It's not mine, I swear. I don't know anything about this." I could feel the dam break as the tears rushed down my cheeks. I took off my eyeglasses and put my hands over my face and cried.

I heard the calm voice of Robinson as the good guy coming to the rescue. "I believe you, Ms. Reynolds." He handed me a handkerchief that he had pulled from his jacket pocket and watched as I used it to dab around my eyes.

"I can give the money back," I told him. I kept crying.

"That's not what we want from you if we did we could've frozen the account and seized the money anytime. What we want is your help."

"What do you mean?"

"Your boy, Antoine is a low level player we've been tracking him for a while. Their little posse is up to something huge and we believe they've got a part for you to play, but we need to get the main players. Right now they're insulated. We could pick him up and see if he'll turn on them, but that's a gamble because if Antoine's suddenly not around the others will disappear."

"I don't understand. You mean they want to use me to launder the two hundred, fifty thousand?"

"No, it's much bigger than that. There's a lot of activity within the group and our intelligence tells us that something's brewing and it's gonna happen soon. My theory is that they need you because of your security clearance. Either they want to bring something into the country that's real big or take something out."

"What kind of stuff do you think they're trying to smuggle in or out of here?" I asked.

"That's not important for you to know right now," Liles jumped back in. He was now sitting on the corner of Rhinehart's desk like he owned it.

Robinson spoke up. "They usually deal in fine art, antiquities, stuff like that. They've been known to smuggle ancient artifacts out of Egypt. Some of us at the department call them, tomb raiders."

He motioned for Liles to get off of Rhinehart's desk. "Sooner or later he's going to come to you with a scheme, asking you to help him move something using your credentials."

"And why would Antoine even think I'd do something illegal?"

Liles brought back that awful, sinister smirk to his face. He made a gesture like he was twisting his arm out throwing a punch, but with a twist at the end. It was sexual. I gave him a look of disgust.

"You don't have to do anything," Robinson said. "You're the bait or maybe the foil. Either way, they'll come to you, show you the easy money or make you think that what they're doing is on the up and up. As for our department, we just sit back and wait and watch until the time is right. Our goal is to expose the brains behind whatever it is they're planning and catch them all with the goods."

He stood up, straightened his tie. Agent Robinson and his anxious partner were leaving. "Here's my card, Ms. Reynolds. Just give me a call anytime you want to talk or if you think there's something I need to know."

"Am I in danger?"

"Nah, we don't think so. I'm not going to lie. There are some dangerous elements in this group, but they need you."

I watched as the two walked out of Rhinehart's office with Robinson leading the way. Liles gave me a parting glance and shook his head. He stopped midway. "I can't believe you didn't suspect that our boy Antoine was up to something. I mean, I've seen him while we've been on surveillance," he smiled. "Let's just say you're not his type."

Chapter Thirteen

I left work that day upset and confused. A visit from FBI agents made me stop thinking about Charity and her problems. Now I was focused on Antoine, trying to connect the dots. A quarter of a million dollars, it was the second time I'd heard that figure in a matter of a couple of days.

Agent Robinson readily accepted my claims that I had nothing to do with Antoine and his gang and that made me leery. I wasn't stupid and I knew that cops often let someone believe they're not a suspect when they actually are. They did this so the person wouldn't change his routine or fly the coop.

This was weighty stuff and I didn't know what to do about it or who to talk to. El was the most logical person because she was an attorney and she worked for the Justice Department, but that was also the reason why I couldn't talk to her. I had a quarter of a million dollars in some offshore bank account---thanks to Antoine.

I started thinking back, searching for clues. I thought about the last time Antoine spent the night at my place and our clumsy copulation effort. I thought about the look on his face when I came out of the shower and caught him using my computer. He wasn't looking at porn, but now I wish he had. It was obvious he was doing something real shady and I needed to know why.

My telephone rang. "Wuzzup, Baby/" It was Antoine.

My heart sank and I knew he could hear it in my voice. "Hello," was all I could say.

"Damn! It's good to hear you, too," he said, sarcastically. I didn't apologize or explain my lack of enthusiasm.

"We need to talk, Antoine," I said, flatly.

"Sure, what about?"

"Can't talk on the phone. We need to meet somewhere but not here. We need to meet someplace public," I said.

"O.K. How about at the Mall near the Monument?"

"I'll meet you there tomorrow after I get off work. Say about six o'clock," I said.

I hung up the telephone thinking that I wasn't going to worry about Antoine and the FBI. It wasn't my problem and I wasn't going to help anyone, not him or the government. I just wanted to make sure that my name wasn't attached to anything---not the money, not Antoine and definitely not some big-time gang.

I plotted the route I'd take to meet Antoine after work. I decided to catch the Red Line train to downtown DC and then hop a cab over to Capitol Hill just in case I was being followed. The thought wasn't out of the question, Apparently Agents Robinson and Liles had me under some kind of surveillance.

By the time I reached the platform at Pentagon City most of the people had boarded the earlier trains that ran in succession every fifteen minutes or so. I surveyed the area looking for any familiar faces then breathed a sigh of relief hoping and believing I wasn't being followed.

I got off at the Connecticut Avenue stop and went into the same routine checking over my shoulder and scoped out my surroundings. I can't explain it but the anxiety I felt about being caught up in Antoine's mess was blending in with the suspense of playing this undercover game and it was giving me a kind of rush. Suddenly I was this big-time actress getting over on The Man like in a Pam Grier movie. The intrigue of it all was a long way from my job as a pencil-pushing bureaucrat.

I hailed a cab and told the driver to drop me off a block from the place where I was going to meet Antoine. I could walk the rest of the way.

The good thing about meeting at the Washington Monument was that the area was wide open and there wasn't anyplace, like a tree or building to use as a shield. And there were plenty of people out there. I saw a mixture of hunched over, suited down Capitol Hill government types making their way home dodging the longhair, shirtless Frisbee throwers. Add some tourists in Bermuda shorts, white socks and straw hats it became the perfect place for a covert rendezvous.

I could see Antoine off in the distance, sitting on a bench with smoke hovering over his head in the dry, thin air like he'd been sending off signals. I was pretty calm up until that point, but then I got scared and nervous. My heart seemed to pump louder with every stride and I told myself to just relax. I hadn't done anything wrong and I realized that I shouldn't be afraid to confront Antoine. If anything I should have been pissed off.

He gave me one of his typical easy smiles when I walked up on him like I was simply making a social call, but his smile quickly disappeared when he saw that I didn't smile back.

"Uh, oh, you look like you about to kick my ass or some' in'," he said.

"Trust me, if I could I would." I took a seat on the bench beside him then looked around to see if anyone was within earshot. "I had FBI agents come to my office the other day. They asked me about you and about how well did I know you."

Antoine leaned against the park bench and puffed on his cigar. He tilted his head back and playfully blew out rings of smoke. "Old black dude, young white cat?"

I nodded.

"They're just sniffing around. Ain't got nothing cause if they did I wouldn't be sitting here right now talkin' to you."

"That's not the point Antoine. It's the fact that they came to see me in the first place and that I'm being spied on all because of something you're doing."

"And you couldn't tell them nothing cause, you don't know nothing."

I clinched my teeth together for a moment, took a deep breath then exhaled hard. It wasn't in my nature to curse or swear very much, but his casual demeanor was forcing out the demons that resided deep within me.

"What the fuck are you talking about Antoine? You don't get it. You used my computer for something shady and you never told me anything."

"Well, if I told you I'd have to kill you," he said with a look that was as grim and serious as any I'd ever seen. His statement rocked me for a moment until I saw his smile return followed by an outburst of laughter. "Look at your face! That's some funny shit Dahlia. I've always wanted to say that to someone like the way they do in the movies." He kept laughing.

"It ain't funny Antoine."

"Look, don't worry about nothing. We ain't doing nothing wrong," he told me.

"Well, what about your gang they say you belong to?"

"Gang? I ain't no banger. Look at me. Look at this face. You think I'd be messing around with that hardcore kind of bullshit? Hell no. It's just their paranoia. Anytime they see a group of brothers living large and ballin' they say the words, gang related. Worst thing I ever done was to catch a little misdemeanor type weed case a couple months ago."

"It doesn't add up, Antoine. I mean, why would they be following you, following me if you weren't doing something illegal?"

"Look, like I've told you, I'm in the music business trying to become a producer and I admit that some of the people I deal with want to stay anonymous and discreet, but their simply investors. It costs money to produce, record and package an artist and I don't know if you've noticed but Chase-Manhattan ain't giving loans or investment dollars to twenty-three year old brothers trying to become the next Jay-Z."

"Well, that's all well and good but why are you using me? Why'd you use my computer to handle your business and most of all why'd you put money in a bank in my name? You put me right in the middle of all this and you need to clean it all up. I don't want any part of this shit."

"The money thing was because I know I can trust you and my investors wanted to make sure that I couldn't touch the money until I had certain things in place. I mean 250 grand is a lot of cheese," he said.

Antoine gave me this real soulful look like he was about to beg for something. "Look Dahlia just chill out for a little bit--- please? The money's in the account just gaining interest. Besides, I can't take your name off it because the people I work with set it up as some kind of trust and no one can touch it but you. When the time is right I'll ask you to withdraw it and you can keep ten per cent for your trouble O.K?"

His explanation didn't make me feel any better about the whole situation nor did it put me at ease but I decided I'd roll with it for the moment. I tried to do a quick analysis of everything and thought about my options but I was very confused.

"I'll need to think about this for a minute. I need to figure out what I'm going to do Antoine."

"Take your time, baby. Like I said, just chill out. I'm in no hurry to do anything and I ain't doing nothing wrong but if we all panic and start looking like we're up to some dirt then the Feds will be all over us trying to make a case,"

I sat up straight, looked right into Antoine's green eyes. "What do you mean 'we'?" I told him. "Regardless of what happens and even if you tell me that everything is legit, I'm not in this. There is no *we* when it comes to me, Antoine."

"Yeah, yeah, I got it."

I looked around the park and down the long corridor of grass lined by trees known as The Mall. At the end of the corridor was the place where Congress met. I studied it for a moment and thought about all of the laws that were being passed there then directed my attention back to Antoine.

"Those FBI guys think you want to use me because of my security clearance. They told me that you and your people are smugglers and one implied that's the only reason you're involved with me. The white guy said that I'm not your type"

He smirked then dropped his head and shook it from side to side. "You see, that's why I know they're just fishing for something with their theories and that kind of bullshit. We don't need any kind of security clearance to transfer money from an island account to my bank account here and if my associates are some kind of smugglers they don't need you to handle their business," he laughed along with his words. "What do they think? We're gonna bring the money here in a big paper sack?"

Antoine rose to his feet, stuck his cigar in his mouth and began speaking to me through clinched teeth. He stroked the back of my neck.

"What the hell do they know about what woman's my type? I've always been interested in you because you're different. There's something there, something under the surface and waiting to break lose. But it's real, not made up. Nothin" fake about you, you're just being you and that's what I like." He glanced at his watch. "I got a run but like I said, don't worry."

"Easy for you to say."

"Speaking of being worried, you seen your sister lately?"

"No."

"She still in town or did she leave?"

"I don't know, Antoine. You know we're not that close. Besides, why do you keep asking me about her?"

"Just curious. I wouldn't want to see any harm come to her."

Something about the question chilled me. It was almost like Derek asking about Charity, but it was Antoine instead.

"Like I said. I can help her. You know, maybe act as a go between with Charity and Derek."

"And those Asian gangsters?"

Antoine shrugged like it was a no-brainer. "I can talk to them to. You talk to your sister, tell her to call me. I'll pick up whatever she's got and pass it on."

My skeptics antenna was out and reading. "What's in it for you, Antoine?" I hesitated then asked another question before he could answer. "And what's this *package* everyone's so anxious to get?"

Antoine sucked his teeth, made a sound like some squirrel. It was annoying or, maybe, I was just on edge.

"Don't know what's in the package for sure. I heard it's not drugs. Some papers or some shit. As far as what I want out of this--- nothing. Don't know why you're so damn suspicious. We're practically family. Can't a brother help his lady without being put under a microscope?"

He stretched his arms and smoothed out his tee shirt. Gave me a studied look and started walking away. He turned around. "Tell Charity to call me. O.K.?"

I didn't answer. Just watched him as he walked.

Antoine receded into the crowd of people who had gathered near the Washington Monument. I knew that he was the kind of man who'd go through them rather than around. His ego would cause the crowd to part and make a path for him as he headed towards Constitution Avenue and probably to the place where he had parked his car. I guess if I were an expert in human behavior I'd conclude that he wasn't worried about anything.

Chapter Fourteen

Charity's message sounded strange. There was an edge in her tone like I'd never heard before. It wasn't fearful, no desperation, but strange. I thought, *maybe she's lonely.*

She answered my telephone call with her usual enthusiasm. "WuzzUp" didn't seem to match her message when she almost begged me to call.

"What's up with you?" I replied.

"I need to talk to you."

I said, "Not over the phone."

"Dahlia, can you catch the train out here? I'll pick you up at White Flint Mall."

"When are you talking about?"

"Now or as soon as you can catch the Metro out this way."

I breathed heavy into the telephone. "Damn, Charity. I just got home. I've had a long day."

"Please, Dahlia." Her tone had shifted to the uneasy shrill of someone who was feeling a lot of pressure.

I thought about my own circumstances. My life wasn't lacking any drama. FBI, Antoine and Charity and Derek were all making me want to run someplace and hide. And on the horizon was Mackenzie Powell. I could think about him and be calm, feel safe.

But Mac would have to be a faraway thought for now. I turned my attention back to Charity who was going on and on about something that had eluded me up to this point.

"I gotta get outta here. I'm buggin' out Dahlia."

I shrugged off her comment because I figured we could talk about things when we met up.

"Hang in there, Charity. I'll change clothes and hop on the train. I'll call you when I'm getting close. Be cool. Don't let anybody see you," I said. "And don't have me out there waiting, all right?"

"Don't worry, Dahlia. I'll be there and I'll be low key."

I laughed. Hung up the phone.

I jumped up from the couch and headed to my bedroom. I pulled off my gray pantsuit and twisted my hips into some jeans. Loosened my hair from the bun and let my curls wrap around my head like a halo. Angela Davis, but not as pretty. With my prescription sunglasses I was no longer Dahlia Reynolds, government employee-conspiracy suspect-sister of a wayward stripper who's hiding out from who knows what.

I took off my watch and rings and put them in my jewelry box that was sitting on my bed. I didn't remember leaving the box there. I always kept it on top of my dresser. It was my habit, doing the same thing day in and day out to the point I was almost anal about things always being in the right place.

I thought it was strange that it was sitting on my bed but nothing was out of place so I dismissed the idea that someone else left it there. I looked around my bedroom to see if anything else was out of place. Although the room was just as I'd left it that morning I still felt uneasy.

My paranoia was taking over and I had the feeling that someone was watching me as I rode the train. There were people on the train, of course, Most were wrapped up in their own worlds, but others seemed too attentive to my presence there.

A young man with his pants sagging way below his waist was standing on the train and holding on to one of the bars overhead. I thought about Derek, One of his boys on a mission to find Charity?

A white guy in a gray suit with nondescript features and a needle nose made me think of Agent Liles. He looked at me and nodded when we made eye contact then he looked away.

I got off the train in Silver Spring about three stops before my final destination. I pretended like I was heading for the escalator that would take me to the exit as I watched others leave the train. I didn't see the young man in the sagging pants get off or the man in the suit leave the train so I doubled back to the platform and waited for the next one.

I saw Charity's car as soon as I walked out of the train station. Black and shiny, tinted windows. She rolled her window down, waved at me and quickly rolled it up disappearing behind the dark glass.

"Thanks for coming," Charity said as I climbed inside the car. I gave her a quick once over. She was wearing everything Gucci except a Cartier watch, diamond earrings and a ring that looked like something for a red carpet moment.

I said, "I guess you don't plan on giving the money back."

"Hell, no. Look what I'm going through. I figure they gonna try and kill me no matter what so I might as well enjoy it."

I shrugged. "You're pretty nonchalant for somebody who's being hunted by everyone, especially a bunch of drug dealers to the Asian mob and no telling who else is after you."

Charity drove over to Wisconsin Avenue, hit a couple of side streets then headed north away from the populated D.C. suburbs and into the country. We passed through some town I'd never heard of named, Poolesville. Her route seemed purposely twisted like somebody running to avoid being shot. After about an hour we finally drove down a hidden driveway surrounded by trees and at the end sat a house that looked something like a ski chalet.

"I'm renting the place," she told me.

I followed her inside looking around. Lush throw rugs on top of polished hardwood floors, stone fireplace and windows everywhere. In the midst of this opulent setting were clothes thrown all over the place. Fast food wrappers and half-eaten candy bars cluttered the home's interior the way bad choices were cluttering her life.

Charity had shopping bags stacked in a corner of the living room. Names like Neiman-Marcus, Lord & Taylor and Saks Fifth Avenue were stenciled on fancy bags. She pushed aside a pile of clothes crumpled on the couch with price tags still on them. "You wanna sit down?"

I plopped down without answering, still in awe. "How much money do you have left?" I asked.

"Lots. I still got around two hundred thousand." She laughed. "A quarter of a million is a lot of loot."

I thought about the money Antoine had deposited in an account under my name and had a fleeting thought about how I'd spend it. Pay off my student loans. I'd buy myself something nice to wear. Maybe, buy a new car, but nothing fancy. Just transportation.

She walked over to the bar and grabbed a bottle of Alize. "You wanna drink?"

I nodded figuring I needed something to take the edge off my own problems. "How much are you paying to stay here?"

She cleared a spot beside me and sat down. "Not much. The guy who owns this place is some old rich dude who comes to the club. He tips me big time, especially when I give him a lap dance. He gets real excited---if you know what I mean---tips me with hundreds. The more I rub this ass of mine on his lap the more money he gives me."

I shook my head, partially in disgust, partially in amazement. Charity took a long sip from her glass then poured herself another drink.

"It's not what you think, Dahlia. I pay him rent, that's all. Cash not ass. That's the arrangement."

"He know why you're hiding out here?"

"Nah. I just told him I needed to get away. He knows about Derek and how he gets rough with me now and then."

I took a sip of my own. "Speaking of Derek, he was waiting for me outside my apartment building the other day."

Charity gave me a matter-of-fact kind of, "I know."

"What! You've talked to him?"

Charity sighed. "Yeah, I called him last night."

"No! Charity, you didn't, did you?"

"I was lonely. I been out here all by myself. I told you I was bored."

"Did you tell him where you are?"

"No. I mean, he asked me if I was at a hotel and I was, at first, but out here I know no one can find me so I figured it was safe just to talk. He asked me, of course but I just told him I was staying with a friend in the city."

"You planning to see him?"

She put her glass to her mouth and threw her head back. I watched her as she emptied a half a glass of booze in one swallow. She poured herself another healthy glass then tilted the bottle in my direction. "No. I'm straight," I said.

"I don't know what I'm gonna do Dahlia. Derek told me that he'd let bygones be bygones. He said a quarter of a million ain't shit to him. Says he makes that in a week."

I said, "What about that Asian dude you robbed? Is he willing to let bygones be bygones?"

"Derek said it's all straightened out. He said he just wants the package I was supposed to deliver. He gets that and the whole thing is forgotten."

"Package? What was it? Drugs?"

Charity shook her head. She stood up and walked over to a cabinet that looked like a place where a man would keep his guns. She opened it and took out a brown envelope. Charity came back over to the couch and unfastened the clasp that kept the envelope closed.

"This is why I wanted you to come out here. I opened it on the way up to New York. Had no idea what was in this when Derek gave it to me." Charity's face turned grim. "You better look for yourself."

She handed me the envelope. I stared at her for a moment, searching her eyes. Worry was hiding behind her dark pupils. Fear was hiding behind mine. My fingers turned eager as I quickly pulled open the flap and reached inside.

There was a manila file folder with my name on the tab. I looked back at Charity. She shrugged her shoulders. I opened the folder then looked down at its contents.

Letters, papers, a swath of cloth and a picture of a man all neatly stacked inside the file folder. I thought: *What does this have to do with me?* My question was answered when I saw that some of the letters were addressed to Stephanie Reynolds, my grandmother.

"I don't understand," I said. "How, how did Derek get this stuff? Where'd he get it from?"

I looked at Charity. "I don't know," she said. "But remember when somebody broke into mom and dad's house?"

I nodded. They had ransacked the house for this? It didn't make sense.

I flipped through the letters still in envelopes, some unopened. They were postmarked from someplace in Thailand and Louisiana and on the outside of the envelope it read: Inmate Number 10034.

Charity was settled deep into the sofa with her hands wrapped around the whiskey bottle. She was now sipping directly from the source, bypassing the formality of using a glass. She had retreated into another world leaving me puzzled and confused.

There was a grainy black and white picture of a man. He had a thick beard, curly Afro and piercing light colored eyes. He wasn't smiling in the picture, just staring straight ahead into the camera. His face was solemn. His eyes almost pleading.

I flipped the picture over. There was writing on the back. It read: To Desdemona, Love Dad.

"Who's this?" I asked Charity, showing her the picture.

She was slumped over with her knees pressed together and her legs in an awkward position. Her head was cocked to the side. The bottle of Alize was teetering on the armrest barely in her hand.

I turned my attention back to the letters and the picture. I couldn't understand why someone would pay all that money for some old letters addressed to my grandmother and a picture of a man I didn't know. But what scared me was the thought that somehow Derek had this stuff that must've come from my family's house. Panic gripped me. I thought about my mother.

Charity was using the name, Desdemona as her alias. I remembered she told me that Nana loved the name, loved Shakespeare, loved the play Othello. I asked myself, so who is Desdemona?

I realized that I couldn't sit there and try to figure it all out. I needed to go home and think, maybe talk to my mother.

"I gotta go home, Charity." But she hardly moved.

I took the bottle out of her hand and put it back on the bar. I came back over to my sister and shook her slightly. "I gotta go."

She made some kind of involuntary honking sound with her mouth and nose then shook her head. "Take the car, Dahlia. Leave it at the Metro station. I'll get it tomorrow."

"How are you going to get it from there?"

"My friend." Her words were slow and drawn out like a bad record. "He's coming out here tomorrow to check on me." Charity shook her head repeatedly. "No funny stuff. Ain't givin' him no booty."

"You going to be all right?" I asked.

"Yeah, yeah. I'm cool. Just lock the door when you leave. I'll get my car tomorrow."

I put the file folder back inside the envelope and grabbed Charity's keys. It was just getting dark and I was hoping I could remember the route we took to get there from White Flint station. I read a sign pointing to Poolesville and I felt relieved. From that point I looked for landmarks. An old diner told me that I was getting close to Route 301 and that would take me back to Wisconsin Avenue. I'd be on the train in a few minutes.

I rode the train with the envelope pressed close to my chest, clutching it with both arms. Letters to my grandmother and a picture of some strange man along with a piece of cloth and a door key were apparently worth a fortune to the man Charity had robbed. I wondered if she gave me the envelope to throw them off her trail and maybe, put them on mine.

Chapter Fifteen

I stared at the picture of the man with the vaguely familiar eyes. He was somebody's father. A girl named Desdemona, Charity's pseudonym. My grandmother must've known the girl.

Maybe, Nana once knew the man whose face stared back at me from a faded sepia-colored photograph with the word Polaroid printed on the edges.

I reached inside the envelope and pulled out the piece of fabric. I'd taken just a quick glance at it when I was at Charity's hideout. Now I could see the cloth clearly and the stitching that appeared to be symbols. A circle with rays---maybe a rising sun. An arrow pointing upward to the sky---depending on how I held the material----was directing me somewhere, maybe heaven.

Simple things that didn't seem to go together couldn't have been worth a quarter of a million dollars. I thought back to the break-in at my mother's house and how nothing was taken, but they did ransack Nana's room. They were looking for something. Apparently this was it and Derek was connected.

I was so engrossed in my thoughts that I almost didn't hear the doorbell ring. I put the envelope down and headed over to the monitor to see who was ringing my bell.

"He's gotta stop doing this," I said, frustration in my voice. It was typical Antoine, coming over without calling, acting like I didn't have a life. My first thought was that he wanted me to withdraw the money when he had just told me that he was in no hurry to get it.

I was feeling a little agitated when I turned on the monitor to see the concierge standing with a delivery man holding a large box.

"Ms. Reynolds," said the concierge. "You have a delivery."

"I'll come right down."

I put the envelope Charity had given me away and made my way to the elevator that would take me to the lobby. I was thinking I hadn't ordered anything and I didn't usually get packages out of the clear blue sky. After the last couple of days and the things I'd gone through I would view this latest surprise with suspicion.

Maybe it's a bomb!

It was an absurd thought but with everything that had happened in the last couple of days I couldn't be sure. A huge sum of money deposited in an offshore bank in my name, FBI investigations, my sister on the run harboring a windfall of her own then passing the baton to old gullible me. A brown envelope with letters from a stranger written to my grandmother and a picture sent to some girl named, Desdemona. It was getting crazier and crazier by the minute.

I dismissed the idea that someone might send something deadly to me. Through the chaos I'd done nothing wrong, committed no crime. I tried to think positive as I rode the elevator. *Maybe, my mother sent me a surprise.*

The last time I'd gotten a gift from back home was when Grandma Nana sent me the family quilt that I kept hanging on my living room wall. That was a total surprise because I always wanted the quilt but never thought I'd have it until both my grandmother and mother were dead and gone. But Nana told my mother she wanted me to have it before she died a few years ago.

But I could tell from the wrapping around the box that this was nothing from home. The box was wrapped in thick, fine paper more like brocade fabric and not old back issues of the Waycross Gazette. It had a silk bow and a white woven envelope tucked inside its seams.

I waited until I was back in my condo to read the card. It read: *I hope you'll come to my little party — Mac. P.S. I realized that you might need something to wear.*

I opened the box to find a dress, a matching pair of shoes and a Fendi purse. The shoes were a size nine, my size. I wondered how he knew. I filed the thought away for the moment, figuring that his skills of observation were finely tuned or it was a lucky guess.

The dress, a Jean Paul Gaultier, was like the ones I'd see in fashion magazines. I figured its price to be around three to four thousand dollars.

I sat down on the sofa and breathed hard and deep, nearly hyperventilating. I didn't know whether to be flattered or angry. I tried to figure out why he sent these things. Maybe, he really was trying to buy my affections but he didn't seem like the kind of man who'd have to pay for his women.

He's a collector. That's what he said. And what do collector's do? They buy what they want whether it's an antique or a woman.

I picked up the telephone and dialed Mac's number. It rang a few times and then his voice mail came on asking the caller to leave a message. "Yes, Mr. Powell. This is Dahlia Reynolds. I need to talk to you. I need to tell you that I can't accept these gifts from you." I left my number although something told me he had it already.

The gifts Mac sent answered the question about what to wear, but I was uncertain whether I should go or return them. I called El and later, my friend Stacy to ask them what they thought I should do. I knew what El would say, "Take the clothes, girl." Stacy was more guarded. She told me people don't give you expensive gifts without expecting something in return.

But that was Stacy, always cautious. I decided that I'd wear the dress and the shoes, sport the purse like I was born to carry a fifteen hundred dollar bag. I was going to the party.

I pulled my hair back trying to give myself a sophisticated look, one that would match my outfit. I put on a little makeup to glam myself up, hid my eyes behind my schoolmarm-looking glasses and headed out to catch a cab to Georgetown.

I was half way to the elevator when I remembered the envelope. I had left it out in the open and something told me I'd better hide it in a safe place. I figured I would read the letters addressed to my grandmother and try to unravel the mystery of it all later.

Chapter Sixteen

Mac's home had a fairy-tale, mystical quality about it like something you'd read about in a gothic novel just not as scary. Old style carriage house that almost took up the whole block and shot five stories into the air. It was a brick edifice to Georgetown's historic past with gargoyles crouching on every cornerstone guarding, I imagine, Mackenzie's fortune.

He said he was an antiques dealer so I figured he had a lot of expensive stuff inside protected by something a lot more reliable than stone gargoyles. I saw the security cameras canvassing the grounds like one-eyed sentries and wondered who was on the other side.

But I was used to being under surveillance. Ever since 9/11 the people in this town had become the most watched population in history with us all getting our fifteen minutes of fame even if we didn't know it.

I took one last look at the cameras as one of the valets opened the door to my taxi and held out his hand. The lenses followed me to Mac's front door and to a stately looking man standing there in a black tuxedo.

He smiled and said, "Welcome, Madam." Then with a slight bow and gloved hand guided me inside. "You are looking very lovely this evening, Ms. Reynolds."

I stopped. "Do you know me?" I asked.

He increased his smile. "It's my business to know all Mr. Powell's guests."

He regarded my surprised expression for a moment then said, "Right this way." I followed him into a large foyer with marble floors and velvet drapes. There were other tuxedo wearing men standing stoic-like each with trays of Champagne carefully balanced on one hand. The men watched the guests closely making sure that no one's glass was ever empty.

"Champagne?"

One of the servers had approached me without my seeing him. I jumped just a little then settled in to a quieted, "Yes, please." I took one sip then opened my Fendi handbag and pulled out a dollar.

He frowned, at first. Then he drew an amused expression on his face. Guess he figured I didn't know any better. "No thank you, Madam," he said.

I watched him walk to the other side of the foyer to a small group of people. Each person accepted a glass without tipping him any money and I realized that I not only embarrassed the server but myself as well.

I glanced around quickly to see if anyone else had seen my social transgression, but as far as I could tell no one was watching. I walked around the foyer nervously admiring the ambience of it all.

The fountain in the foyer was lit up in yellow lights and pushing Crystal not water. There were servers everywhere with trays of appetizers. Mac's guests were dressed like they were in a scene from the old television show *Dynasty*. I thought, *there are pretty people everywhere.*

Everyone was talking and laughing obviously having a good time. It seemed like all the rich and famous were there.

I recognized D.C.'s mayor at the center of a small crowd and looking a lot more relaxed than the way I had seen him on television. He nodded at me and held his drink up as I walked by making my way deeper into Mac's cavernous home.

I noticed Congressman Taylor, chairman of the House Ways and Means Committee and one of the most powerful men in Washington talking a man who looked Middle Eastern. There were two, drop dead gorgeous women about half the congressman's age lurking nearby like they were waiting for him to finish his conversation. And leering at the two young women were several members of D.C.'s professional football team, including Blue Morris.

I thought, *Wow! Mac seems to know everybody.*

The thought made me realize that through all the glitz and glamour Mackenzie was conspicuously missing. I wandered deeper inside hoping I'd see that smiling dimpled face with the flashing green eyes.

Searching through the crowd but trying to be cool about it until my eyes connected with a familiar face. She gave me a cold stare then acknowledged me with a head nod. I remembered her from that very first day, the day I first met Mackenzie at the restaurant with El and a freaked out Charity. I froze in place as she walked towards me. It was the one I called, The Dragon Lady.

"So glad you were able to make it," she said. She forced a smile, but I could tell it was as icy as the cold coming from her violet-colored eyes. She extended her hand towards me. "I'm Sue When. I work for Mackenzie."

"Dahlia, Dahlia Reynolds," I said.

"I know. You must be looking for Mac."

"Just wanted to let him know I made it."

Sue narrowed her eyes, as she looked me up and down. "Nice dress."

"Thank you," I said. "It's Jean Paul Gaultier."

"I know. I picked it out."

I wanted to make myself invisible. But something told me I was being tested. I had to rise to the occasion. I was trying to be a brand new me. "You have very good taste," I said.

Smug look. "Follow me."

I walked behind her like I was under orders. I watched her from the rear for a moment. Her silk dress made Eastern style fit perfectly. A slit revealed smooth skin and a thigh that was taut and robust. I caught a glimpse of a tattoo on her left ankle that disappeared with each forward stride. It looked like a serpent or dragon, which seemed appropriate for her.

I walked faster. I caught up to walk with her side by side. She walked with her chin up and shoulders back. Her long black hair was pulled straight back, revealing a proud slightly larger than average forehead. High cheekbones cut through the room like a pair of knives. I thought: *She's stunning. She works for Mac. Wonder what she does.*

We glided past the pool house where I could hear music playing. It was a live band.

"Mackenzie's in the pool house," Sue, said.

She retreated back into the house without another word. I shrugged off her icy attitude figuring that was the way she carried herself.

I made my way through the crowd, passed the atrium and walked over to the swimming pool. This was the real party. While the people in the house were standing and talking, the folks here were getting their groove on. Nothing old and stuffy here, they were jammin'.

Mac's swimming pool was covered by a temporary dance floor and with a stage that had a ten-piece band grinding out some soulful songs. I recognized Phoenix, a popular local singer leading a jazzy, bumping version of Marvin Gaye's, "What's Going On." The music made my body sway involuntarily and I started mouthing the words to the song. There was a man on stage with his back to the crowd, tuning up his trumpet. It was Mac.

He turned around and immediately hit a solo that could've rivaled Miles or Dizzy in its vibrato and Wynton in its precision. But his demeanor was low key and not showy. It was easy to see that he was having a good time and was in his element up there. And the crowd loved it. With each beat and every burst from his horn they rocked and swayed, throbbing to the music, a unified body moving like one person.

I got closer to the stage to get a better look. Mac was dressed in a black tuxedo and looked like a man ready to model in a wedding magazine. There was a small group of women standing right in front of him, cheering him on with flirtatious smiles. He responded by blowing a few notes and stopping to let the band catch up while flashing that killer smile. His eyes finally caught me standing there admiring his every move. He greeted me with a warm smile and a nod as if to say, I'll be right there.

When the song ended and applause rained down on the band, Mac got off the stage and made his way over to where I stood. He was a little winded from playing but it didn't dampen his enthusiasm. It was clear that he was happy to see me.

He took my hand and said, "I'm glad you made it. I thought you weren't coming."

"I almost didn't. You got my message, didn't you? This is too much," I said, showing off the dress.

"It's beautiful. You're beautiful. It was made for you," he replied. "Look, buying women expensive clothes is something I don't normally do but someday if I have the chance I'll tell you why I did this for you. Besides, it's a small gesture."

"Of what?" I asked.

"My appreciation for just knowing you."

I was smiling and looking into his soulful eyes as he held my hand. There was strength in his hands. Something in them that told me no harm could come my way with him around. For that moment the world stood still. There was no band playing, no crowd of people bumping to what was now non-existent music, just Mac and I standing there talking. It couldn't have been a more perfect setting for a man and a woman who were just meeting and trying to get to know each other without being awkwardly thrown together on a first date. It was perfect until we were interrupted by a woman's sultry sounding voice.

"Hey, Mac," said the voice behind me.

She quickly moved over to his side and grabbed him by the arm like she owned it. I recognized her as the same woman that was with him that evening at Café Alexandria. Her eyes were focused on him, ignoring me as she talked about the party and how she loved his playing the trumpet. Mac listened for a moment and then stopped her.

"Felicia, let me to introduce you to Dahlia. Dahlia, Felicia."

I held out my hand but she gave me a fake smile in return and kept her death grip on Mac's arm. "Nice dress", were her only words. I read between the lines.

I found myself shrinking behind her overwhelming presence. But it wasn't just Felicia's lack of manners that made me feel uneasy, it was Felicia herself. She was downright intimidating. I sized her up. She was model-type beautiful, around forty-years old and holding it extremely well.

Her hair was perfect, short and sassy. She looked like she was pressed from a mold. An African-American version of Mac's employee, Sue When. High cheekbones, full lips, brown skin and a body that would rival any twenty-six year old's including mine. I hoped I'd look like that in fifteen, twenty years.

But it was more than Felicia's looks that intimidated me, it was an air about her like she was the Queen of Sheba and everyone else her subjects. I picked up on it right away, a diva in the classic sense buoyed by a lifetime of being spoiled by men with an attitude as clear as cellophane.

Felicia whispered something into Mac's ear and pulled him away as he gave me an apologetic smile and mouthed, "I'll be back". I was left hanging there alone and feeling slightly dejected. I thought that this was way too much drama for any man. Sue, the dragon lady and now Felicia, the ice queen. Both running interference. Each with an obvious thing for him.

I stood on the dance floor pondering whether I should just leave, but before I could move I was being pulled onto the dance floor. *Screw her and Mac, too.* I jumped at the chance, grabbing something to drink as I followed. The band played and I had a series of men, both young and older surrounding me on the floor and with each dance came another glass of champagne.

For that moment I felt that I was the center of the Universe. *All eyes on me.* This had never happened before. I wasn't blending into the background like someone dressed in camouflage fatigues and standing in a forest or on a sand dune. Truthfully, I loved the attention and it made me feel good not to be overshadowed by El or that bitch Felicia or that bigger bitch, Ms. When.

As the night went on I danced to Prince, Outkast and Mary J. Mac or no Mac, I was having a good time. But it was time to find Mackenzie and tell him I was ready to leave. I walked back into the house passing admiring stares and wishing I'd brought my friends along so I wouldn't feel so alone. I saw Mayor Huff still talking and obviously entertaining the crowd. I figured I could blend in.

A young woman whispered in my ear, "His Honor is talking shit."

I picked up on the conversation as Mayor Huff was debating the virtues of older men and younger women. *That's just great,* I thought.

"Old is better than gold, baby," he told his small audience. "The Hell with Moms Mabley. Talkin' bout ain't nothin' an old man can do for her but point her to a young one. That's bullshit. These young cats don't know how to treat a woman. Me? I'm flowers and candy and expensive gifts. You could say that I'm all that and a bag of chips."

Everyone laughed. "Bag of chips? No one says that anymore," someone said.

"Yeah, you talk a good game Mr. Mayor but I know you can't handle this," a woman said, sticking out her ample rear as she struck a sassy pose with her hands on her hips.

He leered at her ass, reached into his jacket pocket and pulled out his business card.

"Here's my personal telephone number. Call me, we'll talk about it," he said.

Then he turned to someone who was probably a reporter. "If you print this I'll deny everything." His words were followed by a chorus of laughter.

I shook my head and turned around when I heard Mac's distinctive laugh behind me. He was a few feet away talking to one of his Saudi Arabian guests. Felicia wasn't up under him anymore but it didn't matter. The alcohol was my liquid courage and it gave me confidence. I set my eyes on Mac and stepped right to him.

"So, there you are Mackenzie Powell. I thought you deserted me," I told him.

I was ready to forgive his transgression.

"I am so sorry. Felicia wanted me to meet someone and I had to fight to break loose."

He paused and then directed his attention back to his guest. "Dahlia Reynolds, I'd like to introduce you to my good friend, Sheik Khalid Al Amin. I just call him, Al," Mac said.

I was impressed. I was thinking, *A real Saudi prince? Mac operates in rare air*.

"It's a pleasure to meet me. I mean, it's a pleasure to meet you."

My words disjointed and slurred. I was feeling no pain.

"Likewise," Al said.

He extended his hand ready to accept mine and when I gave it to him he gently kissed it. Then he gave me this long look like he was studying my face and that made me feel uneasy even with my senses dulled by the alcohol. Mac could tell that I had had too much to drink and that I was real unsteady on my feet.

"I think you could use a good strong cup of coffee," he whispered in my ear.

He took my hand and led me to the only room in the house that wasn't crowded with his guests. On the way he told one of the servers to bring me a cup of coffee.

I leaned on his shoulder as we walked and Mac put his arm around my waist keeping me upright and steady. Once in his study, I slumped down on the sofa, down so low that I almost disappeared inside its pillows.

"Was that your girlfriend?"

I forced out a drunken inquiry, still cognizant of my own insecurity. He knew that I was talking about Felicia.

"No, she's just a friend," he answered, softly. "How many glasses of champagne did you drink?"

I held up ten fingers and said, "Just two". Mac shook his head and then lifted my feet on to the sofa so that I could lie down.

"Why don't you rest here for a minute? I'll check on the party and I'll be back," he said.

My head spinning, I looked up, gave him a goofy smile.

"I will if you kiss me," I told him.

Without hesitating Mac leaned over as I closed my eyes and readied my lips. I felt his warm lips plant a kiss in the middle of my forehead.

"I'll be back," he whispered.

He turned off the lights and left.

I drifted into an alcohol-induced stupor, something between sleep and veiled consciousness. I couldn't fight it and I couldn't move so I resigned myself to the fact that I would sleep it off.

I don't know how long I was there but my sleep was interrupted by the sounds of someone breathing heavy and deep interspersed with a few moans. Even in my haze I knew that it was the sound of people engaged in some kind of carnal activity. I couldn't see much in the darkened room except the outline of two bodies, a woman leaning forward on the desk and the man behind thrusting himself against her.

It was obvious that they didn't know I was there. It didn't last long and when they finished I heard the sounds of clothes rustling and hurriedly put back in place. After that, murmurs and whispers followed by kisses. I strained to hear their words.

The man spoke: "Anybody see you come in here?"

She laughed. "Fine time to ask now."

I recognized the laugh and the voice. It was Sue. Fear gripped me. I wondered if it was Mac with her. I brushed the thought aside hoping that he would say something else and that I could be sure.

"We can't let anyone know about this, especially Mackenzie."

Hearing that brought me some relief. It wasn't Mac who'd been humping Sue. I held my breath as she spoke. "What? You don't want him to know that you screwed me?"

"I don't give a damn about that. I don't want him to know that I told you about Desdemona."

"Don't worry. I won't do anything to upset your little plan," Sue told him. "And as far as Mac is concerned I don't know her."

"That's good, trust me."

"And what about the girl?" She asked.

"Don't worry, my people are keeping an eye on her. You just follow orders and do what I tell you to do," he answered.

I could see him pull her close. Their silhouette became the two-headed monster---deception and intrigue. For a moment no words were spoken until she broke the silence.

"Just like a man. Screws you and then wants to boss you around. Don't worry about me. I'll take care of my part. You just take care of Mac and Desdemona."

She pushed him away, pulled her dress down and smoothed it against her body. He stood motionless for a long time after she had left the room and I held my breath afraid to make a sound. I was hoping that he wouldn't turn on the lights to see me balled up in a corner of the couch. Instead, he walked to the door, paused and then made his exit.

I wanted to rush out of the room, find Mac and tell him about what I saw but I wasn't quite sure what was going on. I chose to curl up on the couch and wait. As I drifted off to sleep my thoughts were of some woman named Desdemona and my heart sank. All of a sudden the name was resonating everywhere. My sister's alias, it was in the letter to my grandmother, that unusual name was on everybody's lips. I figured it was its time like Stevie Wonder and all the women who named their daughters Ayiesha in the Seventies when he sang that song.

I reminded myself how Sue told the man to take care of Mac and Desdemona and the instruction had a foreboding quality to it. I fell asleep with the words "Mac and Desdemona" ringing in a head that had lost its sobriety. Mac and Desdemona sounded like a match pair like Brad and Angelina, Lucy and Ricky, Bobby and Whitney.

Chapter Seventeen

The light from the Sunday morning sun crashed through and entered the study without mercy, unforgiving in its interruption. I was startled to the point where I sat straight up and then quickly laid back down. I grabbed my head and rubbed at my temples. I couldn't believe that I'd slept there through the night. I stumbled to my feet wondering what happened to Mackenzie.

I surveyed his study looking for signs of life there. His laptop computer was in the middle of a starkly clean desk. The faint glow from the screensaver told me that someone must've been on the computer while I slept.

I looked at the computer screen and decided not to touch it. I turned around and took in the pictures that seemed strategically placed on Mac's credenza. There were pictures of him with famous people---smiling with Bob Marley, another with him talking to Miles Davis.

I saw the familiar face of a very beautiful woman in one of the pictures and I realized that I recognized her. It was Michele Swift, a movie star my mother loved back in the day but had died tragically in a car accident overseas. Mac was standing with his arm around her, both smiling wide, a tropical scene in the background.

I thought if I were only as pretty as she was Mac wouldn't leave my side. I put the picture back down in its place.

A picture of a little boy with devilishly green eyes caught my attention. His hair almost took up the entire picture frame. I figured it was a picture of Mac's son taken a long time ago. I smiled. "What a cutie," I said.

At the end of Mac's picture gallery I noticed a black and white photograph of a group of young men. I picked it up and studied it close. There were eight of them in the picture, some black, some white. Big Afros, long hair and beards, they had the look of musicians like modern day troubadours.

It was a picture of Mac's band. I searched for his image. I saw the face with his same dimpled smile and jade colored eyes flashing at me from more than twenty-five years ago. He was kneeling in the front of the group with another young man who looked like he could be Mac's brother.

I smiled at the sight of seeing them in bell-bottom pants and paisley colored shirts. The man who looked like he could be Mac's twin was wearing a medallion around his neck, but not like the gaudy bling-bling that some of the rappers of my age wore. I looked close to see that it was a St. Christopher's medal, probably his patron saint. It made sense. Mac told me they were a traveling band.

I put the picture down and kept the image of Mac and his friend lingering inside my thoughts. I wondered if the man posing with him was his brother.

I walked out of the study and into one of the halls, followed it towards the foyer and the spiral staircase that led up to the eight bedrooms that Mac said were upstairs. I stopped when I heard sounds coming from the kitchen. "Mac? Mac?" I called out.

I could smell fresh coffee brewing along with the smell of something cooking. I found my way to the kitchen ready to curse him out and to ask him why he left me there. But it wasn't Mac cooking it was Felicia. She was standing over the stove dressed in a silk robe and gown and with her back to me.

"How do you like your eggs?" she asked.

I was a little too shocked to answer so I asked my own questions.

"Where's Mac? Is he upstairs?"

Felicia was pretty matter-of-fact in her reply.

"Oh, I think he went to play golf with the mayor and some of his guests from Saudi Arabia."

"And he left you here?" I was looking very confused.

"I know what you're thinking and the answer is, no. I didn't sleep with him. Mac and I are yesterday's news. I slept in one of the guest rooms upstairs."

I was still foggy brained and slow to process what Felicia had just told me.

"I guess I drank too much," I said.

Felicia smiled. She seemed totally different than the way she was when we first met, even friendly.

"You really like him, don't you?" she asked.

I nodded. "I think I do but I don't know what to think. I just met him and I definitely want to get to know him, but last night he didn't seem that interested," I said.

Felicia listened as she continued to concoct something that I assumed would be breakfast.

"Mac doesn't eat red meat so there's no bacon or sausage, stuff like that. I put some croissants in the oven and there's fresh fruit if you'd like some," she said still scrambling the eggs. "The eggs are those organic, low cholesterol kind and so is the butter he uses. Personally, I like the real stuff, the kind that clogs your arteries to the point where they'd have to put a catheter in me to keep my blood flowing."

Felicia laughed at her inside joke as its punch line drifted over my head. "Forget it. Stupid joke," she said.

"I guess I looked real silly last night. Getting drunk and passing out."

"It happens. I didn't even know you were here until Mac told me this morning. We've all been there. As far as whether he's interested in you or not, I can't say. Mackenzie keeps things locked inside. All the time we were together he never once told me he loved me, but I know he did."

Felicia continued. "Look, sweetie. Be careful. Mac's no different than any other man. He's got good qualities and he has bad ones. How old are you anyway?"

"Twenty-six."

"Well, you're young but old enough to know better. Ever been in love?"

"No."

"All I can say is; be careful. Mac and I used to be an item once but that ended years ago. Like most men his age he's got some baggage and he keeps secrets. Did he ever tell you about Michele?"

I thought about the picture of Mac and his lost actress.

"One thing I know is that he's never gotten over her death. Did he tell you that he was driving the car when it happened?"

"No," I answered.

I watched Felicia intently as she busily poured, stirred and scraped. For a moment I thought that the conversation was a little too heavy, especially considering the fact that I hardly knew Mac and didn't know Felicia at all. On the other hand, she was someone to talk to and at the very least I could pick her brain and maybe learn everything I wanted to know about him.

"Yeah, it seems like he has a lot going on," I told Felicia. "What's the deal with Sue When?" I said.

Felicia scraped some eggs out of the skillet onto my plate. "His personal assistant, that's all. He met her years ago back in

Thailand or Singapore. She's a little on the cold side but smart as hell. She's real good at finding valuable art d' objects, especially precious jewels but mostly, she's tough. Martial arts expert, Sue can kick any man's ass I've ever known. But Mac trained her himself, taught her everything, made her who she is today."

"What do you mean?"

"Well, I heard he found her when she was like seventeen years old working the streets---if you know what I mean." Felicia winked. "Transformed her from a trashy little street urchin to the Miss Thang you see now. He sort of did that with me."

"Oh."

"Just make sure you don't let her intimidate you. She's real protective of Mackenzie. Loyal as a pit bull. She'd probably kill you or anyone else if she felt you were a threat to him."

Felicia laughed behind her words, but what I saw in Sue made me believe there was an element of truth to the warning.

"I know Mac and if you ask me I think he has a special interest in you. And trust me he's not the paternal type. I've been with him. He had me asking my damn self who's my daddy?" Felicia laughed. "Here, eat this and then go up to the first guest room and change your clothes. We've got an errand to run."

Chapter Eighteen

My brain was still full of cobwebs as I climbed inside Felicia's car and we sped down Mac's driveway like we were on the Autobahn. I opened my eyes wide when we almost struck an unmarked car with tinted windows. I made another mental note.

Felicia cursed at the car like it was the other driver's fault but she didn't stop. "They're probably cops or something," she told me.

"Why? Is Mac in some kind of trouble?" I asked.

"Nah, you know how it is. Police are always around where the rich folks live, protecting their stuff and they treat people in 'The Hood' like they're in some kind of leper village. They only go in when they have to," Felicia said. She was changing the subject as quickly as she was shifting gears in her car.

It was the nature of small talk, prying and inquisitive to be sure but I couldn't help but gravitate to the woman I saw as my rival. I thought there was no harm in talking about my life.

Felicia shifted gears seamlessly and the black Porsche zipped down Connecticut Avenue without stalling or lurching forward as we exceeded the posted speed limits. It was hard hearing her with the wind whipping around my ears. I was tempted to ask her to put the top up. But the combination of wind and speed and riding in a convertible sports car was intoxicating so I just leaned closer and strained to hear her every word.

"What do you do for a living?" I asked.

"Oh, a little of this and a little of that."

She was being evasive, but I wasn't going to press her. Whatever she did it was obvious to me that she did it well.

Felicia downshifted and the Porsche whined, let out a high-pitched cry and then deepened into an outright growl like it was fighting being harnessed at low speed. We whipped around a corner, hugging it tight like the car was on a rail. She pulled it out after punching the gear into third and the car lurched forward at nearly seventy miles an hour. My fingers dug into the sides of my seat, making sure that wherever the car would go I'd fly right along with it.

"Nice car," I said.

"Men aren't the only ones who are entitled to have toys," she told me.

Somehow the statement didn't surprise me nor did the aggressive way in which Felicia drove her car. I could tell that she took a back seat to no one including the rich and powerful---especially men who were in that category.

"Where are we going?" I asked.

Felicia looked over at me with a near smile on her lips. "When's the last time you've been to a spa? Girl's gotta' get pampered."

She returned her eyes to the street, shifted gears and accelerated. We were crossing the Key Street Bridge into Alexandria, Virginia and over to Old Town. All the while I was wrestling with my hair that was blowing all over my head.

"We're going to have to do something about that," Felicia said, looking at my mass of curly hair.

If there was a place for a woman to get pampered it was La Femme Spa, a high-priced world of saunas, massages and some of the top hair stylists on the planet. Felicia walked in like she owned the place and she seemed to be on a first name basis with everyone from the receptionist to the manager.

"Give us the ultimate package," she told a beauty consultant. "And for my young friend here throw in a beauty consultation. I want her to have a total makeover. You know---haircut, perm and makeup."

I looked at Felicia. "Wait a minute!" I said. "Who told you I wanted my hair cut and permed? I can't afford this."

"Trust me. You need this. Besides, if you want to get Mac's attention and make him really hot for you, you'll do everything you can to enhance what you already have---he's very particular, you know."

Felicia reached into her purse and pulled out an American Express Platinum Card. "Don't worry. Mac's treat."

We were led into a dressing room and emerged later wearing robes. A steam sauna helped me get rid of the remnants of my hangover. We followed with a massage, pedicure and manicure. Felicia was taken into another room after we finished the first phase of our royal treatment and I was led away to the salon where my hair was washed and detangled.

"You have beautiful hair," said the Asian woman. I watched her study my hair like a scientist. She was running her fingers through my hair, methodically feeling its texture.

"But, you need it thinned and, maybe, a little tint to bring out color. Don't worry, when we finish, you like, very much."

"Are you the stylist?" I asked her.

"Oh no, Mr. Powell say Mr. Sinclair do hair. I prep you," she answered.

El had told me about Raymond Sinclair, the hair stylist to dignitaries, debutantes and stars from Hollywood and New York. Getting him to work on a woman's hair was like trying to get a private audience with the Queen of England. There was a waiting list for his waiting list.

"You Mackenzie daughter?"

I gave her one of those you must be kidding looks.

"The eyes. You have his eyes," she explained.

"No, I'm not his daughter. We're friends." Then my curiosity took over.

"Do you know Mackenzie Powell?" I asked.

She smiled.

"Everybody know him. He come here, say once, twice a month. You know, manicure, pedicure."

"Does he bring any other women here?" I asked.

"Oh, no. Sometime Ms. Felicia come in but not with him. Act like goddess or something. Nobody here like her. All the ladies here love Mackenzie. Men, too. He so-o-o good-looking."

She had a wishful look planted all over her face, like she had retreated into some kind of fantasy and he was the object of her desires. I watched as her dark, almond-shaped eyes took her to some unspoken, faraway place and I knew that it was time for some fantasy interruptus. I cleared my throat hoping that she'd remember that I was there.

"I sorry," she said. Back to reality, she was fluffing out my hair, using her fingers as combs.

After her assessment of my hair she summoned her team and they attacked it like it was Medusa's writhing snakes, intent to lob off my thick mane and make it more manageable. They combed through it and started cutting my hair in big wads at a time. I couldn't see exactly what they were doing but my stomach balled up into a knot each time a lock of my thick curls fell on the apron draped over me. They gave me a light perm, which tingled but didn't burn the way I'd always heard it does.

When Raymond Sinclair came in I was expecting him to be accompanied by an entourage. I also expected him to be pompous and gay, but he was neither. He was tall, handsome and dark-skinned, which made me feel uneasy about him working on my hair. It was like having a good-looking gynecologist looking at me with my legs spread wide open and my feet up in stirrups.

He smiled politely, introduced himself, asked about Mackenzie and then asked me about myself. He wanted to know my favorite colors, hobbies and activities, as well as, what I did for a living.

"I treat every woman as a model for a masterpiece. It's not just a matter of style but a look inward so that I can sculpt a style that brings out your essence," he told me. All the while I was thinking that El would be green with envy because she bragged that she had made an appointment with him three years in advance.

Like a surgeon, Raymond took over and used some kind of comb with blades to rake through my straightened hair. After that, he blew it dry and flat-ironed it into a style that reminded me of the hairdos I admired in beauty magazines. When he finished, the whole team stood there admiring what they'd done. Then they erupted into applause.

I felt a little embarrassed, but also anxious to see the final result. Raymond spun me around to face the mirror as I fumbled for my glasses. My mouth dropped open. The change was so dramatic to the point where I almost didn't recognize myself. What had been a wild, uncontrollable mop of hair that extended past the middle of my back was now a soft, semi-straightened Cleopatra-like hairdo that stopped at my shoulders. Someone said that I was like a caterpillar turning into a butterfly.

"They'll do your makeup next," Raymond told me. "Tell Mac he owes me a round of golf. I want to get my money back. Tell him Lola and I will see him at the fundraiser."

Felicia was in the lobby reading a magazine when I came out and approached her without saying anything. She felt my presence as I stood there with a wide smile. She gave me a quick glance and then at the book sitting on her lap. The double take she gave me said it all.

"Girl, just look at you!" she said.

I struck a pose, did a couple of spins so that my loosened hair would follow and snap back into place. Felicia was beaming like a proud parent watching her child take her first steps.

She said. "Wait until Mac sees you. I think he'll be impressed."

Felicia took my hand and led me out. She looked at me again, trying to fully appreciate the metamorphosis.

"Anyone ever tell you that you have the most beautiful eyes? I mean what are they - green, gray? It's hard to tell with those glasses."

"They're hazel with specks of green." I told her.

"Tomorrow, we make an appointment to see an eye doctor. You should wear contact lenses or get laser surgery."

She was talking like a woman on a mission.

I didn't respond to her directive. I was so excited about my new look that even the suggestion about wearing contact lenses didn't upset me. I was busy looking at my hair and makeup in the car's mirror to the point where I started to imagine how everything would come together if I didn't wear eyeglasses. Felicia watched, amused by my pre-occupation.

"I'll drop you off at home," she said.

I learned a lot about Felicia during the drive home. At forty-two, she had been married and divorced and she didn't have any children and never wanted to have any.

"I'm not the domestic type," she said, repeatedly.

Felicia explained that her career was important but not all consuming and she had been successful at it because, in her words, she had achieved perfect balance between her business and personal life.

"How long have you known, Mac?" I asked.

"Oh, about twenty years. I'll never forget that day I met him. I was walking down the Champs Ely sees and…"

"The what?" I broke in, displaying my lack of worldliness.

"It's a street in Paris," she replied flatly. "He was the most beautiful man I'd ever seen and I walked right up to him and told him. I was modeling over there and we quickly got involved. I thought that he should model too, even though he was almost forty but the agencies over there said he was too exotic looking."

She laughed with the memory.

"I remember an agent telling Mac that they were looking for an All-American type and he got pissed. Told them, 'America ain't just blonde hair and blue eyes, you French pastry jerks.' That was the end of his career there." She laughed.

"What did he do then?"

"He got his hustle on. Got me off drugs. He basically saved my life."

"What do you mean, he got his hustle on?" I asked.

Felicia dumbed up on me.

"I probably said too much," she told me. "Let's just say that Mac knows how to make money."

It was almost dark when we got to my place. Felicia said she needed to use the bathroom so she hastily parked her car and followed me inside.

"Your place, it's nice and quaint," she remarked after coming out of the bathroom. "How much did you pay for it? I know. Rude question but I'm just curious."

"Too much." I left her question unanswered, figured that was really too much information. After all, I didn't ask her how much she paid for her Porsche.

Felicia flopped down on the sofa, the picture of a woman relaxed and in repose.

"Nothing takes the edge off like a day at the spa." She paused. "Nothing, except this."

She was reaching into her purse searching for something. Finally, she pulled out a joint and a cigarette lighter.

"I hope you don't mind," she said.

I said nothing but thought, what *can* I say! It wasn't like I'd never seen marijuana before. In fact Charity and I would smoke on occasion. And, of course there's Antoine. But most of all I didn't want to appear to be un-cool around her.

I watched and said nothing as Felicia lit up, took a heavy toke from the joint and exhaled a cloud of smoke that nearly filled my entire living room. She closed her eyes for a moment and leaned back on the couch. She looked back at me and held out the joint for me to take.

"That's O.K. I'll pass. My job drug tests, you know."

"Right," said a skeptical Felicia. "When's the last time you've been tested?"

"Well, I've never been but just in case. There have been some things going on at my job that makes me nervous about doing something like this. And I don't want to risk being random tested one day..."

Felicia cut me off. "You won't be. This is some good stuff, baby. Not that ghetto shit you folks get on the street. This is right from the source."

My resistance was short-circuited by Felicia's seemingly raw power over me, a power I didn't quite understand. I reached out and we traded the joint from her hand to mine. I took a long hit to show her I wasn't afraid and held it inside until my lungs burned. The smoke fast tracked right to my brain and I quickly felt its effect. Playfully and with a good buzz going, I blew smoke into Felicia's face.

We laughed hard and passed the joint back and forth until it nearly burned the tips of our fingers. Felicia was right about one thing---the stuff was unlike anything I'd ever tried. A couple of puffs on a thin rolled up marijuana cigarette had my head swirling and made my body numb. Time seemed to pause as I sat in a sensory stupor unable to speak and hear.

"You're high."

"You damn right, I'm high," Felicia said laughing harder. "And so are you."

"Yeah," was the only word I could utter and force through numbed lips. My mouth hung open, frozen by the effects of the cannabis. Like a character in a *Cheech and Chong* movie I'd blotted out reality and suspended my animation.

Felicia chuckled as if she had told herself a private joke.

"What's so funny, Felicia?" I asked.

She gave a heavy sigh, blew out empty air because she hadn't inhaled anymore smoke.

"You said you've never been in love, Dahlia?"

"Yeah. What about you?"

"Yeah, once and only once."

"Mac?" I asked.

She nodded. Another sigh. "Loving him put a vice grip around my heart. Squeezed out any love I might've given someone else. I had nothing left to give. Even for my poor ex-husband. Problem was, he knew it. Whenever Mac would call me I came running and the poor schmuck I married would sit there and wait for me to come back to him. I felt bad for him and sorry for myself."

"And did Mac love you?" I asked.

"Yeah, in a way. It wasn't on the same level that I loved him. I'm an adult. I knew that. Where I lost the capacity to love anyone else because I loved only him Mac lost his capacity to love me because he loved so many."

The statement confused me and I guess it was showing all over my face.

"Sweetie. Most men have only one great love their entire lives. All the other women are merely infatuations or lustful connections. Mac has truly loved a number of women but has probably never really been in love."

"Oh, so he's a player." I smiled.

Felicia turned to face me. "There's a difference between players and lovers. Players play. Lovers love. Players make love into a game. A true lover of women knows that the heart is nothing to trifle with."

"Then I guess what you're telling me is the fact that Mac didn't love you meant that he was playing you so by your own definition he's a player."

I sat back after the comment and realized I was being too philosophical. Felicia's intuitive senses must've been working overtime because she laughed hard.

"That's what weed does to some people. Makes them think they're Socrates or Plato, reincarnated, when it's just their brain's all fogged up by the drugs. You know, this is your brain and this is your brain on drugs."

I guess getting high did something else to me because I hadn't noticed that Felicia was steadily moving closer to me. Without a word she put one arm around my shoulders and used her hands to massage my neck.

"You're still a little tense." She whispered.

I nodded, my eyes closed, my head was spinning.

"You know you're very pretty. I can see why Mac is attracted to you," Felicia told me.

Her voice was soft and breathy as she spoke. "Ever been curious?"

I was so into the moment that I barely heard the question or I didn't understand it.

"Curious about what?"

I felt her warm lips on my bare shoulder. Her free hand moved from massaging my neck, down along my breast and was now resting around my waist. Felicia pulled me at the waist as she moved her own body into position, ready to mount mine. I guess she probably thought that I was too high to be aware of what was happening and with my guard down she thought I was there for the taking.

She pulled my face close to hers, our lips just inches from each other's.

"You are so pretty, Dahlia. So pretty," she whispered and puckered her own sensuous lips ready to taste the sweet nectar of youth that emanated from my mouth. Slowly, Felicia moved closer and closer. My breath stilled. My heart pounded hard.

"I've been wanting to do this since the first time I saw you," she said.

She touched my lips with her own. But feeling her kiss shook me out of my drug-hazed fog. I pulled away disengaging her lips from mine.

"What are you doing?" I asked.

My tone made it clear that the advance wasn't welcomed.

But she was undeterred. "C'mon. Don't you ever wonder how it would feel to be with another woman instead of some man treating you like a piece of meat? You should know that nobody knows a woman like another woman and nobody knows how to *satisfy* a woman like another woman."

"So, you're telling me that you're a lesbian, right?"

I leaned back and put some distance between us to take some of the starch out of Felicia's advances.

"No. I'm not a lesbian. I just don't put labels on myself. I am whatever I want to be for the moment. For me, there's a time for men and there is a time for women. It's what I want when I want it," Felicia said. I could feel her conviction in her words.

She was annoyingly matter-of-fact about my reaction as though she was testing me. Maybe it was the drugs but for some strange reason I thought about one of the cats we had on my stepfather's farm, the one that teased and toyed with field mice before devouring them. The cat would trap them with his paws then let them go free momentarily and play for hours. Eventually he would tire of the game, grab hold of their tales, toss them in the air and swallow them whole. His power and self-indulgent sense of superiority over the mice made him the fattest and happiest cat on the farm. I wondered whether Felicia, like that old cat, was just doing this for sport or was she really hungry.

I amazed myself with my own sense of calm about being hit on by another woman. This had never happened to me before. I wasn't upset or flattered and ambivalence was an inadequate description. As beautiful as Felicia was I wasn't attracted to her.

"Well, I'm not there," I told her. "Call me naïve or stupid or even, country but I'll just stick to men."

I was defensive but I stayed calm.

"Oh, sweetie, you are what you are," Felicia replied.

Her voice was soothing and smooth like butter.

"That's all anyone can be in this life. I just figured that a young sister like yourself would be open---given what you have to work with. From what I hear most young brothers are either in prison, on their way to prison or gay. Face it, your choices are limited and if you think latching on to some older man like Mackenzie is the answer, then you really got a lot to learn, baby."

I was O.K. until she mentioned Mac. The comment upset me. Latching on is for leeches and I never thought I was one.

"I think you better leave," I said.

Felicia's reaction was swift. She stood up, adjusted her dress and headed directly for the door. I sat there fastened to the sofa, refusing to move. But I still watched as she stopped in the doorway with one foot inside and her pride standing in the hall.

"I'd be very careful dealing with Mac if I were you," she warned. "Oh, and please do me a favor. Don't tell him about what happened here today, alright?"

She gave my place a visual once-over like she was looking for something or trying to remember the way it looked.

"Love the old quilt you got hanging on the wall. So quaint."

Felicia slowly closed my door and I heard the clicking of her high heel shoes against the hall's marble floors. I listened as the sound diminished with each step until I heard the elevator chime and realized that she would take a slow ride to the first floor and I hoped out of my life.

Chapter Nineteen

I rushed home from work that day hoping that he had called and left a message. My anxiety level rose when I entered my building. I thought of my answering machine's familiar refrain, "You have no new messages."

I could hear my telephone ringing as I approached my apartment door. I fumbled with my keys as I clumsily unlocked it. The telephone sat on an end table right beside my sofa and I literally dove for it with an outstretched arm. "Hello," I answered.

"Hi, darling Dahlia," came an exaggerated greeting. It was Felicia. My heart sank. I know she heard it in my voice.

"Oh, Hi."

"Well, aren't we the chipper one? Hard day at work? Not a problem. Look, I'll be brief. You have an appointment for tomorrow to be fitted for your contact lenses."

I said nothing, allowing my brain to process what I was hearing. I recalled Felicia had mentioned something about contacts that day we went to the spa but I got high and I didn't take her seriously. Now things were clear and I wasn't sure it was a good idea.

I thought about everything that had happened during the last week or two. The dresses, the makeover and now contact lenses, things I couldn't afford to do for myself and now I was beginning to feel overwhelmed by it all, swept away and fearful of being lost in Mac's wake. And what about Mac?

"Are you Mac's secretary? Why doesn't he call me himself?"

Felicia laughed like she was amused by my question. "Mac's out of the country and I'm sure he'll want to see you when he gets back," she told me.

She continued un-phased by my indifference. "Everything's set up for you. Just show up for your appointment and they'll take good care of you. Bye, Sweetie." Click.

I sunk into the sofa still clutching the telephone close to my stomach. I thought about calling my therapist but the situation wasn't exactly an emergency so I turned on the television just to have as background noise and I sat there trying to process the things that were gradually changing my world.

It was six o'clock and the evening news was on the television. *Seven more soldiers are dead at the hands of insurgents. President Bush still insists that Saddam Hussein had weapons of mass destruction.*

Police find a burglar stuck in the heating duct at a local department store. And police have no clues about the man found shot to death behind a local nightclub. Details right after this.

Mac hadn't called me and neither had Charity and that had me worried. I dialed her number. It rang a couple of times followed by her voice mail greeting with some generic rapper in the background. I suffered through Charity's sing-song greeting and quickly shouted into the phone: "Charity! Call me!"

I decided to dial the other number I had for her, her other cellphone. Different greeting, but same result. I put my phone down wondering where she could be and why she didn't answer. I persuaded myself not to think the worst. I decided I'd try and call her again---just in case she had been away from her cellphones.

It rang. I waited. I glanced up at the television. Dead soldiers' pictures on display, fresh faced and too young to die. I was watching the screen. 'Double-U-Bush' was on now trying to look confident but not fooling anyone. He's aged at least fifteen years compared to the six he's been in office.

The reporter was talking in front of Café Alexandria with file footage wrapped around his live report.

The news report said a body had been found behind the club in a dumpster. I thought about all the news of death and destruction and my anxiety level about my sister increased ten fold. Problem, I didn't know what to do about it.

I had been so pre-occupied thinking about Charity and Mackenzie that I almost forgot about the envelope Charity had given me, the one I had tossed aside just before I went to the party. Along with the picture of the strange man with the Afro was a letter. I pulled it out and opened it. I skimmed through it trying to figure out who wrote it and why.

The writer asked about my grandmother's health and told her how much she was missed. I read the name Desdemona once again and there was a question about how she was doing.

It went on to questions about my grandmother's quilt. The writer talked about its history and that the real treasure was what it meant to my family.

I looked at the piece of cloth again. It matched in some ways the quilt that hung on my living room wall like it was going to be added on at some point in time. I repeated my interpretation of the symbol on it: *"Rising sun."* I asked myself what that meant.

I poured the solitary key out of the envelope. It didn't look like a key from my mother's home, but I reasoned that it must be connected to the letter and the other items that were inside.

My grandmother had to have known what this all meant. But the answer to the question why some Asian guy would pay a quarter of a million dollars for the envelope's contents could only come from him---whoever he was.

I dialed a familiar number. My mother answered the phone. Her voice trembled out a "hello".

"Hi, mom."

"Sweetie, I need you to come home. We need to talk. It's important."

Chapter Twenty

There was rudeness in the way the telephone rang. I woke up with a jolt to my consciousness and grabbed the phone. I exhaled a feeble, "hello".

"Hey, Dahlia."

It was a man's voice in a slow drawl. Its tone sickened me as I heard him say my name as I imagined through gold teeth.

"What do you want, Derek?"

"Just a friendly call. We practically family ain't we?"

"Not the last time I checked."

I heard sarcasm in his laugh. "Hear you got something that belongs to me."

"I don't know what you're talking about, Derek." I felt a lump rise in my throat. He had gotten to Charity. "Where's my sister?"

"You tell me."

"If you've done anything to hurt her I'll make sure you pay for it."

Another half-hearted laugh. "What you gonna do, Dahlia? Like I'm s'posed to be scared or something. Look, just give me back my package and nobody including you gets hurt."

"Like I said I don't know what you're talking about."

"Bitch lied to me. You tell her when I see her she's a dead woman!"

"I gotta go," I told him.

"Hope your folks are all right."

He hung up the phone with me still holding my end. I was trying not to panic. My mother told me that they hadn't been able to reach Charity and neither had I, but it sounded like Derek knew about the break-in at my mother's house. I tried to dismiss the idea that he had sent someone to Georgia to find my sister or the envelope, but it was clear that there was a connection. They'd do anything to get it---even kill.

I cursed Charity over and over then felt sorry for her, but it was clear that I had to get out of my place as soon as possible. Even with my building's security I knew Derek and his boys could find a way to get to me. But I had to find Charity before he did. He was closing in on her thanks to her stupidity.

I had to find her first. I figured I'd catch a taxi out to the place where she was hiding and talk some sense into her. Maybe I could let her know just how dangerous this game was.

I couldn't get a flight out until sometime the next day and that was on standby. I couldn't spend the night there alone. I thought about calling Antoine. Maybe, he would come help me, but I quickly nixed that idea.

I threw some clothes in my travel bag then put the envelope back where I'd hidden it. I hurried out of the building hoping I'd find a cab real fast. I surveyed the street out front and stepped out to the curb. A black car with tinted windows was there like it was waiting for me. I knew who it was before he climbed out of the car. It was Derek. He'd called me but he was outside my building the whole time.

Derek and one of his boys a huge man, taller than El's basketball player boyfriend, jumped out and walked towards me. I started trembling uncontrollably like my legs would give out from underneath me at any moment. Still, I couldn't move. Fear had planted my feet like they were immersed in concrete.

They were walking fast with their hands in their pockets. I turned to look at the front door of my building, hoping the security guard was watching but he was nowhere to be seen. All I could think about was they're going to shoot me right here. My whole life flashed by in a millisecond.

Their heavy footsteps were getting louder. I fumbled for my door keys, but it was too late. They were just a few feet away. I looked at Derek and caught a glimpse of the evil piece of steel he was carrying in his hand. I whispered, "Oh, God!"

Then I heard footsteps coming from another direction. I thought they had surrounded me so I wouldn't be able to run. I turned to see who was coming to join them. It was Mac.

"Hey baby. You ready?"

Mac reached for my travel bag then gave Derek and his boy a no nonsense kind of look. They both stopped in their tracks momentarily then continued their march in our direction.

"Hey, Dahlia. Can I talk to you for a moment," Derek said. He tucked his gun back inside his pants pocket.

Mackenzie jumped right in. "We're kind of in a hurry," he told Derek.

"I wasn't talkin' to you, old man."

Mac smiled, but it wasn't the usual one he'd turn on whenever he was being just plain charming. It was that deadly---don't mess with me---smile. It was the one I saw that night at the jazz club when he confronted the man who'd been harassing me. "Hey, bro. Don't want any trouble, but like I said, we're in a hurry."

Mac took my hand and started walking towards his car. He whispered, "Just keep walking."

I heard Derek's flunky say, "Dude's dis'n you, Dee."

"Yeah, I know Scoob."

That was all he needed. I could almost hear him thumping his chest, full of courage fabricated with steel. "Don't walk away from me, bitch! We need to talk!"

I saw Mac's jaws tighten. He put my bag down, turned around and started his walk right up to Derek. "You need to watch your language, son."

"Who the fuck are you? My daddy or something?"

"If I were your father you'd be a better man than what I see here."

Derek shook his head. "I'm a man, alright. You see this. This is all I need to make me a man." He was pointing to the gun that was protruding from his pants pocket.

Mac didn't flinch or retreat one step. He calmly opened his jacket and put his right hand on his gun. "I guess this makes us about equal," he said. "It's a little different standing eye to eye on equal terms. Probably easier to just speed by in a car and shoot out the window at someone standing on a corner. Hit your target or hit a child, it doesn't matter. You're just out to prove your manhood, right?"

I was terrified. I wanted to run, but I couldn't leave Mac there staring them down like some modern day Wyatt Earp. "Let's go Mackenzie." I tugged at his left shoulder, but Mac was riveted to the ground.

"You've got a choice to make here. You can leave and let us go on about our business or you can stay. But if you stay I can pretty much guarantee that you won't leave this place on your own."

Derek was still feeling cocky, but he eased his hand away from his pocket. He whispered something to Scoob and they both turned and started walking back to his car. "You ain't seen the last of me, old school." They kept walking with Mac staring the two young men down until they were climbing inside the car. "Dahlia, don't forget to tell Charity what I said."

We watched Derek pull off with tires screeching and smoke churning from underneath the rubber. I was still shaking and unable to talk. Mackenzie picked up my bag once again and gently took my hand to lead me to his car.

"Where can I take you?"

"I'm, I'm not sure." I took a deep breath and swallowed hard on my fear. "I was going to check on my sister, but then he came by…"

"Who is that guy?"

"Her boyfriend. He's been looking for her because…" I hesitated. I looked at Mac as he started the car. My mouth hung open in disbelief. "Where'd you come from?"

"I was in the neighborhood," Mac said. He added, "Nah, just kidding. I came by to see you. I felt so guilty about the other night at my party. I guess I wasn't a very good host. I would've called but I couldn't find your number."

He started the car and drove off. I sat there not knowing what to say. Finally, I said, "Thanks."

"For what?"

"For showing up the way you did. Derek's crazy I don't know what he would've done if you hadn't been there."

"What's he got against you?"

"It's complicated. There's so much going on in my life it's hard to explain," I said. "Can you help me? I need to find my sister, make sure she's all right."

"No problem. Just tell me where."

I told him how to get to the place where she'd been hiding out. When we got there the house was dark and her car was gone. I asked Mac to wait while I got out and went to the front door. I knocked on the door, rang the doorbell, but no answer. I went around to the back door and knocked again. Still, no one came.

When I came back around to the front Mac had gotten out of the car. He was looking into the house through a window.

"Looks like somebody's been here," he said. "I'll open the door and check and see."

He went to his car and came back with a curved knife. I watched as he put the blade inside the lock and twisted it until we heard the lock pop and the door opened. Nervously, I followed him inside.

I called out her name a couple of times but no answer. "She's gone, but her stuff is still here. She probably went out. She's been going crazy staying here by herself."

"Any other place she might have gone to?"

"Not that I know of. I was afraid she might've gone over to Derek's but he came by my place looking for her so I guess she's O.K. I'll call her a little later."

We left there with me feeling that Charity was fine. Mac had said he didn't see any evidence of any foul play.

"I guess you can take me back home," I said.

"You sure you'll be O.K.?"

I thought about Derek coming back to my place. I didn't feel safe there. I guess Mac sensed what I was feeling. He said, "Why don't we go to my place? You said you're leaving town tomorrow. You can stay there."

"I can't impose."

"No imposition. Looks like you're going someplace."

"Back home to Waycross. I'm hoping I can get a flight out sometime tomorrow."

"You sound like something's wrong. Some kind of emergency?"

"Not sure. My mother called. Said I needed to come home. It's not like her to ask me to come home unless it's something important."

" Look here, I've got to fly to Miami in the morning. I'll drop you off. It's on the way."

"I don't get it. How are you going to drop me off in Waycross, Georgia?"

"I'm a pilot. I'm chartering a plane to go on a short business trip. There's a small airport near Valdosta. Can you have someone pick you up from there?"

"I think so. My mother will come and get me."

"Good. Now I'm hungry. Why don't we stop and get something to eat?"

I nodded.

"I'm sure your sister's fine. You can get a good night's sleep then we can leave early in the morning."

He took me to this quaint little bistro named, Van Gogh's in southwest Washington, right on the Potomac River. We talked over PEI Mussels, roasted vegetable Ratatouille and seared Diver Scallops. The conversation was engaging and although I hung on his every word my thoughts were weighted. I had to talk to someone. I had to tell Mac about all the things I was going through. I just hoped my baggage wouldn't be too heavy for him to carry.

My mood turned sullen and quiet over dinner. Mac picked up on it and asked me what was wrong?

"Like I said so much is happening in my life I don't know where to start. My mother is at the top of the list, but there are other things."

"Like your sister and her boyfriend?"

"It goes much deeper than that. I shouldn't tell you but something's telling me to trust you." I smiled a faint smile. "Maybe, you can give me some words of wisdom."

He laughed. "Is that a crack about my age?"

"Uh, oh. I hit a nerve, didn't I?"

"No, not really, but experience does matter. You can talk to me. Are you in trouble or something?"

The question made me a little edgy. "Why'd you ask me that?"

Mac shrugged his shoulders. "Guys with guns are always a bad sign."

"No, I'm not really. It's Charity. Please promise me you won't tell anyone, please?" I paused. "Besides, you carry a gun."

"Score one for Dahlia. I promise not to say a word to anyone."

Mac did the cross-your-heart thing with his finger.

"O.K. here goes. My sister took money from some Asian guy in New York. She was supposed to deliver two hundred and fifty thousand dollars back to Derek and she kept this envelope with what seems like some meaningless stuff, letters, a picture of some man who looks like he's in a police lineup and a tattered piece of cloth with symbols on it."

"Cops looking for her?"

"No. Some Asian guys. They're big time gangsters in Thailand. Charity would be better off if it was the police trying to find her."

I looked directly in Mac's eyes. He looked confused but he seemed intent on following where I was headed.

"Anyway, Derek, the guy you met tonight is or *was* her boyfriend. He's this crazy-ass drug dealer who beat her up at least once."

Mac clinched his jaws hard. "Go on."

"Anyway, Charity gave me the envelope and I took it home. There were letters from someone in Thailand and in Louisiana written to Nana, my grandmother apparently before she died. I mean it doesn't make sense. She never left south Georgia let alone some foreign country."

"Maybe it's some kind of pen pal," Mac said.

"Yeah, must be a letter from MLK or the king of Thailand if someone's going to pay a quarter of a million dollars for it." I paused. "There's something else."

"It gets deeper?" Mac asked.

"Yeah, real deep. This guy I kind of date or something, named Antoine has got the FBI checking up on me. They came to my job to talk to me. They think I'm laundering money for some smugglers."

Mac sipped his wine. "Smugglers?"

"Yeah, Antoine set up an offshore bank account in my name and he put a quarter million dollars in that account."

Mac said, "There goes that figure again. It seems like two hundred and fifty grand is the going rate these days for almost anything."

"You're being sarcastic, but this is real."

"I'm sorry, but it all sounds like some kind of cloak and dagger stuff---but I believe you. What about the FBI? What did they tell you?"

"Just that their investigating and that they don't believe I have anything to do with the money and Antoine."

Mac stirred his Ratatouille around. He was deep in thoughts of his own. Finally, "So what's the deal with this guy, Antoine? You love him?"

I didn't hesitate. "No. I mean, we had something for a brief moment, but he's got a reputation with women. Besides, he's really not my type. I mean he's a street guy like Derek. Thinks he's a hustler like he says his father was."

"As far as the laundering situation, are you helping him hide money?"

"Oh, no! No way! I'm broke but I'm not desperate. I know it might sound lame but I'd never do anything against the law---not something like that."

Mac gave me a reassuring type smile. "I believe you. You're right, though. You've got a lot going on for someone so young, but your problems aren't insurmountable. Maybe, if you give Derek the envelope that would be the end of it all, but I got a feeling that won't bail your sister out. What are you going to do?"

"I don't know. I don't want to involve you, after all, you hardly know me, but I was hoping you'd have some ideas."

"I know some people who might be able to help. I can handle Derek."

"I think Antoine told me the guy she stole the money was from Thailand. Charity didn't really know. She thinks they all look alike."

Mac rubbed his chin. "Probably connected to the mob people I told you about. Antoine, uh? Does he have something to do with Derek?"

"He knows of him, that's all."

"Well, I'll call the people I know. They have connections over in Thailand. They can probably give me the skinny on the, who and why. If they want what's in that envelope, maybe you can give it to me when we get back and I can work something out to give them what they want and no one gets hurt." He hesitated. "Maybe, if I check out this envelope we can make some sense of it all."

Talking to him made me feel better. I was still tense, but there was a comfort in just being with Mackenzie. It was attracting me to him even more. I guess there's something about a man who can take charge when he has to. Call me old fashion, but I needed that, I needed him.

I thought about showing him the envelope and its contents but decided I'd wait until after I returned from my trip. Besides, I'd left it in my apartment and hidden for safekeeping. There were too many people looking for it and too many questions.

Chapter Twenty-One

I held Mac's hand as we waited for the valet to bring his car and felt a touch of moisture in his palm. I squeezed it slightly as though I was reassuring him and marveled at the power I apparently had over a man who could intimidate any woman. He reacted by giving me a vague smile then focused his attention on a man and woman walking down the stairs from the building and heading in our direction.

The always calm, always cool Mackenzie Powell was having an uneasy reaction as the couple came closer. He shifted his eyes away from the pair like he didn't want them to see his stare, but it was too late. The chocolate man with the familiar soulful eyes was upon us.

"Well, well, if it isn't Mackenzie Powell," the man said.

Mac forced a smile, gave him a slight nod. "Paul," he said.

"Have you met my wife, Mac?"

"I can't say that I've ever had the pleasure," Mac replied.

The woman reciprocated with a polite smile of her own then passed it along to me. I, in turn, wanted to run. I cringed underneath the man's presence and hoped that he didn't recognize me or if he did that he wouldn't call me by my name.

The air was thick with tension and Mac tried to ignore the man as he strained to see if the valet was bringing his car.

"It's been a long time," the man said.

I thought, *it was just the other day* believing he was speaking to me, but when Mac said, "Yes it has been a long time Paul." I realized that I was off the hook.

It seemed that we both breathed a little easier when the shiny black Bentley rolled up in front of us and came to a stop. The man looked at me and narrowed his eyes while I tried my best to ignore him as I hopped inside the waiting car. Mac walked to the driver's side and gave the valet some folded up dollar bills as he seemed to hesitate before he took his position behind the steering wheel.

"Nice car, Mac," the man said. He looked at his wife waiting for her to join him in his appreciation of Mac's exquisite automobile. "This is truly a great country when a man can overcome adversity and achieve whatever his heart desires."

He followed the statement with a broad smile, which quickly evaporated into the stone-faced presence I'd seen in my supervisor's office just a few days earlier.

Mac was in the car and comfortable behind the steering wheel. He inserted the key, turned on its engine and waited as the seat automatically adjusted to his height and pushed back to accommodate his legs. The steering wheel retracted and adjusted itself to Mac's driving preference. He touched the LCD screen and quickly programmed some music and the car's interior lights then leaned over and looked at the man through the window on my side of the car.

"It truly is a great country, Agent Robinson. I hope that you and your wife enjoy the rest of your evening."

With those words, Mac shifted the car's gears and pulled off slowly as I watched Agent Robinson with him watching me through narrowed eyes. The large soulful eyes were gone, replaced by an intimidating scowl that resonated in his stare. He nodded at me, letting me know that I hadn't escaped his scrutiny. The fear returned with the same kind of intensity I had felt that day when he and his pasty-faced partner came to interview me, but it soon went away.

Mac seemed unusually uneasy and barely spoke a word. He loosened his tie and opened the top button to his shirt. "It's getting a little warm in here," he said. "You mind?"

He adjusted the AC and seemed to breathe easy from that point on. I had a million questions about our encounter with the FBI agent, but I wasn't going to ask. I just sat back and let the nighttime air carry us. I didn't want to know why Mac seemed troubled about running into Paul Robinson and I didn't care.

I remembered Mac telling me that he had recently been to Thailand. "Tell me about your trip to Thailand."

"Not much to tell. It was all business. I've got some special and demanding clients there," Mac said.

"Must be a real exotic place. Me? I haven't been anywhere but here and Georgia and of course to Ohio for college," I told him.

"There's a big world out there. I've lived my life to the fullest. I've been places, done so many things. Hung out with Miles at the Montreux Jazz Festival in Switzerland, listened to the great Archie Shepp play under the stars beneath the Great Pyramid in Egypt, partied at Studio 54. If I die tomorrow I'd have no regrets," he told me. He paused. "Well maybe a couple."

I thought about his worldliness, imagined all of the women that must have been in his life.

"Felicia told me you were a womanizer," I said half teasing, half in a serious vein.

I could see Mac with a smirk on his face. He shook his head. "Felicia, Felicia," he said. "Just to set the record straight, I've never been what they call, a womanizer. What you have to understand is that I'm a child of the Seventies and the Eighties. You know, pre-AIDS, women popping birth control pills like Skittles."

I smiled and decided to taunt him. "And they were all over you, weren't they Mackenzie," I said. I don't know why I said that. I didn't want to hear his answer because I knew that it would make me jealous.

"Like I said, it's a big world out there."

I was grateful that he didn't answer my question. Instead, he bypassed the comment and kept talking. "We Americans are so egotistical, believing that the whole planet revolves around us."

Mac clinched his teeth, something I had noticed before whenever he was irritated or just deep in thought.

"You don't like it here, do you? Is that why you're planning to move to that place where you're having your house built?" I asked.

"Oh, you mean my house near Bahia in Brazil?"

"Uh, uh."

"It's not that I don't like it here. It's just that I'm looking for a different kind of life. I'm over fifty and although I don't think that's old, I spend more time looking back than I do ahead, reminiscing about the past and agonizing about the future. I guess what I want is to wipe the slate clean and start over."

"And do you think of marriage in your new life?" I asked.

He turned directly towards me and smiled. "There's a place for it---maybe."

"And children. What about children?" I asked.

"Not sure. Hadn't given that one much thought. I mean, like I said I'm fifty-something and there aren't any kids on the horizon. So even if I became a father in the next two years I'd be seventy when my daughter graduates from high school."

He pushed out a breathy half-laugh. "Her friends would probably ask her if I'm her grandpa."

"And all of those friends would envy her for having such a virile, handsome and distinguished-looking father. I wouldn't be surprised if they all had crushes on you."

I let my mind race twenty years into the future. I'd be forty-six to his seventy with a grown daughter. The thought made me pause and ask him, "Why did you say, daughter?"

"I don't know. It just came out. I already have a son and you know all about that relationship but I've always thought that a father-daughter relationship is special. You know, daddy's little girl. Sons grow up and want to be your competition or your buddy, at least most do but daughters always hold that special place right here," he said, putting his hand over his chest where his heart beat underneath.

I leaned back into his chest where that heart was beating and rested my head on his shoulder while his strong left arm cradled me and I thought about Mackenzie, his little girl and me. We would be a nuclear family, living on a tropical island off the coast of Brazil if only in my dreams.

Chapter Twenty-Two

When we finally got to Mac's house he quickly poured a drink and offered me one, but I declined remembering how I was the night of his party. I was feeling amorous but he seemed to be in no hurry. I followed him into his study and took a seat on the sofa while he sat across from me in his easy chair.

"Why so far away?" I asked.

He smiled. "No reason," he said.

He sat there staring at me, swishing his brandy around in a large snifter but my question didn't move him.

"You're a very beautiful young woman. You remind me of someone I knew a long time ago."

No man had ever told me I was beautiful before so I wanted to savor the moment and let it soak in. I thought about the other three women I knew about who had been in Mac's life.

"Who's that?" I asked.

He sipped from his glass and wiped away remnants of brandy from the tip of his thick mustache. That wistful look I'd seen on his face earlier that evening returned.

"I'm sorry. I shouldn't talk about this," he said.

"It's O.K. I'm a big girl. Tell me."

He paused. "It was a long time ago. I met this little sweet country girl and…"

"You two fell in love?"

"Not quite, but I always wondered about the possibilities."

"I don't know if I should be flattered or insulted," I said.

"It was definitely a compliment."

Mac got up from his chair and sat beside me. I moved closer and kissed him on the cheek and then his neck. He sat almost motionless as I unfastened the top two buttons of his silk shirt and kissed him sweetly on his chest. I stopped for a moment to study the gold chain and the St. Christopher's medal he was wearing underneath his shirt.

"That's nice," I said referring to the medallion.

"It's very special. I never take it off," he replied.

I said, "Why, because of its religious meaning?"

"Partly. St. Christopher is the patron saint of travelers," Mac told me.

I touched it, held its weight in my hand, read the inscription on the back: *To, Ricky* and briefly wondered but it wasn't important. I kissed his face and waited as he turned his lips to join mine. Slowly, his arms engulfed me and pulled my body close to his. I could feel the warmth, the passion growing with every passing second. My heart welled up and my body ached with a sweet pain that anticipated fulfillment.

"Mackenzie, I want you to make love to me," I whispered. With those words I threw myself upon him, kissing his neck and chest while being beckoned by his sensual cologne to taste his entire body. I allowed my hands to touch him and to let my fingers play with the thin patch of hair that rested right above his sternum. Not satisfied my hand found its way lower and felt the fullness that was quickly growing between his legs. I breathed deep, I breathed hard and my body tingled to the point where I wanted to scream. I repeated my request but this time I was almost begging. "I want you, baby," I said.

Mac said nothing and I figured that he was as caught in the moment as I had been. But his actions were too deliberate for someone who wanted what I wanted. He shifted and moved away but not very far, clearing his throat to speak.

"This is difficult, Dahlia. But we can't do this," he said.

His words stung like arrows. I was crushed by his rejection to the point that I wanted to cry but instead, I asked him one simple question, "Why?"

"I can't tell you right now but in time you'll know and understand."

"I get it. You don't find me attractive, do you?" I asked not satisfied with his answer.

He shook his head.

"To the contrary. I find you extremely attractive but I…" He stopped.

Mac stood up and walked towards the door leading out of the room and into the hallway.

"I've got to get some sleep. I want you to stay in one of the guest bedrooms. Give me a few minutes to make sure the room is ready and I'll be back to get you. In the meantime, make yourself comfortable." Those words pierced my heart and I wondered how

Mac could be warm and passionate one minute and so cold the next. He gave me a long look that wasn't detached like his words then turned to leave.

I watched him unable to say a word. He said I was beautiful and that he found me attractive so I didn't understand why he didn't want to make love to me. I thought of all the possibilities. I thought about how much I needed him right then. He could've made me forget about everything else that swirling around in my head and my world.

Maybe he was sick or was having a problem that he was too macho to admit. Or maybe the woman Felicia talked about, Desdemona was really in his life and he was being faithful, but none of it made sense. I walked around the study trying to figure out what had happened. Deep down inside I was hoping that he'd come back and sweep me off my feet the way heroes do in some old movie and carry me off to his bedroom. No words said. No apologies made. In my thoughts, he would simply take me.

I paced the room with those thoughts as my guide, tried to lose myself in the things that made this place his. I walked over to Mac's desk and marveled at its organization. Everything was in place, put where it was for a reason. His laptop computer was in the very center and a paper shredder was on the floor to the right of the desk. His chrome-plated pistol, Mr. Friendly, claimed a spot in the middle of the desk and it made me pause. But I moved on, remembering what Mac had told me about wealthy people needing protection.

I was looking at his pictures again when I heard the sound of Mac's footsteps.

"I'm sorry I took so long. I had to take a quick shower," he said.

I smiled inside knowing that it must've been a cold shower. I decided I wouldn't press him for anything. One thing I'd learned from my friend El was that a woman shouldn't force herself on a man or if she had to then she should do it without him knowing. "Make him think he's in control when it comes to love and sex," she once told me. "It's good for his ego and great for sex."

"Come. The room's ready."

I followed, holding his hand as he led me up the stairs. At the end of the hallway was an open door to what I assumed was his master bedroom. I took a deep breath as we walked down the long hall. My heart was pounding hard and my anticipation was growing nearly out of control.

I thought that he was playing some kind of mind game, trying to make me want him even more. But if that was the case it was a very sophisticated ploy and totally unnecessary because I could feel every part of my body screaming to be touched by him and knowing that the touch would take me places I'd never been.

I started unraveling my hair with my free hand as we walked and loosened the impromptu belt that I fashioned from my shawl. I kicked off my shoes, walked along in a dreamlike state and followed him blindly into the bedroom. He opened the door and turned on the light.

"This bed is very comfortable," he said.

Then he pulled me close and put his arms around me, engulfing my whole body. It wasn't a sensuous hug but more like a father putting his little girl to bed reassuring her that he'd be nearby and that he could exorcise any nighttime demons that lay waiting in a darkened room.

I laid my head on his chest first without speaking but trying to understand.

"I thought you wanted me," I said.

"For sex?" he replied.

The question, abrasive in the way it sounded but I knew that wasn't his intent.

"For love," I said.

He gently pushed me away so that our eyes could engage and they danced back and forth between our thoughts.

"I love on many different levels, Dahlia and it's a word I don't take lightly. For us to fall into bed now would be giving in to the physical without one soul knowing the other."

For a moment I thought, what kind of metaphysical bullshit is he running on me? But when his eyes pierced through my spirit I sensed his sincerity. But it didn't quell my longing to connect with him on that basic and most carnal level of all.

He let go of my arms, gave me a knowing smile and retreated out of the room. I decided that I wouldn't follow him. I undressed and sat on the edge of the bed, embarrassed by the fact that I'd thrown myself at him and he tossed me aside. The old, insecure Dahlia Reynolds would've accepted her fate but the new Dahlia couldn't.

Chapter Twenty-Three

Mac wasn't in his bed when I woke up the next morning. I peeked inside his bedroom, but he wasn't there. I figured he was downstairs probably getting ready to leave.

I made the usual morning pit stop as I made my way to the bathroom adjoining the master bedroom. Mac's bathroom was almost as large as my whole apartment with lots of windows, a Jacuzzi tub, double showers and mirrored walls.

I watched my image pee, checking out the young woman looking at me from the other side of the mirror. My hair still looked great, thanks to Paul Sinclair and his professional styling but my makeup had been mixed with my tears and lost on the pillow. I didn't see it when I got up but I was hoping that it didn't look like the tee shirts that vendors still hawk on Capitol Hill. The ones that read, "I RAN INTO TAMMY FAYE LAST NIGHT". Smudged up face-print of the former television evangelist underneath the words.

I finished and was ready to find Mac when I got curious, wondered what secrets I could find in his bathroom. Mac told me that he wasn't involved with anyone but I knew there was no better place to find evidence of another woman than in a man's bathroom.

I remembered girl talk with Stacy and El and how they said women often leave their personal belongings at a man's place. It was their way of claiming their territory the way animals use urine. Panties and makeup kits were the primary warning signs. They were like pee stains in the snow, obvious and blatant.

I decided to look inside his medicine cabinet for a stray tube of lipstick or some mascara. The cabinet was clean unlike the way most single men kept theirs. No toothpaste stains running down the sides or on the shelves. No lint filled brush. Nothing that said: I'm a bachelor. I don't give a damn.

Everything was chrome and pewter, from the cup that held his toothbrush to the comb that kept every hair on his head in place before he cut it all off. Everything on this side of the cabinet was for grooming and arranged like a print ad for GQ magazine. I dismissed the idea that Mac would harbor some woman's messy eye shadow container or half-used nail polish bottle. But I couldn't resist taking a quick peek on the other side of the cabinet.

This was the side that brought meaning to the words, "medicine cabinet." Small bottles of prescription medications lined the shelves with his name written on the labels. I was hoping to find one with a Viagra label on it. But most of the labels mentioned medications I couldn't pronounce except the ones that ended in "nitrate". I knew that was for the heart.

Mac had a heart condition. It brought home our age difference and the thought that he already had a head start on me in the living department by almost thirty years. I started doing the numbers. Women generally have a longer life expectancy than men by at least five years. Add his thirty and that's thirty-five years I'd have to live without him assuming that he made it to eighty. Suddenly my fanciful thought of a future with him, the one I had conjured up during our carriage ride had lost some of its luster.

Morbid thoughts about Mac grabbed me. Still it now made sense. Bad heart, bad love. Love kills if you do it too hard. I couldn't believe my thoughts, like my mind had a mind of its own. I had to seize control. I needed to go home. I needed to protect my mother. Whatever thoughts and feelings I had involving Mac had to be put on the backburner. I made my way down the steps and into the lower level of the house.

"Mackenzie?"

I called out but not in a loud voice. Instead, it was meek and timid like someone who didn't want to wake the monster.

I called out again. I heard Mac talking on the telephone. His voice was coming from outside and echoing through the atrium from the swimming pool. I moved closer to the sound. He was talking loud, almost shouting. His words were infused with angry expletives leaving no doubt that he was really pissed off.

"What do you mean, I'm the one who's jeopardizing the project? That's *bullshit, man!*"

He took a deep breath as though he was drawing energy from his surroundings, ready to return verbal fire.

"I'm working on that! Desdemona's in a safe place. Don't worry, I'll find her."

I thought there goes that name again. I knew he couldn't have been talking about Charity. She had adopted that name but no one knew about that but me. I tried to put it all out of my mind. I was guilty of snooping and this was obviously something that was none of my business.

"Do you mind if I say something?" Mac said. He continued, "Just shut the fuck up and listen! GODDAMNIT! You know as well as I do that I can deliver just like I promised."

I heard him mention, New York, Miami, Paris and Bangkok several different times during the conversation. Mac started speaking in another language, but I understood Desdemona.

I stood out of view, being patient as he shouted into the phone. But I had to let my presence be known or I'd never get out of Mac's house. I stepped around the corner and walked right into the poolroom.

"Excuse, me," I said softly. "I didn't mean to disturb you. I just wanted to let you know that I'm up."

Mac's tone shifted from angry to soft and smooth. "Hey, young lady. I'll be right with you."

He put a finger up in the air as he held the phone with his other hand. That was my cue to leave the room. I left but all I could think about was the name, Desdemona. Desdemona. Desdemona.

*　　*　　*

Mac dropped me off at my place so I could grab a couple of things I had forgotten the night before. We checked for Derek's car when we pulled up to the building and I quickly ran inside.

I took one last look at my place just to make sure I hadn't forgotten anything. I thought about taking the envelope with me so that I could show Mac but decided against it. I hid it between my mattress and box spring.

I stared at my grandmother's quilt for a moment because it always reminded me of her. I remembered the way she would carefully sew on the different patches as she would tell me about our family history. Returning home for the first time in a couple of years would bring that history rushing back to me.

I walked out of my building and looked for Mac's car when I noticed someone standing near the entrance.

"Going somewhere?" It was Agent Liles, the cocky FBI agent who had to be subdued by Robinson. Somehow he had crept up on me and now he was standing uncomfortably close.

"Ah, yes. I'm going out of town. Is that a problem? I asked. I was feeling invaded and defensive. I wanted to tell him that it was none of his damn business, but I didn't. "Is there something I can help you with?"

He had the same smug expression he had when I first met him and I concluded that it must've been something he picked up at the FBI Academy in the Asshole class. I figured he was at the top of his class in that department.

"You seen your boy Antoine, lately?"

"No, it's been a while. I figure you'd probably know where he is better than I would."

Liles moved from my side and stood directly in front of me, repeated that wicked smile that seemed to be a part of his nature. He looked me up and down then rested his eyes on my face. He was a short man and at five foot, nine inches, almost six feet with my heels on, I towered over him. He was looking up to me. I was looking down on him. It made an interesting metaphor that he probably wanted to reverse.

"You've done something different to yourself. Uhmm, your hair and makeup looks good on you. I guess you must've thought about what I said. You know, Antoine and the kind of women he likes."

I twisted my mouth in disapproval and tried to pretend that the FBI agent wasn't standing there. But he was and I was beginning to feel defiant.

"Look, I don't know why you're here or what you want, but like I told you before I don't know anything about anything and I'm just trying to get back home to see my family, Agent Liles!"

"Whoa, calm down Miss Reynolds. And call me Rick. I just stopped by, just in case he's around. I just wanted to make a social call on my brother Antoine. There's a lot of buzz around him and his crew."

Liles stared up at me and I glared back like we were playing a game of who'd flinch first.

"You know, you've got some real pretty eyes. I never noticed them before. I guess it was the glasses."

"I got em from my dad," I replied.

He took a deep breath like he was trying to inhale a part of me then turned an eye to the suitcase that was on the ground tucked close to my side. "You wouldn't happen to be leaving the country? Ever been to Thailand? I hear it's a very interesting place."

Everything about him reeked of sarcasm. His small talk had a purpose like he was trying to get some information out of me. I was anxious to get away from him. I was hoping that Mac would walk up and take me away but Liles would be the one to leave.

I watched him carefully as he made his way to the familiar looking black sedan parked on the street in front of my building. He stopped halfway to the car then turned to speak. "You know we checked. That quarter of a million dollars that's tucked away in your name can't be traced to anyone except you. We got video, compliments of the Antiguan government. It's kind of grainy and I admit the quality is poor but there's ol' Antoine and a tall, attractive woman in shades making a cash deposit. Just thought I'd tell you. Anyway, have a safe trip."

*   *   *

Agent Liles' visit didn't upset me although I knew that was his intent but it shed some light on the things that were swirling around me and he let me know that Antoine was a key figure in this growing mystery. Someone had hacked into my personnel files and the reason was clear. It was to steal my identity.

Somehow, Antoine and a woman who looked like me went to Antigua to open up a bank account in my name with the help of information gained from my files. His excuse that the money came from an investor in his music projects didn't make sense. I thought about all the reasons why he might have told me that lie and nothing added up but I knew I would have to do something rather than let things spiral totally out of control.

Chapter Twenty-Four

Mac went through a series of systems checks and talked on the radio to air traffic control. When he got the go ahead we taxied down the runway and within seconds were airborne. It would be a two-hour flight.

My mother was anxious to see me and I told her about Mac and how I wanted her to meet him. The thought made me a little nervous knowing my mother the way I do. Her parochial sense of morality would have her question Mac's intentions and not our age difference. But that wasn't important. I was on my way home to a place that I tried to escape and one that carried memories I'd worked so hard to put behind.

I looked over at Mac as he was leveling the plane at our approved altitude. There was the focus in his eyes that's obviously necessary when operating a complicated piece of equipment but now it was easing up and he removed his headphones and smiled.

"You are free to move about the cabin," he said.

"Mackenzie Powell, you are a man of many talents. How long have you been flying?"

"It started as a hobby about twenty years ago. I took some lessons and loved it. I took more lessons, was certified and decided that I wanted to make money flying. I started as a co-pilot for a charter airline, worked my way to pilot and then flew for various corporations flying the CEO's, clients and board members around. It was how I made some connections to do what I do now. Just lucky. I guess I was in the right place at the right time."

Mac checked his gauges once again. "We're heading south. We should be near Valdosta in an hour." He flipped a couple of switches and looked back at me. "Auto-pilot," he told me.

I thought about the heated conversation he was having over the telephone earlier that morning. The woman named Desdemona seemed to keep popping up everywhere. I wondered if Mac was flying to Miami to see her. I decided to ask him right then about her.

"Who's Desdemona?"

Mac's face twisted. I could tell that the question made him uncomfortable but he fought against his surprise at my asking. I could tell that it was a subject he didn't want to talk about but he didn't ignore my question.

"Shakespeare's, Othello. He murdered her in a jealous rage," he said, flatly.

The statement spoke volumes about the subject and about Mackenzie, himself. Whoever Desdemona was he wasn't going to talk about her to me and I would learn at that time, for the first time, that most men keep secrets.

*   *   *   *

We landed a few minutes later. I'd told Mac that my mother would meet us at the airport and drive me back to Waycross and I felt him tense up when I said she wanted to meet him.

"It's a little too soon for me to be meeting your family," he said.

His response came as a heavy thud against my heart. I'd told my mother that I thought I was falling in love---for the first time in my life. In her usual way, she cautioned me about being impulsive and about sex. "No unwanted pregnancies," she said. And now he was telling me that it was too early to meet her as though he knew that the meeting wouldn't be just a casual introduction. I thought about how I was going to explain to my mother Mac's reluctance to meet her as he taxied the plane to a stop and how embarrassed I would be if he didn't.

The airport had a terminal about the size of a small town bus station and one landing strip. Mac allowed the plane's engines to run as he opened its door and helped me out onto the runway.

"Call me when you're finished here. I'll come back to get you."

We walked towards the terminal in silence with Mac carrying my luggage. He stopped at the entrance, gave me a parting smile as antiseptic as a man who'd been washed clean of all emotions. I was falling in love but it was obvious there was no reciprocation. I thought about the loves in his life, the ones I knew about and I wondered if he had the capacity to care about me. I watched him as he walked back to his plane without turning around. It only took him a moment to disappear into the friendly skies.

I found myself standing alone in the small airport terminal remembering the reason I had made the trip. I'd expected to see my mother and stepfather there waiting but they were apparently running late. I wondered if she would recognize me with my new hairstyle and without my conspicuous eyeglasses. I was a woman and looked every bit the part. My life had changed greatly since I'd gone away to college.

I strained to see the familiar blue truck creep slowly into the parking lot and my heart was pounding. It came to a stop outside the terminal door and my mother stepped out from the driver's side. I was relieved to see that Rufus wasn't with her. She greeted me with an array of facial expressions. First a weak smile then a worried look and, finally, frustration.

"What have you done to yourself?" My mother asked as she stood there looking up at me.

"You cut your hair? Wearing makeup? And what happened to your glasses? Did you get your eyes fixed or somethin'?"

I didn't answer her question.

My mother's reaction put a damper on my enthusiasm. I hadn't seen her in two years and I was expecting more warmth and not condemnation. But I quickly overcame it all. She was still a Pentecostal who thought that makeup made a woman a harlot, the Devil's mistress.

My mother looked around.

"Where's this young fella you were raving about? I'd like to see who he is and ask him what kind of intentions he has for my daughter."

"Oh, he had to fly to Miami."

It was obvious that something was bothering her. Maybe it was the living that was displayed with more prominence than anything else. The lines on her face like crevices sown into the earth, irregular and unrelenting made her appear much older than her forty-five years. I thought of Mac by comparison. He had led the good life and although he was older than my mother he looked at least ten years younger.

"I've got to get back home. Rufus is probably worried, you know how he gets," she said.

The blood rushed quickly to my brain and with it came the memories I'd tried so hard to suppress. Rufus, the Almighty. My momma was at his beck and call, trapped in an abusive relationship, trapped by circumstance. She had been a single mother with her own mother in tow and selling her soul. A form of indentured servitude purchased by the only bidder. Rufus, the Almighty.

"Mama, this ain't about Rufus. For once, will you think about yourself first? With everything that's going on in the family and all you can say is that man is probably worried? I don't care if he's worried, Mama. What about all the times…?"

My mother turned and gave me a look of consternation mixed with surprise. "What do you mean, everything that's going on in our family? Is there something you're not telling me? Is Charity all right?"

I didn't want to upset her even more so I decided to talk later. I didn't want to tell her what I knew about Charity or that the reason I came home was because I was afraid for her, my sister and for myself. I probably couldn't have saved any of us but I could play detective and try to piece together this growing mystery.

Chapter Twenty-Five

Memories of home and my childhood rushed back like a freight train ready to jump the track. My bedroom looked the same minus the posters of Whitney Houston and Blair Underwood that once adorned its walls. My old bed seemed even smaller and I wondered how I could've ever fit comfortably in it. But it was nothing when I considered my closet and the claustrophobic times I spent huddled in a human ball, sometimes hiding from my stepfather and other times being relegated to stay there as a punishment. It was both sanctuary and prison.

It was that experience that would later sustain me when prison became my reality. I am like the caged animal, raised in captivity that has never known what it's like to roam free and, therefore, unmissed in the experience.

I slowly unpacked my clothes and placed them neatly in my dresser drawers and hung the rest in the closet. I thought about Mac, the image of him that couldn't escape my mind. The mystery that was Mackenzie left me off balanced.

Alone in my old room, I was now trying to piece it all together. The warnings from Felicia, easy to discount but still worthy of consideration, his refusal to bed me, and my female instincts not yet fully cultivated but being tested were all telling me something. I just couldn't figure out what it was. I repeated the name Desdemona several times, thinking about his refusal to talk about her and trying to figure out who she was.

I realized that I had to put thoughts of Mac behind me for the moment and focus on the envelope my sister had given me and its connection to my grandmother. I decided to walk down the hall to her room. It still had the look of intrusion. The only room in the house that had been ransacked it looked like Hurricane Katrina had touched down and took her wrath out on my grandmother's bedroom. The visual of the intrusion was too strong for me at that moment and I had to leave the room.

I took a deep breath and gathered my courage. This was the first time I had been in her room since she passed away. I remember those times when I would sit and talk to my grandmother and how I could smell her scent, the Jungle Gardenia perfume she wore that

137

was an indelible part of her. I'd inhale and keep the scent inside me for as long as I could. Although it was difficult I knew that I needed to go back into her room.

My grandmother kept a hope chest that she made many years ago from a Dutch Masters cigar box. That box held her dreams both past, present and for the future. And she meticulously guarded it, keeping it hidden---the keeper of Nana's secrets.

There was a certain amount of intrigue in that old box, a mystique about it that somehow gripped my thoughts like the quilt I inherited. Nana kept it in a wooden trunk hidden under the floorboards and under her bed. I remember once watching her struggle to lift the small trunk from its hiding place and then she'd tell me to "skee-daddle" lest I find out where she kept its key.

Whenever I'd ask her what was in the box she'd just say, "You'll learn in time, Dahlia."

I could've opened it anytime I wanted because I had always known where my grandmother kept the key but I didn't.

I guess it was because I simply thought it was a place where she kept her memories, memories irrelevant to the existence of a young girl. I could think of nothing in the box that would've interested me.

I recalled the time when I was nine years old and how I spied on my grandmother, watching as she moved her bed and counted fourteen floorboards from the North wall of the room. And under the fourteenth board, loosened with a butter knife, could be found the little wooden trunk. Its key was taped underneath the bed itself. I guess she thought that if anyone moved the bed to get her hope chest they'd overlook the obvious place to find the key.

The one thing I could always count on was that Nana was consistent and the fact that the place where she kept it would never change. It was like unlocking the clues to a treasure map. After removing it from its hiding place I held the little trunk in my lap and said a prayer. I took a deep breath and used the key to open it and lifted the box from inside, the one that kept the things she held near and dear.

Her hope chest was made "tamper proof" by what seemed like yards of cloth on the outside and heavy gauged plastic meticulously wrapped around its entire outer surface. I was prepared.

Armed with a pair of scissors, I used it to cut away the cloth one layer at a time until I reached the waterproof plastic. It was easier to remove and I cut through it with a single penetration of the sharp end of the scissors. I could see clearly the images of the Dutch Masters who bore a striking resemblance to the descriptions of Alexandre Dumas' Three Musketeers I'd read about in college. Finally, I cut the tape that sealed the lid and carefully pried open the box.

Inside were the things that my grandmother must've treasured above anything else tangible. A tattered Bible, yarn that matched the color of the stitching in our family quilt and her handwritten last will and testament was on top.

There was also a bundle letters wrapped and held together with a rubber band at the bottom of the box. I unraveled the bands and separated the letters. Some were addressed to Nana and others to my mother and each letter bore the same distinctive handwriting. And on each letter appeared the name---Richard Reynolds, my father. My heart seemed to stop when I read the name, but then it began to race again.

Like an archeologist exploring the pyramids of Kush in search of secrets and hidden meanings, I opened the top letter, quietly read its words and instantly became connected to my past. My father had written my mother, asking about her health and the health of their baby daughter. His words were soft and reassuring. He vowed to be devoted to his daughter. *Life's complicated,* it read: *But through it all please remember that my love for her is unwavering.*

Those words hit me like a ton of bricks and not for their content, but their timing. My mother had always told me that my father died before I was born. This letter was proof that he was still alive after I had been born. It was obvious that my mother had lied about his passing.

I dug deeper and opened more letters and in each one he asked about me. Each letter was like a radioactive time clock because it dated and mentioned certain events that occurred in my life. Like the time I fell off my bike and knocked out my front teeth and the times I did well in school.

He wrote three or four letters every year until I was about eleven years old and around the time my mother married Rufus. That's when the letters stopped coming, but had they really?

My curiosity transformed into devastation when I thought about the stories my mother had told me. He was dead to her and she made him dead to me, too. I could feel the anger rising inside.

I wrapped myself up in Nana's bedspread, trying to process what I'd discovered and then figured that there must've been more. Digging deep to the bottom I found a large brown envelope that was stained by time. Inside there were two black and white photographs, both grainy and faded, but I could see the people in them, posing, their faces marked by what must've have been a happy time.

The first was a picture of an attractive young couple. It was the kind of photograph people would take in the drugstore picture machine a long time ago. Like a tinted memory they were two young people posing together in the small booth that captured the soul in Sepia colored strips to be memorialized for all time or at least until the picture faded. Four pictures for twenty-five cents.

I recognized the woman in the picture as my mother, many years ago. Beside her was a handsome, young man in a fancy paisley shirt. His eyes seemed to pierce through the lens of the camera and a bright smile illuminated his face. His ringlets of black hair framed his dark face, which seemed to have been sculpted out of ebony. A Michelangelo rendition of human perfection, he was art brought to life.

I stared at the man in the picture and soon realized that I was looking in a mirror. His eyes were my eyes, his nose mine. And the high cheekbones that made him both noble and refined belonged to me, as well. I had no doubt that I was seeing my father for the first time in my life.

I looked hard at my father's youthful photograph as he posed with my mother and recalled the image of the man in the envelope I'd gotten from my sister. They were one and the same. The man with the deer in the headlights look and thick beard in that photograph was my dad advanced some twenty years later. Same eyes, same bone structure, just more mature.

Suddenly, I realized that the Pandora's Box had been opened and now the evils of the world had been set free. The next picture would confirm that they could never be recaptured. I knew what it was without really looking. I'd seen the picture before, recently and at a place so far removed from where I was that it might as well have been on the other side of the universe. I'd seen the very same picture of a group of young musicians at Mac's house.

The young man in the picture with my mother was the same young man in the picture of Mac's band. He was wearing a St. Christopher medal like the one that Mac had on the night before when I tried my best to seduce him. And the inescapable conclusion made me feel sick.

I remembered when I saw the picture at Mac's house. I assumed at that time that the young man wearing the medallion and wide smile was Mac and now I was really starting to feel sick. I squirmed and mumbled to myself. Nausea grabbed hold of me. I dropped the picture on my grandmother's bed, ran down the hallway to the bathroom and threw up my insides, tried to regurgitate those thoughts and flush them down the toilet.

Chapter Twenty-Six

My mother had lied and the lie had destructive consequences that couldn't have been foretold many years ago when it was first created. No one would've predicted that someday I would unknowingly find the truth about my father and fall in love with a man who was somehow connected to him. I remembered telling Mac about my father, their common background in music, the fact that they were both from Lafayette, Louisiana and he said nothing. I couldn't figure out why.

And what of my father? Is he alive?

I spent a sleepless night turning over the events of the day in my mind beginning with the first time I saw Mackenzie Powell at J. Paul's Restaurant. Was he there by some strange coincidence? That night he was in Café Alexandria's with Felicia. Was that just another coincidence?

I thought about the letter to my grandmother, the one in the envelope that Charity had given me. It was dated just a few months earlier. And the picture---was that really Richard Reynolds, my father?

I knew I had to confront my mother to get some answers. I wasn't sure how or what to say to her but I had to say something. I decided to wait until after breakfast and after Rufus took to the fields in his noisy diesel powered tractor. It would be better to ask my mother the questions that were beginning to consume me after everyone had eaten while she was busy cleaning the kitchen.

No one said a word during breakfast, reminded me that I was definitely home again. Rufus was his usual bubbly self with his face glued to the newspaper that served as a barrier to any conversation. He wolfed down his food and left the kitchen without saying a word to anyone.

My mother believed in big Southern style breakfasts and she spent most of the morning cooking and serving, squeezing in a bite or two as she waited for the pancakes to finish cooking. And I picked over and stirred my grits with my head down rather than eat them, a thing I started many years ago whenever I was upset. It didn't take her long to realize that something was bothering me.

"O.K. Let's hear it. What is it? Rufus?"

My mother's tone was tinged with a little bit of frustration, seasoned by her years of living with that man, I guess. But I detected a new defiance in her, probably a defense built against the docility forced on her through the years.

"You lied to me!" I shot back.

"Girl, what on earth are you talking about?"

"You lied to me about my father, mama. He wasn't killed before I was born, was he?"

I felt the sweat gathering in little droplets above my high cheekbones, a precursor to crying. I tried to choke back the tears that were beginning to well up in my eyes, to choke back twenty-six years of pain but it was like trying to seal a crack in the Hoover Dam with a band-aid. Inevitably the dam will erupt.

My mother's eyes widened. It was a dead giveaway. I'd resurrected a ghost. She stopped what she was doing and with dishtowel in hand took a seat at the table across from me. She used a hand to wipe the sweat from her brow and then used it to form a cover for her face. Then she cried.

"That's why I wanted you to come home," she said. "The break-in---I think it had something to do with your father."

She unveiled the pained expression that had seized her face; put her hands flat on the table. I could tell my words were arrows that found their mark deep inside my mother's heart. I didn't want to hurt her but like they say, the truth sometimes hurt.

"I loved your father. I mean, I barely knew him, but I fell so hard and so deep I thought I was goin' crazy."

She took a hard breath like she was sucking in the painful memories and holding them so they wouldn't hurt me.

"It happened the first time I laid my eyes on him. He was up on stage and every girl in the house wanted him and I felt like every song he played he was playin' just for me. It made me feel special cause' I was this little ole country gal and here he's this tall, handsome man from New Orleans or someplace and he was givin' me that look and that broad grin of his and I was helpless."

I could tell from the way she talked that the stilled waters of her emotions ran deep. Even twenty-six years of not seeing him couldn't satisfy the thirst she must've had then and one that still lingered on. The floodgates were now open and letting go to talk about him I hoped was therapeutic. I thought that it could be the warm springs that would sooth her soul.

"After the show, I waited for him and he comes out with his best friend and he says to me, 'Hey, Girl. Tonight's your lucky night'. I tried to be a good girl and even though he was just passin' through I wanted him to respect me, to court me like he really cared. So I told him it was *his* lucky night and that he had to meet my momma and get her permission to take me out."

My mother's expression turned whimsical. I know that memories like honey leave their residue on everything they touch. They become the sticky fingers that can't be licked clean. I could tell that my mother thought of him often and fondly. Memories both sweet and painful but lacking the sting of the present, faded by the passing of time.

Listening to her talk softened my spirit. I listened while she kept talking, touched by the sweetness of her memories.

"He came by and met Nana and she was so impressed because she thought he was such a beautiful man and because he was a musician. She gave him permission to take me out. I remember he was driving a shiny, black Corvette with the top down and he took me for a drive. I could feel the wind against my face. It was like running in an open field, only much faster.

We went downtown and he bought me a milkshake and we took pictures in a photo booth at the drugstore. Later, we snuck back into my room and that was the last time I saw him.

He told me he'd be back and that he'd write me. I wrote him weeks later and told him I was pregnant. I didn't think I'd hear from him again but he called and said there was no way he was leaving the road and his music career to settle in Waycross. Said I was stupid and naïve. After that he was dead, as far as I was concerned."

The truth confirmed. I asked, "So he wasn't killed trying to get back here for my birth?"

My mother's mouth turned downward. She poked out her bottom lip and shook her head.

"He wrote me and I refused to write back but your grandma wrote him and sent him pictures of you over the years and let him know what was going on in your life.

I made her promise never to tell you and that someday I would tell you myself. But I got comfortable with the lie and I really wanted Rufus to be a father to you, so I never told you. I'm so sorry, Dahlia. I'm so sorry." She cried.

I stood up and went over to where she sat and stroked her face.

"I forgive you, Mama." I said. "Do you know where he is now? My father, I mean."

My mother was still crying as she shook her head and spoke once again. "Don't know. The letters just stopped coming."

"Did you know that he wrote Nana a couple of months ago?"

"No I didn't."

"At least I think it was from him. The letter was from someplace in Thailand."

"Well, if he sent something she never got it. I walk out to the mailbox everyday and if your father sent her something I would've seen it first."

I thought: *The letter must've been intercepted by someone. That's how it wound up with Derek.*

"Can I show you the pictures, Mama?"

She nodded. I opened my grandmother's little box and placed the two pictures on the table and watched as she picked up the dime store picture and longingly stared at the images of the happy couple. She sighed, rubbed her fingers on their images.

"He told me that his father had given him that medallion and that he never ever took it off," she said, touching the St. Christopher's medal in the photo.

My mother then moved over to the next picture, the same one that Mac had in his house. "That was the band. They called themselves, The Soul Persuasion and see, there's your father with the chain and medallion. The fella next to him was his best friend. He was some ol' fancy Creole. Nice fella. Cute like your father. Everyone thought they were brothers. They do look alike, don't they?"

I nodded.

I was pointing to the image of the man I thought was a young Mackenzie Powell. "Do you remember his name?" I asked.

My mother examined the picture again. "Yeah, they called him Mac. It was on the poster, along with the names of the other band members."

She handed me back the picture of The Soul Persuasions. There was Mackenzie twenty-seven years ago posing with his arm around my father's shoulder. I studied my father's St. Christopher's medal I wondered why Mac was now wearing it. My questions had created other questions instead of answers.

I pointed to Mackenzie. "That's the man who flew me down here."

Her mouth dropped open. "He's the one you said you think you're falling in love with?"

"Yes."

She sat there motionless for what seemed like an eternity then she smiled a warm smile.

"Life is strange and full of coincidences. Mac came to visit us after you were born. He was caring and charming. He was a good friend to your father and he came to check on us. Didn't see or hear from him after that."

"I guess then he could tell me about my father better than anyone else and whether he's still alive," I said.

*   *

I took a commercial flight back to Washington the next day so that I could filter through the things I'd learned during my trip home. I didn't call Mac to let him know. I wanted to exorcise the demons that were beginning to pursue me in the form of questions and talking to him now wouldn't help. Questions, like did he know that I was his best friend's daughter and if he did, why didn't he tell me? And most of all, what could he tell me about the man I thought had died many years ago.

Chapter Twenty-Seven

Mailbox Full. That was the message on my answering machine. It was full to capacity with telephone calls. Conspicuously absent were any calls from Charity. El had called a couple of times while I was gone and so had Stacy. But the overwhelming majority of telephone calls were from two men, Antoine and Mac. Their messages were filled with the urgency of men on a mission, trying to make the world standstill for some undisclosed reason.

I wasn't surprised that Mac called after all I had flown back home with money I borrowed from my mother without calling him. But it was the calls from Antoine that worried me. I hadn't talked to him at all the week before I left for Georgia and now he was blowing up my telephone and sounding like a man bordering on obsession.

Hey, Baby, It's Antoine. Where you been? I miss you. Or, *What's up, Dahl. It's Twon. I really need to talk to you. I been thinkin' bout us. Hit me up, O.K.?*

Antoine had left at least ten messages sounding like he was begging for me to call him. It was a far cry from his ultra-cool player persona who'd never show his cards or any emotions. I wondered whether his calls had something to do with the FBI and their investigation or if he wanted his money.

I listened to his messages and shrugged them off. I dropped my bags in the living room without a thought about unpacking. I needed a shower. So many questions loomed over my head. Most were about Mac, some about Antoine and the rest involved my father. I opened my carryon bag and pulled out the pictures I took from Nana's hope chest. Mused over the drugstore photo of my parents and the other one of my father's band and wondered what I'd say to Mac.

I made my way to the bathroom, stripped down, dropped the clothes I'd been wearing onto the floor and ran the water until its heat steamed the glass on the shower stall and frosted my mirrors. Heat was therapeutic and soothing, healing body, mind and spirit. I allowed it to engulf me and lead me away from the things that weighed heavily on my mind.

I was dazed and confused by the revelations that seemed apocalyptic in nature. The world was ending, as I had known it.

There had been warnings, but I didn't understand them. Now I was in bad need of some time to reflect on everything to try and figure it all out.

I changed my mind about the shower and decided to take a long bath to give myself a chance to meditate in the quiet.

I slid into the water and stretched out. Its buoyancy seemed to lighten my spirits and I closed my eyes after laying my head back. I don't know if I'd fallen asleep or just let my mind free itself, but I could've stayed in the tub for hours, oblivious to the outside world until I heard sounds coming from my living room. I mumbled, "Must be Charity." She was using her key again.

"Charity is that you? I'll be right out," I shouted out from the bathroom and waited for her familiar voice to tell me to take my time. But there was no reply.

"She probably didn't hear me," I said as I got out of the tub. I grabbed a towel to wrap around my wet hair and another to dry my wet body, as I listened for Charity. But it was quiet and no sounds of movement came from beyond the closed bathroom door. Knowing Charity, I figured she was sitting on the couch, combing through the back issues of *Ebony Magazine* that sat on my coffee table.

"Charity?" I called her name, again.

I looked around my small place for any signs of my sister. I figured it must've been noise coming from the apartment next door or that Charity had somehow slipped past me and had gone down the hall to my extra bathroom. I walked back down the hall with a little bit of caution in my stride.

"Charity? You in there?"

I glanced around at my bedroom door, but it was closed. I shrugged off the thought that she might be inside because the door would've been wide open and Charity would probably be lying on my bed. I continued walking to the other bathroom, calling out her name again.

No answer.

I flinched when I thought I saw a shadow move, but I wrote it off as a symptom of my fears. I had locked the door to my apartment right after I walked inside and the door was still closed.

But my senses told me that something wasn't right. I could feel a presence even if I couldn't see it. Something told me to look back over my shoulder, but before I could turn I felt the weight of a strong arm grab me from behind, gripping tight around my waist and a gloved hand suppressing the sound of terror ready to spring from my mouth, reflexive as a by-product of my fear. My primal urge to scream had been muffled, quieted by my assailant whom I felt, but couldn't see.

The gloved hand gripped my mouth in a vice made of flesh covered by leather, as his right arm held me with equal force around my waist. Fear had been my companion from the moment I felt his clutch and those tentacles engulfed me and made me more fearful by the minute.

The combination of his covering my mouth with one hand and trapping the air inside my stomach with the other made me a candidate for oxygen deprivation. And the consequence of a lack of air meant a lack of coherency. My mind raced without thinking and searched in earnest for the right reaction.

His grip around my stomach eased up and for a second I felt a little relieved, but it was short-lived as I felt a new reason for my terror. Cold steel was being pressed up against my throat, a flat and wide dispenser of death that had but one function and that was to kill and gut and rip through human flesh with quiet ease. But what I felt was the threatening side of the knife not the killing side and I concluded that it wasn't my life he wanted---at least not then.

"Don't fucking scream! Don't cry. Or I'll cut you, bitch. I'll cut you, deep," he said. His throaty, whispered threats chilled me, made my kidneys weaken and paralyzed all thoughts and functions. If fear had a sound, his voice was it. The irony was that I couldn't scream even if he hadn't told me not to. My screams or any sounds, for that matter, were caught in that space between my vocal chords and my heart with both too scared to move.

"I'm going to ask you one question and for your sake you better tell me what I want to hear. All right?"

His voice and words reflected his total dominance over the situation and over me, too.

I nodded, profusely.

"Where is she?" he asked.

*Where **is** she?* I thought. *Where's who?* I didn't know who he was talking about. He removed his hand from my mouth and waited for my answer.

"Where's who?" I asked.

I thought: *Charity.*

"Don't fucking play with me!" His tone was rife with impatience. "You know goddamn well what I'm talking about. We checked the old lady's room in Georgia and it wasn't there. Like, I said. Where is it?"

His grip tightened and the dull side of his knife was slowly breaking the surface of my skin. I swallowed back my fear, concluded that whatever it was he wouldn't kill me until I told him where to find it. I thought about what he had said about the old lady, my grandmother. I realized that he was the person who'd broken into my mother's house and here he was in Washington on a cross-country quest for something or someone I didn't know. What baffled me most was how he thought that I might have it.

He was breathing hard as I was hardly breathing. His breath was full of garlic and the residue of spicy food filled my nostrils with the smell of curry powder or Creole-style gumbo. When he spoke I caught the scent of his last meal full in my face as it crept from behind and from where he stood. In what seemed like a carefully disguised voice he said, "Let's check your bedroom." It made me shudder and he sensed that, too.

"Don't worry. I ain't gonna rape your skinny ass. Just give me what I want and nobody gets hurt. Understand?"

He spun me around and pushed me down the hallway with the knife at the ready.

"Open it," he directed.

But before I could grab the doorknob he must've noticed my purse and luggage thrown loosely across the living room floor.

"Let's see what goodies you brought back."

He followed me to the living room. I tried to get a peek at him out of the corner of my eye, but his face was covered with a bandana gangsta-style and topped off with sunglasses. A Baltimore Ravens baseball cap covered his head. He was a man without a face or identity. There was no way to describe him to the police.

"Just look at the wall and you won't get hurt. Understand?"

He reached past me and grabbed my carry-on bag, dumped its contents on the floor and rifled through tubes of lipstick, makeup, panties and the precious pictures that I'd gotten from my grandmother. Disappointed, he turned and stalked his way towards me with his knife poised to kill.

"For the last time, where is it bitch," he said. He wasn't looking for Charity so I figured he wanted the envelope hidden between my mattress and box spring.

He spun me around and I felt the sting of his hand's swift contact to my face. There was anger in his blow, meant to punish me for my perceived deception. I braced myself for another one, believing that he would soon finish me with the killing side of the knife he still brandished. I squinted, cried and waited for the end. Held my breath as though I could numb myself by oxygen deprivation.

"It's—it's under my...."

I didn't see him, either. But he came in a blur from a different part of the room. Crashing into and hitting my assailant from out of nowhere. We both were oblivious to his coming as he sent my intruder sprawling to the floor in a heap.

He knocked the knife out of my attacker's hand and it went flying across the room. There were two men on the floor in a death struggle, villain versus hero. And I could see that the hero was Antoine.

He used his six foot-two inch frame like the running back he claimed he was in high school and he drove the intruder into the wall. The heavy sounds of fighting continued as I hid in a corner of the room. There was a loud grunt, followed by stillness and a solitary figure rose from the rubble and ran for the door. It was the faceless assailant leaving in a rush with Antoine sprawled out on the floor. The worst kind of fear grabbed hold of me. It was my fear that Antoine was dead.

I jumped to my feet and slammed the door closed, walked gingerly over to where Antoine was lying very still on the floor hoping for some sign of life. I thought about the knife and wondered if the intruder had managed to somehow stab Antoine. I started to panic as I leaned over him. There was no blood I could see, no evidence the fluid that sustained life was seeping out of him and when he groaned and moved I felt a sense of relief.

"Antoine? Antoine. Are you O.K.?" I asked.

I struggled to roll his two hundred pound frame onto his back and watched as he fought to regain his focus and consciousness. Slowly, his eyes opened and then he squeezed them shut for a moment. He coughed and reached for his side in an effort to quell the pain of a heavy body blow left as a reminder of his struggle with the intruder.

"Is he gone?" Antoine asked.

I nodded while holding his pretty head.

"You chased him out of here," I told him.

I was barely able to speak. My voice trembled and my knees were weak and all I could think about was what might've happened had Antoine not appeared.

I guess it was his persistence in trying to reach me that brought him to my place that evening or maybe he had some kind of insight that I was in trouble. But none of that mattered. It didn't matter to me how or why he ended up at my place. I was in dire need and all that mattered was that Antoine had fought off the boogeyman.

Chapter Twenty-Eight

It took Antoine a few minutes to gather himself. He'd taken a hard blow to his ribs, had the wind knocked out of him. He was now sitting up with his back against the wall and breathing heavy.

"I'll get you some water," I told him.

He took a couple of sips, inhaled deep and let the air out of his lungs. He smiled, slightly and shook his head.

"I hadn't been hit like that since I played ball."

He looked at me. He saw the concern in my eyes, mixed with the residue of the fear that had preceded his heroic arrival.

"You, a'ight?" He asked.

I nodded. I was all right thanks to Antoine, but his question brought back the reality and gravity of what had just happened. Through my attack I never once thought about actually dying, but I realized at that point, watching Antoine recover, that I could've been killed.

"I don't know what would've happened if you hadn't come along. I think he would've killed me."

"Well, the muthafucka's lucky he got that cheap shot in. My eyes were looking for that knife he had when I came in. Did you get a look at him?"

"Nah. He was all covered."

Antoine's face coursed the emotional landscape from anger to sympathetic. He could see that I had only a towel wrapped around me.

"What? He was trying to rape you?"

His anger returned.

"No, I don't think it was about that. He was looking for something, but the strange thing is that I think he was the same guy who broke into my folks' house."

Antoine's mouth gaped open. "You mean in Georgia!" he said. "Shit don't make sense."

I agreed.

"This is the craziest thing I've ever seen Antoine and I'm scared. All of a sudden all kinds of things are happening to me and I don't know why and I definitely don't understand."

I looked around my apartment at the wreckage that was on display as the aftermath from the fight.

"How'd you get in?" I asked.

"Door was cracked open. Question is: How did that guy get in?"

Antoine dragged himself off the floor and walked over to examine the door and then closed it.

"No sign of any force," he said. "Must've had a key."

That was as terrifying as anything I'd heard that evening. The fact that someone had a key to my apartment and could come in whenever he wanted was frightening.

Antoine continued. "You need to get your lock changed."

"And call the police," I added. I walked over to the spot where all of my belongings had been spilled out onto the floor. I started searching for my cellular, buried somewhere in the rubble.

Antoine had a sickened expression on his face like the word, police, was toxic---the five-oh pandemic.

"Hold up a minute, Dahlia."

"What? Why?"

"What they gone do? Nuthin', really. Make a report? Shit like that. Keep us here all night. Or worse, take us down to the station. I mean, what you gone tell them. Dude came in here trying to rob you? You're all right. Trust me, he ain't coming back."

I didn't trust Antoine regardless of the fact that he came to my rescue. He had a ton of hidden agendas, but in some ways it made sense not to call the police. Suddenly, any mention of law enforcement made me distrustful and cautious and I didn't need to be converted from victim to perpetrator. Besides, by the look on Antoine's face it was clear that he didn't want to talk to the police about anything. *Must be tied to the system,* I thought. On probation, parole or outstanding warrants can make a brother phobic about dealing with the law.

"What am I supposed to do in the meantime?" I asked.

He rolled a smile across his lips.

"You can stay at my place. Tomorrow you can get the lock changed and you should tell your condo management about this. File a police report once you figure out what you gone do."

I didn't know what to think when Antoine suggested that I stay at his house. I had always assumed that he lived with his momma like so many lost and aimless young brothers I knew---even if he did drive a fifty thousand dollar car. But the suggestion made sense and I was too afraid to sleep at my place that night.

I threw on some clothes and grabbed an overnight bag and met him back in my living room. He was walking around playing amateur detective, casing the place to see if the intruder had left some evidence of any kind. I told him that the knife slid under the sofa and watched as he retrieved it. It was a large folding knife with a devilish curve. Antoine closed it and gave it to me. "Evidence," he said. "Hold on to it." Satisfied that there was nothing else he moved like he was heading for the door.

"You ready?" he asked me.

I paused for a moment. I was beginning to second guess myself because in that instant I thought about this man that I'd been intimate with and his lies and secrets. But I realized that I had to trust him regardless of what FBI Agent Liles said because if Antoine hadn't shown up I'd probably be dead.

I followed Antoine outside. He looked from side to side for any signs of danger and then helped me into his car. Forty-five minutes later we were pulling up to a row of three story townhouses in an exclusive gated neighborhood near Washington Harbor. Antoine pushed the remote control button inside his Escalade, opening the garage door.

"You live *here!*" I said.

"Yeah."

"With who?"

He laughed. He was obviously amused by the question.

"This is *my* place. Deed, title, taxes, insurance, all in my name."

He led me inside and into a place with hardwood floors, vaulted ceilings and modern recessed lighting. Tasteful art, the kind you might see in an art gallery, and bronze sculptures displayed on pedestals accented the environment.

"This is nice," I said. "Real nice."

I took the tour. Antoine had a shelf full of football trophies as evidence of his glory days, but this didn't surprise me as much as the plaques on his wall. These weren't tributes to his football prowess. Instead, they paid homage to his scholastic accomplishments. Dean's List, Distinguished Student and a Bachelor of Science Degree with Magna Cum Laude honors were his *fete accompli,* a testimonial to academic achievements. I was both pleased and stunned.

"I don't get it, Antoine. You always come across as some wannabee thug. You know, blunt smoking, dick holding brotha from the streets, but this is the real you."

I was holding my breath, hoping that he wouldn't take my comments and candor as an insult.

"I'm sorry," I added.

"No apology needed. It's all about the persona. You know. Street cred. Gotta have it to succeed in the rap game. So I put the academics on the shelf and act like I'm from the hood. It works for me. You know, you're the only person I let see this room," he said and paused.

"So all that talk about growing up in the hood, getting into trouble and going to prison was just that---talk."

"Yeah, if the people I work with knew that I was some geek, nerdy bookworm you think they'd deal with me? Hell, no. They want someone who can relate. Somebody who feels what they feel." He hesitated. "But that case I caught is real. It's just still caught up in the system."

I shook my head, thought about how smart Antoine was, but also, how misguided.

"I think it's about talent, Antoine. If you can write and compose that's all that matters. Putting up a front won't help you make it, but being true to yourself will." I paused. "But you know I kinda understand your logic. The part I don't understand, especially after seeing everything you've accomplished is why you're involved with some shady business that's got the FBI looking at you."

He glared at me for a moment. "Look, I told you all that's on the up and up. They just think that a black man with money is doing dirt. I'm serious about my music."

I rolled my eyes slightly without thinking, an indication of my skepticism. "Music career! What music career? You didn't get all of this from your music, did you?"

"That's not the point and I didn't get this place slinging dope or doing something illegal. I can't tell you all my business but like I said, I'm serious about my music," he repeated the same refrain.

I could see that he was reflecting on what I'd just said. He said, "Let me show you my studio"

I followed him through several rooms and to the rear section of his townhouse. Antoine opened up the double doors and we entered his world of keyboards, computers, microphones and a padded sound room.

"This is where I spend most of my time."

He walked over to the huge mixing board that dominated the area and picked up some headphones.

"I got some beats I gotta mix tonight for one of my artists. You need to get some sleep. Make yourself at home and tomorrow we'll see about getting your locks changed and making that police report."

I went to bed wondering about what Antoine was thinking and how he seemed so different. He wasn't that overactive libido-laden, self-indulgent man I'd known for the past year and although I had questions, Antoine wasn't really a thug. Instead, he was this highly educated, Renaissance man. I could tell that he was hurt by the doubts I had about him and his music, but could he blame me? The law was pressing me about him and there still remained this small matter of a quarter of a million reasons why he put that money in the bank under my name. Like J.C. once said, "If it doesn't fit, you must acquit." I guess I could turn that around and in Antoine's case say: *If the facts don't fit, you must convict.*

I knew I wouldn't rest easy that night. Ironically, it wasn't because of the break-in, that scared me and I was no longer paralyzed with fear. What would have me tossing and turning that night would be thoughts of Mackenzie.

I found myself once again lying in the guest bedroom of a man's luxurious home and it reminded me of being at Mac's house, except the man I wanted, the man I craved wasn't in the other room. All I could think about, despite my ordeal that night, was seeing him. Add the revelations about Mac and my father my anxiety level was at an all-time high.

My thoughts drifted to this growing mystery scripted as my life and I wondered how the puzzle could be solved.

*   *   *   *

I woke up the next morning not to the smell of coffee brewing or Canadian bacon sizzling on Antoine's kitchen island, but to the aroma of cannabis permeating the air throughout his entire house and mixing in with the scent of fresh gardenias strategically placed in almost every room. I wandered down the stairs to the place

157

where food should be cooking to find him sitting in a chair with the newspaper on the table in front of him, smoking twigs, internal combustion.

"Well, I see you're off to an early start," I told Antoine.

He took a puff, allowed a large plume of smoke to exit his lungs and let loose the ten thousand brain cells that were attached to the THC residue.

"It's the breakfast of champions," he said, matter-of-factly. "If it bothers you, I'll put it out. It kind of eases the pain." He was holding his ribs.

"No, it's O.K. You all right? " I asked.

Antoine lifted his shirt to display his ripped six- pack torso and a deep blackened bruise that looked like a cloud.

"I'm fine. Been hit harder playing football and kept playing." He put on his best macho man impression.

"I'll get some ice," I said.

I looked past him to the wall of windows that started from the floor, rising three stories as the rear wall of his townhouse. His place overlooked the Potomac River and the tranquil setting of water and pleasure boats. From here I could see Haynes Point and the Washington Monument in one panoramic view and wondered how a twenty-three year old black man could live like this if he wasn't doing anything wrong or illegal.

I put the ice on his bruised ribs and held it, He leaned back and sighed.

"That feels good, baby."

He had that slight smile and the look of a man whose mind was venturing into the carnal. I felt his hand touch my head with gentle strokes that begged for reciprocation. He wanted me. I could tell. But things had changed since our last mindless, sexual encounter and I wasn't feeling the way he felt.

"Not right now," I told him.

He pulled his hand away, gave me that incredulous look, like *I don't believe you rejected me.*

"C'mon, baby. Brotha went through a lot last night."

"So you feel like I owe you something?"

I was fighting my own indignation at the thought---you saved me so you have the right to screw me?

"Not like you owe me or sump'in. It's just, you know, that's our story. You never turned me down before."

I walked away from him and turned my thoughts out the window and on to the beautiful cityscape that stretched out in front of me. I didn't want to look at him right then, but I couldn't let his comment go without saying something.

"Damn, Antoine. I've been through a lot lately, you know? Some asshole breaks into my place and threatens to kill me and he's probably the same man who broke into my folks' house and you know about my sister and all you care about is sex! I don't believe this shit!"

I still had my back to him, preferring to watch the water and the boats. I could hear the winded sound of his lungs inhaling another long toke, continuing his journey from the not so sublime to the subliminal. From his lofty perch Antoine thought I owed him. Maybe it was the madness of the reefer talking or maybe it was our history that had exalted him and made him think that the bounty of my booty was his entitlement. But times had changed and so had I.

"Look, Antoine. You know there was a time when I felt that it was enough to just be around a man like you, a man women look at and lust for and have you pay a little attention to me. To have you want me was enough. But things are different, Antoine. I'm not the same girl."

"Yeah, I can tell you had a makeover." I wasn't surprised by his sarcastic retort.

His green eyes shifted to a steely gray or maybe it was the sun reflecting through the windows.

"It's more than that, Antoine. It's a paradigm shift." I thought. *Where did that come from? Paradigm?*

"So you learned a new word? Maybe you should have said that it was an epiphany."

Antoine still wasn't trying to disguise his sarcasm.

"Whatever" was my reply..

"Is there someone else? You seeing someone else?" he asked. The question was definitely out of character because he never seemed to care what I did and whether I did it with anyone else.

I wrestled with myself and silence prevailed.

"Yeah, just what I thought. I already called a locksmith. So whenever you're ready we can go to your place and change those locks. I'll go get dressed."

I stood there fuming, but proud of the way I'd turned the tables by standing up for myself. Antoine's joint was the other thing fuming. I thought I'd better put it out so he wouldn't waste any part of his precious plant.

Antoine returned dressed and ready to go, but there was still the issue of the money. It was hanging over my head like a sabre and it was time for me to crawl from underneath its shaft.

"Antoine I need to talk to you about the money you have in that account. You need to get my name off of it. I've got enough to deal with and a friend of mine told me the Feds might think I'm laundering money for you and your so-called, investors."

He gave me a frustrated look. "Just give me a few more days, Dahlia. I'll make the shit right."

"Two days, Antoine. Two days and its got to be straightened out. I don't want to be associated with anything shady."

He twisted his mouth. "You ain't seen shady yet. Just wait. You have no idea."

"What does that supposed to mean? Is that some kind of threat?"

"Nah, just you need to watch who you're dealing with. That's all I can say. Look, I'll take care of the Antigua situation. You just take care of you."

Chapter Twenty-Nine

The ride with Antoine was a wordless journey punctuated by his occasional turning up the volume in his chariot with the twenty-two speakers. I was quiet because I was thinking about Mackenzie and the revelations about my father. I was glad I asked my mother about him. I sat back and started getting into the music on Antoine's CD player.

It was a soulful mix of his music featuring a young female singer. I admit that I was feeling this groove, which reminded me of a pre-hip hop, Seventies jam my mother once played over and over on our cassette player.

"Who is this?" I asked Antoine.

"Some new talent I'm working with."

I was waiting for more from him, thinking that he'd tell me about the artist, but he fell back into verbal silence with the music as the foreground for our existence while we rode in his car. I guess he was still angry. A man like him had only heard the word "yes" from women most of his life and my rejection must've been a hard pill to swallow.

"She's really good."

"Yeah," that was his only word until we reached my place.

I think Antoine and I saw the dark, government issued sedan parked in front of my building at the same time and it made him jittery while it made me curious. It looked like the same car I had seen parked in front of Mac's house and I remembered Felicia's explanation about how the cops protect the wealthy. I assumed that they weren't there that day to protect some secret millionaire living in my building.

We rolled to a stop a couple of buildings down from my place, as Antoine looked like he was studying the scene. Although our attention had been primarily on the unmarked car I quickly noticed that there was a swarm of police cars in the parking lot adjacent to my building. Antoine mumbled, "Looks like some kind of SWAT operation." My instincts told me that it was something else, something personal.

I looked at Antoine and said, "Still think they're fishing?"

He had this scared, nervous look like a kid who'd been caught by his parents with his pants down around his ankles and a Playboy magazine in one hand. He tried to speak, but his nerves were caught in his throat. He coughed, hoping that his testicles would recede back to their proper place and he would have the courage to say something. "Ah, look. I gotta go someplace. I almost forgot, I-I have an appointment."

It was my cue to get out of his car and face whatever was happening inside alone. I gave Antoine a disgusted look, twisted my lips at one corner of my mouth and shook my head. I made the long, slow walk to my building as I heard my "hero" burn rubber leaving the area.

I laughed, slightly as I opened the front door to the building. I thought: *It's probably Mrs. Sloski on the fifth floor knighting the mister with a frying pan.* But the solemn expression on the concierge's face told me otherwise.

I saw them when I came out of the elevator, police in uniforms and plainclothes and in their midst was Agent Liles standing in my doorway. I walked right up to him and said, "What's going on here? Why are you in my apartment?"

"The locals got a report of a disturbance last night. Said there was a fight and that a woman might've been abducted," he said. His nonchalant tone made me skeptical.

"Where's Mr. Robinson?" I asked him.

"If you're referring to SAIC Robinson, he's inside."

I remembered the title on Robinson's business card. SAIC meant *Special Agent In-Charge* and it made me think about the HNIC designation that black folks attached to other blacks in important positions. I walked by Liles and into chaos. There were several officers inside going through my place, turning over furniture and opening drawers with Robinson orchestrating the entire show.

"Why are they doing this?" I asked. My tone was a mixture of shock and anger.

Agent Robinson turned and gave me a matter-of-fact, "We're searching for evidence."

"Searching for what evidence?"

"Can't tell you that," he replied.

'What about a warrant? You got a warrant?" I had enough presence of mind to ask the question despite my horror at seeing my place being ransacked.

"Exigent circumstances," said Liles, who was suddenly standing at his partner's side.

I looked confused.

"It means search incident to a lawful arrest or some other extraordinary circumstance like a crime scene," Robinson explained.

"But I'm O.K. so there's no reason to search my house," I told them.

Liles had that same evil smirk painted on his face. "We didn't know that when we started so we went ahead and did our duty. You know, searching for blood and DNA just in case you really were missing."

My jaws tightened. I gave him one of my own evil stares. "And I just bet you personally searched my panty drawer, didn't you."

Liles shrugged my comment off like I had bestowed a badge of honor on him. I looked over at Robinson, my eyes pleading for help. "I haven't done anything wrong," I told him.

He said nothing as we all watched the uniformed police officers continue rifling through my belongings. One of them reached up to remove my grandmother's quilt from the wall, which in my mind was the ultimate intrusion.

"Wait! My great-great grandmother made that while she was a slave! It's a family heirloom!" I said, protesting.

Robinson signaled to the officer to leave it alone. "I think we're finished here," he said. "Miss Reynolds we need you to come down to headquarters."

"I think I asked you this once before. Do I need to call a lawyer?"

"No, I just need to show you something," Agent Robinson explained.

"And if I refuse?"

"That money in an offshore account makes you a co-conspirator so I think it's in your best interests to come along. Don't worry we'll have someone clean up this mess. Liles can stick around and supervise."

Agent Liles' smirking grin quickly evaporated.

Chapter Thirty

I had seen the J. Edgar Hoover Building many times and never ever wanted to go inside yet there I was sitting in a stark looking office with SAIC Robinson sitting behind an equally stark looking desk. I thought about Mac and compared his desk to Robinson's. I thought about Mac period and compared him to the FBI agent, in general and there was no comparison.

Paul Robinson was attractive and about Mac's age, but he lacked the sex appeal. He was probably a lady-killer back in the day with his soulful eyes set on chocolate skin, but I could see that the years hadn't been kind. I guess it was all of his years chasing criminals as a civil servant. El said it made you cynical. Cynicism makes you old. I concluded that Mackenzie Powell must be the ultimate optimist. I was prepared to proclaim my innocence to whatever crime Robinson thought I might have committed even if I had to subject myself to his cynical eye.

I tried not to look at him, at first, preferring to focus on my hands and the manicure that needed refreshing while I waited for him to open up the discussion. I looked around his office. Robinson had a bookcase stocked with training manuals and crime related books and on top of the case was a Baltimore Ravens autographed football. I heard him rustle through some papers and pull something from his desk drawer, but I didn't bother to look to see what it was.

"You like history Miss Reynolds?"

"I'm always interested in learning new things even if it's about something old," I replied.

He smiled, slightly. "Let me tell you a story that started back about fifty years ago. It was South Africa in the throes of apartheid. Dutch Afrikaners were running things and the black Africans were working the mines as virtual slaves. Anyway, there was one mine in particular that was so dangerous and took so many lives that the people called it 'The Hole of Death'."

Robinson leaned way back in his chair, folded his hands behind his head and continued. "When they started dismantling apartheid in 1990 one of the first things the new government demanded was to have that mine closed. However, in 1911 The Hole yielded the most rare, pure and largest blue diamond ever found. The

164

diamond weighed thirty-seven carats and it was flawless. A blue diamond is extremely rare and this was the only mine in South Africa that produced diamonds of that hue."

He stood up from his desk as though he needed to take a break from his own history lesson. "Would you like some water?" he asked me.

I nodded and watched him open a small refrigerator that was parked under the only window in the room. He retrieved two bottles of water, handed me one and twisted off the cap of the bottle he had for himself. He took a long swig nearly downing all of the water in a single gulp then wiped his lips and returned to his seat behind the barren desk.

"Anyway, the diamond is stolen and winds up in Thailand in the hands of that country's most notorious underworld figure who calls himself simply, Ping. He's a big-time dealer in narcotics."

Agent Robinson finished the last sip of his water, used his shirtsleeve to wipe off its residue from his lips. He cleared his throat.

"I'm sorry, Agent Robinson, but what does all this have to do with me?" I asked.

"I'm getting to that part. I'm almost there," he said. "A couple of Americans in Thailand to make a major drug deal steal the diamond from Mr. Ping. They make a run for it, shots are fired and they get in a big automobile accident. A young actress who was with them is killed, her fiancé presumed dead and his buddy somehow escapes. The diamond is never recovered.

"The man who escaped makes his way back to the U.S. and is arrested by a young FBI agent for high crimes and misdemeanors and he spends five years in one of our minimum security spas and resorts," Robinson laughed. "He had been running a con game. Of course, we didn't know about his involvement in the theft of the jewelry at the time of his arrest. Basically we've been keeping tabs on this fellow ever since he was released from prison and I must say he's done all right for himself. I guess he's an example of what a man can accomplish in this country if he puts his mind to it."

Agent Robinson leaned forward, used his hand as a brace for his chin with his elbow planted firmly on the desk. He inhaled, held it and slowly exhaled like he was using a yoga relaxation technique.

"There's a man who had been in a Bangkok prison for the last fifteen years that we believe is Richard Reynolds, your father."

I was pretty impassive about Robinson's story until he mentioned my father. I maintained a poker face not wanting to let the agent know that I was dying to learn about my father's fate and so badly wanted to connect with him, no matter what he'd done or where he was.

"You still haven't explained why you're telling me all this," I said clinging onto my composure.

"You're Richard Reynolds' only family." Agent Robinson hesitated. "Mr. Reynolds managed to escape from that Thai prison a couple of weeks ago."

I closed my eyes and tried to steady myself. "So you're trying to tell me that my father is alive."

"Don't know. The Thai authorities believe they shot him while he was trying to swim across the river near the prison, but no body has been recovered---yet."

Agent Robinson said, "We figure that if he is alive he'll try to get in touch with you."

"Why?" I said. "I've never even met him?"

"We're aware that he's been writing your grandmother for years."

"So what, you hope to capture him by using me and spying on me?"

"We could care less if we find him or not. The only thing we're interested in is recovering the jewels. Like I said, you're his only family. Odds are that he sent you the jewel back then before the Thai locked him up."

"I was eleven then Mr. Robinson."

"Doesn't matter. I figure you just might know where they are. Over the years the agency has intercepted letters from your father addressed to you or your grandmother. The letters are cryptic with what we believe are clues. Your grandma ever say anything to you?"

I bit down on my bottom lip. This is what I always did whenever I was angry and had to restrain my words. It was my version of biting my tongue. But it was time to speak my mind.

"I don't understand. First, you accuse me of laundering money and now you think I've got some priceless jewelry that my father or his friend stole years ago? Excuse me, but I thought you FBI guys knew how to do the job. It's like you're bungling your way through all this. What are you the Keystone Cops?"

Robinson smiled like he was amused by what I said. "Probably does seem a little haphazard, but I'm leaving no stone unturned. If you don't have the jewels then I believe you, just like I believe you're not in the money laundering business."

"What about his partner, the one escaped?" I asked.

"He's looking for it, too. Actually, that's why we're keeping tabs on your friend, Antoine."

It was a light bulb moment. The break-in at my family's home, my own intruder and even this stiff sitting right in front of me were all looking for a piece of jewelry I didn't have. The FBI had no search warrant. It was just an excuse to search my apartment hoping they'd find the crown jewels in a D.C. suburban apartment. Robinson was law enforcement, but something about him made me uneasy.

"What does Antoine have to do with this?" I asked.

Agent Robinson smiled. "Antoine's a bit player. In fact, we're not sure what his role is. The money he deposited in that bank for you isn't drug money so it's legit except that it might be a violation of Antiguan law to falsify a deposit slip. Otherwise, we think he's some kind of front man. It's the people he works for we're really interested in."

"Who is that?" I asked.

"Your father's, partner. I put him away once and I'm going to put him away again. This time it'll be for a long, long time. You know him as Mackenzie Powell."

I sat in silence for what seemed like an eternity then the questions started accumulating in my mind. "Antoine works for Mac?" I asked the question just to confirm what the agent had told me.

Robinson nodded.

"And Mac is looking for the jewelry?"

He nodded again.

"And they both think I have it?"

"Yes. It was Antoine's job to locate it. They thought that by his getting close to you you'd talk about it and tell him where they could find the diamond. I guess his boss must've figured he wasn't man enough to finish the job. You can imagine how surprised I was to see you with Mackenzie Powell the other night."

My heart sank. I knew then what Antoine saw in me, but the pain came in realizing what Mac wanted and the things he was willing to do to get it. I was sure that Agent Robinson could see my pain etched indelibly all over my face, but he ignored it. Unfortunately, I couldn't. I had to get out of there.

I said in a low tone, "But I don't have the jewelry."

"Like I told you, I believe you don't, but *they* don't know you don't have it," Robinson said.

I saw him look down and watched as he slowly opened the top drawer to his desk. He pulled out a beautiful brown Mahogany box that was about the size of a notebook, but thicker and then gently placed it on the desk in front of me. I sat there in dumb silence.

"The South African government wants the jewelry bad. So bad they've offered a reward of five million dollars to the person who recovers it or tells them where it is. No questions asked. The problem is Ping wants the diamond as well. With him involved it's clear that somebody's going to pay with his life."

Robinson slowly eased the box across his desk so that I could touch it. "Open it," he said. "Please," he added.

I reached for it like I was under some kind of spell, my mind on overload and now de-sensitized to any shock or fear. Slowly, I lifted the box's lid with my eyes opening wider with every corresponding movement of my hand. And there it was placed on black satin, a huge beautiful blue diamond with a chain of a hundred smaller white ones sparkling like it had been harvested from the Milky Way itself.

"I don't understand. This is it. This is the diamond you told me about. It's not missing at all," I said.

Robinson leaned close. "This, young lady, is the miracle of science. Diamonds made by man and his friend, the computer. It's worth about twenty-five thousand dollars and made to look like the real thing," he said. "The guys in the lab call it 'Desdemona II'."

"What? Desdemona?"

"Yeah, that's the name of the original stone."

"I have to go," I said. It was too much for me to take.

Robinson nodded. "I understand. I just want you to do one thing." He looked at the jewelry in the box. "Take it with you."

"Why?" I asked.

"Bait. Mac wants it. You give it to him. I, in return, get him and his cohorts. The Thai government can nab their countryman and maybe one day the real thing will appear."

"So, I'm supposed to just walk up to him and say, 'Here, I know you've been looking for this diamond you and my father stole many years ago,'" I said.

The agent's response was a half-hearted laugh. "I think you can be a lot more subtle than that. Just tell him you found it during your visit back home and you want to know if it's worth anything. Trust me, Mackenzie Powell will know what to do from that point on."

"And what about that Ping guy? I'm sure his people haven't given up looking for the real diamond. They're probably the ones who broke into my house," I said.

"I doubt it but I wouldn't rule anything out. We have the tape from your building's security monitor. We'll be studying it to see if we find some answers. In the meantime we'll make sure you're protected."

I had a parting thought. "I thought you said the diamond, ah, Desdemona belongs to South Africa? You act like it belongs to the U.S. government," I said.

"Just trying to do my duty as a civil servant," he answered.

Chapter Thirty-One

I turned down Agent Robinson's offer for a ride home, choosing to walk around downtown with a twenty-five thousand dollar fake necklace in my purse. For a couple of hours I walked around deep in thought and window shopped without really looking at items in the stores along Connecticut Avenue. I stopped at a small tavern on M Street and drank brandy alone and listened to a sad Billie Holliday lullaby. It only deepened my pain. A short cab ride and some courage later I was standing in front of Mac's house poised to knock on his door.

I had asked the cab driver to wait a few minutes just in case Mac wasn't home or if I might lose my nerve, but his car was parked in front and that answered one of my two questions. Seeing my cab take off and disappear down the long driveway forced me to seek an answer to the second. Did I have the nerve to confront him about the things that had rocked my world since the time we first met?

I thought about what Paul Robinson told me about Mac and realized that a lot of what he said was based on suspicion and speculation. Mac having known my father was real and that was my only truth because I could prove it. Everything else I was told and I would give him the opportunity to explain.

I knocked on the door and waited. Rang the doorbell and waited. Rang the doorbell again and again like a woman possessed. The firewater I drank was my fuel. "Mackenzie! Mackenzie! I need to talk to you," I shouted. Resignation was slowly setting in and I realized that just because his car was there didn't mean that he had to be. With one last knock and kick to that obstinate door I slid down to the step, sat there exhausted and exasperated.

I had my head down sitting in a Lotus position when the door cracked open and I heard a sleepy voice that almost cracked, "Dahlia? Is that you?"

"Can we talk?" I asked followed by, "Are you alone?"

Mac had this puzzled expression, but he quickly opened the door and waited for me to come inside. "I've been worried about you. I've called and called you but all I got was your answering machine and you didn't call me back," Mac said.

He led me to his kitchen and offered me a chair. "I thought you wanted me to pick you up in Georgia." He sat down.

My eyes told him that I wasn't buying what he was saying about being worried but my lips were stilled. All I could think about was that he was a shyster, a conman of the highest order if I were to believe Agent Robinson. I was searching for the right way to tell him the things I knew and to ask him about the things I didn't know. I decided that the best way to do it was to be direct and straight to the point.

Mac stood up and walked over to the refrigerator. He poured himself a large glass of orange juice and motioned to me.

"Can I offer you something? How about a cup of coffee? Tea?"

"No." I breathed deep, mustered some courage that I knew I didn't have before. I said, "I found out something while I was back home." Took a deep breath. "You knew my father, didn't you?"

I watched him pause and stagger just a little like he'd been shot with an arrow. Mac leaned against a counter, sipping his O.J. with his eyes studying me, piercing examination of the young woman sitting at his table, a refugee from his kindness. An ever so pregnant pause delayed an answer. He cleared his throat as I watched him squirm.

"Yes, I did. You must've found out when you went home. Who told you? Your mother?" Mac asked.

I looked over at him, rubbed my temples. "You knew who I was all along, didn't you?"

Mac nodded this time.

"It was all part of some grand plan wasn't it Mac? The designer dresses, spending money on me. First I thought you were just feeling sorry for this little ole country girl. Then I thought maybe, just maybe you really liked me, but it was just a game for you. High stakes like the poker you play or golf. I guess what I need to know is how far would you have gone to get what you want? Would you have screwed Ricky's little girl for this?"

I reached into my purse and pulled out the polished Mahogany box and set it hard on the table.

"What's that?" he asked, pointing to the box.

"Open it. It's what you want. It's the reason you and I are here, isn't it?" My anger was bubbling over.

I watched Mac as he opened the box much in the same way I had opened it at FBI headquarters. He was cautious and moved gingerly as he slowly lifted its lid. But his eyes smiled when he saw what was inside.

"What? How'd you know? I-I don't believe this," Mac said.

"Like I said, my grandmother told me in a way. It's yours as much as it was my father's."

I stood up and started my walk to the front door. I figured that the diamond was all Mac really wanted and that because I wasn't good at deception I would let him know that it wasn't the real thing. I fought back the tears that were trying to besiege me, hoping that Mac would follow me to the door, but a quick glance backwards and I could see that the diamonds had him transfixed and unable to move. Desdemona was the love of his life and I was merely a pawn for this player. I reached for the door, felt the pressure of his hand on my arm pulling me.

"Wait, Dahlia, don't leave," he said.

I reluctantly retreated back to him and stood there waiting for whatever he had to say to me.

"There are a lot of things you don't know about me, about your father and about that damn necklace," he told me.

"You're wrong Mackenzie. I know everything about you, about Antoine, about that piece of rock you treasure."

He looked stunned and shaken. "You know about Antoine?" he asked.

"Yes."

"Please come back and sit down, I've got some things I need to tell you."

We sat on the floor in Mac's foyer facing each other, each in the lotus position. "That rock cost me my best friend and I hated that, but I was desperate to get it back," he said.

"So meeting me was your act of desperation," I told him.

He shook his head. "No, Dahlia, but I had to come up with a plan to get the jewels back and Antoine's way wasn't working."

I thought, *Antoine, Antoine, he was being pimped in a way, trading his body for information.* "So was it part of your plan to almost kill me?"

Mac gave me a heavy sigh. Another arrow into his heart. I could tell that my words carried nothing but pain. I could see a transparent coat of moisture cover the whites of his eyes and wash over his emerald pupils. "I would've never let anything happen to you or your family. That's why Antoine was coming around. His job was to protect you, to make sure that nothing happens to you. I was hoping that you'd like him, that he would like you since you two were close in age, but it wasn't my plan for him to use you. It wasn't my plan to exploit you."

Now it was my turn to shake my head, trying not to lose my thoughts of sarcasm, trying not to be lured in by his eyes. But I looked into those eyes, *damn his eyes, damn him, damn it.*

"It was all part of your plan Mac, detailed and meticulous just like you. So was it your plan to make me want you, to make every organ in my body ache for you?"

"Things like that don't happen according to some plan. I felt the same things for you, but I couldn't act on my feelings. I know it's hard for you to understand this, but that piece of rock in there is my last shot. I've been knocking around this world for fifty years, reaching for the carrot only to have it snatched away from me," Mac said.

I surveyed the area, the interior of Mac's house with all its trappings of wealth and success. "Looks like you made it," I said.

"Dahlia, things aren't always as they appear to be."

"So you figured you'd take the diamond...."

Mac cut me off. "Not just take it. My plan has always been to split it with you no matter what. My plan was to take care of you--- the way I always had."

"What do you mean?"

"Your college and student loans. At one point you owed more than a hundred thousand dollars. Guess who paid that off?"

"You! Why because I'm Ricky's daughter?"

"That's part of it. You know duty and honor among thieves. Your father lost his life because of what we did. I owe him that. I owe you that much."

"But my father..." I stopped in mid-sentence. I decided for the moment I wouldn't tell Mac that Richard Reynolds might still be alive. I had to learn the rules of this game that all of these people including Mac were playing and rule number one was not to disclose everything I knew.

Mac put his hands on mine and regarded the woman sitting in front of him with his eyes. "It's crazy. Here you are this lovely and beautiful woman and I can't think of you as a daughter. I can't think of you as Ricky's little girl. I see you now as someone I long for, someone I can't stop thinking about."

My heart welled up. His words with those eyes dispelled any thoughts that he was acting only out of duty to my father. I realized right then that I really did love him, that it was more than a crush or infatuation. I moved close to him so that I could see his soul through his hazel and green-colored eyes. Kissed him.

And like magnets we were drawn together, our lips in a lovelock as a precursor to our bodies following not far behind. We stood, pulled each other close, arms intertwined and I held on for dear love. The warmth and passion was unlike anything I'd ever experienced.

I gave him a breathy, "I want you, Mackenzie. I've wanted you since that day we first met."

Chapter Thirty-Two

Mac held my hand and led me to his bedroom. In that moment my own demons had ceased to exist. There were no thoughts of my grandmother or the man who'd tried to hurt us or all the intrigue surrounding Desdemona. It was just he and I and the anticipation.

We sat on the bed, kissed hard and groped at each other's pleasure spots hidden underneath our clothes. I stood up in front of him taking off my clothes, one piece at a time, slowly titillating his sense of sight and proud of what I had to offer. His eyes admiringly held my image as his breathing quickened.

His, "we shouldn't do this" was barely audible, but he didn't stop and I didn't want him to. I felt the warm air from his mouth pass over my nipples followed by the wet, stickiness of his tongue tracing slow spirals down to my valley. And he stayed there moving in slow conjugal spirals that twisted me, causing involuntary tremors that shook me to the core.

I was a virgin to this. No one had ever touched me like this. No one had ever moved me like this. I closed my eyes, made an unrepentant plea to my Creator and got lost in my feeling. When it seemed like I couldn't handle it anymore I moved away from his lips and serpentine tongue. We kissed hard again as I absorbed the aftershock that quaked my body and Mac ripped off his shirt and unfastened his pants.

I felt his readiness and then straddled his lap, allowed him to fill me slow and gentle as I sank down upon him. For a moment we just held each other without moving. Our core and centers, fully engaged, were adapting to the newness of this experience. I didn't want to move, just feel my juices surround him, labia growing accustomed to his large phallic presence.

Our stars were fully in Eros when Mac began to move his hips slow and deliberate. His motion, forward and back, side to side made me follow until we were in perfect timing and rocking in tantric-like syncopation. I closed my eyes and leaned back knowing that his strong arms would hold me safely around my waist and our motion continued. I then leaned forward into his awaiting kiss and wrapped my arms around his back and squeezed and held on for dear life.

The sounds of lovemaking dominated the room with its heavy breathing, gasps and whimpers, guttural sounds of people caught in the moment of passion without pretense, adorned with ugly faces. I could feel my transformation from the young woman who lay silent during sex, used solely as a receptacle for some man's prospective progeny to being a real woman fully engaged, enjoying giving as much as I did receiving.

"Do you want to turn out the lights?" I asked.

"No, I want to see your face. Hear you breathe in my ear. Watch your eyes, your mouth. And kiss you as I love you."

With Mac's words, I lost myself in the abyss and felt my body slipping as a torrent of waves began to build and eventually seized it. This was the orgasm my girlfriends had told me about, except words couldn't do it justice. It hit me once and then repeated itself over and over. At first, each wave was more intense than the one that preceded it. It made me want to scream, to pull out my hair, to push myself from underneath him, to savor it all.

A chorus of unintelligible sounds from two people swapping juices until we reached a crescendo and then fell apart, panting and grabbing air like it was our last. My body quivered to the point where Mac quickly composed himself, reached for me, held me, listened to me say, "Ooh, baby" over and over.

We had made love like he had invented it. Made love like it was our last. Coupling and un-coupling three or four times, I lost count, until finally we collapsed. Coition complete like I'd never known or experienced. We lay afterwards, bodies still intertwined as Mac closed his eyes and his breathing became shallow.

For a moment, fear overrode my euphoria and the pace of my heart accelerated. "Mac," I said, quietly.

No response.

I raised my voice a few decibels.

"Mackenzie!"

I sat up, shook him slightly and when he didn't move I reached for the telephone to dial "911". In my angst and hobbled anxiety I heard his deep, rich voice say, "What are you doing?" Softly.

"I thought, I thought something was wrong. Like you had a heart attack."

He smiled. "No, I'm fine," he said. "Just asleep. What? You thought you killed me, didn't you?"

I nodded.

"Death by passion," he joked.

I settled in beside him, comforted in knowing that he was all right and feeling the warmth of his body and the strength in the arms that now enveloped me. For the first time in my life I was feeling complete, satisfied, safe.

I slept through the night, awakened only by the sun washing over my face, signaling that it was morning. My eyes still closed, I reached out for Mackenzie, but felt nothing but the coolness of his satin sheets. I looked across the wide spans of his king size bed, but he was gone. I thought, *He's probably downstairs* or maybe, *he's gone to play golf.*

There was a robe at the end of the bed and I hastily wrapped it around me and went searching for him. I could hear the sound of activity coming from downstairs so I followed it.

"Mac?"

There were men in the foyer carrying furniture and boxes and working hurriedly without talking. The mansion was virtually empty. I looked around only to see a cavernous shell that now lacked any evidence of Mac's existence there.

The three men loading the truck seemed not to notice me as they busily kept their pace and systematically went about carrying out their task. I called out for Mac hoping that he was somewhere in the house, but he didn't answer. Finally, I stood in the path of one of the workers, a Hispanic looking man, and asked him where the owner of the house was. He returned a blank look without a word and I realized that he didn't understand what I was saying.

A fourth man, big and burly, chomping on a thick cigar and armed with a notepad, was coming from the kitchen. He had one of those, *"what do you want?"* expressions all over his face, which made me want to run for the door. But I stood my ground and waited.

"Where's Mr. Powell?" I asked.

He shook his head. "Don't know who you talkin' bout, young lady."

"Mackenzie Powell. The guy who owns this house," I said.

"We were called by some guy named, Richard Reynolds and this is his stuff we're moving."

177

"Must be a mistake," I said in near reflex fashion. "Richard Reynolds is dead, I think."

The fat man blew smoke at his frustration, almost choking me in the process. I could tell that he was in no mood to debate me.

"Well then his ghost must've called me," he said.

"Then tell me, where is Mister Reynolds?" I asked.

The big man shrugged his shoulders and continued to direct the other men to their tasks. What he said made me panic. There was no Mackenzie Powell, no Richard Reynolds and no one else in the house. Mac was gone and so was the Desdemona Diamond.

*   *   *

I dressed in a hurry not quite sure what I'd do next. I knew I had to get out of the house. I wasn't concerned about the jewel---it was a fake, but his leaving hurt just the same. I was wondering what he was planning to do with it. Sell it, I suppose.

The men who'd been moving Mac's things were gone. I figured I'd call a cab and go home when I heard the sound of footsteps echoing throughout the hollowed out house. It was coming from his study.

She was pacing around the room with notepad in her hand, taking inventory or so it seemed of Mac's valuable art collection. She didn't seem to notice me at first as I stood there watching her without making a sound, but she quickly let me know that she was aware of my presence.

"You have a good night's rest?" She said without turning around.

It was Sue doing the things I imagine personal assistants do for their bosses. She kept counting using her other hand with a chrome plated ink pin poised between her fingers. With each count she'd make a note on the pad. Her focus was on the paintings and not on me.

I didn't answer her question. It seemed silly considering the circumstances. "Where's Mackenzie?" I asked.

My question made Sue stop and acknowledge me. She looked at me through narrowed eyes reminded me of a snake ready to bite. "Who knows? Probably Brazil or someplace. What happened? He screw you and leave you?"

I could feel her icy tone even more than I heard it, but I wasn't going to shrink away and let her intimidate me. "I'm just asking if you know where Mac is?"

Sue went back to her business, acting like she didn't hear me. I could feel my frustration build like I could reach over and choke an answer out of her, but I remembered Felicia's warning. She told me that Sue was no one to play with.

Sue replied, "If I were you I'd forget about him. He's got your little trinket and he's gone. Life goes on."

"Little trinket?" I asked.

"The diamonds, you know Desdemona."

"You know about that?"

"I know all of Mackenzie's business, naïve little girl. Did you really think he was interested in you? It was always Desdemona and the twenty million dollars he's going to get for her."

Sue walked over to me and stopped within inches of my face. Her violet colored eyes made me think of lasers. I wanted to run, but I held my ground. She turned her head slightly and used her eyes to examine every inch of my face.

"Richard's little girl. I see it now in your eyes."

My mouth dropped. "You knew my father?"

"Of course I know him. He, Mackenzie and I go back a long way. We've got a history."

"You said, 'know'. As in: he's still alive."

Sue walked away. I could tell that she was now looking at the artwork with a feigned sense of interest. She said, 'Maybe he is. Maybe he isn't."

"Don't play games, Sue. Is Richard Reynolds alive?"

"The answer is in the envelope."

I gave her a hard look. Could feel the muscles in my body tighten. "You know about the envelope, too?"

"Ah, yes. Your little sister did a very bad thing taking it. You don't happen to know where she is, do you?"

"Ah---no. I haven't talked to her since she got back from...."

"New York." Sue When filled in the blank. She walked back over to me, entered my comfort zone and stood there. "Get me that envelope and I'll take you to your father."

"And what if I can't find Charity? Can't get the envelope?"

Sue shrugged her shoulders. "Then you're all dead----you, your sister, Richard and Mackenzie."

I felt the chill in the words she spoke as calm as someone ordering fast food. She walked back over to Mac's art and took inventory of his Romare Bearden, Jacob Lawrence and Andy Warhol paintings.

I headed to the door then stopped. "Why Mac?" I asked. "Why would you have him killed? He's got what you want. He's got what you and your friend wanted."

"Friend?"

"Yeah, the man who had you moaning and groaning the night of Mac's party right here in his study."

Sue looked annoyed. "Little creatures hiding in the dark. Little creatures with big ears. Don't worry about what I do, worry about Mackenzie. After all, you gave him the replica. When they find out, they'll kill him for sure. Get me the envelope, get me the real thing and you all can walk away from this."

I left thinking that I'd have to do whatever I could to save Charity and my father. Mackenzie was a different story. But Sue When had answered a lot of my questions without her knowing. The man who was screwing her brains out was also her business partner. They wanted the real diamonds and they'd double cross or kill anyone who would dare stand in their way.

It was all coming together. I knew the plan. I knew what they wanted. I knew who the players were. Sue had told me the name of her partner without saying it. The question was, how could I let Mac know? And what could I do to stop them?

Chapter Thirty-Three

I left the house where Mac once lived and went home. Or at least to the place I called my home. I sat and waited for my telephone to ring---waited for him to call, but the silence spoke volumes and deep in my heart I felt like I'd never hear from him again. Still I waited at home. And there I found solitude, secreting myself away from the world, crestfallen.

Erykah Badu in the background on my MP3 player singing unintelligible lyrics, an ode to neo-soul and the forgotten classics, but it was not the words or the beat that mattered---it was a feeling.

I tried to call him, but his home number was disconnected and his mobile phone's voice mail repeated the refrain: *the subscriber you are calling does not accept calls from this number.*

Badu was still singing. Made me feel melancholy.

For the next few days or more I rarely left my apartment. I called off sick from my job and barely ate. My sweat suits and tee shirts were my uniform, the couture of the depressed and rejected. The contact lens that had opened my eyes to my new beauty were now stored in saline, floating about in lipid pools of sorrow and my hair had reverted to the curly nest that had coifed the old Dahlia Reynolds. I had become myself all over again.

My mornings meant a queasy stomach, a dash to the bathroom, a quick peek at my image in the mirror followed by my gasping in horror at my metamorphosis. Depression was making me sick and out of touch with myself and my body. Regurgitating the contents of whatever had been in my stomach the night before was the only measure of my existence.

I spent those days watching my security monitor, my only portal to the outside world. I watched the comings and goings of my neighbors, some of whom I'd never seen before others I'd thought had moved. But mostly I watched to see if Mackenzie had somehow found his way to my door.

Badu played over and over until the music became part of my culture or, rather I became part of it.

And whenever my telephone rang my hope sprang eternal, believing that it was Mac only to be dashed down to the reality that it wasn't. It was the usual calls from bill collectors along with occasional inquiries from my friends checking up on me. I allowed the answering machine to speak for me, choosing to listen in discriminating silence and hoping that one of those calls would be from him---with Badu in the background.

My feelings about him ran the gamut---sorrow, rage, longing, lust---a recipe for the gumbo of funk that pervaded my little world locked away in twelve hundred square feet of living space. I guess I could've dwelled there depressed and heartbroken for eternity or for a few days more, but that was the old me. The new one could emerge from the rubble in Phoenix-like fashion, ready to press on and search for some answers.

Answers.

They weren't there in my place. I'd never find them there. My usually pristine apartment had become a reflection of my wretched existence. Dishes piled up in the sink like mountains of neglect spoke of someone who didn't give a damn. I hadn't made up my bed for days, choosing to sleep in a bundle of sheets and clothes that I'd wash, but wouldn't fold or put away. And it didn't interfere with my sleeping.

After a few days of this non-existence I knew that it was time to break the cycle. It was time to wake up. I looked at the family quilt hanging on the wall. Studied it the way El did. Its intricate detail was telling me a story I hadn't bothered to hear. It was a story of survival through horror and oppression, through slavery and Jim Crow yet it hung there proudly, resilient in its proclamation that it had survived. My family, like the quilt had survived and so would I.

I remembered my grandmother's words when we were talking about the quilt years ago. "The treasure is within," she told me. I thought that she was talking about the fact that it was so valuable, but I realized that she meant so much more. The treasure was within me.

I got dressed, turned off Badu and left my place for the first time in days.

Chapter Thirty-Four

"This better be important."

That was the first thing El said when she walked into Stacy's townhouse. She looked around surveying the place.

"This isn't about me. It's Dahlia," Stacy told El. El sat down on the bed beside me, kissed my forehead.

"It's that old guy, huh? What happened?"

El turned to me and said, "Give me details."

I tried to tell her everything while allowing her sharp lawyer's mind to absorb my words. When I finished the story all she could say was, "wow" and then she settled into a pensive expression, her lawyer's mind was turning its wheels.

"Tell me about this jewelry," El said. "Where'd your grandmother get it?"

"Apparently from my father. He sent it to her for safekeeping, I guess."

"And no one knows where the real diamond is?" she asked.

"That's what the FBI agent told me. Some guy named Robinson. He thinks I have it, but I don't. They even have a name for it called, Desdemona," I explained.

El nearly lost the color from her chocolate hued face. She shifted uneasily on Stacy's bed, put her head down and began to wring her hands.

"What is it?" Stacy asked.

"You know where I work, don't you, Stacy?" El told her.

"You know I know you work for the Justice Department," Stacy said.

"We all know where you work, El. Department of Justice," I said.

"Yeah, DOJ, International Crimes Division," El stood up and abruptly headed to Stacy's bedroom door. "I got to go. I have to check something out."

"What's the matter?" I asked.

"It's nothing, really. Just a hunch, I guess. I can't talk about it right now."

El turned and then stopped in mid-stride.

"What's Mac's last name?" she asked.

"Powell. Mackenzie Powell."

El seemed to file that information away in that computer mounted on top of her shoulders and housed inside her perfect bone structured face. Her expression turned grim.

"It's been a rough day. A guy I know who once worked as an investigator with the department was killed. Shot in the head behind Café Alexandria's," she told us.

My heart froze.

"His name was Joe Martin," El added.

I didn't want to say anything right then. I heard about the murder on the news and it happened the same night I was at the club. I thought about the confrontation Joe had with Mac that night, but I dismissed the idea that Mac might have been the one who killed Joe. After all, Mac took me home that night. But still the thought lingered. Did he go back to the club? Could Mac kill a man?

El hesitated for a moment giving her silent condolences to the dead man, as though honoring him was an afterthought then walked out of Stacy's house.

*   *   *   *

"*Shssssh.* I could lose my job if anyone finds out that I'm showing y'all this stuff," El told us.

She was looking around the third floor reading room in the Library of Congress like a not so subtle spy as Stacy and I hovered over the neatly bound dossier that memorialized a man's life.

Stacy laughed.

"You would've been fired a long time ago if they knew about all the times your name was, 'unidentified source' or 'identity withheld' when I report for the Post," she said using imaginary quotation marks drawn with her fingers. "Don't worry, you won't get into trouble."

El's facial expression was solemn. Her words were sincere.

"This is no joke. Wait until you read what's in that file," she told us.

There was a "rap sheet" for Mackenzie Powell that listed a string of criminal convictions. Most were "theft by deception", white collar type crimes and nothing involving any acts of violence.

"It was the theft by deception conviction that sent him to prison."

"Prison?" I tried to act like I didn't know.

"Yeah, it seems that he was a conman. Ran some kind of ponzi scheme that was bilking women out of their money and valuables. He did five years in a minimum security facility outside of Lafayette, Louisiana."

"So, Mister Smooth Mackenzie Powell is some kind of con artist. Damn! I really liked him," Stacy said.

But I wasn't so judgmental in my own reaction to what Mac's file revealed. "People change, Stacy. Besides, when was that? What? Twenty or thirty years ago?" I said in his defense.

I looked over at El and the grim expression still lingered on her face.

"What's wrong?" I asked.

"There's more," El said. "He's a smooth career criminal who might've been the man who broke into your place and held a knife to your throat."

She took a deep breath.

The room became quiet for what seemed like an eternity as we sat there thinking about the unthinkable.

"No, no. He-he's not that kind of man." I said.

But I wasn't speaking with any sense of conviction. *What if Mac was the man who broke into my place and almost killed me and Antoine?*

"Why don't you believe he could do something like that?" El said. "Because you think you've got a thing for him?"

And then her mouth dropped open. El looked at Stacy first and then back at me.

"You didn't sleep with him, did you?"

My response was the silence of the obvious. I'd been convicted without saying a word. *It can't be. He wouldn't try and hurt me like that no matter what he was after,* I thought.

For a moment deafening silence and an air of condemnation occupied us but El, as usual would be the first to speak up.

"What kind of sick bastard would do something like that?" she asked.

"Wait a minute, El," Stacy said in a calming voice. "Let's not jump to conclusions. We don't know if Mac is the man who assaulted Dahlia."

"Yeah, well someone did and who's the likely suspect? That guy, that's who," El said.

"Damn, El! You're the lawyer here. You need to start thinking like one. I mean, c'mon. You read some twenty-year old rap sheet and you're going to condemn the man forever! Whatever happened to rehabilitation?"

"Spoken right from the textbook of the liberal left wing media. Heard the term, recidivist Stacy? C'mon you're the goddamn investigative journalist! Start thinking like one."

I suddenly felt the need to be the mediator. After all, it was my father, my life, my man, I guess. I wanted to---no, I needed to get to the bottom of this intrigue and find the truth, whatever it might be. I stood up and tried to pull myself together.

"You two need to stop. This is about me and I've got to figure it all out. I'm going to find Mac." I said.

El looked surprised. "You're going to do what?"

"I'm going to find him."

El cleared her throat.

"Well before you go off on some wild desperate search for a man I think there's something else you should know."

She reached into her briefcase and pulled out another file folder, plopped it on the table in front of Stacy and me.

El turned to Stacy and said, "If I see anything remotely resembling what's in this file in your rag of a newspaper I'll disown you, Stacy."

Stacy raised her right hand like she was taking an oath of secrecy.

El continued. "Remember I told you about Joe Martin? Well, I didn't tell you everything I knew. I said he was an investigator with the Justice Department. Actually he used to work with our section. He quit and became a contractor, you know, freelancer."

El slowly opened the file folder, revealing several documents inside.

"Joe was working under contract for some wealthy Dutch family. They were paying him to find and recover the diamonds," she said.

El flipped to a document that was stamped "Classified" in bold black letters.

"Anyway. Joe had been involved in ongoing surveillance of a gang of smugglers. He created what we call in the business, a Thread."

"What's that?" I asked.

"Like a family tree, sort of. You know, like that quilt you have except it's for a crime family."

El slid the document on the table then turned away to see if anyone was watching.

"See at the top of the tree is this guy who goes by the name of Ping. He's a reputed mob boss who specializes in the sex trade."

El cut a hard stare in Stacy's direction.

"Don't you write any of this down, Stace."

"O.K. O.K."

"Ping has been trying to acquire the jewels on his own. Thinks he'll enhance his power in the Thai government and that will give him leverage to continue his criminal enterprise."

She pointed to the Thread.

"Underneath Ping are his non-Thai co-conspirators. It gets deeper. Mac's girl you told me about, Sue When is right in the mix."

That revelation stunned me.

I said. "She helps him with his antiques business."

El laughed.

"Yeah, right. She's in the smuggling end of the organization. They bring stuff into the country like designer clothes like the dresses Mac gave you and all kinds of other black market type stuff. They also provide weapons like outlawed AK-47's, Apache helicopters. Hell, they can even get a cruise missile for anyone who can afford it. If that isn't bad enough, they're also the muscle end of the organization."

"So where does Mac fit in all of this?" I asked.

"I'm not sure. He's obviously a freelancer who periodically uses your father's name. ."

I sat there quietly, absorbed in my own private thoughts. I thought about Mac, Joe and Mr. Friendly then about Sue When.

"So do they think that's why Joe Martin ended up dead?" I asked.

"Don't know," El said. "He was shot in the head, three times. That usually signifies more than just someone eliminating another person. That's a sign of anger, passion."

El leaned close. "What do you think, Dahlia? You were there that night, the night he was killed. You said he and Mac got into some kind of argument. They find Joe the next morning with three vent holes in his brain."

The thought settled deep in the pit of my stomach. Mac wouldn't have killed Joe for being a drunken pain in the ass, but he could for another reason. Actually it could've been twenty million reasons to be exact. Either way I had to know.

"I've gotta find him," I said.

El shook her head.

"Girl, this is some dangerous action. You need to keep as far away as you can. You said the jewelry you gave Mac was a fake replica of the Desdemona diamond and if he or his associates find out they'll think you set them up. They'll also think you've got the real one. Either way, you're putting your life in danger, honey."

"Yeah, if he's desperate enough to break into your place and hold a knife to your throat what do you think he'll do if he finds out he's been tricked," Stacy added.

What my friends said made sense, but I was relying on my instincts about the kind of person I thought Mac was. I thought about Agent Robinson telling me that the FBI was reviewing the tapes recorded by the security monitor in my building and I knew then how to find the answer to my questions about Mackenzie Powell.

Stacy and El were still going tit for tat about Mac and how crazy I was for wanting to find him when I interrupted their lively discussion.

"Stacy, El I need your help," I told them.

It was the end of Dahlia Reynolds, victim.

*   *   *

After a stop by El's townhouse and a quick change of clothes, we hopped into the Beamer with the top down and my friend at the wheel, the three of us on a mission. A half an hour later we were sitting in the car in the back parking lot of my apartment building going over last minute details.

"You know what to say, don't you?" I told El.

She gave me a disdainful look. "Girl, I'm a lawyer and he's a man. And unless he's gay he'll listen to anything I say to him."

Stacy groaned. "It's four o'clock in the morning. I should be getting my rest."

We climbed out of the car. Stacy and I were dressed down in black jeans and sweatshirts and El in her come-and-get-this dress. Together we were Charlie's Angel's only chocolate-ized. El went ahead of us walking with small baby steps to accommodate a dress that was so tight it looked like she'd been wrapped in cellophane at a day spa. Add a plunging neckline and six-inch spike heels and she could stop traffic on the Capital Beltway.

Stacy and I assumed our positions behind two large bushes near the staircase that led to the building's front door while El carefully navigated the stairs. We watched as she stood in front of the glass door peering at the security guard trying to get his attention because the door was locked. I could see him from where I was hiding with his head down as he sat at the front desk probably playing video games on the building's computer. El decided that she had to be more aggressive to get the young man's attention.

"C'mon," she said as she knocked on the glass door with her long fingernails. She whispered to the two of us, "If I break a fingernail you guys will get the bill for my manicure."

The security guard finally looked up from the computer after a couple of minutes of El's persistent tapping, got up from his station and cracked open the door. "May I help you?" he asked El.

"Oh, thank you. My car broke down about a block away and I was hoping someone could come and jump me. I mean, help me. You know what I mean, jumper cables?" El asked him in her sexiest winded voice.

"I'm sorry Ma'am, but I'm on duty. I can't leave my post," he answered. "Can you call someone?"

El took a deep breath, allowed her breasts to heave up and down with her cleavage drawing a line from her beautiful face down to her awesome body and back up, again. The capable attorney was now the helpless damsel in distress.

"I would if I could, but my cell phone is dead. I guess I forgot to charge the battery." El poked out her red painted lips into the shape of a perfect kiss and gave him an extra dose of the sad eyes.

The gatekeeper in the uniform was trying to maintain his professional decorum and greeted her with a stern face. I guess he was new on the job. He looked over his shoulder and then around El as if he was checking to make sure the coast was clear then beckoned her to come inside. Stacy and I watched him as he allowed El to walk ahead and we chuckled when he bumped into the door while it was slowly closing.

"She's got him," Stacy whispered.

They walked over to his station and he handed her the telephone and watched as she pretended to dial it. But he could still see the front door.

I whispered to Stacy, "She's got to make him get up from there. He can still see us when we come inside."

Of course we had accounted for every detail as part of our plan. As if acting on cue, El knocked her purse off the desk and all of its contents came spilling out on the floor. She dropped down into a squat and started picking up her things as her dress rode up and stopped just short of where her kitty was peeking out from its hiding place. The young security guard was in a trance. He stared for a long moment then hurried from around his desk to offer his assistance.

"It's time to move," I told Stacy.

We walked like a couple of cat burglars, hunched over in our black outfits as I pulled out my door key and opened the door. Stacy was about to walk inside when I said, "Stacy! Put on your ski mask." Even if the security guard's distracted the monitor would catch our images.

El squatted down on the floor with the security guard hovering over her while Stacy and I made our move. We eased by our voluptuous friend as she nervously kept an eye on us and talked to the guard. The building's office was over to the right and only a few feet away from the guard's station.

El was talking loudly about anything and everything she could think of just to keep him from hearing us. "Have you played NBA Live?" she asked. "I have a friend who plays for the Wizards if you need a ticket." And, "Thank you so much. Did anyone ever tell you, you have nice hands?"

I eased open the office door as we slid through its narrow opening. Stacy closed the door softly and waited in the dark while I searched for the lights. I had been inside the office once to talk to the manager about getting my toilet fixed, but I didn't know where they kept the security tapes. There was a television monitor inside and a VCR recording everything in the lobby. We surveyed the room and concluded that the large metal cabinet in the corner was the logical place. I grabbed the door handle and turned, but it was locked.

"Can't open it Stacy," I said.

"Let me try," she told me. I watched my friend as I listened for any sounds coming from the lobby. Stacy reached inside her purse and pulled out a letter opener that looked like a small sword and inserted it into the door's keyhole.

"What are you doing with that in your purse?" I asked

She shrugged her shoulders. "I get a lot of mail?"

She turned and twisted the letter opener inside the hole until the whole lock popped out. "Sorry," she said.

We opened the door wide. There they were organized neatly according to date, the backup tapes of the lobby and the comings and goings of everyone who entered the building. I quickly found the tape marked with the date of the break-in at my apartment. I put it in my purse. It was time to leave.

We turned out the lights and cracked the door open. I could see El leaning over the security guard with her breasts practically in his face. She was laughing, pointing to something on the computer and he was smiling like St. Peter had just given him a free pass into heaven. We were ready to make our exit when I remembered something.

"We need to erase part of the tape that showed us sneaking in here," I said.

Stacy groaned, "It's going to show us leaving, too."

"I'll be right back. You keep an eye on El and her friend," I told her.

I re-wound the tape and recorded over the section that showed the three of us entering the building with El in her slut suit and Stacy and I in ski masks. I turned the machine off hoping the building management would think it malfunctioned. I rejoined my friend who was looking through the door opening with her hand over her mouth trying to contain her urge to laugh.

"What is wrong with you?" I asked Stacy.

"El, look at her."

I took a position over the shorter Stacy's head and joined her voyeuristic gaze. El was listening to the young man's iPod with his earphones on and dancing like a stripper. All she needed was a pole. I was waiting for the young brother to reach into his wallet and pull out some dollar bills to stuff inside her garter if she had one. The guard was totally captivated by El's sexy dance.

"Put your mask back on," I told Stacy. She looked puzzled. "Just in case he looks up," I replied.

Stacy asked, "What do we do if he does?"

"We run."

We were already watching the recordings by the time El made it up to my place. She walked in saying, "You owe me."

Stacy laughed. "Seems like you owe us," she said. "How much did you earn in tips downstairs?"

El gritted her teeth and gave Stacy a look of feigned disgust. "He wants to take me out," she said. "Little young dude barely out of puberty and he thinks he can handle all of this."

"He is kind of cute," Stacy chimed in. "You should take him up on his offer."

"Wake up Stacy he's a security guard, a nineteen year old security guard. I rest my case."

"She'd chew the boy up and spit him out. The boy's mama wouldn't recognize him after a night with Miss Thang," I said.

El smirked. "I bet you're the only person in the world who still has a VCR. Find anything?" El asked.

"Nah, been fast forwarding through the tape," I answered.

"What exactly are you looking for?"

"Mackenzie Powell. I wanted to see if he came through the lobby the day I was attacked."

Stacy said, "Check her out. Miss amateur detective."

I was intent on finding a clue while hoping with my heart and soul that Mac wouldn't show up on the tape. It was five o'clock in the morning. Stacy and El were both slouched over and asleep in each corner of my couch, but my adrenalin kept me going, my eyes focused steadfast and unyielding on the tape. With the remote control in my hand I hit fast forward and re-wind so often that my fingers were starting to get numb. Then I saw him. Saw that familiar face.

"Bingo," I shouted.

The sound of my voice woke up my two friends. A groggy, Stacy looked at the image frozen on my television and asked about the man in the Baltimore Ravens baseball cap. "That's not Mac," she said.

El rubbed her eyes and focused on my television screen. "I thought your attacker had on a mask."

"Yeah," I said. I was studying the image of the man now frozen in time by the pause button. "But he was also wearing a Baltimore Ravens cap like the one the man on this tape is wearing."

"You know his name?"

I smiled and quietly said, "Yeah, I call him 'Insurance'.

El closed her eyes again and mumbled, "Girl's crazy" as she drifted back to sleep.

Chapter Thirty-Five

Mac had taken the fake jewelry and disappeared. I had to move on. My thoughts turned to Charity. I hadn't heard from her in days. I decided I'd try to call her again.

The phone rang, but this time someone answered. It was Derek. I held my telephone for a moment unable to speak. Finally, I said, "Where's Charity?"

"She's in a safe place."

I imagined Derek's sneering smile on the other end. "Quit playing games, Derek. Put my sister on the phone!"

"You'll talk to her when I get what I want."

"If you want that envelope no problem. You send Charity to my place and I'll make sure you get it."

He laughed. "The stakes are higher now. I want the stones."

"What? I don't know what you're talking about."

"You know damn well what I'm talking about. Get me those diamonds and nothing will happen to your little sister. Otherwise, the bitch is dead."

"I don't have any diamonds."

"You got forty-eight hours, Dahlia."

He hung up.

My worries shifted from Mac and myself to Charity. If I had the diamond I could give it to Derek.

Derek was right about one thing, the stakes had been raised and it was a game that was way over my head and his, too. He was working with someone else, probably the gangsters from Thailand Mac had told me about. I was left wishing I could've given them the fake jewels that Mac had.

*   *   *

I didn't tell Stacy and El about Derek's telephone call because I knew that their first reaction would be to call the police. Actually, I didn't believe that Derek would hurt my sister, but I wasn't sure. He said I had forty-eight hours. He thought I had the diamonds so Charity would be safe as long as Derek and the people who were looking for it were thinking I could give it to them.

There was enough time to figure things out and if everything else failed I'd call Agent Robinson.

Antoine. He knew Derek and although he wasn't the thug I once thought he was Antoine was still out there. He was trying to make his mark in the rap game and he had an Ivy League education and I was one of the few people who knew it. Besides, he was working with Mac.

I thought about the showdown Mac had with Derek in front of my apartment building. I realized that there was a reason Derek backed down and it wasn't just because Mac carried a gun. It was adding up. Mac had a connection to some gangsters from Thailand, possibly the same men that had hired Derek to find The Desdemona Diamond. And I was at the center of everything. They paid a quarter of million dollars for an envelope full of meaningless items that belonged to an old woman, but the jewel was the real prize. Somehow my father's letter, the piece of cloth and some man's picture would lead me to Desdemona's hiding place.

Maybe Antoine could help me to save Charity. I thought he could also help me find Mackenzie Powell.

*   *   *

I was standing at Antoine's front door wondering if I should knock or run. I thought about what I'd say, how I'd phrase the questions.

I inhaled some of the cool night air and pulled in some courage along with it. I remembered something Mac told me about courage when I was anxious about going home to see my mother. He quoted Winston Churchill. "Courage," he said, "is the first of human qualities because it is the quality which guarantees all the others."

I had never thought of myself as being courageous, but I guess optimism and love take courage so in that sense I was brave. I sucked in my courage and I knocked on Antoine's door.

"Chill, goddamnit!"

I could hear the bravado in Antoine's voice from the other side of the door.

"Who is it?" he shouted.

A lesser me would've shrunk away, but I recounted my courage like the lion in *The Wizard of Oz*. It only took a medal of courage to instill it in him. The courage, a placard of words placed on his chest somehow melded into the cowardly lion's spirit and gave him internal fortitude. It was a kind of reversal, strength coming from without rather than within. My medal was the burning desire to find Mac.

"It's Dahlia, Antoine. We need to talk."

I could almost see his eyes roll up and his head shaking through the door. I knew he was thinking: *What the hell does she want?*

Deadbolt locks, unloosed to let me in had some kind of poetic ring to it. Throughout the year I had known Antoine it was his sometimes, intrusive forays into my world, invading my body with his manhood without revealing much of himself that had annoyed me. And now I had erected an emotional barrier to him. I guess it was only natural that he'd be annoyed with my sudden appearance at his door.

"Yeah, wuzzup?" Antoine said through a cracked door.

"You got a minute? I need to ask you something."

He opened the door wide, my invitation to come in as he revealed his shirtless torso. His body glistened from the faint signs of sweat that had gathered in small beads attached to the hair on his chest. They formed a small stream that coursed their way down the thin, hairy road that divided his stomach, cut off by his pajama bottoms.

"Sorry to bother you," I told him. "Were you working out?"

He smirked, not smiled. "Yeah, I been working out."

Antoine looked towards the white leather sofa that made an "S" shape and took up the middle of his expansive living room. I followed his eyes to the point where two young, scantily clad women were perched on his sofa.

I hesitated. "Oh, you're busy. I can call you later," I said.

"Nah, ain't like that. We were shooting all day. That's Tanika and Sherry over there. Models. You know the deal. Part of the perks for being in the video. They get to hang out here."

Antoine ushered me through his living room, passed by the two women.

I spoke trying to be polite. The one named Tanika smiled slightly and Sherry, with her nose in a magazine didn't acknowledge my presence. It didn't matter.

Antoine motioned for me to follow him. I knew where he was heading---to his studio where we could talk in private. But I could hear music coming from that direction and I first thought he was playing one of his beats or songs he said he'd been working hard to produce. Instead, there was someone inside the sound room, a young woman with headphones over her ears. She was mouthing words, apparently to one of the beats Antoine had produced.

"That's Desire. She's working on a new song I wrote," he said.

"She's gorgeous. Got any talent?" I asked.

Antoine gave a look like I must be kidding.

"She's tight. Can sing her lungs out and just turned eighteen. She'll be bigger than Beyonce."

We were looking at the young woman like she was in a fishbowl. I saw her lips moving, heard no sound from her just the beats Antoine had composed blaring through the speakers. Apparently she was rehearsing and not recording. Her glass-encased cage was totally insulated and soundproofed. Desire must've sensed the two of us standing there. She looked over, gave a wide and warm smile.

"Eighteen years old," I said.

"Yeah." Antoine nodded at her as though he was prompting her to continue rehearsing. "She's got a lot of living ahead."

"Yeah," I replied. "I know what its like to be eighteen with dreams."

I realized that I was sounding like someone who'd been on this planet a lot longer than twenty-six years, but I guess the last few weeks had aged me.

"You said you needed to talk to me, so let's talk."

I could sense some hostility in his tone and realized I didn't need to be coy with him.

"I'm trying to find Mackenzie."

Antoine shook his head and looked down at the floor. "I don't know who you're talking about."

I looked hard into his eyes and shook my head. "You can drop the act Antoine. I know everything. And you know I know."

He looked over at Desire in the sound booth, but his thoughts were somewhere else. "O.K. So what. You know I work with Mac. Don't mean I know where he is or like I know about his business."

I smiled, but it was a cynical smile. "Antoine, you know more about Mackenzie Powell than anyone else. Mac's your father, isn't he?"

Antoine walked over to a white leather reclining chair and sat down. The beads of sweat that had illuminated his body were now twinkling under his green eyes like faraway stars. Quiet permeated the room even though Antoine's manufactured beats were pulsating in the background.

"I guess you must think you're some kind of Sherlock Holmes. How'd you figure that one out?"

"Picture of a little boy with green eyes in Mac's study. An old picture of him and his band. You look like him, the way he looked thirty years ago."

"You know what they say, we all look alike."

"It was more than your physical similarities, Antoine. Once I saw all of this, your place, your academic accolades and the things Mackenzie had told me about his son it all added up. He pays for all of this not drugs, not the music. What I don't understand is why you're working against him."

"You don't know what the hell you're talking about."

"Don't I? You should be careful about using my computer. You forget I'm an analyst at the Pentagon. I know something about computers. Getting into your email files was easy."

"So."

"That Asian guy Charity robbed was going to pay a half a million for the information only you could've given Derek. You already had a down payment of a quarter of a million. You figured you'd put it in an account in my name because you could hide it from your father and you knew I wouldn't take it."

"So I guess to you that means I'm double dealing against my father."

"Pretty much. Plus the fact you're working with Derek. He tells you about the confrontation he had with Mac in front of my building? Strange. I know Derek. Crazy brother. He doesn't take to being disrespected. Overcompensates for his underprivileged upbringing. But when he found out it was Mackenzie he backed off.

He knows Mac is your father and although you think you hate him you're not going to let Derek or anyone else harm him."

Antoine looked like he was sulking. He made me think about the little boy he actually was in a man's body. Ivy League college boy with a rich father paying his bills yet he's still ungrateful.

"Hell yeah. I hate him. He wasn't there for me growing up. He left me and my mom."

"My father wasn't there either."

"Yeah, but he's been in prison all these years."

"Mac did some time, too but he's been trying to atone for his sins. Look, I'm not here to play shrink or social worker. I need to find Mac and most of all I need to find my sister."

"Thailand," Antoine said, flatly.

"What?"

"Yeah, she's in Thailand and Mac's gone there to bring her back."

"I don't get it."

"Dumb-ass Derek gave her to those gangsters over there. They said he had two options give em' their money back or get that Desdemona diamond. Otherwise, they're gonna make their money back by Charity working it off."

I stood there dumbfounded for a moment. Then anger. I could kill somebody because I knew the implications. They'd make my little sister a sex slave. "You said Mac went there to get her?"

"Yeah. Heard you gave him the rock. That's what they want. So he took it to trade her for it. Guess the Thai mob don't want to pay the twenty million dollar asking price. That guy named, Ping is some ruthless muthafucka. He flipped the script on my father. They were going to pay Mac twenty million dollars for the jewels---now they're trading a little black stripper for it. I guess he's gotten soft in his old age. A few years ago he wouldn't have cared what they did as long as he got his money."

I thought about Desdemona. It wasn't the real thing. Mac was risking his life just taking it to Ping and if they found out they'd kill him.

"You didn't tell me how I can reach your father."

"Your guess is as good as mine. He's in Bangkok and he's supposed to meet a couple of Ping's men at this warehouse there. I think in a couple of days. I've got the address, that's all. Mac always stays at the Oriental Hotel when he's over there."

He pulled out his cell phone and wrote down the information on a piece of paper. "Here, I don't know what you can do with this, but it's your call. I'm sure if he makes the exchange both my father and Charity will be fine."

I was wishing I felt the same. I was ready to leave, but I had one more question. "Antoine, why were they willing to pay you and Derek a half a million dollars for an envelope with a letter, a rag and a key?"

"There were clues that would've told them where they could find the stones, but I guess it's a moot issue since you obviously found it and gave it to my father."

I thought: *Clues? What clues?*

Chapter Thirty-Six

The first thing I did when I got home was to go to my computer. I removed the firewall and went into the cache of websites that Antoine had visited on the days he used my computer. I quickly found the website to The Bank of Antigua. I used my name to log on, but I had no idea what he used as the password to the account he had set up in my name. I thought about Antoine and the way I knew him and my first attempt was to use his name "Antoine" as the password. *Password rejected.*

I then tried Desdemona, but got the same result. I knew I had just one more try and if I failed I would be denied access. "Think, think, Dahlia," I mumbled. My mind was acting like a computer as I sat there recounting the things Antoine said that were important to him then I typed in *Desire18. Access granted.* I was in.

I read the account balance: $250,000.00. Untouched. I quickly transferred two hundred thousand dollars to an account I'd set up for my mother a few months earlier to deposit the loose change I could spare from time to time just to help. I transferred the rest into my account just in case I would be gone for a long time. I figured I would pick it up in cash the next day. Finished, I shut down my computer, took out the hard drive and put it my travel bag.

I packed my clothes and went through a checklist, made sure I had enough clothes for a long trip. I kept watching the clock and watching my security monitor. Once I had everything I needed I called a taxi.

Nervously I sat waiting, looking around my little home and wondering if I'd ever see it again then my thoughts turned to my mother and sister and I wondered if I'd ever see them again.

I looked at our quilt and studied it. I got out the envelope that had been at the center of all this. I hadn't given much thought to the key that was inside, but I knew there was a connection. Antoine said there were clues in that envelope and I realized that if some strangers thought they could figure out where my father hid Desdemona then so could I.

I studied the key then pulled out my own set of keys. I put the one that had been inside the envelope next to my house key. The ridges and teeth were a perfect match. Someone had duplicated the key to my apartment. The key confirmed the fact that Antoine had been working with Derek because no one else could've gotten it. It also told me that he had given it to the intruder.

Desdemona was somewhere in my apartment.

The piece of cloth I found inside the envelope, the one with the arrow and rising sun was telling me all along where to find the diamonds. I lined it up on the quilt. It fit perfectly in the lower left hand corner.

I remembered my grandmother's words: "The treasure's inside the quilt" and repeated them over and over. The arrow pointed to the border.

I squeezed the padded quilt but felt nothing except its cotton lining. I went to my kitchen, searched a drawer where I kept a few simple tools and found a single-edged razor blade. I needed to cut the quilt right on the seam or risk ruining my family's only heirloom.

Like a surgeon I made a careful incision then separated the sides of the quilt that had been stitched together many years ago by an ancestor who'd lived in bondage. I imagined her suffering and how this brightly colored quilt must've given her a brief sense of liberation. She had created it with a purpose.

I got a chill when I thought about the darkened, gnarled fingers that had pulled cotton in a scouring southern Georgia sun for hours at a time. Her respite was her religion and this quilt. She must've seen the future.

Now my own fingers, ones that had never known real manual labor, were nimbly picking apart my family's past. I pulled at the cotton lining a handful at a time until I'd hollowed out that corner. I forced my hand inside, all the way up to my elbow and felt it. Reached a little further to wrap my fingers around it and gently pulled it out.

I gazed at it for more than a moment. Blue like the ocean against an azure sky its replica failed to do it justice. I took a deep breath and exhaled hard with my eyes closed tight. I sat alone with my thoughts, meditated and prayed.

I didn't know why Nana had never said anything to me about the secret hidden inside the quilt. Maybe she thought I wasn't ready for it or it her instincts told her that I wouldn't know what to do with it. I couldn't sell it on my own. I guess she was saving it for my father, for the day when he would be released from a Thai prison. It would be a kind of reparation for his innocence and lost liberty.

I rose to my feet with Desdemona in my hand. It was time to unite my past, present and hopefully, my future. My father, sister and a life with Mac the way I'd imagined it on a cool spring night riding in a horse drawn carriage, would all come together in Bangkok. This priceless piece of carbonized coal, buried for millions of years only to be unearthed through suffering for the enjoyment of one man's pleasure would bring us all together---or kill us all.

"Thanks, Nana," I whispered.

*   *   *

I spent the night at a cheap motel near downtown Washington, hiding my whereabouts and my movements like a criminal. I didn't call my friends, my mother, I didn't call anyone out of fear that even my mobile telephone could be traced and they'd find me. I slept in my clothes that night cautious, but not afraid. In a few hours I'd be on my way out of Washington, out of the country.

I had checked on flights to Bangkok. There was one leaving at six o'clock in the morning. I didn't book it figuring I'd just show up and buy a ticket at the airport. Everything was working according to my plan and with ticket in hand I flashed my government I.D., made it through the security checkpoint and found a seat in the waiting area near the gate.

I sat with one eye on my magazine and the other on the clock. Occasionally, I'd look around the area where I was sitting checking for familiar or strange faces. There weren't many people traveling that early in the morning, just a couple of women with small children, some Asian-looking young people I thought might be college age and a small group of men in suits who talked loud in some Eastern language I couldn't understand. I was able to relax and breathe easy for the first time since I left Antoine's house.

"Calling all first class passengers for boarding Flight 198 to Bangkok, Thailand". Came the announcement over the loudspeaker.

Next were passengers who needed assistance to board and then she began announcing the rows. I had asked for a seat in the rear of the plane and I would be one of the last people to board. When she called my row I waited so that I could be the last one to get in line. When it was time for me to go I stood up, pulled out my passport and plane ticket and got behind the other passengers to board.

I was focused on making it onto the plane so I didn't notice that there was someone standing behind me until he said, "First time going to Bangkok?"

I answered, "Yes it is" without turning around, but then the hair on the back of my neck stood up. I knew that voice. I turned to face him. "Good morning Agent Robinson," I said.

He greeted me with a subtle smile, but said nothing. I looked around for his partner Agent Liles expecting to see him standing nearby waiting like a coyote and anxious to pick over my bones. But there was no Liles, no uniformed police officers at the ready. It was just Robinson and his soulful eyes.

"Are you here to arrest me?" I asked.

He shook his head. "No. Not right now. I'm just taking a little trip. You know I work real hard. Thirty years with the department and I think I've only taken three actual vacations. I guess that's dedication. But I got a lot of vacation time built up, enough to retire this year and get a nice check."

"And you just happen to be going to Bangkok?" I asked him. I was full of skepticism and he knew it.

He gave me a half-laugh. "Yeah, I think I am. I've got to protect my interests." He pulled his jacket back and displayed the gun he was carrying so that only I could see it. "Even though I'm taking a little time off from work I'm just in the habit of always carrying my equipment. Some people take their computers, others take a Blackberry. I don't think Mackenzie would cooperate with me if I didn't have it."

"Cooperate with you by letting you take the diamond or the money he's going to get for it?" I asked.

Robinson smiled, licked his lips like it was habit and nodded to show his appreciation. "Very good, Ms. Reynolds, I think you've missed your calling. You would've been a good agent. Anyway, I could care less about the diamond. I'll just wait and take the cash."

He stood there staring at me. I could see his soulful eyes turn deadly, but I was cool under pressure. "So this isn't about the FBI and some investigation you're conducting, is it?"

"Oh, there's an investigation. It's just that no one else knows about it," he replied.

"Agent Liles?"

"Young guy, he thinks this is about some major drug smuggling ring. You know it was easy to play on his stereotypes," Robinson laughed. "Everyone around this thing seemed to fit the profile."

"So you're freelancing. A rogue agent," I said.

"Guilty. I've worked all these years for the government and there's something about seeing a slick ex-con walk away with millions that sticks in my throat. Makes me want to spit," he said.

I could sense his contempt for Mac and it was deep rooted. "So you think you're going to go over there and just take the money, huh?" I asked.

"That's about the size of it."

I shook my head, looked down at the floor and listened as they announced the last boarding call. "I don't think so," I said.

Robinson laughed hard this time. "And who's going to stop me?"

I smiled. "You like football Agent Robinson?"

"Yeah, I'm a big fan."

"I noticed the Baltimore Ravens autographed football you keep in your office."

"So what."

"Well, it made me start thinking. For some reason it made me think about the man who broke into my apartment, put a knife up to my throat and threatened to kill me. He was wearing a Baltimore Ravens cap," I told him.

"So what, the Ravens have lots of fans," he responded.

"Like I said, it made me start thinking so I got a copy of the security tape from my building that was recorded the day of the break-in. You know they keep a backup tape, don't you? And I bet you thought the tape you took was the only one. Anyway, I viewed the tape and who did I see walking through the lobby exactly on the night I was attacked wearing a Baltimore Ravens baseball cap?" I said looking right at him.

Robinson swallowed hard. He cleared his throat. "I'm involved in an active investigation so what's your point?"

"Well, my point is, whether it's standard procedure to conceal your identity with a mask and threaten to kill someone with a knife?"

"You can't prove anything, baby girl. So you got a video tape of me, so fucking what?"

"I also have a knife with your fingerprints on it. You see your accomplice, Antoine, gave it to me. You do know that he's Mac's son, don't you?" I paused. "Oh, you didn't know? I'm so sorry. I guess blood is thicker than water or in this case, thicker than the drug case you had against him. The other thing I think you didn't know was that I have a friend, an attorney with the Department of Justice and there is no active investigation. She's holding onto a couple of copies of the tape just in case."

I smiled politely. "You know overall, I think it's better to spend a quiet retirement with a nice government pension than to spend years in prison. My friend calls it burglary, assault, abuse of office, wiretapping just to name a few of the charges."

Robinson said nothing, just stood there dumbfounded.

I smiled, "It's time for me to catch my flight. I don't imagine you'll be making the trip will you?" I reached into my purse, pulled out a copy of the tape and handed it to him. "I thought you might show up, hope you enjoy the show."

Chapter Thirty-Seven

I breathed deep and hard. Three hours was the longest period I'd ever spent on an airplane before this trip and the thought of the twenty-two hour flight made me feel, claustrophobic. I brought a book for the trip, *Their Eyes Were Watching God,* by Zora Neal Hurston. Mac had suggested that it was good reading that night we reconnected in Club Alexandria.

I read some, slept a lot and worried more. My mind was riddled with second thoughts and questions. *This is crazy,* I thought.

The flight was long and tedious, even though the book had captivated my thoughts. I could identify with its heroine. Its combination of tragedy and ecstasy; there were lessons to be learned. Young girl's discovery of self, blooming and blossoming womanhood, defined by life and its lessons, it could have been my story. Hopefully, there would be no tragic ending.

It was nighttime when we landed in Bangkok. This was the real City of Lights. I took a limousine to The Oriental Hotel, held my courage in my chest and took the inexorable step that would forever change my life.

Moments later I was standing in front of the door with the numbers, 1245 staring back at me in polished brass. I hesitated, my hand poised to knock, but suspended by doubt. I hadn't thought about it before, but it occurred to me that Mac might not be alone. I cursed my impetuous spirit, guided by impulse and not logic and tried to think about what I would say to him.

I closed my eyes and tapped, hardly making a sound. I waited. Tried to give him time to answer, but not enough time. Weak kneed I turned to retreat back down the long hall not knowing where I'd go and what I'd do. My steps were interrupted by the sound of the door opening. Mac peeked out, our eyes met, mine fearful, his in disbelief.

"Dahlia? What are you doing here? How'd you find me?" Questions I couldn't answer right at that moment. All I knew was that I was there.

"Come inside," he said.

He peeked down both ends of the long hall then closed the door to his suite. I mustered a weak smile, dropped my head and went inside.

"What are you doing here?" Mac repeated.

"Mac. I know why you're here, to get my sister. I guess I don't understand why you left me without saying anything. You left me like you weren't coming back ever."

He looked down for a moment. "It's not what you think, Dahlia. I had to get out of that house in Georgetown because no matter what happens here, I'm never going back." Mac clinched his teeth. "The Feds were getting a little too close. I *had* to go."

"So you were going to enjoy your island paradise alone?"

Mac answered, "No, I was hoping you'd be there with me. I was going to send for you, but that's all changed."

"What do you mean?" I asked.

"Well, it had always been my plan to sell these guys the diamonds. It was going to be a straight up business exchange, plain and simple. Now things are complicated."

"Because they have Charity?" I asked.

Mac nodded. "They say they're going to kill her and I think they plan to kill me, too."

"So, you're telling me you're just going to walk into a trap."

"Basically, but I think I can negotiate with them. Ping, the top dog here is ruthless but he's a smart man. I trade the diamonds for Charity, plain and simple. It won't be a messy transaction. Killing two people, especially Americans will."

I sat down on a sofa and started to cry. "It's my fault you're in this situation, Charity and I. I know that you could've walked away, did the safe thing and collected five million dollars from the government of South Africa, no questions asked, but here you are ready to walk into a trap and what will you get in return…?"

Mac sat down beside and held my hand. "My actions here aren't entirely self-less. A man reaches a certain age and he starts reflecting on his life, the mistakes, his misgivings. This might be my only chance for redemption. And to you I owe the most because of what happened to your father."

I tossed him the small velvet bag I had carried in my purse all the way from D.C. My face, unsmiling. Defiant.

"What's this?" he asked. Mac pulled the drawstring that seal the bag and poured its contents into his hand.

208

"Desdemona. The real one. The piece I gave you that day is a replica. Robinson had it made. He said his plan was to get you as you were making the exchange for the money. He doesn't know I have the real thing. Besides, I don't think he cares."

Mac studied Desdemona. "It doesn't add up. This is outside his jurisdiction, so why all the trouble?"

"Because he wants the money for himself. He broke into my apartment and held a knife to my throat trying to force me to tell him where it is."

"Well, if I know Paul Robinson, he'll be searching for us."

I shook my head. "I don't think so. I've got enough evidence to make sure that he spends his golden years in a federal joint."

I looked up into Mac's eyes. "My father is alive, I think."

"I thought he had died when the car crashed. Michelle died, but somehow Richard survived. When I escaped back to the States Robinson was waiting for me. I spent five years in federal lockup."

"So you started looking for Desdemona."

"Yeah. When I found out it was never recovered I just put two and two together. Richard had no family other than you and I knew that his daughter was the only person in the world he really cared about. I figured he must've stashed the gems with someone close to you while you were growing up. It wasn't your mother so your grandmother was the logical candidate. When I heard she died, I figured you might have Desdemona."

"So that's when you came looking for me. At least, that's when you sent your son, Antoine."

Mac held his head low. "I'm sorry for all of that. It wasn't supposed to happen that way. I think Antoine got too involved in the job."

"Yeah, he wasn't supposed to screw me, was he?"

"No. And I wasn't supposed to make love to you, Dahlia."

"But it happened, so now what?"

"First thing is to get Charity."

"And my father?"

"That's a different story. I mean, we don't know if he's still locked up here in Bangkok." Mac laughed slightly. "Knowing Richard, he's probably lying on the beach someplace tropical. Brazil would be my bet."

I looked at Mac and knitted my eyebrows together. "Do you know about the envelope? The one Antoine gave Derek?"

"I know that my son and Derek were working on a side deal, but I don't know anything about an envelope."

I walked over and opened my briefcase. I took out the envelope and pulled out the letter and the picture. "Did you write this letter?"

I handed it to Mac. It was dated just a couple of months earlier. He shook his head then looked at the picture. His eyes widened. "Richard!"

"According to Paul Robinson, Richard Reynolds was here up until a few weeks ago. Apparently, he made a run for it and escaped. Robinson said the Thai guards rained bullets at him and he was somehow able to dive into the river near the prison. His body hasn't been found."

"So he might still be alive?" Mackenzie asked.

"Maybe. I'm hoping so."

"The news doesn't make me feel much better. Richard has spent the last fifteen years in prison here for something I did."

Mac turned to face me. "Look, if I make it out of this I'm going to do everything in my power to find him. If he survived his escape then it's likely he's still in the country. Probably doesn't have any money or a passport. I'd guess he's probably hiding out in some remote place or being resourceful and hustling tourists in some place like Pattaya City."

I asked, "And what am I supposed to do while you're trading diamonds and searching for my father?"

"I want you to stay right here. Once I get Charity I'll send her to the hotel and I want the two of you to hurry up and get the hell out of Thailand. You've got some money, the quarter of a million dollars Antoine put in that account. Keep it it's yours. I'm forcing him to make amends for his indiscretion."

"But I want to go with you. Antoine told me about the warehouse and your meeting day after tomorrow. I can help, besides Charity doesn't know you. She'll be more at ease when she sees me there with you."

He smiled. "Makes sense." He picked up my bags. "You must be very tired. It's a long flight from Washington to Bangkok. But it's a beautiful country. You get some rest and tomorrow we'll do a little sightseeing."

Mac pointed me towards the bedroom and like a zombie I walked inside. I stretched out on the bed with my clothes still on. Jet lag and fatigue, a hypnotic combination, were getting the best of me. I groggily lifted my head and looked out into the living room through the slightly opened bedroom door.

I could see him sitting over the coffee table loading Mr. Friendly one bullet at a time. He slammed the clip into the gun's stock and pointed it at some unseen enemy. His hand as steady as a rock.

I fell asleep knowing that whoever was within Mac's crosshairs would meet a certain and fatal end.

Chapter Thirty-Eight

I must've slept for fourteen hours straight. A combination of a long flight mixed with the things that had burdened me, both mentally and emotionally, made me sleep like I was hibernating.

I expected to reach over and find Mackenzie still asleep beside me, but I wasn't surprised when I saw he wasn't in the bed. My last vision of him, before I fell asleep was seeing him with his gun. Nervous energy probably kept him from resting comfortably the way playing golf was his passion and the competition that made Mac rise early on warm spring days to chase a little white ball around on manicured grass.

I got up and made my way to the bathroom for my morning ritual. There was a note from Mac taped to the mirror. It read:

Dahlia-Here I go again. The meeting was moved up to this morning. I didn't want to tell you. I'll send Charity. If I'm not back by noon...well, you know what to do. Love you, genuinely and sincerely, Mackenzie.

All I could think of were the words, No! No! No! "You're not going to leave me again, Mac. Not like this. Not ever."

I dressed quickly and caught a cab to the warehouse district right by the Chao Phraya River near Bangkok's Chinatown off Taksin Road. I had no idea what time Mac had left the hotel or whether he would still be there, but I had an address and a will to make sure he and my sister would be fine. My only question concerned what I was going to do once I got inside the building.

I had the cab driver drop me off around the corner from the place they were supposed to meet. I didn't want anyone to hear me coming.

There were several cars sitting in front of the building marked 140 and with symbols that were probably written in Thai. I thought: *What am I going to do now? Just walk in?*

I started walking around to the rear of the building figuring that if I came in through the back I'd go unnoticed until after everything was over. There were windows on the building's side, but the glass was painted with white paint. I noticed that the lower windows were streaked and somewhat transparent like the painter

212

was in a hurry to finish. I found an old wooden box and pushed it right up to a window then stood on top of it to see inside.

There were two men standing with their backs to the front door. One was holding two metallic cases. Mac was facing them. His facial expression was stoic and unflinching. He nodded his head a lot and although I couldn't hear what they were saying it seemed that their words weren't hostile.

Where's Charity, I thought. I scanned the place then saw a hint of light brown skin and blond hair. She was nearly blocked out standing behind the two Thai men. It was my sister wearing a wig. Heavy makeup painted on her face had her looking like a doll made up with crayon by some five-year old. Her mascara was melted around her eyes and ran black rivers down her cheeks.

I gasped in disbelief at the sight of her, but at least she was alive. I watched as one of the men escorted my sister to Mac's side then held out his hand. Mac gave him a velvet bag then watched and waited.

I could see the man empty the bag's contents into his hand. It was the jewel. He held it up to the light then nodded in the direction of his friend. It seemed like everyone including myself were beginning to breathe a little easier with the exchange. I started climbing down from the box when I was greeted with the words, "We meet again, Ms. Reynolds." It was Paul Robinson.

He was holding a gun pointed right at me and I realized that he wouldn't hesitate to use it. "Care to join the party?" he said.

I walked in front of him without speaking and not knowing which side he was on and how he was going to play out this scenario. I thought I had disposed of him.

"Guess you're kind of surprised to see me, aren't you?" He asked me.

"More like astounded. I guess the idea of going to prison doesn't really bother you, does it?" I replied.

"Oh, I don't think it'll come to that. You see I figure I get that rock and cash it in for the reward and I can take a page out of Mac's book. Buy my own island paradise some place where I can't be expedited and live happily ever after."

He walked me around to the back of the building. "Open it," he said. He whispered, "Be smart and no one, especially you and your sister will get hurt."

"What about Mackenzie?"

"Can't make any promises on that end. We'll just have to see."

We walked quietly into the building coming up behind Mac and Charity. We were just a few feet away when Robinson grabbed me around my waist, the way he had grabbed me back at my apartment, except this time he put the gun to my head.

He shouted, "All right. Nobody moves, nobody gets hurt!"

Using me as a shield he leveled his gun at the two men who were there to trade Charity for the Desdemona Diamond. Before they could react Robinson fired off a couple of rounds with deadly accuracy. I saw each man drop to the floor one at a time curled up quickly into a fetal position.

Agent Robinson returned his gun barrel to the side of my head. I glanced over at Charity who was crying hysterically and calling out my name over and over.

Robinson said, "Easy Mac. I want you to reach real slow inside your jacket and take out your gun with two fingers."

I watched him in horror. Mac held the weapon gingerly by the handle.

Robinson had his weapon pointed t Mackenzie. "Now just drop it on the ground."

Mac did.

"Hands up and slowly. I mean, real slow. Slide that piece over here with your foot."

Robinson loosed his grip from around my waist, letting me go so that I could run to my terrified sister. I looked into her hollowed out eyes and saw the horror hiding behind them. She had been through an unspeakable ordeal. Her eyes told me that much. Charity locked her arms around me and wouldn't let go. She sobbed.

I looked back over at Mac who was shaking his head as if to say, "You shouldn't be here."

He returned his gaze to Agent Robinson, who stooped down, still with his gun pointed in our direction, and picked up Desdemona. He examined the jewels then smiled. "This is the real thing." He said to me, "I knew you'd find it. Good work."

Mackenzie said, "You got what you wanted Paul. Let the women go."

"Oh, I wouldn't worry about them Mac. If I were you I'd worry about my own well being."

I could see Mac's face harden. "What you gonna do, shoot me?"

"You guessed it. You know Mac. I've worked my whole life trying to enforce the law, put away bad guys. You know, keep the peace, defend democracy. And what do I get? A fucking gold watch and a pension that can't outrun inflation. I'm almost sixty and that's young in my book. How can I live on five grand a month for the next twenty or thirty years?"

Paul Robinson was seething as he spoke. I was now whimpering along with Charity, fearful of what he was going to do. But Mac was cool.

"So killing me is going to make your life better," Mac said.

Robinson laughed loud. "It'll make me fucking richer and for me that's better."

"Tell me who told you I'd be here. How'd you know? Was it Antoine?"

"Damn Mackenzie, you really underestimate me. I guess you think that because I'm a public servant I'm stupid or something. News flash, brother. Yeah, I had some help, but from a friend of yours."

He shouted, "Come on out and join us, my dear."

I heard the sounds of footsteps in the form of stiletto heels walking hard, the sound of her steps echoing throughout the entire warehouse. There was nothing subtle about the walk. I had watched her confident stride before. That self-assured way she walked telling the world she was better than everyone else.

Mac looked in the direction of the sounds, but I kept my eyes on Agent Robinson as I clutched Charity. I heard him say, "Sue?"

"Mackenzie, baby. I'm so sorry it had to happen this way, but it was inevitable."

Mac shook his head in disbelief. "You and him? I don't believe this."

Sue said, "Believe it Mac. You did so much for me, getting me off the streets as a young girl. You taught me so much and you could've had it all---me, Felicia and the money, but you chose to throw it all away."

"So this is the thanks I get, huh Sue?"

I listened equally stunned by her being there and her betrayal. I reached deep inside to find the courage to speak. "So, you're just going to kill us. Is that it?" I asked.

Robinson looked at Sue then back. "No. We're going to take the jewels and leave. I've already contacted the Bangkok police. They should be here any minute." He pointed to Sue. "But we'll be gone. I'll leave the locals to figure out who shot who. By that time we'll be long gone. I hear Sao Paulo is a great place this time of the year."

He handed Sue the diamonds. "Put these back in the velvet sack, baby. I'll meet you in the car. I'll grab the money."

"Don't worry baby. You need to keep your hands free. I'll take the jewels and the money. I'll meet you in the car," Sue told him.

She took Desdemona in her hand and started her killer walk towards the front door. Robinson's smile turned deadly. His eyes narrowed. He waited until Sue closed the big double doors then opened fire. He shot three or four times, maybe five, I lost count. Mac reeled and went down.

I watched in horror as his chest heaved and his breathing became shallow. I let go of Charity and ran to the body that was now lying prone with his chest rising and falling slower and slower.

Charity screamed and pulled off her wig as I hovered over Mackenzie pleading with him not to die. I shouted at Robinson, "You killed him!"

Robinson seemed unaffected. He walked over to the two Thai gangsters, put a couple bullets into each then laughed like he enjoyed the killings. "Like I said, I'll leave the local cops to figure this out. You know, the Thai are like us---an eye for an eye—this is death penalty stuff. Either you or your little sister's going to fry. I guess the two of you better figure out which one gets it."

He looked down at Mackenzie, saw the blood oozing from his wounds onto the floor. "Ain't so fucking pretty now, are you Mac?"

Agent Paul Robinson turned around and started his own confident walk to the door. I could hear him laughing a sinister laugh devoid of any guilt. I looked down at Mac. His eyes were now white. I couldn't see his green pupils because they had rolled up and were hidden behind his lids.

I screamed, screamed loud, so loud that I didn't hear the crack of the gun nor did I see its cold steel projectile when it hit FBI Agent Paul Robinson in the back. All I knew was that he hit the floor with a heavy thud. Actually, it was more like a butcher slapping a

216

side of meat down on a concrete block. Dust flew from underneath his body. His face planted into the concrete floor, arms stretched out from his sides and his own gun still in his hand.

I looked over to Charity. She was trembling, shaking uncontrollably. Her grip was tight around the butt of Mac's gun with the barrel still pointing towards the fallen FBI agent. A trail of smoke slowly rose from its barrel and framed a small cloud around Charity's face. The smoke and blond wig gave her a ghastly appearance like an apparition who'd vaporize only to disappear.

"My God! Charity what did you do? What did you do?"

I ran over to her and took the gun from her hand. My mind was racing out of control, but calm had to enter the room. I couldn't help Mackenzie, only his gods could do that now, but there we were---me and Charity with a dead federal agent and a couple of Thai gangsters with bullet riddled bodies. Two black girls from the States, one looking very much like a prostitute.

I thought, *Sue, where is she?* And ran to the door. There was no car there other than Mac's rental and the mobsters' limo. Sue had taken off probably before Paul Robinson took that bullet in his back. I thought about the irony, not in his dying, but the way he'd double-crossed only to be double-crossed. Poetic justice?

I ran back to my sister. "Get it together Charity," I said. She was breathing real hard and twisting the manufactured yellow hair that capped her head. "You gotta listen to me and listen good. If you don't we're gonna die here. You understand?"

She shook her head, but I felt like her mind was someplace else. "Just stand there," I said. "Don't move."

I took Mac's gun and wiped away at any fingerprints then tossed it into a water barrel that was rusting in one of the rooms we had passed through to get to the front of the building. I came back and gently twisted Robinson's gun from his cold, dead hand and wrapped my fingers around the stock.

Finally, I rifled through his pockets and found his wallet. I removed any identification he had that linked him to the FBI. I figured the longer it took them to discover he was a federal agent the longer it would take to send out a dragnet to find us. I went over to Charity.

"Charity! We gotta split up. I want you to leave. Get out of here, O.K.?"

Charity said through trembling lips, "But I don't have a passport Dahlia. How am I going to get out of the country?"

"We'll have to figure that out, sweetie. I've got some money. We'll find a way to sneak you out. I hear if you've got cash you can buy anything here."

I reached into my purse. "Here's fifty grand. I want you to take it and disappear. Get out of Bangkok. We'll have the cops and the way I see things shaping up the Thai mob will be looking for us, too."

I walked over and stared at the two men who had brought Charity there. I presumed they were her kidnappers. "Which one is Ping, the boss man?"

Charity shook her head. "Neither. These two work for him." She looked at me with pleading eyes. "I'm scared Dahlia. I can't do this by myself. Can't we just leave?"

I rubbed her face. "This is the best way, honey. It's going to be a lot easier to find two African-American women in Thailand together than one female tourist. You stay low key and I'll find a way to get you out of here. Catch a train south down to Pattaya City. I hear there's a lot of American and European tourists down there. You won't stick out as much."

"What about your friend?" Charity said looking at Mac.

"I don't know. I don't know. I can't just leave him there." Heavy sigh, a heart felt and heavy sigh. I thought for a second. "You're going to have to trust me on this one, Charity. We gotta put him in his rental car."

Charity looked at me real hard. "What do you mean, put him in the car Dahlia?"

"We've got to carry him to the car. We can't leave him like this Charity. They'd put him in some strange morgue. His family would never know what happened."

"And us dumping him in some car will be different?"

Charity was thinking again, but that wasn't what I needed. I thought about my own father who might've ended up in a watery grave after he escaped from the same prison my cab had passed on the way to the warehouse. Dumping Mac's body unceremoniously in the same river might be a fitting way to bury him. But I didn't know.

"Tell you what Charity. We'll put him in the trunk and you can take the car to the train station and just leave it there."

"Then what?"

"Take a train and leave town. I'll call Antoine and let him know what happened and where Mac's body is. He'll come get his father."

Charity was trembling again, even more than when she shot Agent Robinson. I led her over to Mac's body. We couldn't lift his two hundred pounds so we dragged him out to the car and somehow managed to put him in the trunk. "The police will be here any minute. I want you to drive out of here slow. Don't speed and do exactly what I told you."

She nodded. I watched her pull away as I waited with Robinson's gun in my hand. She passed right by the squadron of Bangkok police cars rushing in my direction. When the police arrived I lifted my hands in the air.

"Drop the gun."

I did. I sat on the ground and cried. I thought about Mac knowing that I'd never see him again. And wondered if Charity would escape or follow me to an uncertain fate.

Chapter Thirty-Nine

Peering at the courtroom from inside my glass box, gerbil-like expression seized my face. Not some unwitting sheep for the slaughter. I know the consequences. My fate was in his hands.

My glass box was confining---even claustrophobic. My attorney told me it was for my own protection. The glass was reinforced, able to withstand bullets or bombs. He said, "Your victims were dangerous men with even more dangerous friends."

I wondered: *So why the shackles and leg irons?*

But they were in the penalty phase of my trial. The prosecutor arguing for the death penalty, my attorney pleading for my life. My was fear un-abiding, still recovering from the shock of the judge's declaration: *Guilty!*

And now a courtroom full of hostile faces with strange slanted eyes. I'd seen the likes of them back in the States. The biased, "they all look alike". I had uttered those words more than a few times. But here I was an anomaly. I was book-kon pai nok to them. Foreigner. Negro. I imagined that they thought all black people look alike.

I studied the sea of faces on the other side of the glass. Brown skin permeated the room with curious eyes attached. But I was searching for something familiar, the faces that had been there throughout my trial, the faces I knew.

Stacy smiled tight and nervous as her eyes met mine. She and El held hands. El hid behind dark sunglasses. She tried to force a happy expression across her face, but it wouldn't come. Instead, she quickly dropped her head and reached for a handkerchief stuffed deep inside her purse. She used it to catch a tear that had appeared from underneath her glasses then she quickly resumed her rigid posture. She nodded to me behind the glass as if to say, "Hang in there, sweetie."

The judge entered the room wearing his usual black robe and white wig, a hangover from when the British were there and when lawyers were called, barristers and judges, magistrates. Everyone in the courtroom rose to his feet in one unified motion. Stacy nearly dropped her pen and pad, but gathered herself quickly. She looked at the stoic El who kept her dark glasses on. They both sat down when the judge nodded.

He said something in Thai and my attorney and the prosecutor quickly walked to the judge's bench. The lawyers nodded and whispered. My lawyer glanced over at me. Smiled. It seemed to bolster my waning confidence.

Is that a good sign? I wondered.

The lawyers took their seats.

Two armed policemen approached my glass cage and unlocked the door. One of them motioned for me to follow him to the table where my lawyer sat with his head down. His eyes were riveted on the documents he'd placed there in front of him.

I shuffled my feet one step at a time as leg irons constrained my walk and evoked thoughts of my ancestral legacy of chains and bondage---coming to America. Middle Passage voyagers shackled and festooned in iron arriving to some foreign land without celebration. I kept my head down the way they had some four hundred years ago. But I was a prisoner in Bangkok, Thailand and this is the twenty-first century.

My lawyer gave me a polite smile then returned to his business as I sat down beside him. I rubbed my arms after the guards removed my handcuffs, regarded the rings now embedded deep into my skin. My arms bore the marks of bracelets locked too tight.

I turned to look at my two friends sitting there behind the rail in the galley area. I mouthed the words, "Did you find my sister?"

Stacy shook her head and whispered, "I love you."

I nodded and said, "I love you, too."

The sea of brown faces erupted into a chant. "Death! Death! Death!" They shouted.

I sank low into my chair, looked at the armed guards and somehow felt a little reassured. Thailand was no true democracy but mob rule wasn't their form of government either.

My attorney handed me a set of headphones so that I could understand every word through a translator. I placed them around my mass of curly hair then watched and listened as the prosecutor spoke first. His staccato cadence in Thai was neutralized by the translation coming through the headphones. The voice, female, was clear and in perfect English and almost soothing.

But the prosecutor's words came through as harsh. Translated, he said, "The Negro prostitute ruthlessly murdered three men. Two Thai, one American. Shot down in cold blood. Motive? Robbery."

My heart sank low. I put my head down, tried to fight off the tears building inside. Those words cut deep on many levels. False accusations---murder, prostitution, losing the man I loved, my hurt could not be greater and my life was hanging in the balance. I sat there sniffling, wiping at my tears with both hands and everyone but my two friends oblivious to my condition.

Stacy reacted and leaned over the rail that separated us. She handed me a tissue as the guards drew menacingly close, hands on their weapons. Stacy opened both hands, gave them a defiant, "What?"

I was hearing through my headphones but not really listening, but I had to listen, had to gather myself. The prosecutor was making his points in rapid-fire fashion. I heard him say two of the victims were well-respected Thai businessmen who had been acting in the service of Thailand's king when they were brutally cut down.

I looked at my attorney for his reaction. He cracked a smile then said in English, "More like Thai gangsters than businessmen." He put his head back down covering the papers on the table with his eyes.

I thought about Mackenzie lying on that cold warehouse floor and how Charity and I struggled to conceal his body. I thought it was a gallant move at the time---that we would save him from an ignoble end, but that was the thoughts of the panicked. Being left in the trunk of a car or dumped in the river was no less ignoble. And Charity? Where is Charity?

It was my attorney's turn to speak. He talked about my youth. I was too young too die. And that she had been an important employee of the United States government.

The crowd shouted, "Spy!"

The judge sounded his gavel. "Silence!"

My attorney said, "She had no motive to kill those men."

The judge said, "Robbery."

"Of what? The jewels were never recovered."

"That is not the issue here, counselor. Besides, the police found her leaving the warehouse with the murder weapon in her hand. No one else was around. Mitigation is the issue. Tell me why I should not sentence her to hanging."

Those words made my heart pound hard, beat like a drum reverberating through my body. I felt nauseous. I clutched my stomach and rubbed it hoping the sick feeling would fade away, but it had become a daily occurrence. Today was no exception.

Chapter Forty

"You can put my bags over there," he said.

"Yes, boss," replied the bellhop. The little man dressed in the hotel's colors of blue and gold, bronze nameplate read, *Non Dook Kim*. He kept the same toothy grin that greeted his guest downstairs in the lobby, continued non-stop during the elevator ride up to the twenty-sixth floor of the Oriental Hotel.

At first the guest thought it was the kind of gratuitous smile he'd usually get from someone expecting a big tip, but the bellhop was going beyond the call of duty. He smiled and nodded profusely and kept his eyes fixed on his guest, even as he removed suitcase after suitcase from his cart.

Eventually, the guest became a little annoyed over the attention, but he didn't want to be rude and tell the man to stop smiling. When the bellhop finished positioning the bags over near the living room closet he stood quietly with one hand behind his back, the other readied to receive a tip he'd hope was in U.S. dollars.

Non smiled even broader as he waited, watched intently as the guest took off his jacket. Removed his tie, slowly emptied his pockets and pulled his shirttails out so that they hung past his waist. He breathed a heavy sigh of relief.

Exhausted from the long flight the man wasn't thinking about anything except maybe to relax and have a drink in his room. He looked around, saw the wet bar fully stocked just as he'd ordered.

For a moment the man who was going to occupy Room 2633 for the next week or two, maybe three (his reservation was open ended) seemed to have forgotten the grinning bellhop. Non stood at attention through smiles and obvious admiration, but growing anxious. He cleared his throat.

The man, now sitting on the sofa was taking inventory of the things he'd removed from his pants pockets. A wallet and a money clip with a wad of bills, loose change and some keys. The bellhop faked a cough then snapped to attention, his smile unabated.

"Oh, I'm sorry," said the guest. He pulled a hundred dollar bill from his clip and placed it in the other man's eager hand.

"Thank you," he said. He gave his benefactor a courtly nod then said, "I see every movie you make." His accent was thick although he obviously had a great command of English.

"Excuse me?"

"Ah, yes. Every movie, every movie. Me see them all. You much better looking in person, much better. Mustache look good." He snapped the smile right back into its place.

The man looked confused, but Non didn't seem to notice. Star struck, a worldwide epidemic. Cable television, satellite and the Internet were the culprits, viral contagion spreading throughout the four corners. He had heard the comparisons from other observers.

He took a heavy breath, too tired to play along with the bellhop's infectious case of mistaken identity.

"No, no. I'm not him."

But the bellhop was convinced that his guest was the movie star he idolized. He smiled politely, watched as the little man in the blue uniform backed his way out of the room. He knew Non would tell his friends and family that he had carried the bags of a famous actor that day.

Now alone, he could survey the room. Furniture made of teak with fourteen carat gold accents, bronze handles on the bureau. Marbled floor entrance bordered on all sides by lush, cream colored carpeting. Scented orchids carefully placed in a crystal vase was the centerpiece of the dining room table just as he had ordered. He walked over to the table and leaned close, smelled the flowers to exorcise the stench of jet fuel and bundled humanity.

The lacquered table with seating for six had no hint of dust or fingerprints and there were original works of art on the walls. It evoked thoughts of his home.

A painting by Gauguin was on the wall by the table. It depicted a smiling woman from the tropics with a flower in her hair, her pose reminded him of Mona Lisa turned exotic and alluring.

Degas guarded the adjoining living room. Chinese vases on stands held the corners. There was a Remington statue of a man on a horse made of bronze and positioned on a pedestal, the only offering to Americana in the room.

He walked over to the windows and opened the curtains. His suite overlooked the Chao Phraya River on one side and his balcony wrapped around and turned a corner so that he could see the Emerald

Buddha and Arun Temple on the other. He nodded his approval at the breathtaking view.

He tore himself away from the window. He'd have plenty of time to appreciate Bangkok's beauty up close and personal. Slow deliberate steps took him into the bedroom where he noticed the thick terrycloth robe placed gently on the bed. Dropped his shoes, socks, shirt and pants on the floor then covered up with the robe. Rubbed his eyes, felt the sting in them and stumbled to the bathroom in search of the sink and the mirrors.

Using his fingers to hold open one eye and then the other, he deftly removed the brown lenses that covered his pupils. He squinted then held his eyes closed for a minute to give them time to adjust. Greenish, hazel colored eyes now stared back at him the way they'd always had for the fifty-five years he'd been on Earth. He'd need the contacts lenses when it was time to leave Thailand.

Cold water on his face, followed by a cold towel to ease the puffiness around his eyes would give him just enough of a boost so that he could unpack his suitcases before he lay down for the evening. He stretched and walked slowly back out to the living room and the wet bar, poured a shot of Cognac. It was Courvoisier VSOP 1935, Pre-War liquor. No ice, always straight. Took a healthy sip then put the drink down on the bar.

He walked over to his suitcases and lifted one to carry back into the bedroom, stopping to grab his keys on the way. This was the smallest of his four suitcases. He'd carried it on the plane held close and not allowing it to leave his sight for a moment. He popped it open, looked at the suitcase that appeared to be filled from corner to corner with men's colognes and toiletries then unceremoniously dumped the contents on the bed.

He searched around for something he could use to remove the metal plate underneath. He thought about the place settings on the dining room table. McGiver type improvisation---butter knife as a screwdriver. A butter knife would do fine.

There were four screws, one at each corner that fastened the metal plate and held it firmly in place. He twisted and turned each screw nearly bending the blade of the knife as he mumbled, "This is a pain in the ass", but he kept at his task. It couldn't wait until the morning.

With the last screw undone he pried the metal plate open and stood there for a moment to take inventory of his inventory. There were one hundred dollar bills with one hundred per stack and each secured by a bank wrapper. He thought; *five thousand dollars per stack, times a hundred stacks equals five hundred thousand dollars in untraceable bills.*

He'd put this money into the safe hidden behind the Degas painting on the wall where they told him it would be when he made his reservation. He would use the money at a later time.

After he removed the money from the suitcase and placed it in the safe, he picked up the velvet Crown Royal Whiskey bag and examined its contents, smiled and placed them back in the bag. It would also go into the safe.

Finally, he took out the holstered Les Baer, brought it from its hiding place. He pushed a button on the side of the stock and let the clip fall into his other hand. He counted one through seventeen as each un-discharged bullet popped up into the air and onto his bed. He wanted to be sure that his pistol's seventeen children were all healthy and accounted for.

He raised the Les Baer with his right hand and held it out at shoulder height. Felt a shot of pain course its way through his shoulder. He winced. Grabbed his shoulder with his left hand, administered his own version of therapy. Although there was little evidence of his wound from the outside he could feel the residual sting the bullet had left inside his right shoulder even though he felt he'd been healing fast.

He re-positioned the gun to shoot from the hip the way the old cowboys did in Western movies. Not an accurate way to discharge a weapon but if he had to then he would have to. He thought briefly about holding it with his left hand, but that was for the cane that kept him balanced. He could walk without it, but the steadiness to his stride was just returning and his crutch had become a crutch that made him feel that he needed it.

He put the bullets back in the clip and re-holstered the gun. The clip would go into the safe along with the money and other valuables. He intentionally left the bullets separated from their mother who might later send them screaming out, piercing air and flesh or anything else that got in their way if he had to use her. But he hoped it wouldn't come to that. God, he hoped it wouldn't come to that.

With the clip now safely secured in the safe, he searched around for his most valuable possession he'd brought on this trip, his passport. For a moment panic seized him until he remembered that he had placed it in one of the pockets of his carrying case, the one that he used to tote his laptop computer along on the flight.

A zipper unzipped and Velcro pulled apart revealed his passport and the other two that he brought along with it.

He looked at his photo and read the name aloud, "Solomon Fortunada". It had a certain ring, he thought. He would be Solomon Fortunada to anyone and everyone as long as he was in Thailand.

Solomon opened the other two passports, thought they were professionally done, looked authentic. He smiled at the familiar face in one of the passport photos and studied the face of the stranger in the other. Thoughts both kind and sweet rushed through his brain, but tinged with desperation. Time was not his friend.

Solomon, as he called himself, placed the three passports inside the safe, set the code that would unlock it at his command and closed the door. The Degas would hide it from any unlikely intruder.

He walked barefoot as his feet absorbed the lushness of the thick carpet with every step until he found himself back at the dining room table. Another purposeful sniff of the orchid arrangement and he was back at his boyhood home in Lafayette, Louisiana in his mother's garden. Back there, smells of Creole foods, jambalaya and e'toufee owned the air inside his father's house, orchids possessed the outside. Sleepy and very southern Lafayette was a far cry from Bangkok, Thailand.

Chapter Forty-One

Sunrise over the Chao Piraya River and the light illuminated the water. The easy moving river played with the light from the sun like children running along the shore trying to avoid the tide. He watched intently, allowed the images to dance with his thoughts. The placidity of the scene brought along with it the irony of his presence in Bangkok. His purpose in being there was for anything but peace and tranquility.

Solomon stepped off the balcony to his suite on the twenty-sixth floor of the Oriental Hotel. Heights made him skittish, gave him a mild touch of vertigo to go along with all of the other physical maladies that seemed to have besieged his body. He was in his pajamas. It was six in the morning.

He'd slept about fourteen hours straight, but the rest was needed. Solomon walked over to the wet bar, opened the fridge and poured himself a large glass of cranberry juice, then an equally large glass of tomato juice. It was time to take his medicine. Dragging his left leg behind his right without the benefit of his cane he headed to the bathroom.

He stood in front of the mirror with a case in his hand filled with pills of various colors, part of his daily ritual. Antibiotics and painkillers, mostly, and the nitrate based medications for his heart. He used the tomato juice to ease the burden of swallowing the pills one after the other and when he had finished his ritual he stood there eyeing himself in the mirror.

Solomon used his hands to pull at his face trying to rub out the creases that had become permanent lines. He smiled. "Character," he told himself.

It was time for Solomon to examine his body. He took off his shirt and studied the small circular mark carved into his right shoulder. It served as a reminder that he should always take great precaution in everything he did from this point on. This would be especially true during his stay in Bangkok. And, of course, trust no one.

His right hand appeared as his left one in the mirror and he used it to rub the fist-sized discoloration that was now a permanent feature on his right side, just below his ribcage. The mark was angry and dark against his copper colored skin, a further reminder of the encounter that almost took his life.

Solomon took his hand and smoothed back his hair, which was thinning just a little. He thought; *you're not getting any younger*. He thought about his mission there and what he would do once it was over, but that was premature thinking.

He had to do what he'd set out to do.

Do the things that brought him there a few weeks before he had recuperated fully.

Solomon's thoughts were interrupted by someone tapping at the front door, but he hadn't heard the knocks at first. It became louder and more persistent. He reached for the empty Les Baer stashed underneath his pillow. He thought for a moment about opening it, the safe, grabbing the clip that housed the seventeen belligerent children and bring them home to their mother, but he held her empty at his side because he wasn't really expecting trouble, not here.

"Who is it?" he shouted through the door loud enough for the world to hear.

"Room service, Sir."

"That's O.K. Don't need any."

Solomon recalled the "Do Not Disturb" sign he'd placed on the handle outside the door and shook his head. The knocking ceased, housekeeping had retreated, but he knew they'd be back.

His cellular rang, but it was all the way back in the bedroom. At first he thought about letting it ring. He'd find out who called by checking his messages, but he realized that it might be his contact person. He was told that the call would come sometime later that day or even, later that week. Solomon decided not to take any chances. He needed to walk fast and get the phone, uncertain that his contact would leave a message or a number for him to call.

"Hello," he said without checking his telephone's caller I.D.

Man, where in the hell are you?

The man on the other end didn't need to identify himself. Solomon knew his voice well.

"Where do you think I am, Bakari?" he shot back.

Uhmm, let's see Rio? Cairo? Or maybe, you're at the jazz festival in Switzerland. Hell, how am I s'posed to know?

Solomon laughed. "Sorry, you must be calling me for a reason."

You didn't answer my question.

"There's a reason, Bakari."

Well, you know as your attorney the things you tell me are always held in the strictest of confidence.

"The less you know the better," Solomon said.

He knew Bakari Lomax would pry and pry, hoping that he'd get some answers, but Solomon also knew that attorney-client privilege could only be stretched so far. Besides, the secrets of a client can be beaten out of anyone.

You just got out of the hospital. I thought when you asked me to help you get those passports that you weren't going to do anything until you were fully recovered and you're telling me you're out of the country?

"I never said I was out of the country, Bakari."

I know you. You didn't get those passports just to sit at home and convalesce.

Solomon heard the impatience in his lawyer's voice, but it was typical. Bakari had always been a protective guardian of his affairs.

Well, the reason I called is that you got an offer on your house, but it's under market value.

"Take it," he said without hesitating. "What about the other stuff, the collection?"

That's easy to move for what you're asking. I hope you don't mind me saying this, but it seems like you don't plan on coming back.

Solomon said, "I don't, Bakari."

The comment stilled the lawyer's tongue, a rare occurrence. He heard the tone in Solomon's answer, wasn't sure how to interpret it. Solomon imagined Bakari's face looking uneasy as he fumbled around for the right words to say.

Morbid thoughts, my friend. Morbid thoughts.

"Not necessarily. I might like it over here. Might plan to stay," Solomon said.

Bakari laughed this time. It was a nervous laugh. Solomon knew it.

I'd ask you over where, but you seem determined not to tell me. You want me to put the money in the same account?

"Yeah, just in case," Solomon answered. "And put a quarter of a million in the account I told you about. Maybe, that'll help get his career moving." His mood became reflective, somber. "How long have we known each other, Bakari?"

Since that time I helped you out of that jam. What? Twenty years ago?

"Yeah, it's been a long time. You've been a good friend and a better lawyer."

Yeah, and you've been a better friend and a piss poor client. Bakari laughed hard. *Look whatever you're doing I just want to tell you that if you need anything, anything at all let me know. O.K?*

"Who do I always call when I'm in a jam?" Solomon said. He switched gears, needed to make sure the instructions were clear. "Go ahead and close on my house. Don't haggle over their offer trying to get more money. I'll make plenty. Just make sure everything is final by the end of the week."

I don't know. You're talking inspection and closing in that short period of time. Can't happen.

"Make it happen, Bakari. Tell them if they close I'll knock off another hundred grand. Give em an incentive. Talk to you later."

Yeah, I'll make it happen. Bakari Lomax, Esquire paused. *We'll talk later. You can count on it.*

Solomon folded up his cellular and stood still for a moment. His thoughts caused him to linger on his own words like they were an oral last will and testament.

*   *   *

A hard knock at the door.

His patience wearing thin.

Room service, he thought. He marveled at their persistence, but he'd tell them to come back later, once again. He threw open the door ready to tell them in the rudest way he could that he didn't need his bed made or fresh towels, but it wasn't room service. It was a girl.

She stood at his door with her fist still poised to deliver another knock, but she froze there like she was suspended in animation. She forced a smile to greet his frustration. Looked scared for a moment, but managed another wide smile that overcame any appearance that she might've been startled by him.

"Yes, may I help you?" he said.

She stepped by him, walked into his suite like she belonged there, like he was expecting her visit. He turned around and watched as she took a seat on the sofa.

"I'm sorry, you must be in the wrong place," Solomon told her.

She kept her wide smile like her cheeks were strained and hurting from the effort. He thought that she didn't understand him. He tried to think of the words in Thai that would help him to communicate with her, but she spoke first.

"My name Lulu," she said. "I here for you." Still smiling.

Solomon raised one eyebrow and said, "Excuse me?"

"I here for you," she repeated.

"What? You're here for me? Who sent you?" he asked.

The girl, Lulu, crossed her legs, allowed her dress to rise up far beyond her knees to show her young brown thighs. She was Thai that was obvious and young, real young.

"I here for you," she repeated a third time. He was getting the point.

It was still morning, but she was made up like she was going out to party in the clubs or maybe she'd been out all night. Either way, Solomon didn't understand why or how she happened to be there. He thought about the elevator and how a key was needed to access the penthouse level of the hotel. He closed the front door and followed her into his suite, took a seat of his own in one of the chairs that faced the sofa, separated by a coffee table.

"I don't know who sent you or why, but I didn't ask for any company," Solomon told her.

Lulu put on a sad face, but Solomon knew that fabricated expression. She poked out her bottom lip and turned her eyes downward like a Geisha performing in brown face.

"Lulu's boss, say you need company. Me take good care of you," she laughed behind her words. "Take *real* good care of you. Suck you real good, love you real good. Do anything you like."

He looked at her without smiling. "Who's your boss?"

"Boss name Ping. He say Lulu gift for Solomon. I take real good care of you, please?"

Solomon mumbled, "I should've known."

She rose from the sofa and walked over and stood directly in front of him. Lulu was wearing a tight black dress with a plunging neckline to show her cleavage. Deep red lipstick painted over her full lips stood in stark contrast to her dark skin, dark even for a Thai woman. She was wearing false eyelashes that flitted like butterfly wings in a contrived attempt to be alluring.

Solomon sat there as she un-wrapped her hair taking out the pins that held it up one at a time. Black and flaxen, her hair fell over her shoulders in one fluid motion like a black waterfall. She tossed her head from side to side to loosen her tresses and dropped to her knees as she positioned herself between his legs. She took one hand and used it to snake its way along his leg and up to his thigh. He grabbed her hand and held it tight and firm.

"You tell Ping, no thanks. Tell him I don't do business this way."

Lulu shrunk away. "I cannot tell him that. He say, Lulu gift to Solomon. He think I do something wrong. He beat me if I offend you."

Solomon sat back in his chair, rubbed his hand over his chin. He looked at her hard through all the makeup. Lulu was a young girl, probably no more than sixteen or seventeen years old.

"How long were you supposed to stay with me?" he asked.

"Ping say me stay two, three day or how long you want Lulu to stay."

Solomon knew enough about Thailand and the Far East to realize that sex trade was serious business. Tradition and gestures of gratitude were even more serious business and to reject such a gesture might sour his deal and undermine his reason for being in Bangkok.

"Get up," he told her. "Look, tell Ping. No, I'll tell him I don't do business like this. You can stay here for a day or two, but no funny stuff, all right? There's plenty other things to do here in the hotel."

He remembered that there was a sauna downstairs, movie theatre, swimming pool.

"The sofa pulls out. You can sleep there. O.K?"

Lulu nodded.

"I've got a lot to do while I'm here so you can make yourself at home until you think you can go back to wherever you go without feeling that you're going to catch a beating from Ping or anyone else. Understand?"

She gave Solomon a genuine smile this time. He could see the delight in her eyes like the kid she really was.

"You bring any clothes?" he asked.

She walked back over to the place where she'd put her purse down on the floor beside the sofa and pulled out something that resembled a slingshot. Lulu waved it in the air without stating the obvious. Solomon shook his head. He walked back into the bedroom, pulled out ten one hundred dollar bills from his money clip.

"I've got some things to do on my computer. Take this and go to one of the gift shops or the mall next door. Buy yourself something, ah, that has more material. Have you had anything to eat this morning?"

"No," Lulu told him.

She reached out and took the money. It would be converted into thirty-five thousand *baht,* in Thai currency.

"What bout you, Solomon? I bring you food from downstairs, no?"

He shook his head. "I'll eat later."

He watched the young girl as she walked out of the suite and he hoped out of his life. A grand was worth it to avoid the headache of still another young woman that he'd have some kind of duty and obligation to protect. They were beginning to stack up like playing cards precariously positioned to make a paper house. Pull the wrong card and the whole house could fall down. Solomon knew that if he wasn't careful he'd get pinned underneath the rubble.

*   *   *

He soaked his wounds and his thoughts under the pulsating water. Ping had sent a very young girl to entertain him, but Solomon didn't trust their motives. Maybe it was a small test designed to try his patience as he waited to meet with them. Or perhaps Ping was hoping to catch him with his guard down and use the girl to take the thing he'd come there to trade.

Solomon had a lot to do while he was in the city and just a few days to do it. There was no time for or interest in debauchery.

He got out of the shower, towel dried his body and let it drop to the floor. A few stretches were part of his morning routine. He started with his damaged right shoulder. With his elbow pointed toward the sky he used his left hand to stretch his right arm back as far as he could take it until the pain became so familiar that it was beyond the point of being tolerable. He grimaced, made a short grunting sound and then allowed his arm to slowly return by his side.

Solomon repeated the movement nine more times then stood on one foot trying to bring his left leg back, bent at the knee so that his hand could reach it. In the hospital they had used an elastic band to wrap around his ankle and would tell him to pull it until his knee could bend. Solomon wished for the elastic band.

He bent slightly at his waist to the left side and reached for his ankle. He caught it with a hard grip and pulled. Solomon gasped at first then he pulled his leg back until his eyes began to water. The doctor had told him that if he ever wanted to regain full motion in his leg to run or play tennis, even golf, he needed to do this every day.

Repeated the motion, repeated the pain until he couldn't stand it anymore. Finally, Solomon collapsed on the bed, did a few stomach crunches to take his mind away from the pain. He was lying on the bed still and breathing deep when he heard the sound of the television coming from the living room.

I didn't turn that on, he thought.

He reached under his pillow for his gun, but remembered he had put it down on the wet bar when the young girl entered his suite. This was after he told himself that he would be extremely cautious from the time his plane had touched down in Bangkok. Another bad move could get him killed for sure.

Solomon grabbed his robe and threw it around his body. A few careful steps in the direction of the living room and a peek around the corner and he could see the young girl with the remote aimed at the television, surfing channels in rapid fire motion moving from one station then to the next.

"I thought you were going to get some breakfast," he said.

She turned and smiled without showing any teeth. "Lulu wait for you. You need food, too."

Solomon did a quick visual inventory of the area, starting first with the spot where he'd left his gun on the wet bar. It was there, untouched and undisturbed. That was the only thing he was concerned about even though the clip was in the safe right behind Lulu. He walked over and picked it up then put it in a pocket of his robe as she seemed not to notice.

Lulu's gaze was locked on the television. BET Uncut was being broadcast on the tube. Solomon couldn't hide his disgust. He wouldn't let his daughter if he had one watch the show.

"Just give me a moment. I'll put some clothes on," he said. Lulu was bobbing her head to the beat, acting like she was in a trance.

"I be right here waiting," she said, almost singing.

She walked ahead of him down the hall toward the elevator. Solomon was using his cane, but was right behind her. Lulu looked like a full-grown woman with curves like a Coke bottle and long legs made tight from hours of walking the streets, he thought. Legs accentuated by her stiletto high heel shoes. She had kept her hair down and from the back reminded him of someone he had known not so long ago. It was a woman Solomon had spent one rapturously glorious night with a few weeks earlier.

Lulu turned to face him with lips that looked like a rose in full bloom. "You like eat in hotel restaurants? There are many."

"I'm flexible," Solomon said. "But first we have to get you some more clothes. Something a little more appropriate.

Chapter Forty-Two

Solomon watched with some amusement as Lulu pranced through the mall making stops at stores with names like Harrah's and Givenchy until he steered her into a Banana Republic store a block away from the hotel on Charoen Krung Road.

I must be getting soft in my old age, he thought. *She's not my daughter. Hell, I don't even have a daughter---remember the plan.* But the plan was ad hoc and flexible. Providence sent Lulu his way. He had to make the best use of her.

The first items she picked were some hyper-short shorts, to which he shook his head. Next came a halter-top that was just a swath of cloth meant to cover only her breasts. His straight face stopped her in her tracks. She retreated to the dressing room only to return in the same micro-mini dress that she had worn coming in.

He led her to a section in the store that had clothes with a more casual, conservative look that he thought a seventeen-year-old should wear. With Lulu in the background making faces, Solomon selected several pairs of brown, green and blue cargo pants, a jean skirt that stopped at mid-knee, blue jeans and some girly-looking blouses. He piled the clothes into her arms and pointed her back to the dressing room while he took a seat just outside.

It was time to rest his leg and to check his cell phone for any messages in case Ping had called and he hadn't heard his telephone ring. He snapped the phone closed when his voicemail told him that he had no new messages.

Minutes later Lulu came out wearing blue cargo pants, a white blouse with flower patterns and a pair of oval shaped sunglasses with a white frame. She smiled, did a pirouette for him to see. He nodded his approval.

"Try on the other clothes," he said.

He had already resigned himself that he was going to buy her anything she wanted and as long as the clothes he selected fit they were hers to keep. Lulu came out wearing one outfit after the other. Solomon was relieved to see her in something besides her hooker outfit.

As Lulu was making what he hoped was her final trip to the dressing room, Solomon handed her his handkerchief.

"Do me a favor. Wipe off your makeup and lipstick," he told her.

She frowned and pouted, but snatched at the pieced of cloth and stomped back towards the dressing room. Moments later she was standing in front of him wearing the blue cargo pants and white blouse with the flower pattern. She handed Solomon his once white handkerchief that was now tie-dyed with smudges of red lipstick and black mascara. Lulu also took the added measure of pulling her dark hair back into a ponytail.

He smiled.

"I'm hungry," he said.

Lulu walked to the cashier with enough new clothes to last her a month or two. She reached into her purse and retrieved the ten one hundred dollar bills Solomon had given her, but he was ahead of her. He handed the cashier an American Express Platinum card. The cashier, a forty-something woman with a mole over her top lip gave him a smug look.

"You have I.D?" she asked.

He pulled out his driver's license, handed it to her and wondered if her European or white American customers had to undergo this kind of scrutiny. The woman with the mole put his credit card and driver's license side by side then flipped both over where he signed his signature.

"Name do not match," she said, her mole moving up and down with every word like the bouncing ball in an old sing along movie.

Solomon cursed under his breath. He realized that the woman with the active black mole was correct. He thought briefly about the mistake he had made when he left his gun out in the open the time Lulu first came to his room. The errors were piling up. *Must be the medication,* he thought.

"Look, that's O.K." He grabbed both his credit card and driver's license in one motion. Put them in his wallet and brought out another wad of bills. "How much in U.S. dollars?" he asked.

She took out something that looked like a calculator and punched the buttons. "One thousand, seven hundred and fifty-two dollars, U.S," she said.

Solomon peeled off several hundred-dollar bills and a fifty to go with them. He reached inside his pocket and found two one dollar bills, handed the money to the woman who had a confused look on her face. He figured her suspicions about the different names on his credit card and his driver's license were getting the best of her. He just hoped that she wouldn't remember the names and would forget his face.

He glanced over his shoulder at Lulu who didn't seem to be aware of the goings on at the cash register. Fortunately, there was full-length mirror nearby. The young woman was admiring herself while tuning out everything else.

Solomon stood there like an anxious bank robber watching the cashier bag the clothes. He needed to get out of the store and disappear, make himself fictitious and nameless the way he had when he became Solomon Fortunada. When the woman finished putting the items in the bag he turned to Lulu and said, "Let's go."

He pushed his cane ahead and dragged his bad leg behind as fast as he could go. Now Lulu with bags in both hands was having a hard time keeping up with him. He said, "Shit!" a few times under his breath and shook his head as he walked. "Last time. It's the last fucking time!"

A man with a cane and a young girl in hasty pursuit carrying bags like they'd gone to the pre-Christmas sale at Macy's in New York were moving through the plaza and into the lobby of the Oriental Hotel. Solomon checked over his shoulder to see if anyone had followed as he had from time to time during their hasty retreat back to the hotel. He let out a relieved breath of air and settled down in a leather chair in the lobby.

"You make Lulu breathless," she told him as she grabbed a chair beside his and dropped her bags in front of her.

Solomon was breathing hard. He gave her a sarcastic, "Yeah, I have that effect on women."

Lulu smiled and winked. "Me know," she said. "You take breath away make women go ga-ga over you. Lulu like you very much, make Solomon feel very, very good."

She had a flirtatious look about her that made him think for a moment that he wasn't just another john that paid her to flatter his ego and massage his penis. The moment quickly passed.

"You hungry?" he asked.

Lulu had her head down. The upside down smile had returned. "I thought you like me," she said. "You buy me stuff, pretty things. You like me, no?"

"Like a daughter," he told her. This was the first time he really thought about what it might've meant to Lulu for him to buy her things. She was a young prostitute and he had known young prostitutes when he was a young man in the States. Gifts were interpreted as a gesture of kindness and often more. He couldn't tell her that it was neither. He couldn't tell her that he had a reason to do the things he did for her that day. Motive and intent are sometimes synonymous.

*   *   *

Lulu wolfed her food down, chewing with her mouth wide open and talking in between chews as Solomon watched. It seemed as if she was trying to impress him with her savvy street sense and worldliness. She talked about her johns and laughed at their desires. When he had had enough he told her, "Let's talk about something else."

"I want to go to States someday," she said.

"And what's stopping you?"

"Have to pay off contract. Must pay them three hundred and forty thousand *baht*."

He thought that must be like a million dollars to her, but she could buy her way out of the life for a mere ten thousand dollars in U.S. money.

"How well do you know Mr. Ping?" he asked.

"He bad man. Him work with bad people. They kill everybody. They kill girls who try to quit or run away."

He frowned. "What did he tell you about me?" Solomon asked.

Lulu kept up her voracious consumption of the food piled high on her plate, shoveling it into her dainty mouth in big bites. She swallowed hard, drank tea. "He say you important businessman from States. He say treat you good."

Solomon rubbed his chin, thought about the things Ping had told Lulu.

She added, "He say for me to make sure you are who you say you are."

"Why? Did he tell you that I might not be the man I say I am?"

She shrugged her shoulders and kept eating.

Solomon was trying to read between the lines, assess the threat level that Lulu represented to him. He knew enough about her in the short time they'd been together that he could buy her loyalty.

"Why you have gun?" she asked. "Do all Americans have guns?" Her preciousness was showing.

He laughed slightly. "If you believe everything you read or see on television."

Solomon realized that Lulu would report to Ping that he was armed, that he was ready to do battle if it came to it.

"I'm a secret agent," he told her. They both sat on his words for a moment then laughed.

Lulu had an easy, hair trigger laugh. Solomon wondered if it was genuine or whether she was just acting---like the times when she was strictly entertaining. He wouldn't know the difference.

He studied her every move as she ate and talked. He thought about the two passports stored in the safe upstairs in his room and the photos of the two women. Lulu bore a strong resemblance to one of them although there were ethnic differences. But they were similar in height and build. Lulu's hair was straighter and then there were the eyes. Both had skin the color of darkened honey. Both women had an honest looking smile.

She asked, "Do you use gun in business?"

"No, never."

"Then why have gun?"

Solomon's look turned serious. His jaws tightened. He spoke without really talking to her.

"I need to right a wrong," he said. He took a sip from his coffee cup, put the cup back on the saucer, kept his eyes cast downward at the table. What had been a light-hearted morning was now coming to an end. It was time to get back to business. "I need you to me a favor," Solomon said.

"Anything. I like you. You good man."

"There's money in it for you. Enough to buy your way out of Ping's contract."

Lulu bounced in her seat anticipating an assignment from this man with a gun. Another film noir classic. "What is it?"

"I need you to watch someone for me. Kind of look after her."

"Where is she? She your girlfriend?"

"No, but somebody I'm very close to. She's locked up in the prison across town."

Lulu looked confused. "What? You want me to go visit her there?"

"No. I want you to keep an eye on her for me. I want you to go to jail."

Lulu's mouth dropped open. Half chewed food coated her tongue. "You crazy. Lulu don't want to go to jail."

"For ten grand? Half now, the rest when you get out."

"How long I stay there?"

"Couple of days, that's all" Solomon paused. "There are risks."

Lulu laughed out loud. "I risk my life everyday for fifty baht. Ten thousand dollars U.S. will buy my freedom. It worth risk."

Solomon spent the rest of the day waiting for Ping to call. He was starting to get anxious, which was something he didn't usually feel.

He had sent Lulu away so he could think. She had gone to see a movie, probably something like Transformers with subtitles in Thai. He thought for a moment that she might not return to his room, but for some reason he knew that she would.

When she returned later that evening he gave her some orange juice to drink while he sipped on Courvosier. He had pulled out the sleeping sofa for her, said goodnight then went to bed. Solomon could hear the television playing videos on MTV through his closed door. When he woke up the next morning the T.V. was still on and Lulu was gone---so was the money in his wallet, about five thousand dollars.

Must be a down payment on her ten thousand dollar ticket to freedom, he thought.

He didn't panic or become angry. He reached for the hotel telephone and dialed the hotel's operator. "Give me the Thai police department," he said.

Solomon opened the safe hidden behind the Degas painting, took inventory. Everything was untouched. The two hundred and fifty thousand dollars cash was still bundled in its place. So was the clip of bullets. And most important of all the three passports and the velvet Crown Royal bag with its contents were still there.

The police told him he'd have to come down to the main station, which was on Samsen Road about a block away from the

Dusit Zoo and the Thai House of Parliament. He could fill out a report there. He was told if they found her she'd be arrested and that it was a serious offense in Thailand. Crime had a direct correlation to the tourist industry and that was money in Thailand. Young girls selling their bodies brought tourist there, stealing from visitors kept some of them away.

"She won't be hard to find," a police officer told him.

Chapter Forty-Three

Solomon had been in Bangkok for three days and Ping hadn't called. The mob boss had sent the girl, Lulu as an offering of some kind and all she did was to steal five grand from Solomon's wallet and disappear.

He filed a complaint with the South Bangkok Police Department along with a detailed description. They knew her well. Solomon was told through a translator that she'd be arrested. After that came the profuse apologies.

He thought about the cashier with the bouncing mole at the Banana Republic and the discrepancy between the names on his credit card and driver's license. He wondered if she had reported him to the police even as he sat there filling out a complaint form. He relaxed. She had no evidence and he had paid for Lulu's clothes with cash so there was no harm done.

He thought of Lulu, mostly wondering if she'd be locked up when they caught up with her. For a moment he thought about Ping and Lulu, her relationship with the man and how she said the gangster owned her with a contract that was no less than indentured servitude. But Lulu wasn't picking cotton or toiling in some hot field knee deep in rice plants---she was selling her body.

Solomon thought about the money he could get for the jewels. There was enough there to be both selfish and altruistic. With twenty million dollars he could set up some kind of program for wayward girls in Thailand to help get them on the right track---if he got the money. Of course it was a fanciful thought. There were girls like Lulu all over the world, including in the U.S. of A. Men like Ping exploited them, took their innocence.

Solomon spent the rest of day in his hotel room waiting for his telephone call and moving his funds around from his U.S. bank accounts to secret accounts he held in the Bahamas, Brazil and Switzerland. He had bought a pontoon airplane and made arrangements online to have it shipped to his new home. If everything worked out well he'd return to doing something he loved, flying puddle hoppers somewhere in the Caribbean or the South American coast.

He later opened up the safe, took out the other two passports he had put there and grabbed the ammunition clip for the Les Baer. He thought that the children were better off in the belly of their mother so he inserted the clip, facilitated their reunion.

He sat on the sofa with the passports in front of him. Opened them one at a time and regarded the photographs of each of the two women in them. Repeated the oath he'd made to them without their hearing. Made it from his hospital bed. Solomon swore on his best friend's grave that he'd make them safe again.

He would use the passports to secret them out of the country, but he wasn't sure where they'd go from here. He had decided that he'd give one girl five million dollars and the other two. They could go anywhere they wanted, anywhere but the States.

It would be a tough decision for either woman not to return home. They had family and familiar things there.

Solomon thought of the only family he had, his son. He wondered if the younger man would miss him if something happened or if he never returned. They weren't close and in the twenty-three years they'd been father and son there was never an attempt to reconcile their differences. Maybe a quarter of a million dollars would be the olive branch they needed, but Solomon had his doubts.

He switched gears back to the young women whose passports he was holding in his hands the way he might be holding their very lives. One girl he didn't know. She was safe, as far as he knew.

He thought of Ping, wished that he would call.

The other girl was as good as dead. But Solomon had made an oath to save both women and he'd take on the devil himself to live up to it.

He looked at her passport photograph and the smiling face that was lifted from a picture in her college yearbook. A not-so-creative photographer had made it easy to take the picture and place it on a forged passport, but forged or not it was her picture, her image all the same.

Solomon thought about the night they'd spent together and how she had rejuvenated feelings in him that he thought had died long ago. In his mind he could feel her skin, smooth and silken. Touch her breasts, taste their sweetness, taste the nectar that flowed from the place that made all things about her sacred. Her delta, like the Nile's cradling all of civilization.

He had never longed for a woman before, not like this, but the longing ached. Feelings of love mixed with the carnality of their coupling made him want to see her again even if it was just to save her and send her away from this place.

He could feel himself stiffen at the thought of her, which was kind of reassuring. His medication had made him flaccid in the face of Eros and it was good to know that his body was adjusting.

His telephone rang. It was timely.

He sighed heavily, gave himself time to regain his composure then answered. "Hello."

Mister, ah, ah. I mean, Mister Fortunada.

"Ping?"

Yes, I call like I say. I trust you enjoy gift.

Solomon held back. Ping the Pimp made his stomach churn. Didn't want to tell him that the gift of a young woman wasn't what he wanted or needed. Most of all he didn't want to tell him that she was gone.

"Thank you, very much," he replied.

Please take your time. Enjoy girl long as you want.

Ping's comment let Solomon know that Lulu hadn't gone back to him and that she might be somewhere hiding out or in jail already. Either way, he was relieved.

Ping said: *We are ready to complete transaction. Can be there in hour to see her.*

"What? You mean, Lulu?" Solomon was feigning ignorance.

Ping laughed. *I see you keep sense of humor.*

Solomon knew that Ping could care less about the girl when it came to the prize secreted away in the hotel safe.

"Yeah, gotta have it under the circumstances," Solomon said. "You got the money?"

Must see gems first, Ping answered. *Not like last time.*

"That's fair. You come---alone, check out the stone. When will I get my money?"

Neither man said anything immediately after the question, but the ball was in Ping's court. Solomon waited.

My benefactor say he have money in one week.

"Good enough, but you know I keep the merchandise until I get paid," Solomon said.

Ping said: *We will exchange money for merchandise at appointed time. I will bring specialist with me to view gems.*

247

That made Solomon's chest tighten. Alone, he could handle anyone one on one, but if there were two it could be a problem.

"Just you this time, Ping. Just you," he said.

Impossible. I will need the merchandise evaluated.

"Or?"

Or no deal.

Solomon knew he wasn't in a position to call the shots this time. He needed Ping and his associates to fulfill their end of the bargain more than they needed the stones. He needed to get the girl before they could find her. She was their ace to be played.

He picked up the doctored passport he had made for her. He'd leave all twenty million dollars, let them keep it and the gems, too if it meant that he couldn't save her.

"All right. You come and bring your man along, but I don't want no shit to jump off here. You read me?"

Ping laughed through the receiver. *No shit, no shit.* Repeated the word like a child hearing it for the first time.

Solomon figured his remark didn't translate well in the Thai brain.

*   *   *

Solomon didn't have much time to get ready. He went into the bedroom and opened one of his suitcases, pulled out a vest made of Teflon with a rubber undercoat and put it on. Covered it with the thick bulky robe with the hotel's monogram on it then tied the robe.

He stuck his gun in a pocket so that it would be easy to grab if he needed it. Next he opened the safe, retrieved the Crown Royal bag and stuck in his left pocket. He was ready.

There was a knock at the door exactly one hour from the time he'd talked to Ping. Solomon took cautious steps and opened the door to his hotel suite slowly. A small studious looking man entered first. He wasn't Thai. He looked East Indian. Probably was the gemologist Ping mentioned as his expert rare jewels appraiser.

The man stood about five foot, six inches tall and couldn't have weighed more than a buck twenty-five. He had very dark ebony skin and unruly straight hair. Solomon sized him up, figured he was past sixty and non-threatening in his gate and demeanor. The man gave Solomon a quick smile then released it to resume his straight-faced purposeful expression.

He was followed by Ping with the baldhead and perpetual sneer that could be construed as a smile or---a sneer. Ping was a large man by anyone's standards. He bore a striking resemblance to Oddjob, the villain of James Bond lore. Word was he wasn't to be trifled with or trusted, either.

Solomon greeted him with a handshake then quickly put his hand in the pocket of the robe where his gun was playing a lady in waiting.

"Welcome," he said to his guests.

Neither man responded to Solomon's greeting, instead each grabbed a chair at the dining room table as the two carefully perused the room.

"This is Mister Goel," Ping said.

Solomon concluded that Ping wasn't totally devoid of all social graces. He nodded in Mr. Goel's direction. Goel returned the non-verbal salutation.

Ping asked, "Where's the girl?"

"Oh, Lulu. She went to see a movie. Figured you'd want your visit here to be kept under wraps," Solomon told him. He stayed straight faced without any hint that he was telling a lie.

Ping dipped his face downward and back up again. The sneer remained as though he and Dick Cheney had been cut from the same mold.

"We meet at last, Mr. Fortunada," he said. "You look nothing like I pictured."

"Meaning?" Solomon asked.

Ping sized Solomon up allowing his head and eyes to scan over him. "You taller. No wild hair," Ping said.

"What? You mean like an Afro?"

Ping smiled hard and nodded his head several times as Solomon's jaw tightened. *Might as well have been Bojangles,* Solomon thought. He stared at Ping, wondered about his view of people from different cultures.

"How old are you, Mr. Ping?"

"Fifty-two."

"Guess you must watch a lot of old movies from the U.S., Huh?"

Solomon took a seat at the head of the table like he was a foreign dignitary hosting a state dinner. That Ping and Goel had gravitated to the table couldn't have been better as far as Solomon was concerned. He could sit there with his gun at the ready and neither man could see his hands underneath the table. Problem was---he couldn't see theirs either.

Goel appeared nervous. Solomon figured he was an honest jeweler somehow drawn into a den of wolves. He tapped his foot incessantly while Ping and Solomon made small talk. Finally, he gave Ping a look as if to say, can we get on with this?

Ping said, "Mr. Fortunada I'd love to socialize but my friend here is in a hurry. Can we please examine the necklace?"

Solomon bowed slightly and reached for the bag in his pocket. Put it on the table. He tightened his grip on the gun in his other pocket with his unseen hand. Ping smiled.

"A rather humble presentation for such a prize." He was referring to the Crown Royal bag that held probably the rarest diamond on the entire planet.

Solomon smiled as he loosened the drawstring and opened the bag. "In this case the presentation is in the form of its beauty. *Inegal Beaute.*"

He allowed the necklace to slide out of the bag onto the black lacquered table. For a moment all three men sat very still without speaking. All eyes trained on the large blue diamond pendent surrounded by a string of perfect white gems. But the blue diamond was the centerpiece. Blue like the oceans or an azure sky. Intoxicatingly blue like no other diamond ever unearthed from a South African mine. This was the Holy Grail of stones and now it was on a table in front of them

So mesmerized by her beauty Solomon expected the men to fall to their knees. It was the same reaction he'd had when he first saw the gem many years ago in Costa Rica. Goel swallowed hard, his Adams Apple moved like a snake. Ping said, "It reminds me of a constellation."

He made a gesture with his hand and Goel nervously reached inside his jacket pocket. Solomon gripped his gun, but kept it hidden. An eye on Goel, an eye on the gems.

Goel slowly reached for the stones, stuck a jeweler's magnifying glass in his eye and studied them. He confirmed its authenticity with a nod toward Ping and gently placed it back on the table.

Solomon quickly picked it up and put it back in the bag. "Satisfied?"

The two men nodded their approval.

"Now that we have that out of the way I want to know exactly when we can conclude our business," Solomon said.

Ping said, "In one week. Just like before."

"And the girl? You'll promise her safe passage when I find her?"

"The girl is different story," said the sneering Ping. "My benefactor was very hurt by her actions. Those men were trusted associates of his. It will not be as easy as I first thought."

"And the girl? Will you promise no harm will come to her?" Solomon was putting the bag with the gem back inside his pocket as he spoke, repeating his original question to emphasize its importance to him

"Let me see what I can do. I can help you with the other woman. That is not a problem," Ping said.

"It's a package deal. The women and the money or no deal."

Ping stood up and Goel followed on cue. "You put high price on loyalty, Mr. Fortunada. You would kiss away twenty million dollars?"

Solomon said, "It's a package deal, Mr. Ping."

He let those be his final words on the subject.

"I will see what I can do, Mr. Fortunada. In the meantime tell me what we need to do to assist you with the other girl."

Solomon took a deep breath, let the air ease out of his lungs slowly. "I'll need a contact person on the inside. I'll also need two men, clean cut with no criminal records and a van."

"Done. I will call you in the next day or two to give you details. You'll have to make all the arrangements yourself. These people will want cash."

"No problem."

Solomon walked Ping and Goel to the door with both hands in his pockets. Ping gave him a parting glance, the sneer still prominently displayed on his face, but even more sinister than it was before.

After they were gone he put the security latch on his door and walked into the bedroom. He opened another suitcase and fumbled around until he found a velvet bag with the Crown Royal emblem on it just like the one he'd thrown out onto the table for his guests to see. He dumped the second bag's contents on the bed then placed the gems he'd shown Ping on the bed as well.

"Almost an exact match," he said in a near whisper. He took the gems out to the wet bar, put them in the bottom of the ice chest then filled it with ice and stuck a bottle of Champagne inside. Solomon put the chest in the refrigerator. The manmade copy of the blue diamond necklace would go inside the safe.

He flipped open his cellular. Said: "Dial: Sigmund."

Autodialed beeps running the musical scale then a ring.

Gute Morgen

"Sigmund, it's me."

Hearty laughter through the receiver end of his telephone let Solomon know that Sigmund was happy to hear his voice. *Where are you, my friend? Are you still in the States?*

"Bangkok. At the Oriental."

Ah, ha! You are my first class friend.

Solomon laughed this time. "I just got in the other day. Is everything all right there?"

Did you get my message? Sigmund hesitated, waited for Solomon's answer then said, *Obviously you did not. The girl's left a few days ago. Has not returned.*

Solomon felt the vise that had gripped his heart and squeezed it tight. "Do you know where she went?"

Can't say for sure. She's young. She gets tired of being here---although she loves the children. She might have gone down to Pattaya City. Young people love the beach and nightlife there.

"This is bad news, Sig. How'd you let her leave like that?" Solomon said. His tone was filled with frustration and fear.

She left while I was asleep. Don't worry. She'll be back probably tomorrow or the day after. After all, where's she going to go? She'll be back.

"I hope so, Sig," Solomon said. He realized it wasn't Sigmund's fault. She'd left probably out of boredom. She was young, probably didn't understand the danger. Or thought it was safe to go there after four months in exile. "Pattaya, huh?"

Yes. On the gulf.

Solomon knew the place. Thailand's adult playground. The young prostitute, Lulu had talked about Pattaya like it was some kind of paradise, but she was locked up in a Bangkok jail, far away from an idyllic beach resort.

He closed his telephone thinking about the things he'd heard about the city. Cabarets, discos and go-go bars abound. People everywhere enjoying the nightlife. It would be hard for a young black woman from America to go unnoticed. She'd be easy to find, but that cut two ways.

Chapter Forty-Four

Night sweats and bad dreams. The white-hot sting of a bullet can never be forgotten unless you don't survive it.

But Solomon Fortunada had cheated death, although just barely. His nightmare was a recurring one that haunted him nightly.

It made his sleep restless.

He woke up that morning later than his usual six a.m. rise from the almost dead-like sleep he needed to help with his recuperation. He woke up to pills and medication, stretching and thoughts of Ping. Solomon could smell betrayal all over him.

Even if Ping made good on his promise to help the stench of betrayal would still resonate all over the man. Judas probably had that kind of smell.

It was that kind of betrayal that set him up. It wasn't Ping who pulled the trigger, his henchmen did his bidding, which made the architect of their clumsy plan even more diabolical. Like a general perched high on a hill and away from the fray, looking on from a distance while others made the ultimate sacrifice. Ping had relied on others to do his dirty work.

Solomon smiled at the irony. He had been the hunted and now he was the predator in camouflage.

About twelve o'clock noon Solomon heard his telephone ring in his hotel room. He answered. Hopeful. Full of expectations.

The voice on the other end said, *Hello, Mr. Solomon?*

"Yes," Solomon answered.

My name, Too-Pak. Ping tell me to call.

Solomon laughed slightly. He thought about the Thai obsession with American hip-hop culture. "How you spell that? He asked.

English spelled "T-o-o, hyphen, P-a-k".

Too-Pak coughed into the telephone. *Mr. Ping say you have big business for me and my friend.*

Solomon thought that if he called his friend, Biggie, or some other rapper he'd hang right up. "Yeah, can't talk over the phone. Can you meet me here at the hotel?"

Yes. No problem.

"See you at the bar right off the lobby. Say three o'clock?" Solomon told Too-Pak. "Bring your friend with you."

Yes. What you look like?

"Don't worry, I'll find you."

*   *   *

Solomon arrived at the bar about fifteen minutes early. He ordered water, Artesian Springs in a bottle. And found a table near the back of the room, but kept a clear view of the door leading inside. Settled into a chair. Watched and waited.

There was a table full of Westerners or Aussies with youngish-looking Thai women not too far away sending rounds of shots and toasts, no doubt, to their respective countries. Solomon heard, "God save the Queen" shouted in a raucous roar, topped off by clinging glasses with the overflow spilling on the floor. He shook his head, thought it was a little too early in the day.

One of the men, large with thick looking features, held his glass up high and nodded in Solomon's direction. He downed his drink as he threw his head back like a Brahma bull in heat, finished it with a loud "ah" sound followed by a hiccup and a belch that nearly made the room rumble. He beckoned Solomon to join his group with a hand gesture and pulling his head back like he was reeling him in on a string. Solomon smiled politely.

"I'm waiting on somebody," he told the guy.

"Ah, it's a bloody Yank," the man said. His demeanor changed abruptly. "What's the problem, mate? Too good to drink with us?" He turned to his friends and said, "Mister Pretty Boy over there thinks we're not good enough to bend the old elbow with his bloody Yankee ass."

He slurred every other word, but Solomon could feel a hostile undercurrent vaguely masked by alcohol and the company that surrounded the man and his friends.

"No, that's not it, my friend. Like I said, I'm waiting on someone," Solomon replied.

Up until this point the rest of the group was totally immersed in their tribute to Bacchus, the god of wine and good times, but their brutish friend was single-handedly shifting their attention to "the bloody Yank." One of the women waved in Solomon's direction, said, "C'mon, kon a`-may-ri-qaa. Come have drink."

Solomon shook his head, not at her invitation but because he knew that her friend, full of testosterone and alcohol would take it as the final insult. He sipped his water and coolly waited.

The large man with the thick Cro-Magnon brow and bulldog jaws threw back another shot of courage and plodded over the short distance between his table and Solomon's. Still with another drink in his hand and brains in his pocket, the man stood over Solomon.

"Me la-ahh' dee says she would la-ike for you to join us, mate." He belched to break up his words. "Ahnd me thinks it would be a fucking bloody insult and a mee-stake on your part to ignore her kind gesture and disrespect us."

"I'm sorry, I didn't mean any disrespect to your wife," Solomon said.

The man laughed. "Me wife? Are you fucking kidding, mate? Me wife. That little chink whore ain't my wife! Now ah thinks you really disrespected me. Now ah'm gonna demahnd an apology."

Solomon shook his head, rose to his feet faced the man who was about an inch taller than his six-foot, two inches and fifty pounds heavier. Stood within six inches of the brute, could smell his breath, mixed with onions and alcohol. He didn't care if the man weighed four hundred pounds---sitting down is always a distinct disadvantage.

"Look, I don't want any trouble. So why don't you just get back to your friends and I'll forget you were ever in here," he said.

Solomon's voice was low, his demeanor calm, but there was a tone in his words that spoke of malice and bad intent. The Aussie was sizing him up, appearing not to be threatened or intimidated by the smaller man standing face to face with him. He looked down, saw the cane Solomon carried, made an evil smile like a twisted jack-o-lantern.

Turning to his friends and cohorts, he said, "Think ah'll hav ta go out and teach this crippled Yank a lesson. Maybe, I'll just mess up his pretty face."

Solomon nodded. He was up for a duel. This guy was getting in his way and he had little tolerance for bad manners and worse behavior. He followed the big man through the back exit that emptied into a back alley along with the establishment's trash. The man's entourage followed.

Solomon watched, still maintaining his cool as the man rolled up his sleeves. He cleared his throat, a signal that he needed his instant adversary's attention. He leaned on his cane and narrowed his eyes, allowed their green hue to shine right through the enemy.

"Way I see it, we're at a fork in the road, my friend," Solomon said.

The man's thick lips, now made into a snarl, barked, "And what's that?"

"Well, you can be the bigger man and forget that, as you say, that I *disrespected* you and your crew. We all go back into the bar. I buy you and your friends a round and ya'll move to another table on the other side of the room so I can't see you."

Solomon relaxed. Let out some air and grimly said, "That's the road most people would take if they were in your shoes. You know the road most traveled."

The man stood ready in attack mode with his body leaning forward and his fists knotted into two large fleshy balls. "Ahnd I guess you're gonna tell me that I'ya got ahn ahss kicking waiting down the other road."

Solomon laughed out loud and pointed at the man with his cane. "Have we met someplace before?"

The big Aussie lunged. Fortunately he came at Solomon's right. Solomon pivoted away like a matador, let the raging bull pass by and felt a small gust of wind follow. Sidestepped with his foot extended he sent the man sprawling to the ground.

Solomon got ready for the next charge. It came with a little caution and deliberate movement instead of the full-fledged charge like before, but moving slower would be the man's undoing. Solomon used his cane to brace himself then brought his right knee right into the man's solar plexus. Solomon's opponent made an "oomf" sound then dropped to his knees trying to suck in the air that had abruptly left his body. He followed with a crushing blow to the man's face for good measure and better insurance.

The big Aussie's friends had been standing by watching, sure that he could easily take care of the Yank with the cane. Two of them started moving towards Solomon. A flash of steel caught his eyes. Solomon turned to face them with his eyes on the knife one of the men was holding. He shook his head giving them a non-verbal warning, but they moved closer. He grabbed the brass handle of his cane with his right hand and its shaft with his left. In one motion he unsheathed the sword hidden inside.

"You fellows are at the same fork in the road your buddy just faced, except you with the knife have raised the stakes," Solomon said. He glanced over at the big man still on all fours, still trying to breathe. "Your mate obviously chose to go down the wrong road. You probably won't be as fortunate as he is."

They looked over at their friend, looked at Solomon and the long blade he had poised and ready. Their scowls softened as they walked past him and went to the side of their ailing comrade. They helped the big man to his feet and with cautious eyes directed at Solomon dragged their friend back into the bar.

Solomon returned the sword to its rightful place transforming it back to a cane. He smoothed out his suit and walked back inside. He watched the small group of revelers as they left the bar then settled into his chair and took a sip of his bottled water. A waitress came over to his table.

"Can I get you something else?" she asked Solomon.

"No, I'm fine."

"Glad those people gone. They not stay at hotel. Just come to drink and be rude. Manager say they not welcome here."

Solomon smiled, took another sip. "Yeah, made me want to leave," he told the waitress. "Have you seen two men come in here like they're looking for somebody?"

"Yes, they at bar." She pointed.

Solomon looked over at the two men he figured Ping had sent over to help him, Too-Pak and his friend. One of the men, probably Too-Pak had a baldhead, mustache and goatee. The other man wore shoulder length hair and looked like he needed a shave. Neither man had the look Solomon wanted. He couldn't use them for the job he had to do. Besides, they were Ping's men. Solomon couldn't take any chances with men he couldn't trust.

He watched them as they looked around the bar. They turned their heads every time someone else came through the front door. One of them looked at his watch then motioned to the other that they were through waiting. Solomon watched them leave satisfied that he had made the right decision, but he'd have to find someone else to do the job he needed.

He left the bar and walked into the lobby of the Oriental Hotel. He kept his guard up just in case that big Aussie might return or the two men Ping sent had doubled back to find him. Solomon looked around the huge lobby, saw a familiar face with a wide smile. The man was standing with another man, both dressed up like palace guards. They walked right up to him.

"I told my friend I carry bags for you. He not believe me." The bellhop was nodding repeatedly at Solomon.

Solomon smiled, gently. He was ready to tell the two men that he wasn't who they thought he was, but something told him he shouldn't. He looked at the other bellhop, who had a wide smile to match the one plastered on his friend's face.

Solomon smiled and said, "What can I say? It's me, live and in person."

Both men nodded repeatedly this time like a pair of bobble-head dolls.

Solomon put on a studious expression like he was sizing the two men up. He circled around them rubbing his chin with his free hand. Saying, "Uh-huh. Yes, yes. I think you two will do just fine."

They both stood quietly as Solomon walked around them until he completed a full circle. "You fellas ever do any acting?" he asked.

They both shook their heads. His bellhop said, "Me watch lots of movies. Big fan, big fan. Me see Training Day three time. *I, Robot* four time."

"Well, I'm shooting a movie here in Thailand. You guys would be perfect for the part."

The two men were now giddy with excitement. The other man clapped his hands and started jumping up and down.

"Is that why you have cane?" he asked.

Solomon paused. "Ah, yeah. I'm in character. I play the part of a hero with a major flaw he has to constantly fight to overcome." Solomon looked amused. "What are your names?"

His bellhop said, "Non Boo Jang and my friend here is Bok Jon Nong."

"Pleased to meet you Non and Bok. Look, I'll need you to…"

Non broke in, "We play good guys or bad guys?"

"Good guys. Always good guys," Solomon answered.

Non looked confused. "But in Training Day you not good guy. You bad, very bad."

"New movie, Non. Like I was saying we'll get together in the next couple of days. I'll get you your costumes." He looked at Non. "What are you about a medium?"

Non nodded. "Bok same size."

"O.K. Meet me day after tomorrow here in the lobby."

Solomon headed for the elevator that would take him back up to the penthouse level.

"A boss? Boss?" It was Bok.

"Yes."

"Can we have autograph? Show wife. She big fan, too."

He was holding out a pen and a piece of paper. The giddiness was still obvious like he was ready to spring a leak.

"Sure," Solomon said.

He signed the piece of paper and resumed his walk to the elevator.

"Ah, excuse me, boss."

Solomon turned around.

"You sign paper, *Solomon Fortunada.*" Bok had a nervous smile.

"Yeah, like I said before I'm in character."

Forty-Five

Solomon reflected for a moment on his confrontation with the big Australian. He thought about what might've happened back in the alley, like if he had hurt the man real bad---or worse. He'd end up in a Bangkok jail and everything he had planned would go down the drain. He'd be like fresh rainwater mixing with raw sewage and come out stinking to high heaven.

But it was a calculated risk, one worth taking. First of all, Solomon feared no man, never had. It wasn't like him to back down after being called out. What made it worth risking everything was that it was a test he needed. He didn't know how his leg would hold up or if he had the guts to test it and he was probably looking at a much bigger challenge from Ping and his associates. Solomon knew he had to be ready.

He was back in his hotel suite content with the feeling that everything would go according to plan. He recounted the things he'd have to do. He'd use Non, the bellhop to drive the van but first he needed to find one. It would have to look official, the van that is.

Solomon went over to his computer and found a picture of an ambulance, the kind they use in Bangkok. Next he checked the pages of an English language telephone book for a list of ambulance companies. He decided that it would be easier to rent an ambulance for a day than to buy one and have it painted.

He found a company located not far from the hotel on Sathon Road, but first he stopped at a Fedex/Kinkos and had some business cards printed. He had the name of the famous actor printed on the card and his title as: ACTOR – FILM PRODUCER.

Solomon was slightly amused that he was going to impersonate a Hollywood movie star. It wasn't part of his plan, but he calculated that it would work better than his original one. He took the card to the Kon Bok Ton Ambulance Service and presented it to the owner. When the man didn't respond with the kind of recognition that the bellhop gave him Solomon talked about other big time stars as though he knew them personally.

"Your ambulance will be in a movie that'll be shown all over the world," Solomon told him. "Imagine what that'll do for your business and your own reputation."

"What about Red Carpet?" The man asked.

Solomon looked stunned, like he didn't believe the question. "Are you kidding me? Of course, you'll get the full treatment. You know, Red Carpet, limo, the works. I can even set you up with a date. Who's your favorite Hollywood actress? Halle? J-Lo? What about Angelina? You name it she's yours."

The man nodded and smiled widely like he wanted all three famous women. Solomon was now having fun with his ruse. He had tried many a scam over the years, but this was one he probably enjoyed the most---even though the stakes were higher than any game he had ever played before. All the others were strictly just for money.

*   *   *

Solomon left Kon Bok Ton Ambulance Service satisfied that his plan would work. He caught a taxicab back to the hotel. It cruised by the local prison. He studied the place for a moment, had the driver take another loop around the block, slow and methodical. He muttered low so the driver couldn't hear him. "Hope I don't wind up in there. Or worse."

His next stop was at a clothing store for women where he bought two very plain, but identical gray trench coats and blue and white bandanas. The coats were both Size Six. He also bought two pairs of white-rimmed sunglasses. Paid cash for all the items. Took them with him in a big bag.

Solomon asked the cabdriver where he could buy uniforms like the ones the ambulance drivers wear. "They're part of the costume wardrobe for my actors," he told the driver.

"Take you right there, boss," the driver said.

He bought two uniforms, mediums. Loaded them into the cab. He checked his watch. It was time to get back to his hotel room.

*   *   *

He smelled it as soon as he got off the elevator, that faint smell of deceit and betrayal masked by cheap cologne probably bought at some little shanty-like spot in Chinatown. The hallway leading to his suite was empty although it was only a little after five o'clock in evening. Solomon had shopping bags in one hand, cane in the other. His antennae broadcast trouble.

The door to his suite was ajar. *Could be housekeeping.* But there was no cart out in front of his room and no smell of air freshener wafting down the hall. He walked gingerly towards the door, softly placed his bags down. He thought about his gun, wished he'd packed it and had it ready in his hand, but all he had was the cane and the long blade concealed within.

He used it, the cane, to break the plane of the entrance to his suite as he followed cautiously behind. His eyes swept across the room stopping at the dining room table, the sofa, the kitchen and the wet bar. Silence, stealth and caution were his only allies if there was an enemy somewhere inside. His heart beat hard. Solomon held his breath and opened the closet near the entrance. It was empty.

He looked back in the direction of the sofa. The Degas was pulled away from the wall, but still on its hinges and the wall safe was wide open. Solomon walked over to the wet bar. It was locked. He used a key to open it and retrieved the loaded Les Baer patiently waiting for his hand to caress her. He felt some comfort with her in his hand.

Solomon peeked inside the open safe. It was gone. He breathed easy knowing that his decision to remove the valuables from the safe was a smart one. The Crown Royal bag with the replica was missing and he was relieved, even happy it was gone. Thieves had taken the bait.

With gun in hand he opened the refrigerator. Things had been moved around like the intruder had rummaged around for some kind of late afternoon snack, but it was obvious this was his first stop before he found the safe. Solomon pushed aside a plate of tuna tartare left over from dinner the night before and a Styrofoam box with the remains of a steak carcass and scrambled chicken embryos, Lulu's legacy before she flew the coup with his money. He dumped the box in the trash.

The ice bucket that he'd carefully and strategically placed on the back shelf of the refrigerator appeared undisturbed, but he needed to look inside to be sure. Solomon lifted the bottle of Rioja Reserva out of the ice bucket and sifted through the ice with his fingers as he looked carefully inside the frozen stack of cubes. His heart raced for a minute but there was no panic gripping him. He forced his fingers through the ice until he touched the bottom of the bucket and felt the stones. The jewels were perfectly camouflaged with the blue coating on the inside of the bucket and the ice surrounding it.

He pulled out the bejeweled necklace, examined it closely just in case his intruder was really clever and traded the fake gems Solomon had put in the safe with the real ones he was now holding in his hand. He checked the clasp that closed it, it was real.

"Good thing the thief wasn't a wine drinker," Solomon said with a smile. "He would've known that no one keeps a good Rioja in the fridge."

It was his inside joke. He laughed then silence. Stood still and let his senses re-evaluate his hotel suite relying mostly on his hearing.

He heard the splashing of water striking the marble floor like it was coming from some place far away, faint at first, but growing louder as he edged his way towards the bedroom. It sounded like hands clapping in rhythm to some unknown beat, steady and getting still louder as he entered the bedroom and moved to the bathroom next to it.

Solomon had a death grip on the Les Baer, safety off and ready to introduce her and the children to whatever was behind the door and inside the bathroom.

He stepped off the carpet from the bedroom on to the marbled floor, his gun leading the way. There was liquid under Solomon's feet that moved and rippled with each step. Felt the floor's wetness as the water overflowed into his shoes. He flipped on the bathroom light and looked down at the floor. Water, now rose-colored infiltrated by swirling patterns of red like an artist's palette out of control. It was blood.

The sunken bathtub with the Jacuzzi motors along the sides, normally pushing sensuous bubbles through the water had pink foam crested on top. The jets that had probably massaged and titillated many hotel guests before now were spewing a bloody concoction over the sides of the tub on to the floor.

Solomon could barely make out the image of a face submerged in the water and foam, but it was unmistakable that there was a body underneath it all. He flipped the switch shutting off the underwater jets and the water stilled and the foam cleared. The face, now unobstructed but still submerged stared up at him. Mouth and eyes wide open like a fish that'd met a twisted fate drowning in its natural element.

Water mixed with blood covered the body. Fully clothed his white shirt was now pastel. The image, both surreal and psychedelic to Solomon, body covered in water turned fuchsia looked like something in a Warhol experimental movie. Dark-hued skin was showing through the water. Solomon paused and stared.

He reached into water that looked like a witch's boiling cauldron with both hands, grabbed the man by the shirt and pulled the upper half of his body out. It was Goel, the little Indian jeweler. Solomon released him, Goel re-submerged limp and lifeless. A sick feeling gripped Solomon as he abandoned his cane and gun and hurried out of the bathroom.

He opened the patio door and stepped outside, breathed the evening air as he left the smell of death blended in water behind him.

He leaned on the fence that surrounded the patio, breathing deep and deliberate until the nauseous feeling evaporated. Solomon looked around and at the river below and the cars on the road beside the water. Sounds of sirens broke through. He could see red and blue lights swirling and flashing on top of cars that had now stopped abruptly in front of the hotel. They'd be at his door in minutes.

*   *   *

They pounded on the door like they could make a hole in it with their fists. "Police! Open up!" they demanded. More pounding.

"I'm coming!" Solomon shouted so that his voice could be heard and to show the people on the other side of the door that they owned no monopoly on impatience. He ran his fingers quickly through his hair and tightened the belt around his robe. Coughed and cleared his throat like it was full of the thick mucus-like matter that gathers there during sleep. With eyes half closed he opened the door.

"Yes, may I help you?"

There were two Thai plainclothesmen standing there with faces stern like the parish nuns that taught Solomon back in Lafayette. They flashed badges to add weight to their presence there. One of the men spoke. "My name is Martin Giapong. My partner is Pong Jak Kim. We were called about a possible disturbance coming from this suite."

Solomon scratched his head, kept his eyes squinted and yawned for effect. "Nothing going on here. It's been quiet all afternoon," he told the detectives.

"Mind if we come in look around?" The one named Giapong asked.

Solomon shrugged his shoulders. Stood there like he was trying to decide whether to let the men in or not. He slowly yielded away from the partially opened door, let it swing into the room to allow the men to enter. "I take it you guys are detectives?" he asked. They nodded. "Unusual for detectives to respond to a simple disturbance, isn't it?"

No nod or verbal response this time. They walked into the suite, hands in pockets, heads on a swivel. "Nice place," Giapong said. "Must cost you thousand dollar U.S. a night?"

"Twelve hundred if you have to know," Solomon replied. He took a mental inventory of the two men believing that he'd see them again soon.

Giapong, first name Martin was short with an angular face narrower than most Thai men and eyes rounded rather than oval or like almonds. Solomon figured that his facial structure along with hair that was incongruently dark brown, not black, was due to the coming together of Asia and Europe to make a baby of mixed race.

The name, Giapong was clearly Thai. Martin came from the Brit or Aussie roots of his mother. Solomon concluded that he probably straddled the fence riding between the two cultures, but not completely accepted by either. Men like that always had something to prove.

Pong Jak Kim was nondescript in his features, a great asset for a detective. He had a forgettable round face, too much hair on the top of his head and a height that made him neither short nor tall. He stood in one spot inside Solomon's hotel suite doing that detective thing---snooping around, but only with his eyes. Solomon kept a wary eye on him.

"Detective Giapong, you didn't tell me why you came to my suite...other than something about a disturbance. What? Music too loud? Television blasting?"

The detective smiled, but not the kind that showed he was amused. It was a wry smile with ulterior motives behind it. "Somebody call about fight. Say heard screaming and shouting. He looked up at Solomon, regarded his face. "What happened?" he asked, looking at the small pink bandage stuck on the end of Solomon's chin.

Solomon forced a weak smile. "Cut myself shaving."

"Mind if we look inside the bedroom?" Giapong asked.

Solomon twisted his lips and nodded. "Be my guest." He could feel a distinct lump inside his throat, swallowed it away as he followed the two men into the other room.

Giapong stood near the entrance with Solomon beside him as his partner walked around the bedroom and then entered the bathroom. "No towels," he said.

Solomon painted a disapproving expression across his face. "Yeah, twelve hundred dollars a night and still can't get decent room service."

His eyes caught the small drop of blood that stood out against the white marble floor at about the same time Pong Jak Kim noticed it. Solomon had missed a spot. He wasn't surprised that he had. He intercepted the question he knew was coming.

"Like I said, I cut myself."

Giapong slid the bedroom closet door open, saw nothing but a couple of suits, white shirts and several pairs of slacks along with two pairs of shoes. He gave his partner a head signal motioning him back into the living room. Once again, Solomon followed them.

"If there's nothing else I'm going to get comfortable. It's been a long day," he said.

Giapong nodded and reached for the door that would take them out of the suite and into the hallway. Mr. Kim was still surveying the surroundings. He looked at the sliding doors that led out to the patio, walked over to the doors as though his instincts were pulling him in that direction. "Some view," he said.

Solomon watched him with his nerves coming loose. He could feel his heart beat heavy against the inside of his chest as Kim opened the patio doors and stepped outside. The detective stood close to the rail and looked down over the side. "Long drop from here," he said.

"Guess it would be if someone jumped," Solomon said.

"Or was pushed," the detective countered.

Solomon said nothing, just watched as Kim walked the length of the patio and took a moment to look over the side after every other step or two. He looked at Giapong, shook his head.

"How long you here for?" the detective asked.

"A few days on business then back home to L.A."

The detective seemed to study Solomon's face. "You know you look like man they found in river near the prison. He escaped a few months ago. They find him the other day."

"I would guess that if he was in the water for a few months his body would've been pretty badly decomposed."

"He was a black man. An American."

Solomon smiled. "I guess there's some truth to the saying that we all look alike. Even the dead and rotting ones."

Giapong didn't laugh at Solomon's attempt to add some humor to the situation. "Maybe, he was your brother, no?"

"I'm an only child."

"We did not recover your money," Giapong said.

Solomon's eyes narrowed with his face drawn into a puzzle. The thieves didn't find the quarter of a million in cash he stashed away. "Money? I'm not sure I follow you, detective."

"The money girl take from you. You know, five thousand dollar. You file report. Remember?"

Solomon nodded. "Oh, yeah, that money. I didn't think you would."

Giapong flattened his hair with his hand, threw a Dick Tracy detective style hat on top of his mixed black and brown hair then pulled the hat down tight over his head. Grim face peeked out from underneath. "Girl name, Lulu, in jail now. She steal no more."

"I know," said Solomon.

He watched as Giapong finally opened the door and followed his partner out into the hall. He knew they'd be back, but he could breath a quiet sigh of relief.

"Enjoy your stay in Bangkok," Giapong said. He let the door close behind him. The heavy door sealed Solomon away from the two detectives..

Solomon quickly peeled the bandage from his chin, a hasty but effective way to avoid questions concerning an errant drop or two of blood he might've missed during that frenetic effort to clean the place before the police arrived. He waited inside his suite until he felt that they weren't standing in the hall waiting for him to come out.

When he thought the coast was clear he made his way out of the room, down the hall and pushed open the door marked "Laundry Room". There was a big white canvas basket with wheels on it and towels stacked high. Solomon moved a couple of towels until he saw the dark ashen face of Goel and his unfocused eyes looking out into the nothingness of being dead.

He lifted Goel out of the basket, moved his body a few feet to the laundry chute and into the opening that was just large enough to accommodate the body of a small man. Solomon said a short prayer, would've played Taps if he'd had a horn. He watched the body slide away like a burial at sea.

Goel's body would be right there in the laundry room for the housekeepers to find him. After all, room service had been lousy.

Chapter Forty-Six

There was a knock at Solomon's hotel room door. No, more like tapping, subtle and non-intrusive. He thought it might be Detective Giapong returning to ask more questions or hoping he'd find whatever it was that brought him to Solomon's door the first time. A dead body perhaps, but it had been ditched.

Solomon grabbed The Lady, held her at his side and went to the door, peeped through the little glass hole. There was a man standing there with that same cynical sneer and staring hard at the door's peephole from the outside. It was Ping. Solomon asked the question anyway. "Who is it?"

"Ping, Mr. Fortunada. We need to talk. I'm alone."

Solomon opened the door slowly. His gun now held slightly in front of him greeting Ping with its cylinder pointed at the man's chest. Ping entered the room hands held high, the sneer still unabated. "I am unarmed," he said.

"Keep your hands up," Solomon told him. He closed the door, kept a watchful eye on his visitor. "Take off your jacket and empty your pockets."

Ping complied.

Solomon patted the other man down the way the police frisk criminals, the way he'd been frisked many times as a young man. "Turn around," he said. No gun stashed in Ping's belt or hidden inside his pants where waist and tailbone meet. Satisfied he said, "Have a seat."

Ping plopped down on the sofa with the Degas hanging over his head, but firmly back in place against the wall. "Can I put hands down now?" He asked.

Solomon responded with a simple head nod and took a seat in one of the chairs across from Ping. He said nothing, waiting for Ping to speak first. Solomon hadn't called their meeting.

"You very clever, Mr. Fortunada."

"The same can be said about you."

Ping crossed his legs with his foot and ankle one leg t-boned at the knee of the other. He showed expensive Italian made shoes with no socks. His brown ankles were ashen and thick.

"I get right to point. My benefactor is very displeased…"

Solomon interrupted. "The displeasure is all mine."

Ping's sneer widened into a full blown smile. "Then you know that my people were here."

Solomon raised the gun, painted a picture of a man ready to use it. "You left your calling card," he said.

"Ah, poor Mr. Goel. He honest man."

Solomon rested the Les Baer on his lap, brought his hands together and let his fingers intertwine. "That's why you had him killed? An honest man not to mention the fact that you tried to set me up with his murder."

Ping nodded this time. "You no problem for us in jail."

"I guess it would've been a good plan," Solomon said.

"Like I said, you clever man Mr. Fortunada. You switch jewel. I have fake and you still have real one, yes?" Ping flattened out his hands, palms up like he was ready to plead for the stones. "Break-in not personal, just business."

Solomon's jaws tightened. "That's not how I do business. You know, double-cross first. Apologize later."

Ping unfolded his legs and sat back against the sofa then leaned forward with his hands resting across his knees. "What is that American saying? No honor among thieves."

Every move he made caused Solomon to flinch just a little, keep his weapon at the ready just in case.

He wanted to end this dance and get right to the point. "What do you want Ping?"

"The jewel. That not changed. We are businessmen. A little indiscretion should not change that," Ping said.

"A mere indiscretion, thieves without honor. Is that what you call it Ping? You break into my room, think you've stolen the diamond and kill a man hoping that I'd take the fall for it?" Solomon said. "Well, that's not how I do business. You want to deal with me then no more *little* indiscretions. Most of all I want you and your boys to stop trying to find the girl and I want safe passage out of Thailand for the both of us."

Ping shook his head. "I cannot do that. The girl? I cannot do."

"Can't do or won't do?" Solomon said.

"Cannot do. Girl make big mistake that day. Those men were valued and trusted employees." Ping's sneer evaporated.

Solomon gave him a solemn expression, "I lost my best friend that day at the warehouse." He breathed deep. "I'd say we're more than even. In fact, I'd say that my loss was greater. Let the girl out of the country, promise me that no harm will come to her and we've got a deal."

"Of course, as you know I was not there that day. Your friend Mackenzie Powell's death was so unfortunate. You should know that my people had nothing to do with it," Ping said.

"I realize that. I know that it was a rogue FBI agent who shot and killed Powell but someone in your organization tipped him off. He knew that the deal was happening and the fact that he showed up at the warehouse was more than a coincidence."

Ping shifted uneasily on the couch. "We promise no harm to you. You deliver diamond. We pay money. Girl another story."

Solomon put his hand over the Les Baer but he didn't grip her. He thought; *I can pop him right now. I've got three reasons--- two young women and a broken body at the top of the list---but I wouldn't be able to get out of the country if I did.*

Ping smiled. "Trust me," he said.

"You called Detective Giapong, didn't you?" Solomon asked.

"Giapong work for big boss. You give gems, Giapong go away."

Ping had a cocky, self-assured expression. He tilted his head back and looked down his nose at Solomon. Solomon did a fast re-wind to that fateful day. He felt the white-hot sting of a bullet piercing through his shoulder, exit wound as big as a half dollar. Another bullet exploded in his left knee. Four months later he could still feel it. Then there was the third shot that careened into his side. It could've been his deathblow but for the invention of Teflon.

Solomon could kill Ping right then, a bullet right through that sneering, pompous smile he carried. Kill him for the girl. Kill him for what his men did to them. For redemption and for revenge and Ping would never know why. The man, Mackenzie Powell, was dead as far as Ping knew.

Solomon brought himself back to the moment and to Ping's offer. "What kind of assurances can you give me? " Solomon asked.

Ping snorted. "This is Thailand. We find her if we want to. She still in country. We still have passport. She not go anywhere."

"No promises, huh?" Solomon said.

Ping shook his head. "Not unless you promise to deliver first. Otherwise, if my people find girl first---then you have no choice. Or we kill girl, you keep jewel. No option."

"Give me some time to think about it," Solomon said.

"Time of essence. Give you two days. That's all," Ping said.

Solomon moved his hand from over the gun, made some sort of pyramid with both hands pressed together then put them to his chin. He leaned forward with his eyes looking down on the carpet. He spoke: "And the money? I'd want you to transfer it into my account. No cash transactions here."

"We make it easy. You deliver diamond, money deposited anywhere you want."

"Deal. We'll meet in two days. I'll have the merchandise. You have proof that the money is on deposit to my account," Solomon said.

"Deal." Ping leaned forward, extended his hand for Solomon to shake.

Flesh pressed against flesh, transaction completed.

"As measure of good faith, I tell you that there is word of American girl in Pattaya City. She work in club there. You find, everything O.K," Ping told Solomon.

He stopped at the door. "You should know that girl sent for you name Lulu in jail now." He gave Solomon a genuine smile. "Say she stole money from rich American. Not you, no?"

Solomon shook his head. "Not me. Too bad, she seemed like a nice girl. Too bad she's mixed up with the likes of you."

Ping scowled. "This Thailand. Girls like Lulu have few options in life."

Chapter Forty-Seven

Solomon packed his bags knowing that he had to check out of the Oriental Hotel. Ping and his henchmen, probably in the form of Detective Giapong, would return to find the diamond and kill him. Most of all, despite the promises and assurances Solomon knew he was in a race to find the girl before they did.

He took only those things that were necessary. Things he needed to finish the job and get out of the country. The loaded Les Baer was at the top of the list, followed by the passports and the cash he'd hidden away in the false bottom suitcase.

He found Non, the bellhop in the hotel lobby. Non smiled when he saw Solomon, his exuberance still there.

"Hey, boss. You looking well today. Are you leaving?"

"No, just going to tour the countryside. I need to look at some other locations for the movie."

Non said, "My friend ready for part. Can read script now."

"We'll do that later. I've got your costumes here in this suitcase. You and Pak will play the part of ambulance drivers."

Solomon handed Non the case and a card. "You can pick up the ambulance we're using in the film at this address. We'll be ready to shoot in three days. I'll call you here to tell you where to meet me. O.K.?"

"Very good, boss. We be there on time. My family very excited."

Solomon smiled. "Now I can't have anybody else on the set so make sure it's just you and Pak. There's an envelope inside the suitcase. There's a thousand dollars for each of you. Do a good job and I'll make sure you get to Hollywood to see the movie at the premiere."

Non had a big grin, which he kept as Solomon walked away. Solomon gave the bellhop a parting glance and a thumb's up sign hoping that the little man had bought into his charade.

There was a Hertz rental car counter off in a far corner of the hotel lobby. Solomon opened his wallet and found his reservation card then checked to make sure that the credit card he would use matched the name on his driver's license. There was a pretty young woman with jet-black hair working behind the counter. She had a metal nameplate on her dark blue jacket that read: *Nancy Wong. Reservation Agent.*

Solomon figured she was Korean, judging by the name and that she was probably fluent in several languages, a skill useful to her occupation.

"Solomon Fortunada. I have a reservation," he said.

She had that customer service kind of smile, the way they probably taught her to greet all patrons. "Do you have a reservation number?" she asked without a hint of an accent.

He handed her the card and watched as she punched numbers on a keyboard and stared at the computer screen facing her. "Ah, yes. I have it right here. I see a mid-size vehicle. Three days. Drop off at the airport."

He nodded.

"Driver's license and major credit card, please," she said. She punched in the letters and numbers on the cards and waited for the machine to digest the information and do whatever computers do to verify data.

Solomon was breathing uneasy, but maintaining a cool exterior. A few seconds later the printer spat out a card that Nancy explained was the rental agreement and asked him to sign or initial in four different places. When he completed the agreement she tore off a portion and handed it to him. "This is for your records. The car's a Toyota parked around the rear of the hotel in Lot K, Space 11."

She handed Solomon the keys. "Do you need a map, Mr. Fortunada?"

He shook his head. "No, I pretty much know where I'm going."

A few moments later he was driving through the city. He parked the car near Skytrain Station off Krung Thonburi Road and waited. He checked his watch. He was a few minutes early, but that was good. He could make sure the area was safe, feel assured that no one had followed him there.

Eight o'clock and a solitary figure appeared as a shadow and walking in the direction of Solomon's car. Lumbering more than walking the person approached the car as Solomon studied the figure in his rear view mirror. He pressed the brakes once and then eased his foot off the pedal. The red lights were the sign.

In the darkness he couldn't tell whether the person approaching was male or female. That made him a little uneasy. If it was a man one of them was in the wrong place and Solomon knew it wasn't him. But as the person came closer he could tell that it was a woman.

She stooped down to see inside his car, nodded straight-faced without a verbal greeting. Solomon signaled for her to get inside.

Large, puffy face with eyes that appeared as slits like they'd been carved into a pumpkin with a razor. Her lips were small and tight. He could tell that they weren't meant for singing or much conversation. Her gray pantsuit gave her an androgynous bent, made him think the question, male or female was legitimate inquiry.

"Mister Fortunada?" she asked.

"Yes," he said. "I don't need to know your name. It's better that way."

She agreed. "I hear you need help."

"Yes," Solomon said.

"It cost big-time," she said.

"How much?"

"Ten thousand U.S. dollars."

Solomon knew he'd pay ten times that amount. "Agreed. I'll pay you ten now and another five grand as a bonus after the job's done. Where and when do I meet you?"

She said, "Three days. You meet at side entrance. Paperwork will be ready."

Solomon nodded. He handed her a stack of bills. "Count it if you like."

"Me trust you. Have honest face," she said.

"Thanks." He reached into his pocket and pulled out his cellular phone, held it open and pointed at her. A small flash of light captured her image.

"What's that?" she asked.

"Just needed your picture---just in case," he said.

She seemed unconcerned as she reached for the door handle to let herself out of Solomon's car. "Three day. At twelve o'clock noon."

He watched her again as she faded back into the darkness. Heavy footsteps were taking her in the direction of the Skytrain, up wooden stairs to the platform and probably to her home. Solomon's long list of things to do was growing shorter.

Chapter Forty-Eight

Solomon guided the car out to the city limits. With every turn he checked his rearview mirror looking for headlights. He drove down narrow side streets, away from traffic in a circuitous route.

Made his trip unpredictable like the flight of a bumblebee.

Still checking his rearview mirror, assured that no one was following, Solomon headed to the Bangna-Trat Highway. It was a two and a half hour drive to Pattaya City from Bangkok, but he had a stop to make on the way.

About a half an hour into the drive Solomon saw the sign, *Chon Buri*. He took the exit there. His eyes searched for familiar landmarks like the ruins of that old Buddhist Temple that eerily stood at the top of a hill. He drove on graveled, earthen streets until he reached it.

Stared at the empty edifice for a moment and its ancient tribute from the children of a different god. Mumbled his own respectful prayer as he drove by. "Deliver her safely---and me too."

The temple's open windows like empty eye sockets watched the city and its inhabitants.

He drove slowly down an empty side street that ran past the building. Dimly lit, flat roofed houses dotted the narrow street. He imagined the inhabitants asleep. It was after midnight.

A few more turns on increasingly narrow streets then onto a gravel road. He saw a sign by a dirt driveway. It was in English and German with Thai symbols underneath the words: Dr. Sigmund Gehrig.

Solomon pulled into the drive and stopped the car a few feet away from a small white building. The lights coming through the windows cast a yellow glow outside, made the house look warm and friendly. He climbed out of the car with his cane in one hand and his briefcase in the other. He pushed himself to the front door.

He knocked. More like an unobtrusive tapping than a knock, but with the kind of persistent tapping that would draw the attention of anyone inside the house.

Moments later the door cracked open. A tall robust bearded man appeared. He stood there with his eyes squinted not saying a word. He hastily put on his spectacles, caught the image of his guest clearly then his face erupted into a huge smile.

"I'll be damned," he said. He swung the door open wide, grabbed Solomon with both arms and gave him a bear of a hug that nearly squeezed the life out of him.

Solomon said, "Sigmund" then broadcast a smile of his own.

He pushed Solomon away, but held him by the shoulders with his hands. "When I got the call from you I was shocked," he said. "When you left here I thought I'd never see you again. But then again, I knew you'd be back. Welcome, my friend. Please come in."

Sigmund examined Solomon with his eyes like a doctor proud of his recovering patient. He studied Solomon's deliberate steps then led him into the living room with an arm around him. Sigmund's smile evaporated as he watched, but quickly returned when he felt Solomon's eyes looking at his face.

"How's the leg? Still bothering you, no?" he said.

Solomon shook his head. Smiled. "More mental than anything else. But I'm adjusting. Couple of months and I'll be doing a Russian jig." They both laughed.

"I'm happy to see you doing so well. For a time I thought…." He hesitated. "It's good to see you doing well again."

"Thanks to you, Doc. How's the clinic doing? Solomon said.

"Very good, thanks to your generosity. The money you sent from the states helped us to buy a defibrillator and an x-ray machine."

"It's the least I can do."

Doctor Gehrig gave Solomon an admiring once over. "Where are my manners? I have a rare Reisling I brought back from Germany. I'll get you a glass."

He scurried off to the kitchen and returned with a bottle and two Mason jars. Solomon shook his head. He smiled at the sight of the jars. He thought, *hundred-dollar bottle of wine sipped in containers better suited for Louisiana brewed hooch.*

"It's the best I could do," the doctor said.

"It's not the glass, it's the wine. If it's good in a crystal goblet it's good in a jar," Solomon said. "Growing up in Lafayette, Louisiana a Mason jar was like fine Italian made crystal."

Sigmund Gehrig settled into a large leather chair directly across from where Solomon was sitting. Solomon studied the chair's familiar worn arms, rough- hewn edges, remembered its shiny seat and back. An outline of Sigmund's ample frame was permanently etched into the leather like he'd sat there for an eternity.

Solomon thought back to when he was healing, through morphine hazed days and restless nights and how that old chair was his constant. Sigmund's chair evoked memories of home. Brown worn leather like his Creole grandfather's hands made to comfort him, to sooth his aches and pains. Through fever and delusion Solomon would look at the chair and believe he was in Louisiana rather than some medical outpost in a foreign land.

"You look well---except for the limp," Sigmund said.

"I'm getting better everyday." Solomon took a sip. "And how have things been going around here."

Sigmund sighed. "Well, as the only doctor in a town of ten thousand I stay very busy."

Solomon grunted. "You could be relaxing on some tropical beach, living life without a care or worry. You've surely earned that."

"Helping these people is all the reward I need or earned." Sigmund sank low into the chair, stroked his white beard with his free hand. "And a good glass of wine now and then," he added.

Solomon reached for his briefcase and popped it open. He handed Sigmund a box wrapped in cellophane. "Open it."

Sigmund's eyes lit up, glowed like a child's on Christmas. His large fingers eagerly un-wrapped the cellophane. He put his glasses back on then put the box up to his nose. Inhaled deep. Closed his eyes savoring the aroma.

"Fresh from Havana," Solomon said.

Sigmund lifted one of the silver cylinders from the box and screwed off its top. He tipped it upside down and let the long, brown cigar slide gently into his waiting hand. He sat there staring at it, paying homage to it. "How, ah, where did you get these?"

Solomon smiled. "I've got friends. They're yours."

"I don't know what to say. It's been so long since I've had one of these. You mind?"

Solomon shook his head. "They're yours."

Sigmund bit off the end of the cigar, spat it out then reached for his lighter. He eagerly lit the other end. Puffed hard as the smoked billowed around his head like a cloud and he was some kind of Norse god descending from Valhalla. "Care to join me?"

Solomon shook his head.

"I'm sorry. I almost forgot about your condition."

"That's O.K." Solomon said. "I've got something else for you."

He carefully removed the false bottom from inside the case and took out several stacks of the hundred dollar bills secreted inside. He put ten stacks on the table that separated the two men. "It's a hundred grand. I want you to have it," he said.

Sigmund examined the stacks of neatly wrapped bills on the table in front of him. "I can't accept this, my friend. You have already been very generous---too generous."

"You saved my life, Sigmund and you've been taking care of the girl, protecting her."

"I didn't do anything for money. And the girl, she's been a big help to me here. The children love her. I think she has a knack for this stuff. You owe me nothing."

Solomon shook his head. "I owe you just like I owe her. If it wasn't for her I wouldn't have even made it here that night. I'm a man who believes in settling my debts, both good and bad."

Sigmund let out a breath of exasperation. "If she were here I'm sure she'd say the same thing. You don't owe anyone anything."

Solomon laughed.

Sigmund detected his sarcasm. He lifted his massive frame from the chair, paced around the room puffing his cigar like a diesel engine. "And the debt you've come here to settle isn't just about the girl, is it?"

"No."

"Revenge is a price that's too great to pay, my friend. Revenge begets revenge until there's no one else left. You kill those men, their associates will kill you, eventually." Sigmund rested a large friendly hand on Solomon's shoulder. "You survived. That is revenge enough."

"Revenge is for what they did to my friend," Solomon said.

"Killing them won't bring your friend back," Sigmund said.

Solomon wanted to change the subject. "You said she isn't here."

Sigmund nodded and let out a heavy sigh. "She's gone to Pattaya Island. She's been there before. She's young, restless. Can't blame her for wanting to get away from the smell of rubbing alcohol and antiseptics. There are the clubs there. Young people everywhere."

Solomon nodded. "And go-go bars and prostitution."

Sigmund shrugged. "That's Thailand. She's a good girl. I don't think she'll get into any trouble there. Don't worry."

Solomon thought: *Trouble will find her.*

"I'm not concerned with her getting into trouble. It's just that there are dangerous people who might...."

"Who might harm her to get to you," Sigmund said.

"Exactly. But there's more to it than that. I need to find her Sigmund."

The doctor looked at his cigar. It had burned itself out while the two men were talking. "Mark of a fine hand rolled Havana cigar. They burn themselves out if you don't puff on them." He laughed. "You'd never hear of any Cuban falling asleep with a Havana in his hand and his house burning down around him."

Sigmund lit the cigar again. Puffed, then inhaled deep, exhaled then puffed again. Blew a plume of smoke away from Solomon. "You think she may be in danger, don't you?"

"Yes, Sigmund. They have a reason to harm her even if they were not trying to get to me. I didn't want to say anything to you. I figure the less you know the better. Besides, I knew that she'd be safe here with you. I don't think anyone in Thailand knows this place exists, except for the good people who live here."

"Well, then you have nothing to worry about. You and the girl can stay here as long as you like," Sigmund said.

"It's more to it than that. The men who are my enemies have the police working for them."

"Corruption in Bangkok is nothing new. A bad cop has no loyalties. You can pay them off. They leave you alone."

"I wish it was that simple, Sig. They killed some poor jeweler and tried to set me up to take the fall. Soon, the entire police force and the Thai army will be looking for me."

"So, I guess you're not staying through the night."

"Nah. Gotta find the girl."

Solomon finished his glass of wine then placed the empty Mason jar on the table near the money he'd left for Sigmund. "She ever tell you the names of any of the places she stayed at or frequented when she was in Pattaya before?"

"Like most young people she goes to the clubs. You know discos and dance clubs on Beach Road. She said the Hard Rock Café there reminded her of being at home in the States. She also told me about a new place there called, Blues Factory on Soi Lucky Star. Of course there are a slew of discos on Walking Street."

"Where does she stay when she gets down there?" Solomon said.

"Usually, Beach House."

Solomon rose to his feet. "I need you to do me another favor, Sig."

"Anything for you."

Solomon reached inside the case and pulled out the Crown Royal bag. He emptied its contents on the table. Sigmund's mouth gaped wide open. "How in the hell! I thought it was lost. I thought they took it from you the night you were shot!"

Solomon shook his head. "I need you to send this to this place." He gave Sigmund a small piece of paper. "No one will ever know. But you need to send it out first thing in the morning."

"I don't understand. If this is what they are looking for and they will pay you, why are you sending it out of the country?" Sigmund said. "They get what they want and everyone is safe."

"I wish it was that simple. Problem is, they'll kill the girl and me even if I just give them the stones."

Sigmund bit down on his bottom lip, made his lip flushed red. "That damn thing is a curse for you. Think about it. It's left a trail of blood behind you---your friend, your lover, those three men in that Bangkok warehouse. Damn it man! You barely escaped her fury yourself! And eventually, it will be the end of both you and the girl."

He plopped right back into his worn out leather chair, put his hand to head, lamented over the jewel's past. "You need to get rid of it. The thing's a curse. It's brought misery to everyone who has touched it and it has touched. Look, I'll contact them, tell them I have it and that you're long gone back to America."

"That won't end it Sig."

Solomon looked at Sigmund's eyes. He saw a cloud there like someone had sucked the life out of the old doctor.

Sigmund shifted his head, cast his eyes downward. "You're not bringing her back here, are you?"

"Too dangerous, my friend."

He watched Sigmund walk back over to his leather chair. He reached inside the crease between the cushion and an arm and pulled out an old German Luger.

Solomon looked at Sigmund with an amused expression. "What are you going to do with that Sig? How old is that thing? You must've got it from the Kaiser himself," Solomon said. "I know she's been safe with you, but its time for her to leave this place. Time to leave Thailand."

He opened the case and took out one of the passports he'd been carrying. "I've got a passport for her. She may not be able to return to the U.S. for now but I can get her to France or England."

Sigmund released a boyish smile. "Germany's a good place."

"Haven't ruled it out, but I don't know if she's ready for a Teutonic life of beer and brats," Solomon said.

Sigmund patted his rotund middle. "It was good to me."

Solomon reached back into the case and pulled out the Les Baer and the clip that held her children. He slid the clip inside the pistol. Locked it. He took out the holster and strapped it around his shoulder then covered it with his jacket.

"Make sure you take the money with you," Sigmund said.

Solomon opened the front door, refused to acknowledge his friend's rejection of his gesture.

The doctor watched Solomon as he made his way gingerly to the car. "You take care of yourself, you hear." He hesitated. "Tell me something?"

Solomon stood still.

"The girl. She is your daughter, no? That is why you risk your life for her, isn't it?

Solomon returned Sigmund's question with a subtle smile then climbed into the car without saying another word. He watched the warm yellow glow of Sigmund's house dissolve into the night air as the world turned black with a flick of a light switch.

Solomon pulled out of Sigmund's property with his head on a swivel checking for car lights or a glint of metal that might be caught by the moon's glow. He retraced his path down a narrow street, past flat roofed houses and by the old Buddhist Temple with the empty eyes that stood guard over the town of Chon Buri. Said a silent prayer then headed to the Bangna-Trat Highway and south. It would be after midnight when he'd arrive at Pattaya Island.

Solomon thought of the irony. Pattaya Island, a tropical paradise for many contrasted by Pattaya Prison in the heart of Bangkok. He thought there must've been a reason why the Thai named a prison after a tropical paradise or maybe it was an example of some sick Thai humor.

Chapter Forty-Nine

Solomon glanced at his watch. It was almost one in the morning and Pattya City was still awake. He decided to check into the Beach Hotel first, ask a few questions then hit the streets to look for the girl if he had the strength.

The sign in front of the hotel read "Reservations Only", but Solomon knew that there is always a footnote that should be posted on any sign in Thailand. It would read: Cash is king. You got cash then you're king.

He walked into the hotel lobby, eyed the surroundings. It wasn't The Oriental but it was nice and quaint, the kind of place young partying tourists from Europe and the States would gravitate to because it was right on the Pattaya Bay.

Solomon strode right up to the front desk and the sleepy eyed young man sitting behind the counter. Solomon figured he was about twenty years old, maybe even younger. Probably surfed the bay during the day and acted as part-time tour guide whenever he could coax some young women on holiday to spend their money. Getting laid was probably easy especially when hotel rooms were at a premium.

Black hair pulled back into a ponytail with a few strands dropping over his round face he used one arm like a crutch for his head. He had his head down. Sleep was getting the best of him.

Solomon slapped the counter with one broad hand. The kid jumped and pushed his body upright. He curled his lips, said, "What the fu…?" Looked up at the tall American standing in front of him then cleared his throat. "May I help you?'

"Need a room," Solomon said.

The young man gave Solomon an impassive shrug. "No rooms. You come back tomorrow."

Solomon leaned close and pointed to his watch. "It's already tomorrow."

"Nice watch. You come back in afternoon. Maybe, room available then."

Solomon reached for his wallet. The young man flinched a little like he might've thought that Solomon was reaching for a gun.

Solomon returned with a faint smile. He figured the young desk clerk was probably a satellite MTV/BET victim like Lulu with stereotypical notions about African-American culture the way it's generally portrayed in videos. Sure, he was a black man with a gun, but he wasn't going to use it to get a hotel room. Instead, he peeled off a hundred dollar bill and placed it on the counter.

"How bout you move check-in time to right now?"

The clerk smiled wide. He acted like he was checking the hotel registry for this game of cat and mouse. "Ah, yes. Just notice. We got cancellation. Bungalow on beach is vacant. How many nights?"

"Two," Solomon said.

"That be one...ah, no. That be two hundred dollar."

"Here's three. The extra is for a wake up call and privacy," Solomon said.

"Privacy?"

"Anyone asks I'm not here. Anyone asks you let me know. Understand?"

The clerk nodded.

Solomon reached into his jacket and pulled out a passport booklet. He opened it on the desk and flipped it around so the clerk could see the image inside. "Seen this girl?"

The young man's eyes displayed recognition, but his stilled lips wouldn't commit him to an answer.

Solomon peeled off a fifty-dollar bill, the equivalent of a week's pay. "Maybe, this will help you to remember."

The young man nodded. ""Pretty girl. Yes, me see her here last night. She check out this morning. She meet friends from the Caribbean. Jamaica I think."

"Any idea where they were going?"

"I see them guys here all the time. They surf. Hit clubs hard. They come every year to Pattaya."

"You didn't answer my question."

"Lot of foreigners stay at condos on the other side of the Bay. You might find them there catching waves in the morning. Night, they with crowds on Walking Street, hitting clubs and bars."

Solomon pulled the passport away and placed it back in his pocket. "You say these Jamaicans or whatever come here every year."

"Right."

"I take it they don't just come here for the sun and sand."

The clerk shook his head. "They do business. Import-export."

"Were you here when the girl checked out?"

"Sure, I here."

"She looked stressed?" Solomon asked.

The clerk frowned, looked confused.

"Did she look like she was having a good time or a bad time?" Solomon exaggerated his smile. "Was she smiling when she left here?"

The clerk nodded. "Ah, yes. She very happy. She with black man. Him tall, like you. He spend night in her room. They drive off in big, black Mercedes with his friends."

Solomon held his breath. "Who were the friends?"

The young man lifted his shoulders and rounded them back into the poor posture he'd had when Solomon first approached. "Young guys with dreads. You know, like island guys."

"Could any of them have been from the U.S.?"

"Don't know. I never hear them talk."

Solomon picked his leather case off the floor and waited as the clerk retrieved a key to his room.

"You have to sign book," the clerk said pointing to the hotel register.

Solomon said nothing. He turned the book around and signed his name. Scanned the page quickly with his eyes. Saw the name, Desdemona Reynolds handwritten near the top of the page. He took the key and started towards the door.

The clerk smiled wide. He still had the money in his hand. Four hundred bucks could be stretched far here. Ganja for a week, a new surfboard. The clerk would party the money away. He regarded the tall American with the cane and distinctive limp.

"You have good evening Mister Richard Reynolds."

Solomon kept walking. Sleep would be best right then. In the morning he'd scour the beach and find her.

*   *   *

He slept in his clothes. The sun shook him like a lover wanting to copulate once again before she'd scurry on home. She'd leave him still tired and begging for more---sleep. His sleep was like morning sex, gasping for that last taste of coition, hoping that it might be enough to last until the next time. It wasn't enough but Solomon had to get up, tired or not.

He stretched. Not much shoulder pain this time. He went through his routine then showered. Cargo pants with big pouches on the sides and a linen shirt left open would be his uniform for the early morning. Solomon topped it off with a white straw hat, gangster style. Sharp, but utilitarian. It was already nearly ninety degrees outside and the sun was beating down on him like Tyson in his heyday.

He climbed into his rental car. Had some second thoughts about leaving the Les Baer in his room, but if "Desdemona" was just hanging out with a couple of Jamaican drug dealers he wouldn't need any firepower.

He walked the beach for about an hour. No girl, No Jamaicans. Plenty of brown skin, but not that kind of brown.

Too much exposure in the sunlight could be a bad thing. Not the sun itself. Solomon wouldn't crack, but an American roaming the beaches might get noticed. Those Bangkok cops who worked for Ping hadn't given up trying to find him. He knew it. Detective Giapong seemed like a relentless soul driven by mob money. He'd go to the end of the earth to find the man he'd set up as the killer of the little jeweler.

Solomon retreated to a café for coffee and breakfast. He sat on the patio sipping and eating, watching people watching people.

He caught a glimpse of what looked like a lion's head. Hair plummeting down a man's back in thick black rolls---clumped and knotted. Glistening black skin with small beads of sweat resting on their shoulders like jewels. The pace of Solomon's heart quickened. He was one of a small group of young black men.

He picked up his cup and walked over to the group. He stood by them in silence until one of them noticed him. He was short and brown wearing an Afro like Solomon himself once wore back in the Seventies.

"Can I help you brudder mahn?" Afro said.

Solomon gave him a cordial smile. Tried not to look threatening. "I haven't seen many brothers here. Just thought I'd stop and say, hello."

Afro said, hello then returned to his conversation with his two friends. Solomon stood there patiently.

The young man with the dreadlocks looked up at Solomon. He extended a long arm and pointed to an empty chair at the table. "Come join us, Pops. We just hahvin' some morning java. You must be American. Where you from?"

Solomon took a seat, rested his cane on the edge of the table. "D.C."

"You here on holiday?" asked the tall man with the dreads.

"Not exactly." Solomon pulled out Desdemona's passport picture. "I'm looking for this girl. Seen her?"

All three young men leaned over the picture, one snickered. "That's a fine ass woman. Your daughter, Pops?"

"Yeah. She got separated from her momma and me last night. We just want to make sure she's all right."

Tall dreadlocks said, "She legal, right?"

Solomon nodded.

"Then you got nut-tin to worry bout."

Solomon's face tightened. "I don't know what it is about this place. I can't get a straight answer from anyone. The clerk at the hotel said she left yesterday with three black men."

Dreadlocks said, "So, you figure she left with us." He gave his friends a cruel smile then looked over at Solomon. "I'd say dat's a case of racial profiling, brudder mahn. Me friends and I don't take kindly to dat so just take you old ahss away from here fo' you get hurt."

Solomon stared out into the distance then looked around the café. "You're right. I apologize, my young Jamaican brothers. You brothers have any children?" he asked. "If you do then someday you'll understand."

Dreadlocks waved Solomon away. "Sounds like you got a problem and we don't got de answer so get da fuck outta here before you gets hurt."

His friends leaned menacingly towards Solomon. He took a long sip from his coffee. "Hey, I'm sorry, my brothers. I don't want any trouble. I'll just finish my coffee and go."

He put his cup down on the table as the young men resumed their conversation like he had already gone. Solomon stood up and reached for his cane. He quickly pulled the blade out, placed its sharp tip right into Dreadlock's hair, just enough to touch the base of the young man's neck. He looked around the café and at the crowd that seemed oblivious to the man with a sword ready to impale his young adversary into the table.

Solomon whispered, "Look, my *brother*. You got a choice. Either you can take this blade right through the back of your neck and eat the rest of your croissant off of it or you can tell me where I can find the girl."

Dreadlocks seemed too scared to move. He sat rigid with his back straight. "Are you fuckin' crazy, mahn? Look around. Dere's people everywhere. No way you get away wit dis, mahn." His boys did a slow rise from their chairs then hesitated.

"You're probably right, but you'll be dead or paralyzed. Either way it won't change the outcome of our little meeting if you don't tell me what I want to hear. So I want you to tell Frick and Frack to sit back down and put their hands on the table where I can see them."

Dreadlocks nodded to his two friends and they eased back into their seats like a pair of trained Dobermans.

"Yeah, me wit her last night. But she ghosted on me this mornin'. Me get up and she gone. Haven't seen her."

"Heard you been hanging out with her for a couple of days. She must've told you something like where she was going."

"She say nut-tin, mahn. Bitch fine, but freaked out like she see ghost or some-teen."

Solomon leaned on the blade just a little.

"Ow! Fuck mahn! What is your problem?"

"Bitch. You called her, Bitch!"

"I'm bleeding, mahn!"

"Just a surface wound. Now I want you to tell me in the nicest way you can. Any clues about where she was going?"

"Nut-tin mahn. Just she say saw dis cat from Thailand. Got real nervous. I say me boys got yo' back, Sweet thang, but she act scared, real scared."

"Describe him."

"Describe who?"

"The guy she saw."

"He Thai. Big. Bald head. Look like some kind of movie villain."

"What else?"

"She say she trying to get back to the U.S. Needed money real bad."

290

"Did you give her any money?"

"Mahn, what you tink I am? Some trick or some-teen? I told dee bit---, I mean, I told dee young lady dat I couldn't help her. But shit, she had heat! Mahn she scared me waving dat piece around. Glad she gone."

Solomon stood there then looked around the café. The waiters and patrons were suspended. They all looked like a still life painting. He smiled, politely then bowed. "Ladies and gentlemen, you have just witnessed a scene from the upcoming Hollywood movie, *Thailand Vice*. The camera's are hidden in the car parked out front."

The room stayed quiet then one by one the patrons began clapping until they erupted into a hardy applause. Someone shouted, "Oscar! Oscar!"

Solomon bowed. He pressed the blade against Dreadlock's neck. "Bow," he said.

The young man with the braids dipped his head and gave a sheepish smile to the audience. He waved one hand and reserved a scowl for Solomon. He spoke out of the corner of his mouth. "Me ain't bout to forget dis, old man."

"I hope you don't," Solomon told him. "Don't get up. I can see myself out."

Solomon put the blade back into his cane and moved steadily in the direction of the "camera-car." He thought, *Ping's here. Probably with that damn detective. I need to find her fast and leave.*

Chapter Fifty

Solomon's worst fears had come to roost. Ping was in Pattaya City, probably with Detective Giapong running interference with the local constables and in hot pursuit of the girl. He hoped seeing Ping might've spooked her into going back to Sigmund's place. He flipped open his cellphone and dialed.

"Sig?"

Yah?

"It's me. Hey, I'm down here in Pattaya. Ran into some young Jamaicans. Say they'd been hanging out with the girl."

Well, you know she's young. She have fun. That is good.

"She's not back there with you is she?"

Nein. Sigmund let out a heavy sigh. *You are troubled my friend?*

"Yeah. The men I told you about are down here. They may have found her."

What are you going to do?

"Do what I have to do. I'm going to find her---find them."

They'll kill you both. You can't do this alone. I'll come there. I will help you.

Solomon laughed. "And what are you going to do? Threaten them with that old blunder buss you keep hidden under your chair?"

I may not be able to hit anything with it but it will scare the hell out of anyone within a mile.

"No. They need you there. It's too dangerous. I'll find her, give them what they want."

Silence.

They will kill you both.

"That's a chance I'll have to take. I've run out of options, Sig."

There are always options. Call the authorities. These men are not above the law.

"They **are** the law here. Did you mail that package for me?"

I did, but they will want the jewels. If you had them maybe you could negotiate with them. I could come there, tell them that I know where it is and if they want it they'll let you both go.

"You'd come here and the townspeople would no longer have their doctor. Look, don't worry. I'll figure something out. The Jamaicans said she took off when she saw Ping and his cohorts. She's got a gun and as we both know she's capable of using it."

They know that as well, my friend.

"Look, I got a go. Do you have someplace you can stay for the next couple of days?"

Hah! This is my home. I make my stand here. No place else. If they come here I will be waiting.

"I know you will, Sig. I know you will. If you don't hear from me tomorrow call my lawyer. O.K?"

The one you had me mail the package too?

"Yes. He'll know what to do. And can you do me one more favor?"

Anything.

"If this doesn't work out please go to Bangkok. Tell her what happened. Tell her I tried to do the right thing. Most of all, tell her that my lawyer is going to help her and not to give up hope."

*You will tell her these things yourself, my friend. You are, as we say in my language, **entschlossen**. You are a man of great resolve.*

Solomon let out a half-hearted laugh. "It'll take more than resolve to get through this."

And prayers.

Solomon closed his cellphone without saying goodbye to Sigmund. There was something symbolic about praying and in his case, morbid.

He thought about Sigmund's last words. Solomon wasn't a praying man. He'd always thought that prayer was for the desperate or the needy, but maybe this was that point in his life when prayer was all he had. He hadn't talked to God in fifty-six years even when he was looking at the wrong end of a gun. Maybe it was time, he thought. Or maybe, it was too late.

Chapter Fifty-One

The lobby at the Beach Hotel and Resort was quiet save the incessant ticking of the large wooden clock that seemed to be the centerpiece of this tropical respite for the travel weary. But for Solomon Fortunada the scene reminded him of something out of an old Western movie. Tombstone's or Dodge City's ghostly prescient reminder that the good townspeople disappear when the bandits come to town.

Solomon moved with caution through the lobby and over to the front desk. No clerk in sight, the whole place seemed deserted. He thought, *maybe they're between shifts*. But all he wanted to do was check in case anyone called.

Maybe, someone had told her that he was in town looking for her. Maybe, her Jamaican friends had warned her about the older black man with a distinctive limp and a cane that doubled as a sword. She'd come looking for him, he thought. Her fear alone would be the reason.

He hit the bell. Hit it again. Waited.

Seconds later and the office door opened. The sleepy eyed clerk who'd checked him in the night before must've been taking a nap. He rubbed his eyes, scratched his head.

"Long night?" Solomon said.

The kid smiled, slightly. "Yeah." He gave an Eastern style greeting, head bowed for a milli-second. "How are you Mr. Richard Reynolds?"

Solomon smiled at the young man's formality. And the name. No one had addressed him as Richard Reynolds in a long time. "Just wanted to check to see if anyone called me."

The clerk turned and walked over to a small rack of boxes. Went to the one marked with the letter, "R".

"No nothing for you, Mr. Reynolds but men came here. Have picture. Say, 'Have you seen this man?"

"What did you tell them?"

He laughed. "They show picture say man name, Solomon. I say, never heard of man name Solomon. I say, no. Not see man in picture. Not a rat. Besides, you pay me not to talk, right?"

"What did they look like?"

"One say he cop. Show me card with name, Detective Giapong. He have big mean looking man with him. Bald head, angry smile. Don't think he police."

Solomon muttered, "Ping."

"They looking for girl, too."

"Really?"

That was good news for Solomon. They hadn't found her yet, but the news added to his sense of urgency.

"I see girl before I come to work. She in restaurant wearing sunglasses, looking scared."

"Where?"

"On Walking Street."

Solomon thought that it must've been the place where he confronted her Jamaican friends.

"Was she alone?"

"Yeah. But she keep looking around. Hiding behind newspaper. She have strange look on face. Leave fast."

"Did you see the Jamaicans anywhere in the restaurant?"

"No. They not there. Cops not there either."

Solomon reached for his wallet and pulled out three crisp hundred-dollar bills. He handed the money to the young clerk who returned the offering with a look of confusion.

"What this for?"

"It's part insurance, part gratitude. Have any idea where I might find her?"

The clerk folded the bills and stuck them inside his pants pocket. Solomon knew it would go the way of the other money he'd given him. The young man would spend it in a big way and would probably have a hangover the next day to match the one he was fighting through this day.

The clerk smiled wide. "She probably go to club tonight. Most Americans go to Hollywood Disco on South Road. You find her there---for sure."

The young man put his head down like he was studying the pages of the hotel register laid out before him then jerked his eyes upward at Solomon. "Oh. Almost forget. There was one other."

"What are you talking about?"

"Another one. Another woman looking for you. Asian, very beautiful. Not Thai, though. Maybe, she Vietnamese. Not sure. She speak English, no accent."

"She leave a name?"

Solomon asked the question but he already knew the answer. It wasn't good news knowing that some Asian woman was looking for him. In fact, her coming there was bad news and dangerous--- probably more dangerous than Ping and Detective Giapong prowling around town trying to find the girl and the jewels.

"You very lucky man, Mr. Solomon. Woman real hot. Much sexy."

"Yeah, I know. You didn't tell her anything, did you?"

He shook his head. "She say she girlfriend. Want to surprise you. Flew all the way from U.S. just to see you."

He opened a wide smile.

"She have raincoat on. Act like it open without knowing. She show body, nice and smooth. Black fishnet stockings and nothing but bra and panties underneath."

Solomon could see that the clerk was now totally lost in his thoughts and oblivious to anything going on in the world for the moment. He snapped his fingers like a hypnotist restoring his subject to reality. The kid jerked his head and brought his mind back to the moment.

"Seeing a little skin didn't make you tell her about me, did it?" Solomon said.

The young man feigned indignation with a frown and twisted lips. "No, no way man. I tell her I don't know any man name, Richard Reynolds. Then she mention another name. Ask if man name Mr. Reynolds or Mr. Powell stay at hotel. I say, no."

Solomon imagined how the woman must've tempted the young clerk, but that was her way. She had grown up the way of the seductress, getting what she wanted with a smile and alluring dark eyes. She figured she could beguile the clerk who could only dream of being with a woman like her and he'd tell her anything she wanted to know.

Solomon left the lobby thinking that leaving without the girl was not an option. He decided to stop at a café near the beach to meditate and think over a shot of Courvosier.

Bad guys everywhere. Sue When had come from the States, she could be working with Ping or freelancing. Either way, the risk to him had increased ten-fold with her being in Thailand. He ran over his plan quickly through his mind. Find the girl. Get the hell out of Pattaya City, back to Bangkok and then leave the country forever.

*　　*　　*

He took a minute to survey his rented bungalow as he stood near the swimming pool just outside the hotel lobby. He thought about checking with the desk clerk one more time to see if anyone had returned there looking for him. But he didn't.

Solomon had had second thoughts about leaving his gun in his room but he decided that it was better not to tote it around during the day. It was hard to conceal wearing light beachwear.

He had hidden it inside his room just in case some nosy maid might see it. Even if someone like Ping had managed to get inside his room he figured they wouldn't find his weapon.

He cracked the door open slightly, peeked inside then jerked his head back. The room was just as he'd left it. He held on to his cane with his right hand on the handle and left on the shaft. A false sound or movement from inside would make him draw the blade like Zorro. But the blade was no match for a nine-millimeter.

He looked down towards the floor for the thin black thread he had tied across the doorway. It was still intact. Solomon closed the door behind him. A darkened room greeted him. He kept it that way just in case someone might pass by and think it was occupied. There was dim light from a full moon cascading its way through a slightly open curtain. It was enough light to see.

But the stillness of his surroundings mad him uneasy. His senses heightened by something close to fear spoke loudly that all wasn't well. The faint smell of perfume violated the clinical aroma of hotel. Solomon was now wishing he hadn't left his gun in the room. He made a slow movement towards a lamp near the bungalow's front door.

"Don't bother turning the light on."

Solomon froze. "Sue When?"

Moonlight coming through the window, between the crack in the curtains reflected its glow off chrome-plated death. He could see the image of her hand and a gun coming together like they were one.

"I like the name Solomon Fortunada. It has a certain ring. Why don't you have a seat *Solomon?*"

She waved the gun like it was a conductor's baton. "Slow and easy," she said.

He sat in a chair about six feet away from where Sue was sitting. The light from the moon was cast directly on his face so that she could see him. "Too bad about the kid at the front desk."

Solomon took a deep breath. "What do you mean?"

"Him not telling me you were here, he'd still be alive. And you, I guess you're slipping or getting tired. You registered here under Richard Reynolds? Didn't you think someone would check?"

Solomon acknowledged with a head nod. "You must've killed him while I was down at the bar. Let's get right to it, Sue. What do you want?"

"Two things. I wanted to see for myself that you were still alive. The other is the jewels."

"I don't get. Correct me, if I'm wrong but from what I hear you took the twenty million dollars Ping and his people were going to pay for Desdemona."

Sue leaned forward into the moonlight so that Solomon could see the intensity in her eyes. She wanted him to see that she was holding the gun with a purpose. "They don't know I took the money. I guess they think that little girl ran off with it after she killed everyone in the warehouse."

"So it's greed, huh."

"Twenty million is good. Forty is better."

Solomon forced a subdued laugh. "You really think they will pay you another twenty million after they lost their money and still don't have the diamond?"

"Different buyer. And you're going to give me Desdemona." Sue paused. "Actually I'm going to take it."

"I don't have it."

"I think you do and if its not here you'll tell me where I can find it. You know the cane's a nice touch. Makes you look distinguished. I must say you look real good for a man who's presumed to be dead."

"They say I'm resilient. The cane is necessary. One of the bullets I took was in the leg. It's coming back but I don't move as well as I used to."

Sue took a deep breath and nearly let out a sigh. "You know I'm going to kill you, don't you?"

He nodded.

"I don't have many options. I don't want to kill you but you know I have Ping's mone…"

"The girls know that you have it, too."

"I don't think either one is in a position to talk to Ping. I guess what I'm saying is that I've got to kill you either way--- whether you give me the real Desdemona or not. So you might as well let me have it. She's no good to any of you."

"I'd see you in hell Sue before I'll give you that stone!"

"It'll be a good place for us to finally re-unite, to be together after all these years. You know when I said you were slipping I really meant it. The black thread across the door? You've been doing that since I first met you. What is it, a prison thing? But leaving your gun here in the bathroom for me to find it? You never would've done that fifteen, twenty years ago."

She raised the Les Baer with her other hand, but didn't point it at him. "I'd never shoot a man with his own gun."

Solomon said, "I didn't think guns were your style. A stiletto blade at close range. Guns are so antiseptic, so impersonal."

Sue laughed. "You are *so right*. Besides, I'd never mess up that pretty face of yours with a big hole going right through it. You know, live hard, die young and leave a beautiful corpse."

She put the Les Baer on the table between them, but out of Solomon's reach. She kept an eye and her own gun trained on him as she reached inside her purse and pulled out a wicked knife with a curved blade.

He laughed with a hint of contempt. "You actually think I'd let you rip me up with that thing?"

"I still have the gun. I can shoot you at any time." Sue reached inside her purse once again and pulled out a pair of handcuffs. "Put these on just in case." She tossed them over to Solomon.

He caught them with one hand as he slid his cane between his legs. He clamped one cuff on his right wrist and the other on his left. His mind was turning, trying to think of something, think of a way to stop her. But he was quickly running out of options.

Sue rose to her feet. She used her foot to move the table aside. Solomon watched his Les Baer move further away along with the table. It didn't matter anyway. Her chamber was empty. The children were in the clip and hidden under his mattress. Sue moved easy with a sensuous kind of rhythm about her as she drew even closer to where Solomon sat anxiously.

"I imagine it's been a while since you've been with a woman." She loosened her coat and allowed it to fall to the floor at her feet. Sue gave Solomon the full view, the view that the young desk clerk had only caught a glimpse of, the one now held behind his dead eyes.

"What is this some kind of sick fantasy?" Solomon asked.

"Yeah, probably. I could ride you then kill you. Watch you go soft as the blood leaves you."

Sue dropped to her knees and moved towards Solomon. She reached for his belt buckle with one hand while the other held the knife at the ready.

"You don't really want to do this, Sue."

"The sex?"

"No. You don't really want to kill me."

"You're right." She unzipped your pants then moved between his legs and laid his cane to one side letting it rest on his thigh. She said, "So many years. So much wasted time. You could've had this. You could've had me."

"We can still be together, Sue. We'll leave this place start a life." Solomon's words were labored and breathy.

"As long as you're alive, baby neither one of us is safe. You know the people here in Thailand. They'll track us down and kill us no matter where we try to hide---especially if we're together. Alone I don't exist, they don't look for me. With you dead, the trail goes cold."

With those words Sue started kissing Solomon on his neck then worked her way over his collarbone and chest. With each soft kiss he felt the corresponding sting of her knife's blade as it took a different course along his side. His chest heaved at the touch of the knife and he held his breath.

"No sudden moves baby or I'll finish you off before I'm finished," Sue said then went about her task.

What would have been pleasurable was being overridden by pain. The blade was cutting him, his fluids ebbed out of his body, breathing deepened. Solomon said, "S-S-S-Sue! Don't!" But the knife touched him deeper.

He thought; *this is it!*

But Sue was engrossed in her pleasure-pain adventure, so much so that she didn't feel his subtle movements as Solomon grab hold of his cane with his cuffed hands. He slid the blade out from its shaft and held it low waiting for the right moment when she was deeply absorbed. He had a pained expression on his face as he searched for her eyes but she was engrossed in her task with her head now buried in his lap.

He shook his head from side to side fighting thoughts of regret against his own need to survive. One subtle move with his hand and he plunged the blade into her side. She gasped hard, rolled her eyes upward to meet his. He shook his head. "I'm sorry," he said.

Solomon watched Sue as she gently fell to the floor. Her breathing shallow, blood spewing from the precise incision on her side. A breathy, "I'm sorry, too."

He quickly found the key and removed the cuffs from his hands then made his way to the bathroom, washed any evidence of Sue off his body then came back for her lifeless corpse. He placed Sue in the bathtub the way the little jeweler in Bangkok had been unceremoniously dumped in Solomon's hotel bathroom. He gave her, her last rites, mumbled a prayer for the damned.

He picked up the Les Baer and loaded the clip. He brought along five extra clips as a back up and Solomon thought he could take out a small army.

The clubs on Walking Street usually didn't start drawing customers until nearly midnight. After that people would drink and dance at a frenzied pace until the morning. If he had any hope of finding the girl he knew it would be in one of Pattaya's many dance clubs.

Money and a passport with her photo on it gave him an advantage over Ping and the others searching for her. He could flash her picture around town and offer cash for any credible information. Solomon figured it wouldn't take long for someone to tell him that they'd seen a young African-American woman shaking it up at one of the city's discos. But he also realized that Ping and his paid for detective would be asking the same questions.

Solomon, however, was hoping that she'd be smart. Hoping she was hiding out. Hoping most of all that she'd gone back to Sigmund's home running scared---but he knew she hadn't. Sigmund would've called, told him she's safe. Besides, she was a young woman who'd been cooped up working at a medical clinic in a small village outside of Bangkok. Cleaning bedpans and changing diapers for sick children and sicker adults would drive anyone to take a chance just to let her hair down.

He convinced himself that she was safe, that no one would find her before he did. It was a chess match, though. If Ping and Giapong find her he'll know. They would come there to his nice little bungalow off the Gulf of Pattaya and find him, try to barter or trade her for the jewels.

They'd know where to find him despite the hotel clerk's denials. The young man had told them he was there, Solomon knew that much. He'd given Solomon up to them, had the page with his name in the hotel registry open for them to see. But he had carelessly left it open on that page and Solomon had seen the name, Richard Reynolds, too. Ironically, the kid had died for not doing as much for Sue.

She had a way about her, a way of being persuasive when her good looks weren't enough. He had always thought of her as a beautiful rose with deadly thorns. She could kill without remorse and her flower would still bloom.

Chapter Fifty-Two

Hello Boss.

Solomon strained to recognize the voice. He glanced at the number displayed on the screen of his cellphone. It was Non, the bellhop at the Oriental Hotel.

"Oh, Non. How you doing, man?"

Fine, boss, fine. I call to tell you I pick up vehicle tomorrow. I'm so happy. Me and friend ready for movie part.

"That's good. I'm in…" He paused, thought better than to tell anyone where he was. "I'm out of town looking at other film locations. I'll be back in Bangkok tomorrow or the day after."

Very good. Me very, very excited.

"I'm glad. Maybe the next time I shoot a movie in Bangkok I'll write you in for a starring role."

Solomon wanted to amuse himself with Hollywood talk, but Non seemed like a nice guy, too nice to jerk around by making false promises of stardom. But he had to keep up the ruse, keep the little bellhop on board.

He added, "Now even if I don't make in time for the shoot you do exactly what I told you to do."

What about cameras and makeup? Who direct me?

"This is a reality type movie, Non. All you do is drive to the place where my crew will be shooting. The cameras are hidden, so don't worry about them. A large woman in a uniform will come out of the building along with the actresses. You help the girl on the gurney get inside then take off. The large woman in uniform will tell you where to go. O.K.?"

Got it, boss.

Solomon could sense his exuberance through the telephone. "Remember, once you reach the destination that's the end of your part. Don't stick around or mingle with the crew or other actors. Remember the cameras will still be rolling so I want you to take off fast. I'll call you later, if I'm not there and let you know when the screening will take place. You ready to go to Hollywood?"

Ah, yes, yes. Me ready to go. Can't wait for family to see me on big screen.

"Good. I'll see you in a couple of days"

Oh, oh boss. Did you know man got killed here at hotel?

Solomon hesitated. "No, didn't know that. What? Some kind of accident?"

No, boss. Man murdered right here. Never happen at Oriental. No trouble. Never!

"Did they catch the person who did it?"

No, not yet. Say American kill man over some business deal.

"That's sad, Non. Hope they catch the bastard."

Solomon closed his cellphone. He looked out the window from inside his rented bungalow. Non's call had jolted him from his nap, but he needed to wake up and set about his task of finding the girl. He had two days to make it all happen.

He thought about how everything had to go like clockwork. In the midst of it all he'd have to avoid Ping and Detective Giapong, get the girl and get her back to Bangkok. Of course the ruse with Non had to go on without a hitch or the plan would be doomed.

He took a deep breath and put the Les Baer to rest on the table. Ping knew he was there and Solomon had expected him and who knows who to come bursting through his door any minute. He had fallen asleep facing that door with gun in hand.

Solomon would open fire on anyone who'd dare to enter. He just hoped it wouldn't be the housemaid.

*   *   *

One more telephone call to Sigmund before he'd hit the streets of Pattaya searching.

"She make it back?"

Nein. Now, I am starting to worry. I would come there and search for her, but I have sick children here. I cannot leave them.

"Sigmund, don't worry. I'll find her."

But you are running out of time.

"You're right, but I don't have a choice. I've got to find her and get out of here."

You might have to make a choice, my friend.

"And what choice is that, Sigmund?"

Can't tell you, but you may not be able to save both of them.

Solomon inhaled and released his breath hard out into the air and into the telephone. "Can't choose, Sig. How can I make a choice?"

It's a difficult position for you to be in. I wish I could help. I'm attached to her. She's been here with me ever since...(pause) Well, you know, but I can't tell you.

"Well, if I don't find her by tomorrow and get back to Bangkok in time then they're both lost."

Let me tell you a story, my friend. Maybe it will help you. There was a man standing on the shore. The ocean out in front of him. Suddenly, he sees a small boat capsize. There are two men on board---one very large, the other very small.

The man on the shore is not a great swimmer and regardless of what he does he can save one man, but the other will surely drown. What do you think he will do?

Solomon laughed, slightly. "Save the little guy?"

No, no. He saved the big man, even though in doing so it put his own life at risk.

"And the meaning of this little parable?"

Well, he saved the large man because he figured that although his burden would be heavier, the thought of the small man dying would not lay as heavy on his conscience. You're right, it's a parable. More like a metaphor. You must make the choice, if you must, that will not lay as heavy on your conscience.

Solomon laughed. "Parable, huh. You made that up."

Hey, I'm German. My name is Sigmund. What would you expect?

"I thought you're an M.D. not a shrink."

Out here, to these people, I'm a little bit of both.

Sigmund's words stayed with Solomon as he began his preparations to go out and roam the streets and nightclubs of Pattaya City. He wouldn't have to make a choice between whose life he'd save, but he realized that sometimes choices are made for you.

He made his way to the dresser and looked in the mirror. Regarded his features. There were a few extra lines around his eyes that weren't there when he first arrived in Thailand. He tried to smooth them away with his fingers, but resigned himself to their existence. His face was becoming a landscape sown with the seeds of worry and anxiety.

His thoughts flashed to another place. A tropical setting, an island of peace where death didn't linger over him. Not the unnatural kind.

He dressed himself in a silk shirt and white cotton pants. He wrapped his holster around his left shoulder then slid the Les Baer inside. Concealed it with a navy blue sports jacket. Topped off everything with a white straw hat with a wide brim. He looked at his image in the mirror, smoothed the brim down Al Capone style. If he had to go down he'd look good on the way.

One last goodbye to Sue and he left the bungalow on the beach. Police cars were pulling up to the hotel lobby. Solomon knew that the young desk clerk's body had been found. They'd search every room and bungalow at the hotel, find Sue's lifeless body and make a connection. They'd go back to the hotel registry and see the name, Richard Reynolds, which would send them into a frenzied search for the man they presumed to be dead, lying somewhere deep in the river near the prison.

Chapter Fifty-Three

Four horsemen.

Four apocalyptic horsemen bearing down on me. Horses with nostrils flaring breathing fire, angry hooves and body armor coming right at me. Hooded riders without faces urging them on and I can't move.

I'm standing over bodies with a gun in my hand. Carnage all around me and I can't move.

"Dahlia! Dahlia Reynolds! You all right?"

A voice breaks through into my sub-consciousness. It's Lulu saving me from myself.

"Wake up, Dahlia Reynolds! You have bad dream."

I force my eyes open, shake the images from my thoughts. I must've been talking in my sleep. I'd had this dream before Lulu arrived next door. And each time I'd awaken, my body cold and wet, my cotton jumpsuit sticking to me like a second layer of skin. The only difference this time was that I could tell one of the riders was a woman.

"Sorry, Lulu. You're right I was having a nightmare. I have them all the time, ever since I've been in this place."

"Lulu have bad dream sometime."

"Yeah, I guess everyone does. Mine are intense, scary. Sometimes I wish I was already dead. When I see them coming after me the way I do in my dreams I just wish it was all over. I don't want to dream anymore."

I think about what I just said, pose a question that I know Lulu can't answer. "Do you think we dream when we're dead?" I ask.

"Yes, we dream, always. I learn as little child that mind has no limit, go beyond this Earth?"

I laugh. "Are you sure you're only seventeen?"

"You go anyplace your mind take you," Lulu tells me. "In my culture we say, be still like a mountain and flow like a great river."

I ponder her words, but the quote confuses me. I can't draw out any real meaning to them. "What does that mean, Lulu?"

"Different things for different people. For me, it mean let spirit change where you are not other way around. Be many things at same time. Be like mountain, be strong. Flow like river, change as things change."

Her words make me think. I can meditate out of my dreary existence, take myself to a different place. Although Lulu quoted the words of someone else her insight amazes me and she sounds much older than seventeen.

"What do you plan to do when you get out of here?" I ask her.

Silence.

She hears me, but doesn't speak. Thinking.

Finally.

"I go back to work. Hope to earn money. Someday me go to Hollywood."

"You want to be an actress?" I ask.

"No, Lulu make movies. Tell stories. I like your stories Dahlia Reynolds. Someday I tell your story in movie."

I think about what she says realizing she'll have plenty of material by the time my story finishes. And she has her own story to tell, which is probably more interesting than my own.

"Lulu, why can't you just leave, quit working the clubs and streets, quit looking for boyfriends and leave?"

"Not easy. Lulu must pay to leave work for good. It costs more money than Lulu have. Take five more year to pay man who owns contract for services."

"And what would happen if you just left town when you get out of here?"

"They find Lulu. They many, many men evil men. They kill Lulu if I run. Torture family.

"What about the police? Can't you call them and tell them how you're being forced to sell your body?"

I hear her laugh quietly.

"Seriously, wouldn't they protect you? You're still a child in most societies. There are laws."

"Here, no law to help me. No police to help. The men I speak of own police like they own Lulu. Police laugh, turn heads, put money in pockets. The big man, how you say, boss? Real important man in Thailand. Very rich, very important. He above law."

I guess government corruption is universal. I understand now why she feels trapped. Lulu's plight is no better than my own. Sure, she may not die in five or six months, but her future seems as bleak as mine.

Lulu has been in Pattaya Prison for three days now and I haven't seen her face to face. We eat, shower and relax for a few minutes everyday in the courtyard without crossing paths. At times I think she avoids me preferring to talk under a cloak of anonymity.

Chapter Fifty-four

"Hear they find man's body in river not too far from here. Say black man been shot. Think he's prisoner who escaped months ago." Lulu goes quiet for a moment. "Maybe, your sister dump Mac's body. Maybe, they find Mac in river."

"I don't know Lulu. I haven't heard from Charity. I hope she isn't dead, too."

I wait for the jailer who brings our food daily with a rude shove through the opening underneath my jail cell door and a scowl instead of garnish. But judging by the setting sun it is still early for dinner.

I used to think that the prison officials wait until dark to serve us dinner so we can't see the garbage they feed us. I guess it's their way of being merciful. But it's amazing, the adaptability of the human spirit that makes the stuff they call food not only palatable, but sometimes tastes good---sometimes. Or is that only in my mind?

As usual, dinner is forewarned by the jingle of keys strapped to the jailer's belt and like Pavlov's dogs the sound makes my mouth's saliva moisten my tongue, my anxious juices wash my gums and push themselves down my throat and back up again. Today, more than any other, I'm hungry. Still, I'm a patient animal and while I hear the cries of others believing that we all will be fed early I don't join in their chorus. I never do.

I hear Lulu's door clang open, orders given in Thai and the shuffling of her feet. I rush to my door and peer in earnest through the hole, trying to get a glimpse of the young woman I know without ever seeing her face.

I still can't see her face but I can tell that she's young, real young. Lulu is tall, about my height and her complexion is dark like mine. She waves with her chained hands.

"I am free now, Dahlia," she says while passing. "May the gods protect you."

Chapter Fifty-Five

Solomon Fortunada parked his car a few blocks away from the main drag in Pattaya City. The place they call Walking Street is part street festival, part sideshow. The street is teeming with westerners, many there for the *katoey cabarets*. This is where the transvestites or "ladyboys" present the illusion of being female.

Solomon knew that he wouldn't find the girl here, too crowded. If she was still in Pattaya it was likely he'd find her off the beaten path in one of the less obvious clubs located on Soi 6 or Soi 8. There were ex-pat clubs there with more of a western flavor and fewer girls to fight off.

He took a deliberate path to Soi 6, tried to ignore the catcalls from the young Thai women who lined the street.

"Hey handsome," they called out. Most were dressed in ultra-short skirts. They'd hike them up high as he passed by, turn around and show brown fleshy half-moons. "You like this ass?"

Solomon smiled. "Love it, but I'm not in the market, sweetheart."

He quickly realized that exchanging words with them could be a mistake. They followed him with persistent calls. "Show you good time, baby. Ooh, you so-o-o handsome. Too handsome to walk alone. You need two, three girls, handsome. Three girls, one hundred baht. O.K.?"

Solomon shook his head. He reached inside his jacket pocket and pulled out a passport. He opened it up to the picture of a young black girl inside. Showing the girls the picture he said, "Tell you what. You find this girl and I'll pay you one thousand baht."

The three women studied the picture with open mouths. "No. Not see her before," they all said.

"Well if you do you can find me in one of the clubs on Soi 6." Solomon stuffed his hand into his pocket. He gave each woman ten dollars, the equivalent of about a thousand baht. "Find her and I'll give you ten times this amount."

The women nodded and watched as Solomon used his cane to push his body forward. He found Soi 6, a long street with many bars and nightclubs. Flashing signs and neon lights lit up the street like daylight. He read the signs as he made his way through the crowd.

Solomon paid the cover charge to get inside a place called, Insomnia Disco. He walked inside a large hall with a pit for a dance floor surrounded by a balcony. It was a perfect place to stand and survey the crowd. R & B music was pulsating through huge speakers with a bass beat that made his heart pump to the rhythms.

A group of young men and women were standing nearby. One of the women, a brunette with heavy makeup and her dark hair streaked with red and blue accents smiled at him. He motioned to her and she quickly walked right up to him.

"Have you seen this young woman?" he asked.

She studied the picture, but he could see recognition in her eyes. "You American?"

Solomon nodded.

"Your daughter?"

"A friend."

"She's hot. I just saw her over at Lucifer next door. Girl can dance."

"Was she with anyone?"

"Not that I could tell. She was having a good time. Every guy in the club was trying to dance with her."

"Thanks."

"Any time, player. You coming back? I hope you do."

She gave Solomon a seductive smile. Good for the ego. He put the passport in his pocket and made his way back out to Soi 6 and over to Lucifer's.

Once inside Solomon knew he was in a race against time. If she had been that obvious other people would notice her, the wrong people. Ping and Giapong, his detective was out there somewhere searching.

Solomon fought through the crowd and made his way to the dance floor. Same pumping music, hot sweaty bodies twisting and gyrating most seemed oblivious to the tall man with the cane. He was bumped and jostled more than once as he headed to the middle of the dance floor and where the crowd was thickest.

He saw a flash of cinnamon colored skin, barely clad in a mini-skirt and halter-top. She had her eyes closed and she let her head and body sway to the music. She looked very different than she did the last time he'd seen her, but it was her there was no doubt in his mind.

She didn't seem to be dancing with anyone particular, just dancing. Her partner was the throbbing beat pulsating from the club's huge speakers.

He stood there watching, not wanting to interrupt her freedom orgy. He understood. Young girl. She'd been cooped up for months. She was letting her hair down.

She must've felt his eyes because she looked over in his direction, did a double take then a big smile. Her eyes wide open she rushed to him and threw her arms around his neck. She squeezed hard, so hard that she nearly choked him.

"You're back! Oh my god. You said you'd be back and you came back for me."

Solomon nodded. "Hi Charity."

She said, "Uncle Sigmund said you were here, but I didn't believe him." She kept squeezing.

"I wish I could enjoy this reunion but we've got to get out of here."

Charity released her grip. "Oh, please. Just let me dance one more song. I haven't been out in so long."

"I wish we had that luxury. We have to get out of here, get out of the city. Others are looking for us."

As if on cue, Solomon thought he saw a flash of a familiar baldhead. He strained to see into the crowd, found that unmistakable sneering smile. It was Ping and Giapong moving towards them fast with guns drawn.

Solomon grabbed Charity by the hand. "Let's go!"

He pushed their way through the crowd as the two men followed them in hot pursuit. Solomon turned to see Giapong looking for an opening in crowd to fire a shot. He dropped his cane and unleashed the Les Baer from its holster, but didn't slow down.

Bodies flew out of the way as their pursuers were parting the crowd like Moses going through the Red Sea. Solomon said, "Their getting closer!" He saw the fear in Charity's eyes that familiar fear he'd seen just a few months earlier.

"What are we going to do?" she cried out.

"Keep moving."

Giapong shouted, "Stop! Police!"

The crowd reacted by moving out of his way. Solomon was now almost dragging her behind him. They were almost at the door where the bouncers stood vigil over the line of people waiting to get inside.

"Take my arm," he told her.

He reached inside his pocket with his free hand and pulled out a wad of hundred dollar bills. "What's that saying you young people use? Make it rain?"

He threw the money straight up in the air, let it drift to the floor right in the middle of the crowd behind them and in front of Ping and Giapong. There was a stampede. People were shouting, "Money!" as they feverishly pushed and grabbed at one another. The crowd quickly swallowed up the two men in their midst and made the route to the front door impassible.

Once they were outside of the club Solomon said, "Keep walking and don't look back."

"Your cane. You're walking without your cane," Charity said.

"Don't need it, I guess. It was more of a crutch than anything else. I guess in my excitement I realize I can walk fine without it."

They found his car and sped out of Pattaya City. Solomon's stunt would only buy them a little time. Soon, the pursuit would be on and they'd come screaming down the highway after him.

She asked, "Where are we going?"

"To International Airport outside Bangkok."

She sat back in the car with a mixture of relief and worry etched on her pretty face. "Am I going home now?"

"Eventually. When it's safe," he said.

*　　　*　　　*

He handed Charity a passport and airline ticket then gave her a Gucci travel bag. "Go inside the ladies' room and change. Bring the bag back with you."

She nodded.

He waited nervously until she returned. When she handed him the travel bag he gave her a suitcase. "There are clothes inside and enough cash to last you a couple of years if you spend it wisely."

Charity looked at her airline ticket. "It says, London, England."

"For now. I've got some friends there who'll be waiting for you. The lady teaches theatre at Cambridge. I hear you're smart and talented. Make the most out of it."

"And what about you? Where are you going?"

"I'm staying here for a little while longer. I've got some unfinished business."

"My sister?"

Solomon said nothing, just smiled.

"Tell her I'm sorry."

"You'll get a chance to tell her yourself real soon. I promise." Solomon surveyed the area near the gate where Charity would get on the plane and fly safely out of Thailand. He looked at the young woman. "I owe you my life, you know. If you hadn't gotten me to Sig I'd be dead."

Charity smiled. "I guess we're even cause you risked your life to save me."

"What can I say? I'm old school. I believe in those old values," Solomon said. "Sigmund is very proud of you. He told me how you helped him at the clinic. You're going to be fine. Remember that. We'll work on you getting back home. O.K?"

She nodded.

Charity waved as she entered the boarding ramp as Solomon's chest filled up with pride. He felt like a proud father sending his daughter off to college.

Solomon breathed a sigh of relief as he watched her walk to the gate and then into the boarding ramp. He took the Gucci bag to a locker and put it inside. He tucked the key away in a pocket and walked without a limp to his waiting car.

Chapter Fifty-Six

Solomon sat in his rental car in the prison parking lot gathering his thoughts and building his nerves. It was early, about seven a.m. and he was right on schedule. A side door to the prison swung open and a large woman dressed in uniform walked out and towards his waiting vehicle.

She looked a little different than she did the last time he'd seen her, probably because it was daylight. But her facial expression was still stoic and unsmiling and masculine. He watched intently as she approached the car. He greeted her in Thai.

"Everything's ready," she said.

He reached inside his pocket and handed her an envelope. "This is the other half. Care to count it?"

She looked around then shook her head. "There are cameras everywhere, as you already know. I trust you."

She handed Solomon a badge and a nametag. "Wear this. You go anywhere inside. No one ask questions."

She looked around and pointed. "Tell them to park ambulance over there."

He looked in the direction of a door that was marked with an exit sign written in Thai. He nodded slightly to let her know he understood.

Solomon waited until she had re-entered the prison walls then he pulled out his cell phone. "Non?"

Yes, yes. Boss?

"Yeah, I'm back in Bangkok at the prison. You got the ambulance?"

Yes boss. We ready.

"Very good. Be here in one hour and park by the north door just by the parking lot. O.K.?"

Yes, boss.

"I hope you're ready. Now remember the cameras are going to be on you and the vehicle at all times so you've got to play it natural like you're really medics attending to an emergency. So stay straight-faced, no smiling and don't look into the cameras."

Got it boss.

"Just remember the cameras are hidden. I'll be directing, but out of view. Once they load the body on the gurney into the vehicle you take off. Turn on your sirens and go straight to the airport. The actress playing the nurse will take the patient into the airport and you guys take off. Understand?"

Yes. Yes. This so exciting.

Solomon was smiling when he said, "You just don't know, Non. Everyone at the hotel will think you're a star. No more bellhop for you."

He closed his phone and took a deep breath. It was time to go inside.

He displayed his badge and nametag to the guards at the front desk. He was searched briefly with a body pat down and a request to open his briefcase. He then signed his name, Solomon Fortunada, Attorney at Law, New York City.

He followed the female guard who'd just met him outside. She walked ahead of him without speaking, still no thought of a smile. When they arrived at a room with a brown wooden door she gestured for him to go inside.

Solomon sat at a table in a room with two chairs and nothing on the walls. He waited patiently while trying not to appear nervous or anxious. He was tired and wanted to sleep, but the sound of the door opening snapped his brain into gear. He gestured for her to have a seat and they both waited until the guard who'd brought her there left the room.

He looked her in the eyes as she chewed her gum. Her expression was the same as it was when he had seen her last. There was no hint of stress or burden, but he figured that her experience there in the prison wasn't a pleasant one.

"Hear you're getting out of here in about a half an hour."

She nodded and kept chewing.

"I hope you learned your lesson. It's not right to steal."

Her eyes and mouth drooped downward. He could see her repentant spirit even if it was a manufactured one. He thought, *good actress.*

"You took five thousand dollars, U.S. That's a lot of money, Lulu."

"I know," she said.

He smiled. "Everything you need is inside the ambulance including a change of clothes. Check inside the first aid kit. You'll find another five grand."

She was beaming all over.

Solomon said, "You understand that if this doesn't work you may wind up back here."

Lulu nodded.

"But whatever happens you won't be here for long. And either way you're going to school in the States, right?"

"Yes, yes. UCLA film school."

"And no more selling your body. You take the rest of the money and buy out your contract."

Lulu used her fingers to make an imaginary cross on her chest. Solomon thought the gesture was unusual for someone who was a practicing Buddhist but she'd been around some western influences.

She rubbed his hands then squeezed his fingers. "Thank you so much, Solomon Fortunada."

"Thank you, Lulu. See you on the other side."

He called out for the guard he had paid to lead Lulu out of the prison and to freedom---even if it might be for the short term.

Chapter Fifty-Seven

I listen for other sounds, but I only hear the keys and something inside tells me someone is coming for me. My heart leaps, garnering hope that the keys will unlock my door and a voice tells me in English that I'm free to go home. The door flies open and my jailer, a large woman, stands there in the doorway not smiling. Her imposing, hulking figure menacingly pronounces her non-verbal communication that someone wants to see me.

"You have visitors," she finally tells me.

Those are her only words. She steps to the side, allows me to pass through the narrow space between her body and the door and then closes it hard. "Follow me," she says.

My heart races. I have no idea who's there to see me, but it doesn't matter. I'll accept anyone just so I can see a face and talk to someone other than myself.

The guard leads me to the room where prisoners meet with their lawyers and tells me in broken English to sit at a small table and wait. "Sit! Dey be here."

But it's hard to sit still. I twist and move in my chair trying to contain my happy anxiety. My first thought is that it's my mother. She writes me often, telling me that she's thinking about making the long flight to see me even though she's scared to fly and has never been on an airplane. I try to think about anyone else and I remember how the jailer referred to my guest as "they" and her use of the word "visitors", as in more than one. And my excitement's dulled when I think that it's probably my lawyer and his interpreter.

The door cracks open and I see a familiar face followed closely by another set of warm eyes and a smile. I start to cry.

"Girl, look at you," El says. She hugs me with strong and passionate arms.

I shake my head. "I can't believe you're here." Still crying.

Stacy greets me next and strokes my head, gives me still another hug.

"And I can't believe you would look so good," she says.

For a moment it's like we're back home. Our tone is light and no one would ever suspect that our reunion is being held in a prison in a faraway land. They both squeeze me until I'm nearly oxygen deprived and then we all settle down at the table.

"So, tell me. What's going on back in DC?" I ask. Stacy is almost gushing with enthusiasm.

"I got a promotion," she says.

"You still getting married?" I ask El.

"Yeah. We haven't set a date yet, but you're going to be there when I do. I want you to be one of my bridesmaids," she says.

I smile feeling flattered by her gesture, but I'm saddened by my present circumstance.

"Don't wait on me." I tell her.

El reverses her cherry smile. Her mood now somber. With earnest eyes she tells me, "I'll wait no matter how long it takes."

Those words bring us all to tears. We hold hands, crowd our emotions into that little room and cry in unison. A big collective tear washes over us and dampens our spirits. Stacy is the first to break this orgy of sadness with words of encouragement.

"You're going to be there. Trust me," she says.

I can tell that she's searching for something to say, something that will lighten our mood. But I beat her to the punch as I swallow back my feelings of doom and gloom. El's perfect body with that bubble butt is my foil.

"I hope you're going to have your wedding dress custom made," I tell her, laughing.

"Why?"

"Because they're gonna have to have some extra material for all that you're dragging behind you."

We all laugh. Our chorus of tears now erupt into laughter, a joyous song like Handel's Messiah.

They're allowed an hour to visit and it's over in what seems like only minutes. It's time for them to leave. I'm overwhelmed by their gesture. They'll spend nearly two days in the air on their roundtrip flight just to spend an hour with me.

Stacy and El turn serious. "I'm writing a story about you in the newspaper. My editor let me research your case and I found out some things about the men they say you killed. Those guys were real sleaze bags, involved in child prostitution, smuggling and all kinds of unsavory enterprises. I'm hoping that by exposing him our government will get involved and get you out of here," Stacy says.

"Yeah, and I'm still working with my people at Justice," El joins in.

"By the way, I had someone who owed me a favor. I found you a new attorney, an American who knows the ropes here in Thailand. He's here, so don't thank me," she says, smiling.

El and Stacy give me another parting embrace and we stand there afraid to let go.

"Don't worry," Stacy says. "We're going to get you out of here." "I have something to tell you."

I look longingly into her eyes. I'm fighting to get the words out, but there are none. Stacy waits to hear an answer, but I hesitate. I take a deep breath. "I'm pregnant." I display my growing torso by lifting up my prison suit.

El and Stacy stand speechless with their mouths slightly open. I can tell by their facial expressions that the questions are mounting. Stacy speaks first. "But who…when…how?"

"I could answer that but I won't, not right now. I just want you both to promise me that if I don't make it out of here you'll make sure my baby is taken care of. Promise?"

They nod.

Stacy shrugs it off and allows her question to fall into the void we know as silence.

"We'll see you real soon. I promise," she tells me.

The door to the room opens in front of them and my friends start making their exit. "Wait!" I tell them. They both stop. "Big hug," I tell them.

And in our huddle I say, "Please look after him, my son and if you see that momma's having a problem raising him then take him, alright? Promise?"

"We promise."

"Last thing. Stacy, can you stop by my old place and get my family quilt and keep it, just in case," I say.

"Shoosh." she tells me. "I'll get it but when you come back home I'll make sure you get it back."

I turn to El, whose red, teary eyes betray her pretty smile. "Thanks for paying my mortgage, but I want you to sell it for me. It's gone up in value. Give my mother the money."

She forces a smile, sniffles.

"Don't thank me. Thank Walter. I keep telling him that he can do more for others with the twelve million he gets every year for bouncing a stupid basketball."

Smiles.

El takes my hand. "Don't worry. I'll look out for your mom."

I choke back my tears, didn't want them to have an image of me crying as their ever-lasting memory of me. I smile weakly and wave with just my fingers. I mouth the word, "goodbye" without making a sound and watch as they fade away. My jailer stands guard until my friends are out of view. I'm ready to return to my cell.

Chapter Fifty-Eight

"Wait here!" The jailer tells me. "Your lawyer here."

I sit at the table. My back is to the door, but I can hear heavy footsteps approaching. It's the sound of a man in full stride. He walks into the room, says something in Thai to the jailer, which causes her to promptly leave us alone. Head down, I'm too afraid to look up at him.

He sits across from me and opens his briefcase, rifles through papers until he finds a legal pad and places it on the table. I don't want to see his face, didn't want him to see me. Instead, I train my eyes on the table and the yellow legal pad. Next, I watch his hands, strong and brown reach down into his case and from it he retrieves a lacquered ink pen. I catch a glimpse of his head as he reaches into his bag, see his salt and pepper colored hair. There's an eerie familiarity about the man but I quickly dismiss the thought that it was him. But it *is* Mac.

Unbelievably and unmistakably, Mackenzie, like he's returned from the dead. My first thought is that the months I've spent in this hellhole have caused me to take leave of my senses. He's dead. I watched him die. Watched and held him as he took his last breath. My stomach turns and I nearly convulse from the shock of seeing him alive. But it truly is him.

That dimpled smile is now framed by a thick mustache. His green eyes glow and make something inside me move. My heart flutters and my mind is trying to understand the incomprehensible.

"You died. I saw you die," I shake my head in a rapid motion as though I can shake the vision of Mackenzie from my eyes.

Mac's wide smile illuminates the room.

"I'm not an aberration although the news of my demise has been overstated on more than one occasion. But it's me, live and in living color."

I reach over and touch his hand, checking to see if he's real. I feel their smoothness, still without a hint that he'd ever done anything more with them than pick up money or swing a golf club. It's Mac, all right.

"But Robinson shot you. I saw you die," I tell him.

I'm truly dumbfounded by this, which causes my breathing to sharpen, a precursor to the panic attacks I'd experienced for almost my whole life. But I'm determined not to let that happen here.

"Where were you? How could you leave me here all this time thinking that you were dead?"

"It's a long story and we don't have much time. And the name is Solomon Fortunada now. So don't call me Mac." He whispers.

"Long or short, I want to hear what happened. Tell me how you survived."

"I'll tell you but we have to hurry, O.K.?" he says.

He takes a heavy breath, unbuttons the top two buttons on his shirt and pulls out the familiar St. Christopher's medal, the one he got from my father.

"My patron saint plus I was wearing a Teflon bullet proof vest. I got hit in the shoulder and my knee---that was the worst. The bullet that would've killed me hit all Teflon. Knocked the hell out of me and caused my weakened heart to go into arrest. I guess you and Charity were too nervous to notice that I was still breathing although barely.

"She had pulled the car down to the river and was ready to roll it in with me in the trunk when I started pounding from the inside. Got a hand it to her. She grew up right then. She found a friend of mine, a doctor outside of Bangkok and after a couple of weeks of convalescing I'm doing fine, almost."

"And Charity? Is she...?" I was almost too afraid to ask.

"She's on her way to London right now. She wanted to see you all this time but she'd been hiding out and a visit wouldn't have been very wise. My friend Sigmund took good care of her. I went back home briefly so that I could heal totally and I just got back here last week."

I sit back in my chair too stunned to speak. Then I ask, "And my father, do you know where he is?"

Mac's face is solemn and tinged with sadness. "Dahlia. Remember when I told you not to trust Paul Robinson? Well the truth is he was trying to set you up by telling you that your father was in this same prison."

"So, you're telling me that Richard Reynolds is not alive."

"Yes."

"But the man they found in the river was that him?"

"Yes. I'm sorry. Richard tried to escape but he didn't make it. He would've been in here for the rest of his life."

"Why do you think he never wrote me the way he wrote to my grandmother?"

"She died unexpectedly. The letters he sent to your family's house were intercepted by Robinson. I bet if you had read them you'd find that he was trying to get to you."

"You really think so?"

"Know it. If you only knew how much your father loved you. That's the reason he sent the diamonds to your grandmother in the first place."

"I don't understand."

"We stole Desdemona, but had no idea what to do with the jewels at the time. We were trying to get out of Thailand, didn't want to risk going through customs so we mailed them to your grandmother. It was kind of our insurance in case something happened. We never planned on prison and the accident."

"I guess you never planned on the FBI getting involved, either."

"Probably can't count Paul Robinson as part of the agency," Mac says.

"That was a cruel thing Robinson did. It was like he was playing a game."

"Trust me, Dahlia. It wasn't a game. Robinson was deadly serious about getting Desdemona and cashing in, one way or the other. He was trying to play every angle. He didn't count on Ping grabbing Charity. I guess the joke was on him."

"So how did he know so much?"

"Sue, my former assistant. She knew everything, except where the jewels were, that is."

"And Sue. What happened to her?"

"She took off with the fake jewels and the money."

"Money?"

"Yeah, twenty million. Ping's men had the cash that day in the warehouse. Of course, her partner Paul Robinson shot them and the plan was that he'd kill me, take the cash and blame you and Charity for the crime. Ping still thinks Charity killed his associates and that's why he was trying to find her and the money. Robinson and Sue weren't part of the equation. Robinson's dead and Sue disappeared. Until…"

I ask, "Until?"

"She was in Pattaya just yesterday looking for me, or least looking for Solomon Fortunada. I think she suspected it was me all along and that I didn't die that day."

"Well if she has the money why would she try and find you?"

"She did find me. She wanted to kill me because she figured I was the only one who could tell Ping that she had his money."

"But you're here. What happened?"

"Let's just say I talked her out of it."

"She loves you."

"Probably but her love of money was greater."

Mac reaches across the table and takes my hand. "Look, we can talk about all of this later because we don't have much time to talk. I'm going to get you out of here," he tells me.

"Get me out? How?"

"You're going to have to trust me on this, all right? Take this."

Mac hands me something wrapped in a small piece of plastic and closes my hand over it.

"Take the orange pill when you get back to your cell. It'll make you feel sick, nauseous, you'll throw up. Tell them you're pregnant and you think you're having a miscarriage. They won't take any chances because the infirmary here isn't able to handle that kind of medical emergency," Mac whispers.

I think for a brief second, how does he know? He can't see through the clothes I'm wearing. Of course, I realize that Mac doesn't know that I really am pregnant. This is just part of his plan. "Mac, I need to tell you something." It was time to tell him.

I see anxiety wash over his face. "I'm sorry, Dahlia. It'll have to wait. Leave everything up to me." He hands me a rubber balloon filled with some kind of fluid.

"Put this inside of you just before the nurse comes to check on you. Make sure you untie the string at the top."

I look confused. "Inside me?" I ask.

Mac nods. "Yes, inside you and I don't mean swallow it, O.K.? There'll be an ambulance here for you. Once inside, take the blue pill. You hear me? Take the blue pill! It'll make you feel better, but you'll still be shaky. The ambulance attendants and the guards will take care of you. They'll give you a change of clothes, take you to the airport. Meet me at Gate 27, O.K.?"

326

"Mac, I want to tell you something. I really am…"

"Save it. We'll have plenty of time to talk, later," he interrupts me before I can complete my sentence.

Mac closes his brief case and stands up. Gives me a smile. He straightens his necktie and smoothes back his hair, Miles Davis' interpretation "Birth of the Cool" come to life.

I return Mac's smile with a weak one of my own, fighting back tears. Apprehension is the dominant expression I wear. Mac's plan is a bold one to be sure, but I have nothing to lose except my life and now, his too. He tunes into my feelings as though he's read my mind. He mouths a reassuring and silent, I love you, and then taps on the door to alert the guard that he's ready to leave. He falls into lawyer mode when the large woman returns to take me back to my prison cell.

"Well, Ms. Reynolds. I will be working on your appeal and I'll let you know something of my progress in the next week or two. In the meantime, keep the faith," he says.

I almost laugh.

Minutes later, I'm back in my cold, dank jail cell, alone. I tuck away the plastic "lifesavers" that Mac has slipped me. Two pills, one orange, the other, blue. Take one first then take the other. I can hear his emphatic instruction---"once you're inside the ambulance, take the blue pill! The orange one will make you sick and you'll get a fever, the blue one will make you feel better."

I take a deep breath, exhale slowly, lick my lips and pop the orange pill into my mouth. I suppress my gag reflex, pills had always been hard to swallow, and force it down my throat. Mac didn't say how long it would be before it takes effect so I sit on my cot, wait and listen to my body.

Fifteen minutes, a half an hour and then a full hour pass and nothing happens. Then it starts with a subtle rumble in my stomach, followed by dulled pain. Nauseated, I roll on my side clutching my stomach and holding him. He is still, apparently unaffected.

I call out for Lulu, at first until I realize that she's gone then I call out to the guard on duty.

"Help! Help! Something's wrong! My baby!"

The response is uncharacteristically quick. The large female guard unlocks my cell door, calls for help in Thai. I can't understand her, but I hear the word, "baby" in English. Soon, the prison nurse appears, looks confused as the guard explains. She pulls out a thermometer and checks my vital signs. She opens my legs, slaps on thin, rubber gloves ready to explore my uterus, but there is blood trickling down my legs.

"Call an ambulance!" The nurse tells the guard while she attends to me.

They quickly carry me out of the prison by stretcher and I'm put inside the waiting ambulance driven by two men dressed in Bangkok Police Department uniforms with an ambulance attendant inside to help me. I'm still reeling from the effects of the pill I'd taken. Sweat drenches my body and face even though the night air is cold. The attendant dabs my face with a cool towel and speaks in halting English.

"You all right. Take pill now," she says.

I un-wrap my fingers from around the piece of plastic that contains the blue pill, swallow it and nod to the attendant. She's a young Thai woman about my age, complexion and height and dressed in a white hospital looking smock. She watches as the pain and nausea subsides and smiles approvingly when it's obvious that I'm feeling better.

"You change clothes now," she tells me as she helps me out of my prison clothes into a blue dress. Next she hands me a long gray trench coat that covers my body and hides my bulging stomach.

"Wear this," she adds.

She then hands me a bright red bandana to cover my hair, leaving my long ponytail hanging loose down my back.

"We take you to airport now," the girl explains.

The young woman has a familiar tone in her voice, one I've heard before. And now I can see her face clearly.

"Lulu?"

She smiles and nods profusely.

"Mackenzie, I mean Solomon had you planted here at the prison to help me?" I ask.

"Yes. To watch over you. To help you."

She's the girl I've been talking to in the prison cell next to mine. I want to ask her how and why, but I realize that this is all part of Mac's plan and only he knows how it will be played out. I say a silent prayer, put myself in the hands of God and Mackenzie Powell and sit quietly as the ambulance speeds to the airport and hopefully, to freedom.

Chapter Fifty-Nine

The airport in Bangkok is no different than most large airports in a post-9/11 world. Like everywhere else in the world, there's an overflow of people, but here most are from the Far East rushing to make their flights to who knows where in a whirl of organized chaos and a sea of brown skin. Added to the mix are police, federal agents and various security personnel and it is business as usual.

The ambulance that carries me speeds onto the airport grounds and right up to the terminal. There are no sirens blasting to warn of my coming, just the red and white vehicle rolling to a gradual stop curbside. I sit in the back trying to let the second pill take its full effect. I can feel my baby move, which comforts me.

Lulu goes into action in a manner that is unmistakably well-coordinated, planned and done in typical Mackenzie Powell fashion. She opens the back door to the vehicle and looks outside. There's a police officer directing airport traffic and standing in the middle of the road just a few feet away. There are other officers dressed in white jackets, swinging batons, walking two deep shoulder to shoulder. They're on "watch" patrol, looking for anything suspicious like a bomb or a prototype terrorist, whatever that means.

Lulu stands still for a moment, watches two officers motioning drivers to keep moving. One splits off from the pair, approaches a recalcitrant driver in a late model Mercedes Benz who seems oblivious to the signs that read, "No Parking" and written in Thai and English. The cop taps on the passenger side window to get the driver's attention while his partner looks on.

Lulu motions me to "come on" while the police are distracted, sensing that this would be our best opportunity to enter the terminal unnoticed. She pulls out a wheelchair. One more peek at the police officers and Lulu steps out of the ambulance grabs the wheelchair and puts it in position for me. She then motions for me to join her.

"You sick," Lulu reminds me.

In other words she's saying, act like you're sick and take it easy getting out of the ambulance. I'm aware enough to know what she means. I gingerly step out of the vehicle, sit in the wheelchair as Lulu takes control. She pushes me in the direction of the terminal. Although there are access ramps for wheelchairs the closest one is about a hundred feet away.

There's a sense of urgency in the air. And I can tell with Lulu there will be no diversions. She struggles to pull the wheelchair with me loaded in it over the curb and into the terminal. She motions for the ambulance driver to come and help, but the vehicle is empty and we can see the driver and his sidekick retreat and melt into the crowd. Although she's tall and fit, Lulu struggles with my weight and that of the wheelchair.

I notice that our struggle has drawn the attention of one of the police officers and he casually saunters his way over to the spot where the pretty young woman in a nurse's outfit is trying to overcome the curb with the wheelchair and me in it. My heart races uncontrollably and with each step drawing the police officer closer comes the feeling that I should just stand up and run inside.

The officer nods at Lulu as he approaches and smiles while reaching for the chair's handles. She gives him a nervous smile in return, but it quickly evaporates as she watches him take control and pull me over the curb. Once up on the sidewalk he turns me around and straightens out the chair. I can't understand what he's saying, but I conclude that he's asking Lulu if she needs help getting the chair inside the terminal. Her nervous smile returns, but she shakes her head telling him, no. She then follows with a courteous nod the way they do in the East to express their gratitude.

I exhale slowly as the officer tips his hat, looks directly at me and makes a military-like about face and walks back to his partner who's still arguing with the Mercedes Benz driver. I ease out a sigh and Lulu resumes control of the wheel chair and we head towards the door. But as the doors swings open I hear footsteps running and a man's voice calling out.

"Sa-wad-dee, Miss. Sa-wad-dee."

It's the same police officer approaching us once again.

I want to tell Lulu to keep walking and to push faster, but he's on us too fast for any kind of reaction other than to stop and wait. I put my head down, trying to appear even more ill hoping that he hasn't recognized me. He stands directly in front of us, blocking the entrance with his hand resting on his holstered gun and his legs spread wide.

"Khun Cheu Arai?"

The officer directs a question to Lulu.

"Dii-chan cheu, Lulu." She responds.

Her voice quivers with a very rational fear of what might happen next. She nods, swallows hard and waits. I'm trembling all over.

"Sabaai Dee Mai?" he asks her.

"Sabaai Dee." Lulu responds.

She laughs. It's a nervous laugh.

I sense without looking that Lulu's becoming relaxed in the presence of the officer. I quickly conclude that if she is a prostitute, then talking to the police is a routine occupational hazard. I try my best to relax, wait and listen.

The officer says something else to Lulu that makes her laugh and he joins her, apparently impressed with his own wit. Now I know exactly what he's doing and the reason why he stopped us. He's hitting on her.

She plays along with him and even becomes flirty to stoke his fire and distract his attention away from me entirely. But it's clear that time is becoming our enemy and Lulu will have to extricate herself from the situation and the amorous officer. She asks him for pen and paper, writes something, hands it to him. He reads, smiles and nods as he backs away.

"Yin dee tee dai roo jak," the police officer says.

He's now walking to his waiting partner. His head held high with a stride full of confidence and bragging rights to be sure.

I look up at Lulu and force a smile of my own.

"What was that all about?" I ask.

"He ask for my phone number. I give him phone number," Lulu replies. "I hope he not know number to Pattaya Prison kitchen."

She laughs.

Lulu rolls me into the airport and tells me to get out of the wheelchair. She gives me one last look as she walks away and heads back outside and to a destination that I hope isn't back to the prison.

"Good luck," are her last words.

For a moment I stand there, my feet riveted to the floor trying to regain my composure, but it's only for a moment and I snap back realizing that I must move. I waste no time looking for Gate 27. A sign in Thai and with English written in small letters, points me to the concourse and the moving sidewalk that would take me to the place where I'm to meet Mac and to my anticipated flight to freedom.

The motorized walkway pushes me as my rapid steps quicken my pace. I wobble a little from the uncertainty of my feet and use my hand to hold the rail and keep my balance. All the while I try to keep my head down and blend into the crowd of humanity that's moving equally as fast.

A tall, African-American girl in Thailand should stick out like Oprah standing in line at a McDonald's in Compton, California and I'm aware that I'm drawing attention. I hurriedly put on the sunglasses that Lulu gave me and tuck the scarf I'm wearing further down over my forehead. With my brown skin and soft ponytail I hope that I look like just another Thai girl going on a trip. But my problem is that I don't have any luggage or even a purse to carry and I wonder if that's enough to arouse suspicion.

Feeling self-conscious, I wrap the trench coat around my torso and hold it close. An occasional look up to check the nearest gate number lets me know I'm getting closer. I'm approaching Gate 24. I take a quick glance in that direction and then eyes straight ahead, avoiding the discerning watch of the police who are stationed at various points along the way with guard dogs poised to react to whatever threat their canine sensibilities can detect.

They make me nervous and I feel that I'd have to get there soon or have a heart attack from the tension and the pressure. My breathing is deep as though there is a shortage of oxygen. It's a pattern that seems to be the only constant I've experienced since seeing Mac at the prison. It's the only thing I can do to calm my nerves and it isn't working very well. *A shot of Vodka would help*, I'm thinking, but I don't have the money to buy one or time to stop. Besides, I'm pregnant.

I look up, check out my surroundings, staring without staring at the police. I can see the sign telling me that Gate 27 is just a few feet away. I step off the moveable sidewalk. My momentum pushes me to the point where I almost fall, but I adjust and hope that Mac is waiting. With anxious eyes I explore the seating area looking for the tall, brown-skinned brother with the ponytail and sensuous eyes. He's there, just as he said he would be. I can tell immediately that he is calm.

My spirit is lifted at the sight of him sitting in the boarding section with his head down, deep into a book. I feel like running, but instead I walk up on Mac gingerly. My heart is pounding so hard I wonder why he isn't jolted by the sound. He smiles when he notices me, but quickly returns to his book. With a slight motion of his head he directs me to take a seat. It's Mac's way of telling me not to draw attention to us. So for the moment we seem like strangers until he reaches for my hand on the armrest nearest him and clutches it. Mac's strong grip is the reassurance I need. I breathe easy for the first time in months.

"Glad you made it," he says in a near whisper without looking in my direction.

Mac keeps his eyes fixed on the pages of his book as though the whole world is inside those pages, but I realize his act is part of the diversion.

Our physical connection is brief and he relaxes his hold on my hand, pulls a smile that only reaches a corner of his mouth and continues to speak without looking directly at me.

"We'll be boarding in about twenty minutes," he tells me.

I watch as he pulls an envelope from inside the flap of his book and hands it to me.

"Your boarding pass and passport are inside," Mac says.

He looks down at the floor and at the garment bag that's strategically placed between us.

"That's yours, Dahlia." Mac says, looking at the bag by Gucci. "We don't want anyone getting suspicious because you boarded without any luggage."

I pretend not to notice as he carefully slides the bag close to me so that I can grab its handle. I study Mac's face and embrace the moment. For four months I thought he was dead and now here he is rescuing me. We're leaving this place that had been a hell to me and we're leaving together.

Mac obviously feels my eyes watching him because he abruptly lifts his head, giving me another dose of those lady killer eyes, but he's now frozen, trance-like and unmoving. He's looking at something or someone behind me. I can hear a commotion, see uneasiness overcome his calm face as his eyes dart back and forth around me and fasten on what is unseen from where I'm sitting.

My eyes say to him, what is it? I start to turn and look, but Mac shakes his head, saying, "Don't turn around." He rises to his feet and reaches out for my hand.

"Take your bag and come with me. You see the ladies' room over there?" He says.

I nod.

"I want you to go in and go inside a stall. There are clothes inside the bag. Put your scarf and coat inside your travel bag and change clothes and take your hair out of that ponytail. Wait fifteen minutes and come out. Go directly to the gate. They should be boarding by then and get on the plane. O.K?"

"But Mac, what about you?"

"Listen, Dahlia! You have to do exactly what I tell you. It's the only way, all right. Just trust me."

I turn enough to see that it's the police and security officers with dogs and they're moving at a feverish pace. Armed with assault weapons and what appear to be pictures in their hands, they're moving from one gate area to the next, looking at the picture and searching. It can only mean one thing---they're looking for me.

Mac gives me a reassuring smile, but there's urgency set in his eyes.

"Whatever you do Dahlia keep your head up, but don't look anyone directly in the eyes and go right to the gate. Get in line and get on the plane."

"And where will you be?" I ask.

He smiles, "On the plane, of course."

He kisses me gently on the lips and pulls me in the direction of the bathroom. The police are getting closer, but don't seem to notice the tall African-American couple making their way through a hoard of shorter Asian people.

My thoughts are full and anxiety high, but I do exactly as Mac tells me. I make my way into the bathroom without looking at anyone and without seeing where Mac has gone. I quickly look for an empty stall, lock the door and sit on top of the toilet, waiting and listening.

I wait a few minutes then take my trench coat and scarf off and open the bag to put them inside. There are other clothes inside for me to wear. I make the change and comb my hair so that it lies straight down, framing my face. My transformation is complete and I know it's time to leave and, hopefully, board the plane undetected.

I open the door to the toilet stall, peek out and cautiously step outside. Although I am feeling more at ease, I hold my breath, say a prayer and prepare myself for whatever might greet me in the terminal.

My heart quickens when I hear the sound of someone opening the door to the stall beside mine. It's Lulu! Our eyes meet, but before I can say anything she puts her finger to her lips telling me to be quiet. I watch as she puts on a trench coat identical to the one I had been wearing, pulls her hair into a ponytail and then ties the same colored scarf around her head. She tops off her look with sunglasses, the ornament of espionage and disguise. Lulu smiles and waves goodbye as she holds her head up high and leaves the bathroom.

I wait a few moments and make an exit of my own. Take a peek outside with the door slightly cracked open and without hesitating walk directly to the gate to get in line. Once again, my heart races and I feel a lump rising in my throat as I stutter-step my way in the line to the person taking boarding passes.

"Passport, please."

That's the voice of the woman holding my boarding pass. Reaching into the envelope Mac had given me I find my passport and pull it out without opening the little booklet and hand it to the woman. She looks at my passport and then at me. I hold my breath and try to still my heart.

The woman's eyes narrow as though she's trying to look right through me and at that point I know something's wrong. I wait while she looks at my passport and the picture and at me. One more look and I wish I'd used the toilet while I was in the stall. I'm so nervous that I can feel the pressure from my bladder trying to take over and exert control over my body functions. I squeeze it back, trying to win the battle of wills over my own body.

It's taking too long. Here I am. Arrest me. But just when I think the ruse is over and I'm caught, the woman takes out a rubberstamp, places a seal on my passport and motions for me to move on.

"Nice picture, Ms. Richards," she tells me.

"Ah, what?" I ask.

My voice resonates surprise. *Ms. Richards?* I try to adjust to my new name, my father's name. Apparently, Dahlia Reynolds doesn't exist anymore, at least for now. Her demise is obvious because the Thai government holds my passport under that name.

As I walk down the ramp and to the plane I open my passport and view my photograph with curious regard. It's me, to be sure, and my new name, Desdemona Richards, is prominently displayed. A sigh of relief is the only reaction I can muster.

A couple of shaky steps and I look to see if Mac is in line, but he isn't there. Something tells me to double back, but to stay in the tunnel leading to the plane. Straining my eyes and my neck to look out into the terminal I can see him now.

There are nearly a hundred police and security personnel surrounding him. His hands held high in a submissive response to having an arsenal of guns pointed in his direction and standing right beside him is Lulu in her trench coat and ponytail.

I want to run back, but I remember Mac's words, consider the consequences and hope against hope that he will find a way out of this and join me. But it's very clear that there's no way out. I've lost him again. My heart sinks low as I drag myself onto the airplane bound for a destination I hadn't bothered to find out.

I hold back my tears and find my seat. Mac put me in the first class section, plenty of room for me to relax if I could. I take out a magazine as other passengers get on the plane and pretend to read still watching for him to board. The seat beside me is empty and that brings me some comfort knowing that Mac was planning to be there, too.

But I figure that as long as the plane is still at the gate there's a chance that he'll make it, as well. With each passenger I steal a glance from behind my sunglasses and as each meander their way to the back my heart sinks further. I watch as the flight attendant closes the door and feel the jolt of the plane moving away from the gate. But then the plane stops. My heart races once again.

The pilot announces that there has been a slight delay and utters an apology. I feel the sensation of moving forward as the airplane repositions itself back at the gate. Now my mind is racing. *The ruse is up. They're coming to get me.* Those are my initial thoughts then I smile with easy confidence.

Mackenzie has freed himself. He's coming to join me. I sit back in my seat feeling apprehensive and exhilarated at the same time and watch as the flight attendant maneuvers the door to open it. I ask myself what's behind the closed door; devil or angel? I take a tissue from my purse and dab at the sweat gathering underneath my eyes and feel the rush of heat that has overtaken me, a by-product of my anxiety.

I think about retreating to the restroom to hide, but I realize it would be an effort in futility. The Thai police would force the door open only to find me cowering in a corner. It's clear that I'm trapped and my only option is to sit there with my head down, listen and wait. I hear feet shuffling down the aisle, slow and methodical, pausing at every row until they stop near me.

I pretend to read my magazine burying my eyes deeper into its pages as I wait to hear someone call my name, praying that it's Mac. In the corner of my eye I can see a solitary amorphous figure, but I avoid trying to discern whether it's him or the police. Instead I flip through the pages of my magazine, as though I'm unaffected by whatever it is that's going on around me.

I hear the sounds of struggle. The flight attendant rushing from her position behind the cockpit is wrestling with something. I hear her words, "Let me help you" then the door to the overhead compartment slams shut above me. I know then that it's not the police. I smile, steal a look knowing that it must be him only to have my heart sink again. It's not Mac. It's a woman I met when I first flew here to Bangkok, the one from Iowa.

She takes her seat, smiles at me with empty recognition. Apparently she doesn't remember the well coiffed black girl who had listened to her nostalgic tale of broken dreams and a love lost.

The flight attendant closes the airplane with the kind of finality that tells me that no one else will board this plane and no one will leave it until it lands at its destination. We're jerked away from the gate as the jets whine.

Once the plane taxies and makes its ascent to the skies the pilot speaks through the PA system.

He says the usual things that pilots tell their passengers. "Enjoy the flight." "Sorry about any delays." He then reminds us that our ultimate destination is Bahia, Brazil.

One last look out the window I can see Bangkok at night, the city of lights and I wonder if Mac is somewhere in all that constellation of manmade illumination. I realize that we'd reversed our lots and circumstance. Mac's freedom for my life and I question whether the trade off is fair. He is Prometheus paying the price and willingly sacrificing all for me and my baby and I understand that the depth of his love is immeasurable.

EPILOGUE

FIVE YEARS LATER. Sitting on the chaise lounge with its black and white swirling design and an umbrella that lets in just enough sun to soak my bare arms and legs I've just finished reading James Baldwin and I'm confounded by the writer's complexity of thought and his allegorical examination of black people in America. I allow my mind to absorb the words, both prophetic and profound, and place the book on my lap.

It's deep reading, probably not the kind of book one reads while sitting on the beach on an island off the coast of Brazil watching the waves play tag with the sand and my young son a willing third party to the game. But I'm not on vacation. This is my life now, uncomplicated and uncluttered. My focus is being the best mother I can be. With every wave brought in by the tide I cast a discerning eye towards the curly haired little boy.

Back in my book and thoughts I hardly notice that he's running to me and shouting in a high-pitched voice, warning me that someone's coming. I look to the ocean. I can see the yacht now anchored about four hundred yards out in the water. A rubber dingy with a motor is chopping through the waves and periodically becoming airborne. It's unusual to see anyone come ashore here after all it's a private beach, the hallowed ground where Mac had built his dream home.

I stand up, clutching my little boy's hand as we watch with interest and I'm unable to suppress the smile growing on my face. Our visitor comes into full view. He runs the little rubber raft ashore and jumps out while it's still moving. I can see his bright smile even from a distance and I eagerly wave my hand to greet him.

I see my son look up at me and then at the man who's approaching. To him it's a stranger, but he can tell that I know the man and I'm happy to see him. We're both watching intently as our visitor takes big strides right up to us and I hug him as though my life depends on him being here.

"It is so good to see you," I say.

"Same here."

"I knew you were coming, but I thought you'd be here tomorrow."

"Yeah. I got a little anxious so I told the charter captain to make a beeline here."

I look him over, smile broadly. "You look good," I tell him.

"So do you. It's been a long time."

He looks down at my son and rubs his hand through the little boy's hair. Smiles.

"He looks like me when I was that age."

I nod my agreement. "Yes. I've seen those old pictures of you."

I squeeze out a sigh full of reminiscent thoughts.

"It is so good to see you,"

I'm repeating myself, probably my nerves mixing with my excitement.

I said, "I watched you on television a couple of months ago. Congratulations."

He shrugs. "Ain't nothing, really."

"Yeah, right. Grammy Award winner. The talk shows and gossip columns say you're going to marry that cute little young lady you're producing. Desire? Right?"

"Can't believe everything you read, can you Dahlia?"

He musters a shy smile then tells me that the gossip was right on point. He looks out onto the clear, aqua ocean.

"She's on the boat."

"Congratulations. Are you going to bring her here so we can meet her?" I ask.

He turns his head towards the boat, licks his lips and smiles.

"Yeah. I just wanted to talk to you first. You know, set the stage. I didn't want to just spring her on you guys plus I wanted to meet him," he says looking at my son.

He looks around at the sprawling open-aired home that is our backdrop.

"Nice place," he says.

"What can I say, it's comfortable and isolated. A good place to raise him," I reply.

I can't take my eyes off of him. I guess my admiration is clear. He kneels down, reduces his six-foot, two-inch frame to three feet. Faces my son, eye-to-eye.

"You don't know who I am, do you?" He says to the little boy.

My son looks down at the sand, shaking his head and tells him that he doesn't.

"Well, you will. I'm your big brother, Antoine."

My son beams and tries to repeat his brother's name. It's an abbreviated version and sounds as though he's been practicing for this occasion.

"Twon. Twon." He repeats the name.

Antoine stands up and looks at the house.

"How's my girls, Stacy and El?" he asks me.

"They're both fine. You know El married Walter not long after I moved here. I couldn't come back to the States so the whole wedding party came here, everybody. It was a beautiful wedding right here on the beach."

Antoine nods his head. "I bet it was. This is like paradise here."

"Yeah," I say. "El had a baby girl last year. She's spoiling her rotten."

Antoine laughs. "And how's Stacy?"

"She's doing great. Still single. You know she's city editor now."

"Yeah. I read her byline all the time," he tells me. "And what about your sister Charity?"

"She's an ex-pat like the rest of us. She loves living in Europe."

I add, "You've really grown up."

"So have you, Mrs. Powell. Where is he?" Antoine asks.

"Inside, he's making gumbo. He's been crazy with excitement, waiting for you to get here. Go on in. Surprise him."

Antoine takes a step towards the house and then hesitates. "You sure?"

I nod. "I'm sure."

"He never told me how he got out of that mess in Thailand," Antoine says almost pleading for the answer to his unspoken question.

I give him a knowing smile. I say, "You know your dad, Antoine. It was a lady who saved him."

"Really?"

"Yeah. A beautiful woman named Desdemona."

340

"Figures. That's my pop."

I watch as Antoine disappears into the house, knowing that it will be a happy reunion between father and son. I turn my thoughts to what I just told him, about how Desdemona had saved Mac and realize the truth in my statement. She bought his freedom and Lulu's, as well. It cost a million dollars, but it was worth every penny.

I always laugh when I think about Nana acting in cahoots with Mackenzie. He told her that it was part of my inheritance and that it was for me to use as I saw fit if anything ever happened to him. Nana had made Desdemona's whereabouts her little secret and no one else knew---until I figured it out, that is.

My grandmother didn't know her value, just thought she was some pretty jewelry my father wanted me to have. But I collected the five million dollar reward offered by the South African government.

And Desdemona? We're inextricably tied together. One of the documents I discovered in my grandmother's box was my original birth certificate, the one I'd never seen. It read: Mother – Mahalia Lewis, Father – Richard Reynolds Richards, Baby's Name – Desdemona Dahlia Reynolds. It seems that the treasure that was Desdemona was with me all along.

I often think about how she touched so many lives. My grandmother, who was chosen as the jewel's keeper became part of an international game of intrigued, deception and murder. And then there were those who actually lost their lives because of it like my father and Paul Robinson and, of course, Sue. No one knows who else fell victim to the diamond's charms. We had all paid a price for something made of minerals and gold and regarded as priceless, but in the end there was a cost.

But some of us reaped the benefits of having Desdemona touch our lives and in the end we were rewarded. Lulu, for example, is no longer a street prostitute. She's a film major at UCLA and almost ready to graduate, thanks to the Powell Foundation.

Mac has a small seaplane that he uses to charter people around the coastal islands and to our home that doubles as a bed and breakfast. And the government of South Africa proclaimed that it was eternally grateful for Desdemona's return. We take great pride in knowing that she's on display for the people of South Africa as a reminder that the quest for riches should never be at the expense of human suffering.

Our lives are now simple and uncomplicated, the way Mac had always wanted. And when I'm not reading I'm working on my own novel. It's a story of a woman's growth and maturity and how circumstances can dictate who we are and what we become.

I turn my attention back to the little boy and call out.

"Ricky! You be careful. Don't go out too far in the water, O.K?"

He waves. Shows that big dimpled smile.

I nestle back into my chair. Open my book and muse over James Baldwin, Zora Neale Hurston and Countee Cullen and their respective messages. I let their words play with my thoughts the way my son is playing with the water. The tide laps at my toes and touches my spirit and like the sea the words are eternal.

Made in the USA
Columbia, SC
20 July 2019